Sweet Temptation

"I intend to marry you, Evelyn MacGregor," Adam said.

Eve swung back, stunned, and wondering if she had heard him correctly. Mesmerized, she could only stand there frozen, his devil's dark eyes upon her.

Adam reached out and pulled her to him. Somehow she found a voice to force out the words. "Stop this, Adam. Please. This is wrong. You have no right to do this to me."

"I have more right than any of those bastards you were willing to give yourself to. You belong to me, Eve. You're mine," he whispered hoarsely.

He lowered his head. His lips were firm and the pressure deepened until she was breathless. His mouth took possession of hers, forcing her lips apart. She gasped for breath, and his tongue drove into her mouth. Eve tried to push him away, but his arms closed about her like a heated vise. She struggled and attempted to cry out, but the words were forced back into her throat by his plundering tongue.

Eve became aware of a tightening within her in response. The realization of what it meant horrified her. *Dear God, was she beginning to respond to this devil's touch?*

ANA LEIGH

PARADISE REDEEMED

LEISURE BOOKS　　NEW YORK CITY

This book is dedicated to my son David.
Thanks, Dave, for having the vision
to see I shouldn't stop with one.

A LEISURE BOOK ®

December 1989

Published by

Dorchester Publishing Co., Inc.
276 Fifth Avenue
New York, NY 10001

Printed in the United States of America.

CHAPTER ONE

**Sacramento, California
1843**

Evelyn MacGregor had never before owned a gown as fine as the one she was wearing. The full skirt of the lavender dress flared out around her on the carriage seat. A white bonnet, embroidered with purple and yellow flowers, was perched on Evelyn's head. Her raven-black hair hung to her shoulders in clumps of curls on each side of her face.

Trembling with excitement, the twelve-year-old folded her hands in her lap and forced herself to sit quietly. Her round violet eyes, ringed with thick dark lashes, glowed with anticipation in a young face radiant with joy. Eve was unaware of how adorable she appeared to the couple seated opposite her.

Mary MacGregor Rawlins glanced at her husband and smiled with pride. Daniel gave her hand an understanding squeeze, raised it to his lips, and placed a light kiss in the palm.

1

The affectionate gesture was not missed by Evelyn. Her smile deepened as her happiness intensified. She shifted restlessly in her seat in an effort to release some of her pent-up energy.

Mary Rawlins was aglow with her own happiness. Just turned thirty, she was an attractive woman. However, her dark hair and blue eyes paled in contrast to the vivid coloring of her daughter. Mary's unique beauty was internal. It came from a serene ambience. People were always comfortable in her presence.

Daniel Rawlins had sensed this quality about Mary MacGregor the first time he met her. The forty-six-year-old financier had been a widower for eleven years. While visiting the home of a business associate near Yerba Buena, he had fallen in love the first time he laid eyes on the Scottish servant woman. The fact she had a twelve-year-old illegitimate daughter did not lessen his ardor. He married Mary after a week's courtship.

Observing that the young girl was on the verge of bursting with expectation, Daniel leaned over and patted Eve's hand. "We're almost home, honey."

Eve smiled shyly and dropped her eyes. She was still timid around him. As the child of a domestic servant, Eve had been raised to remain as inconspicuous as possible in the household where her mother was employed. Her station in life had always been clear to her. Now suddenly this man had come into their lives and lifted the shawl of anonymity from her shoulders.

The carriage passed through an iron gate and traveled up a long lane. Eve leaned out the window, flagrantly gawking at the huge white house with stepped roofs and hipped dormers. Attached wings at either side were set back slightly from the front of the original structure. Her eyes were wide with astonishment as she gaped at the imposing manor. She knew that Daniel was wealthy, as evidenced by the fine gowns he had bought her mother and her. But this house was even finer and larger than the one in which they had worked in Yerba Buena. He had to be as rich as a king, Eve thought with wonderment.

The instant the carriage halted, before the coachman could climb down from his seat, Daniel jumped out to help his wife and then reached up a hand to Eve.

The door to the house opened. A lean, gray-haired, liveried servant greeted him cordially. Daniel handed the man his top hat. "Is my son home, James?"

"No, sir. Mr. Adam is not expected for several hours."

"James, I would like you to meet my wife," Daniel Rawlins said proudly, putting an arm around Mary's shoulders.

If the news came as a surprise to James, the man remained unruffled. He nodded politely. "It's a pleasure, madam."

"And this is her daughter, Evelyn." Eve curtsied to acknowledge the introduction.

"How do you do, Miss Evelyn."

James began to eye them with discretion. It was evident, despite the new finery they were wearing, that the two females were not gentry. A young girl raised in the upper class would not curtsy to a servant. "Shall I show the ladies to their rooms, sir?"

"No, I want to introduce my wife and daughter at once. Will you please assemble the staff in the drawing room? Come, my dears." Daniel took each of them by the hand and led them into a richly furnished room. Carved pilasters framed the doorway, and an expensive Oriental rug covered the polished wooden floor.

Mary laughed nervously. "This is going to be difficult for me, Dan. I'm not used to this new role." Her speech was patterned with a slight Scottish burr.

"You're my wife now, Mary. I'm sure you will soon be comfortable."

James soon appeared, followed by four uniformed women and three men. The sudden marriage of their employer had come as a surprise to the servants, but they all appeared friendly and courteous. After the introductions, they returned to their duties.

"Now, was that so difficult?" Daniel teased. He slipped his arm around Mary's shoulders as they began to climb the wide carpeted stairway to the floor above. Eve followed behind, her fingers stroking the smooth satin finish of one of the hand-carved Chippendale banisters.

"Wait until they find out that I was a kitchen helper myself," Mary warned. "They'll sing a different tune."

"Hush, love. I won't tolerate an inappropriate remark about my beloved."

"Oh, Dan," Mary sighed, as they paused in the hallway above. "How can you avoid it? Your friends and servants alike will scoff at your marrying a servant girl. What is your son going to say? Even I don't understand why you wanted to marry me."

Daniel put his fingers under her chin and tipped up her face to meet his warm gaze. "Because I love you, Mary Elizabeth." Glowing with the warmth of her love for him, Mary slid her arms around his waist and buried her head against his chest. "And I love you, Dan. I can't believe anyone as wonderful as you even exists. Don't let me wake up to find it's only a dream."

Eve's eyes were brimming with tears as she watched them. She had never seen her mother look so happy, or so beautiful.

Unintentionally ignoring the young girl's presence, the two newlyweds stepped into the bedroom. Daniel closed the door behind them. Eve remained staring helplessly at the closed door, uncertain of what she should do. She was jolted out of her distress by the sound of James discreetly clearing his throat behind her.

"If you'll come with me, Miss Evelyn, I'll show you to your room."

Eve followed him down the hallway to a sunny room which overlooked the front lawn. "Mr. Rawlins thought you would be comfortable here, miss."

Eve glanced around at the cheerful room decorated in soft hues of green and yellow. The room radiated warmth. A white canopied bed, draped in pale green, stood against one wall. A beautiful paneled armoire occupied the opposite wall. Two yellow and green chairs stood in front of a white marble fireplace, and a gilt-edged mirror, extending to the ceiling, hung above the mantel.

"Oh, it's so beautiful," Eve enthused. "I've never seen anything this beautiful before."

"May I bring you a tray or cold drink, Miss Evelyn?" James asked solicitously. He liked the young girl. She appeared to be sweet and unspoiled—*and well-mannered*, he thought with relief.

Eve was too excited to even think about food. James forced back an amused smile when she replied, "Oh, no thank you, Mr. James, I'm not hungry."

"Very well, miss. Dinner is at eight o'clock."

As soon as he departed, Eve removed her hat and sat down on the bed. The tester bed felt like feathers after the long trip in the carriage. With a contented smile she lay back, snuggling into its softness, and despite her exhilaration, was asleep within minutes.

Eve awoke with a start and sat up. It took her several seconds to acclimate herself to her surroundings. She got to her feet and crossed to the fireplace. A brass clock on the mantel indicated it was half past seven. James had said dinner was at eight. Eve hurriedly smoothed her hair and dress so as not to be late.

She poked her head out the door and peeked down the hall. It was empty. The door to Daniel's room was closed. Eve was uncertain whether she should go downstairs or wait to be summoned. She did not want to rap on the door in fear of disturbing her mother and Daniel, so she began to walk slowly down the wide stairway.

She hesitated when she reached the bottom. There was no sign of James, or any of the servants. She heard the sound of raised male voices coming from a nearby room. Since the door to the room was closed, she knew the men had to be shouting for the sound to carry so far.

Embarrassed, Eve was about to return to her room when she heard the mention of her mother's name. Curious, she moved closer and recognized the voice of Daniel Rawlins.

"Adam, you know nothing about Mary MacGregor. Why do you presume to judge her?"

"I know all I have to," a deep voice shouted. "Good Lord, Father, a maid in Remington's house! Every one of his guests have probably bedded her. I can't believe you married her. Pay her off and get rid of her. All she's after is your money."

Eve became consumed with indignant rage. How dare this man say these horrible things about her mother? She wanted to storm into the room and strike him in the face.

"I'll not hear another word, Adam. You know nothing about this woman," Daniel Rawlins declared. It was obvious he, too, was indignant.

"That's right, Father, but I intend to find out the truth," Adam Rawlins shouted.

"I've already told you the truth. I know Mary would not lie to me. The man who fathered her child deserted her."

"The man *'who fathered her child.'* You didn't say *husband*, Father."

Daniel cleared his throat. "Mary wasn't married."

"Oh, my God! I can't believe you're so gullible. How many others were there before you?"

"Adam, I have been very lonely since your mother died. I didn't realize how lonely until I met this gentle woman. I love her, and I insist you treat her with respect. She is your mother now, and Eve is your sister."

"Never!" Adam Rawlins shouted. "I will never call that God-damned fortune-seeking whore *Mother* or her bastard offspring *Sister*."

The door opened suddenly, and a young man came storming out. Tall and black-haired, he looked like the devil incarnate to Eve. He stopped abruptly at the sight of her standing there. The eyes blazing into her own looked as black as sin. For a brief moment their eyes locked in a scathing, mutual glare.

At that moment Eve hated Adam Rawlins and

vowed to herself never to forgive him for the bitter, unkind accusations he had made about her mother.

He turned away, strode forcefully across the hall, and loudly slammed the front door behind him. Weeping with tears of rage, Eve raced up the stairs to her room.

Not realizing anyone had overheard the argument with his son, Daniel Rawlins sank sadly into a chair. Adam was so headstrong. He sighed with relief that Mary had not accompanied him when he had come downstairs earlier.

Two days later, Eve was alone in the drawing room when Adam returned home. Daniel and her mother were shopping when the disheveled, unshaven, and somewhat tipsy young man entered the room. Unaware of her presence, Adam walked over to a table and poured a drink from a crystal decanter. When he turned and discovered her sitting on the couch, he leaned his hip against the table, studying her intently as he sipped his drink. Eve's round violet eyes remained impassive as she returned his stare.

When he finally spoke, his speech was slightly slurred. "Tell me, Miss MacGregor, does your mother have the same eyes as you do?"

Eve wanted to get away from the nasty man. She rose to her feet to return to her room.

"Don't let me scare you, little rabbit. *Mi casa, su casa.*" As if suddenly discovering a hidden humor in the cordial Spanish invitation, Adam began to laugh aloud. "My house is your house, Miss MacGregor." He staggered to the bottom of

9

the stairway. "My house is your house." The sound of his insulting laughter followed her as she fled up the stairs.

There was no sign of Adam Rawlins at dinner. Since Daniel and Mary were taking a short cruise on a company-owned ship the following day, this would be their last dinner together for several weeks. Eve was relieved it would not be spoiled by the presence of Daniel's despicable son.

Clara Marshall, a tutor and governess whom Daniel had hired for Eve, joined them for dinner. She was an older, heavy-set woman with graying hair and a pleasant smile. Eve liked her instantly.

"Now, honey," Daniel assured Eve when he said goodbye to her that evening, "if you need anything while we're gone, just ask my son, Adam. I have instructed him to make certain you are happy while your mother and I are away." He hugged and kissed her. "You have no idea how long I've wished for a daughter."

"Thank you, sir. Have a pleasant trip," Eve said politely. Her pleased smile revealed the happiness she was feeling.

Later that night her mother came into her room and sat down on Eve's bed, gathering her into her arms. "I'll miss you, sweetheart. This will be the first time we have ever been apart from the time you were born."

"I'll miss you, too, Mum, but you mustn't worry about me. Mrs. Marshall seems very nice. I want you to have a very good time. And I'm going to study hard while you're gone. I want you to be proud of me."

Mary Rawlins' eyes glistened with tears. "I am proud of you, darling. I don't deserve such a wonderful daughter. And now the Lord has blessed me with Dan, too." She hugged Eve tighter. "We're all going to be so happy together."

The image of Adam Rawlins' spiteful face flashed across Eve's mind as her mother kissed her several times before departing.

In the days that followed, Eve saw very little of Adam Rawlins. During the few meals he took with her and Mrs. Marshall, Adam would stare at Eve with sullen and brooding eyes. The servants were surprised by his treatment of Eve. If they were aware of her background, they apparently thought nothing of it.

In scattered conversations with Mrs. Marshall, Eve found out that Adam was twenty-two years old. His mother had died when he was eleven. Mrs. Marshall seemed to have a high regard for him, mentioning several times how hard Adam worked at running the family's affairs in his father's absence, so Eve kept her opinion of him to herself.

Adam never spoke to her. Most of his messages were conveyed to her through Mrs. Marshall or James. Therefore she was surprised when Mrs. Marshall knocked on her door late one evening to inform her that Adam was waiting to speak to her in the library.

"What's wrong, Mrs. Marshall?" Eve asked at the sight of the woman dabbing at her eyes with a handkerchief. "Did that nasty man say something to hurt your feelings?"

"Mr. Adam will tell you, my dear." She turned away, sobbing.

The thought of having to be alone with Adam Rawlins was horrifying to Eve. Seeing Mrs. Marshall's distress added to her trepidation. She knocked on the library door, then, not waiting for his permission to enter, opened the door. The room was dark except for the light from the burning logs in the fireplace. Adam was sitting at his father's desk. His elbows were propped on the desk top, and his head was buried in his hands. For several moments he remained in that position while Eve waited for him to speak. She could feel her anxiety mounting with every passing second.

He finally raised his head. "Sit down, Miss MacGregor."

Eve walked stiffly to a chair and sat down. Adam got to his feet and moved to the fireplace, where he proceeded to stare at the flames for what seemed an interminable time to Eve.

"Do you have any relatives, Evelyn?" he finally asked.

"Eve-lyn," she corrected politely. "My name only has two syllables. You're pronouncing it as if it has three." It gave her a minor satisfaction to be able to inform this arrogant man that he was wrong about something.

She could have saved her breath. The expression in the dark eyes never wavered as Adam waited for her reply to his question. "I have my Mum," Eve finally answered.

"Other than your mother?"

"No, there are no others. At least, that's what she has always told me." She raised her chin defiantly. "And my Mum doesn't lie."

"I'm afraid I have some bad news."

His tone alarmed her, and her heart began pounding like a drum in her chest. Her eyes widened with panic at the look on his face when he turned to face her.

"I have just received word that there was a fire on board the ship. Your mother . . . and my father . . ." Adam paused momentarily to clear his throat ". . . perished in the fire."

Eve's eyes welled with tears. She sat stunned, staring at him in disbelief, unwilling to accept what he was saying. She jumped to her feet. "No, I don't believe you. This is some more of your cruel nastiness." Her voice began to raise hysterically. "Why are you saying these horrible things? My Mum isn't dead. My Mum wouldn't die and leave me." Tears streamed down her cheeks as she began to cry openly. Adam reached out a hand to her, but she slapped it aside. "Why do you try to hurt me? You're spiteful and mean. I hate you, Adam Rawlins. I hate you."

Sobbing, Eve ran from the room, past the servants who had assembled in the foyer. Most of them were crying and dabbing at their eyes. Even the usually unperturbable James was tearful.

Mrs. Marshall was waiting for Eve at the top of the stairs. The woman opened her arms to the stricken girl, and Eve rushed into them. They sat down on the top step and she hugged Eve to her breast, holding her and patting her back comfortingly. The broken-hearted girl continued to weep in her arms.

For some time Adam Rawlins remained at the bottom of the stairway listening to Eve weeping. Finally he returned to the library and closed the door.

Eve was a sorrowful, pathetic-looking little figure at the memorial service for Daniel and Mary. She sat alone, huddled in a chair watching and listening to the people as they paused to express their sympathy to Adam. She resented all of them. They were all friends of Daniel Rawlins. None cared about her mother. She had to bear that grief alone.

A stunning blonde woman, who had been clinging to the arm of Adam Rawlins for most of the day, walked over to Eve and introduced herself as Laura Raymond. She offered her sympathy and then returned to Adam's side.

When the minister began to eulogize Daniel Rawlins, Eve felt a hatred toward the man who had married her mother. Why was everyone saying these wonderful things about him? Didn't they know if it were not for Daniel Rawlins, her Mum would still be alive? It was his fault her mother was on that ship when it burned.

Eve's resentment was only a temporary reaction. She soon found herself remembering how kind Daniel had been. How much he had loved her mother. She recalled the sight of her mother's face glowing with radiance that Daniel Rawlins had brought to it, and Eve's young heart began to weep for him also.

When the last guest departed, Eve sought the solitude of her room to cry herself to sleep, as she had done every night for the past week. She was about to retire when James rapped on her door to inform her that Adam wanted to see her in the library.

Eve had a feeling of dread as she entered the huge room. It was as if it had all happened before, and she would have to relive it all again.

Adam was seated behind the large oak desk reading a document. She noticed how tired and drawn he looked, realizing for the first time that he, too, had suffered a great loss. Nevertheless, she found it impossible to feel any sympathy for him. Her beloved Mum had gone to her death with this man's curse still ringing in the air. He was a disciple of the devil.

Adam put aside the paper he was reading when she was seated. "Miss MacGregor, I have just read the will my father executed before . . . he left Sacramento." He cleared his throat. "Your mother failed in her attempt to procure

15

any appreciable amount of my father's wealth for you and herself. Father did, however, leave you a small dowry for when you wed."

Adam paused, as if expecting some outburst from her. Eve felt too numb to even look at him. What did she care about money? Her Mum was dead. Daniel Rawlins' money hadn't kept either of them alive. Could all the money in the world bring them back?

"My father made another provision for you," Adam continued. "This house is to remain your home until you wed, and I am to see to your welfare."

Eve looked up to see the sardonic gleam in his dark eyes. "It appears, Miss MacGregor, I have become your legal guardian."

CHAPTER TWO

Sacramento, California
1847

The United States was embroiled in a war with Mexico the fall day Evelyn MacGregor returned to Sacramento from Paris. The war had scarcely touched California. A few battles had been fought in the southern part of the state, but the intense fighting had been in Mexico. Life in Northern California remained unchanged.

Her carriage passed through the iron gate and rambled up the driveway between two neatly trimmed rows of hedges. Its destination was the tall white house a short distance ahead.

Eve closed her eyes recalling the first time she had seen that house. The delicate lines of her face curved into a tender smile as the vision of her mother, radiant with happiness, flashed across her mind. Lost in the poignant memory, she was unaware of the tears that began to trickle down her cheeks.

The woman sitting opposite her smiled with compassion. "There is always such a sweetness to coming home. Particularly after such a long absence, Eve."

Eve's smile was enigmatic. "Actually, it's more of a bitter sweetness, Simone."

Simone Lisle regarded Eve with a bemused look. The Frenchwoman was a twenty-five-year-old spinster, considered unmarriageable in her native country. Her nondescript angular features and light brown hair had little to offer in the line of beauty. Her pale green eyes were slightly myopic, often requiring her to squint.

An orphan like Eve, Simone had been a cook's helper at the exclusive boarding school which Eve had attended in Paris. Coming from a similar background, Eve had gravitated naturally toward Simone, rather than the rich and pampered classmates with whom she felt she had nothing in common.

When it was time to return to America, Eve, after much cajoling, convinced Simone to accept a position as her traveling companion.

Now, as Eve stared reflectively at the large house, it seemed unchanged from the time she had left. *Had it been four years since the death of her mother? Four years since she believed her world had ended?*

Adam Rawlins had not harbored the remotest intention of having his life disrupted by the presence of a twelve-year-old. He had immediately dismissed Mrs. Marshall and shipped Eve off to France for a two-year education at Madame Toulaise's Academy for Young Ladies. The long trip around Cape Horn and across the Atlantic had taken almost a year. The return trip added another. So that now, at sixteen, Eve was finally returning to California.

"Welcome home, Miss Evelyn," James said with pleasure as he assisted her out of the carriage.

It was evident to him how much the young girl had changed. Her black hair and violet eyes were still as startling as ever, but the child's body had blossomed into that of a woman. Her rounded breasts filled the red-and-gray plaid bodice she was wearing.

James sensed more than just a physical change in Eve. She now had a confidence that had been lacking in the grief-stricken girl who had left four years earlier.

"Thank you, James. How good to see you again." Eve's round violet eyes sparkled beneath a bonnet tied fetchingly at the side with a red satin bow. "I would like you to meet Mademoiselle Lisle."

"Good day, mademoiselle," James said coolly to the woman standing beside Eve. Adam Rawlins had informed him that Eve was bringing a Frenchwoman to add to the staff. James saw no need for another servant in the house, but he was not inclined to argue with his master.

Eve glanced hesitantly at the front door. *I might as well get the unpleasant task out of the way,* she thought dismally. She took a deep breath and expelled it in a sigh. "Is Mr. Rawlins in the library?"

"No, Miss Evelyn. Mr. Adam has been gone for several days. I have no idea when we can expect him." James picked up the luggage and entered the house.

Well, you didn't think he would be here to greet you with open arms, did you? she thought with amusement. She felt as if she had received a stay of execution. At least she would have some additional respite from the unpleasant man. During her entire stay in France, Adam never once exchanged a personal greeting with her; his correspondence had been handled through his secretary, Richard Graves. There was no doubt in Eve's mind that the kindly old man was the one who had been responsible for seeing to her needs.

That night Eve climbed gratefully into the white bed with its remembered green canopy. The bed was the one thing in the house she cherished. It had been her only refuge during the tragic days following her mother's death.

And after stretching out between the sheets, Eve realized how good it felt to be home again— even if *home* meant sharing it with Adam Rawlins.

The following morning there was no sign of Adam at breakfast. Their trunks arrived from the ship shortly after. The two women began to unpack the comfortable wardrobe she had accumulated with the generous clothing allowance that Graves had provided for her.

At the sound of approaching hoof beats, Eve glanced nervously out of her bedroom window. She sighed deeply; the dreaded confrontation with Adam had arrived.

The tall, slim young man who stepped out of the carriage was a complete surprise to her. He was dressed neatly in a dark suit and gray beaver top hat. Her nose curled up in distaste. "For heaven's sake, Simone. It's Stephen Wright."

The Frenchwoman abandoned the task of unpacking to peer out of the window. "What is he doing here?"

Eve was anxious to fall in love and marry. She had no intention of remaining under the same roof with Adam Rawlins, and hoped she could find a husband quickly. However, Stephen Wright did not fit her qualifications.

He was a lawyer whom Eve had met on the ship. The young man had come West to earn his fortune, and had pursued her persistently from the time their ship left New York.

He was handsome enough, but too self-confident and aggressive. Despite her repeated attempts to discourage him, the man had remained undaunted.

Eve continued at her task. "I'm going to let him wait," she said to Simone. "He has no business coming here. I told him on the ship I wasn't interested. Maybe if I let him cool his heels awhile in the drawing room, he'll get discouraged and leave."

"I don't think you'll be that fortunate, *chérie*." Simone laughed lightly. "Mr. Wright is a very persistent man."

"Well, he's wasting his time."

An hour elapsed before she completed her unpacking. Finally, unable to put it off any longer, Eve knew the time had arrived to confront her unwanted caller. She crossed to the door of her bedroom with a determined stride. "I was hoping that I had seen the last of Mr. Wright. Well, I'm going to get rid of him right now."

Adam Rawlins awoke with a start. The clock on the mantel indicated it was almost noon. He had returned home in the middle of the night and collapsed exhausted on the couch in his den.

For a few minutes Adam lay quietly mulling over the events of the past four days. Over a thousand acres of timber must have been lost in the fire. The fact that none of his crew had been injured was the only consolation, because a fire that severe could easily have resulted in the loss of men as well as trees.

Adam rose wearily to his feet. There were a dozen things to do. He had to get hold of Graves at once. The campsite was destroyed and would have to be rebuilt. In the meantime, several dozen men were living in makeshift tents.

Preoccupied, he slowly mounted the stairs, his thoughts jumbled as he began formulating the necessary priorities.

"Good morning, Adam," a pleasing feminine voice greeted him in passing on the wide stairway.

"Good morning," he responded automatically without raising his head.

Adam mounted several more steps, then stopped abruptly and swung around, almost losing his balance. Katie Callahan, the upstairs maid, never called him "Adam." And she certainly never smelled of French perfume.

He studied the back of the woman who had just passed him. Even in his weariness, he was not immune to the fetching sight. Black hair hung to a tiny waist, emphasized by a tightly fitted bodice that came to a point in the back. A full skirt, flaring over a crescent-shaped bustle and numerous petticoats, disguised the size of her hips. Adam was no stranger to the mysteries of the female figure, and guessed their slimness.

Eve stopped at the foot of the stairway. Her angry glance swung up to meet the astonished look on his face.

Adam couldn't believe his eyes. Good heavens, it was Eve MacGregor! In the turmoil surrounding the fire, he had forgotten she was arriving home.

Adam sucked in his breath at the sight of her. In the brief glance he caught before she turned away, he could see that her face was exquisite. The incredible violet eyes, which he remembered as round and sorrowful, now glowed with fury; and the thick dark lashes ringing them made her eyes appear more vivid in color.

Eve was seething. She thought that after four years, Adam would at least have the courtesy to welcome her home. But all he could grunt had been a "Good morning." Oh, the man was loathsome.

Why did she expect him to be any different? Eve fumed. Adam Rawlins would never change. He was a totally self-serving individual, who never considered anyone's interests but his own.

James had shown Stephen Wright into the drawing room. The young man was standing in front of the fireplace absorbed in studying a portrait of David Rawlins, the man who had built the house and amassed the Rawlins' fortune fifty years before. He spun around with a pleased smile when Eve entered.

"This is a surprise, Stephen. I didn't expect to see you again." She did not offer her hand to him.

Ignoring the slight, Stephen hurried over and grasped it, bringing her hand to his lips. "I was devastated without you, Evelyn. I couldn't stay away a moment longer." He attempted to take her in his arms, but Eve managed to elude him with an adroit step to the side.

She addressed him with firmness. "I thought I made myself very clear, Stephen, when I refused your offer of marriage."

Her words failed to dissuade him, and to her further chagrin, he smiled confidently. "I knew you didn't mean it. I am certain I can convince you to the contrary."

His smugness amazed her. "Stephen, you

tried for nine months to convince me to the contrary. What makes you think you can succeed now?"

She sat down on the couch, immediately regretting the move as Stephen plopped down beside her. "This is why," he declared. Before Eve could guess his intent, he grabbed her in his arms and forced a kiss on her.

Eve fought to resist, but he pushed her down so that she was lying on her back with her arms trapped uselessly between their bodies. His kiss was suffocating. No matter how much she struggled, she couldn't free her mouth.

"What in hell is going on here?" The voice cut the air like the frigid chill of an Arctic wind.

Stephen Wright bolted to his feet, enabling Eve to sit up. Their glances swung to the tall figure of Adam Rawlins standing in the doorway.

Flustered, Stephen cleared his throat. "I must be on my way, Evelyn. I will call again tomorrow." He hurried from the room with an embarrassed nod in Adam's direction. Adam ignored him, his attention fixed angrily on Eve.

"Well, Miss MacGregor, I see reading and writing wasn't the only thing you learned in France."

Mortified, Eve rose to her feet. She knew how incriminating her actions must appear, but she was still too angry with Adam to care what he thought. Adam appraised her in a slow, deliberate inspection that caused her to blush under the insolent scrutiny.

His gaze finally returned to clash with the irate glare in her eyes. "And I see you're still as despicable as ever, Adam. You haven't changed a bit in the last four years."

Adam's gaze swept over her in another brazen perusal. "The same can't be said for you, Miss MacGregor." His mouth curled into a lascivious smirk. "I can see that you *have* changed considerably in the last four years."

Eve had encountered lewd stares from the ship's crew, as well as the young men in France, so she was aware of the effect of her round curves on men. Yet, she did not understand why she found the ribald innuendos of Adam Rawlins so disturbing. She was determined not to give him the satisfaction of knowing they bothered her.

While Adam poured himself a glass of brandy, Eve took the opportunity to study him. Her memory of Adam had been through the eyes of a child: a jeering Satan with black eyes glinting in an evil face. Seeing him now after a long absence, Eve realized how false that image had been. His features were more rugged than narrow, with a long, straight nose and square-set jaw hinting of obstinacy rather than craftiness. His mouth was wide with firm lips and not the remembered thin slit slicing into a cruel jeer.

But her biggest surprise was the discovery that his eyes were not black, but a deep sapphire.

In all, it was not a perfect face, but it wasn't a wicked face either, Eve realized grudgingly. In fact, she conceded with astonishment, were it not for the narrowed smirk he was wearing, he would be quite handsome.

At the moment, however, the face was smudged with soot, sporting several days' growth of beard.

"From your appearance, Adam, it seems you are still abiding in a habitual state of inebriation."

The dark eyes filled with amusement. Quaffing the liquid in the glass he was holding, Adam poured himself another drink. "Sorry to disappoint you, Miss MacGregor. I've spent the last four days putting out fires at my lumber camp. It appears I should have stayed at home to tend to the fires you have been setting right here in the drawing room."

Eve said a silent blessing for the long hours Madame Toulaise had spent instructing her in decorum. It was the one redeeming grace which now prevented her from picking up the closest object she could reach and throwing it at him. She elected, instead, to force an impassive smile on her face. "It's a pleasure to be home again, Adam."

She walked very slowly out of the room, knowing that his brooding stare was following her every step.

Eve was dressing the following morning when Stephen Wright's carriage appeared in the driveway. She finished dressing and had just reached the top of the stairway when Stephen came out of the library. She stood dumbfounded when he departed without even a backward glance.

Hurrying downstairs, she was about to rap on the library door but then changed her mind, and barged in. As she suspected, Adam was in the room. He was engrossed in reading a letter.

"Did I just see Stephen Wright departing?"

His dark gaze shifted to her over the top of the paper. "Don't you bother to knock, Miss MacGregor? I believe that is still considered the civilized approach when entering a room with a closed door." His attention returned to the letter.

Eve sighed in exasperation. "I'm sorry." She clenched her teeth to keep herself from uttering any other retort. "What did you say to Stephen to make him depart so abruptly?"

Adam laid aside the letter. "I simply gave your Mr. Wright some very sound advice."

"Oh?" she said uneasily. "Just what advice did you give him?"

Adam leaned back in his chair with a complacent smile. "I offered him two pieces of profound wisdom on how to succeed in business. The first was to caution him of the importance in doing the proper research and preparation on a project. Never to accept anything, or anyone, at surface value, because appearances can often be deceiving."

Eve eyed him suspiciously. "I assume you were referring to someone specific, Adam?" She knew what his reply would be.

"*You*, of course, Miss MacGregor. Your ardent young suitor was surprised to discover you are penniless and not the heiress to the Rawlins fortune."

"I am certain it gave you a great deal of pleasure to call it to his attention." Her voice was laced with scorn. "You said you gave him two pieces of advice. What was the second?"

"I also advised Mr. Wright how foolhardy it is to make an enemy of someone who is wealthy and influential—and also smarter than he."

"Who just happens to be *you*," she added with icy scorn.

"Exactly." A grim frown replaced the complacent smile. She could see how intimidating he would appear to an opponent.

Eve could feel her anger building toward eruption. Her eyes widened in disbelief. "You threatened him."

"I don't see it as a threat, Miss MacGregor. Mr. Wright just had to examine his priorities. You or his career?" His brow arched cynically above his dark blue eyes. "Bliss with poverty . . . versus . . . misery with success." In a sign of dismissal, Adam picked up the letter and resumed reading.

Unbeknownst to Adam, the thought of not having to suffer any more of Stephen Wright's unwelcome advances came as a relief to Eve, but she was furious that he presumed to interfere in her life. She was seething with rage. "I can't believe it! I would think you would be grateful to get rid of me. You wouldn't have done it if you weren't trying to make my life miserable, Adam Rawlins. You enjoy being despicable."

She spun on her heel and stormed from the room.

CHAPTER THREE

Eve was at her wit's end the following morning trying to decide how to entertain herself. After breakfast, Simone had taken herself off to the kitchen, having volunteered to show the cook how to make French pastry. There had been no sign of Adam since the confrontation in his den the previous day. Eve thought it was just as well, because she was still smoldering over his brazen interference in her life.

Bored, she wandered out to the Rawlins' stable where the carriage horses, riding mounts, and the formidable Equus were quartered.

Equus, an enormous black stallion belonging to Adam, petrified Eve. She considered the huge, snorting beast a perfect counterpart for the devil who rode it.

There was no sign of the groom, so she began to pat the head of one of the bays. The beautiful animal was one of a matched set used as carriage horses. The black stallion in the nearby stall eyed her cautiously before finally snorting its displeasure.

"You're just as unpleasant as your master," she chided.

The stallion's ears suddenly perked up accompanied by a loud neigh. To her dismay, she saw what was exciting the horse. Adam Rawlins was crossing the lawn to the stable.

Eve had no desire to see him, especially alone in the stable. She looked around for a place to hide. Her only option was the hayloft. Lifting her skirts, she scrambled up the ladder leading to the loft.

She reached the top just as he entered the barn and was able to peer through a crack in the floor to observe him. Her heart was beating so loudly, she felt certain he could hear it.

"What are you so excited about?" Adam asked.

For a moment Eve thought he was talking to her, until she saw him pat the head of Equus. The black stallion snickered with pleasure, his teeth snatching an apple Adam held out to him. "I told you I'd get you an apple, didn't I?" Adam chuckled.

Eve watched spellbound as Adam picked up a brush and stepped into the stall. He began to curry and groom the horse.

The fitted shirt and trousers Adam was wearing made Eve aware, for the first time, of the lithe, muscular body, usually concealed under conservative suits.

As he worked, his dark hair tumbled over his forehead, giving him an almost boyish look. She did a swift calculation and realized Adam would be about twenty-six years old by now. She began to wonder why he hadn't married. Or maybe he had, she thought wryly, and no one had bothered to inform her.

Eve continued to watch in wonderment, marveling at his gentleness with his horse. Adam whispered soothingly to the animal the whole time he groomed it. *If Equus were a cat, he would be purring,* she thought cynically. *What a shame Adam can't show the same kindness to human beings.*

"I think we can both use some exercise, boy," Adam mumbled to the horse. Within minutes he had the animal saddled and led it out of the barn. Eve climbed down from her perch as soon as she heard the horse gallop away.

Feeling foolish for having spied on Adam, she said nothing of the incident to Simone.

As it happened, she saw very little of Adam in the week that followed. He rose early and left for the office before she came downstairs in the morning. He often joined them for dinner in the evening, but it was a stuffy, uncomfortable affair, with Adam being politely civil to Eve during the meal. As soon as Adam finished eating, he would excuse himself and disappear behind the closed door of his den for the rest of the evening.

Despite his reserve toward Eve, Adam was always cordial to Simone, which added to Eve's frustration. Whenever she saw him smiling, or chatting casually with Simone, her blood came to a quick boil.

Several weeks after her return from France, James informed Eve that Adam had returned to the lumber camp and was not expected to return for two weeks. It was as if a load had been lifted from her shoulders. She couldn't understand why she was so tense in his presence, but it was a relief to know she would not have to suffer him for two weeks, at least.

The day following Adam's departure, Eve went out to the stable. She brought Equus an apple and the horse immediately snatched it out of her hand. "Well, you could offer a 'thank you' or even a 'how do you do,'" she scolded.

Undaunted, she returned each day and repeated the act. Eve could tell that the horse was beginning to respond to her. By the end of the week she got nerve enough to reach in and pet him.

Equus drew back and began to stamp around in his stall. At once the groom, Will Higgins, was at her side, warning her not to get too near the horse when he was nervous.

"He's missing Mr. Adam," Will said, calming the animal with several reassuring pats on the head. "Equus always acts up when Mr. Adam is gone for any length of time."

There was no explaining the loyalty of dumb animals, Eve reasoned to herself as she returned to the house.

The following day, on her morning trudge to

the stable with an apple for Equus, she was taken by surprise at the sight of Adam. She quickly stepped into the shadows before he saw her. Adam was dressed in the same casual fashion as the first time she had seen him there. His shirt sleeves, rolled up to his elbows, revealed the dark hair that covered his arms. A similar dark patch could be seen on his chest at the partially opened front of his shirt.

Absorbed in shoeing the animal, he was unaware of her presence. She stood in the shadows watching his steady, sure hands scraping and fitting the shoe. Perspiration dotted his forehead, and he raised an arm to wipe his brow on his sleeve.

He looked so out of character, yet so completely at peace. She found it hard to believe he was the same man she loathed so passionately.

Equus sensed that she was there and raised his head with a snicker. It was enough to attract Adam's attention. He looked up, so she had no choice but to step out of the shadows.

He nodded, then returned to his work. Eve felt ill at ease. She had no idea how to explain her presence to him, so she walked over to the stall of one of the bays. Equus, however, kept up his snickering, waiting for the apple he had grown accustomed to receiving from her.

"Why don't you give him the apple, so he'll quiet down," Adam suddenly said. "I'm trying to get a shoe on him."

"How did you know?" She sauntered over as nonchalantly as she could.

"Will told me you've been coming here every day."

Damn the man! He has spies everywhere. She couldn't have any secrets from him.

Eve dug the apple out of the pocket of her skirt. She wanted to depart the scene as quickly as possible. The stallion lunged for the handout as soon as he saw the apple. Still half-frightened of the huge beast, she jumped back, crashing into Adam. She reached out, grasping his shirt, to try to keep from falling. They both tumbled to the floor.

Eve found herself trapped beneath him. The faint aroma of his shaving lotion teased her nostrils and she opened her eyes to discover their heads were only inches apart. The expression in his dark eyes was guarded. "Did you hurt yourself?"

"No, I'm fine. I'm sorry. It was clumsy of me."

Adam got to his feet and reached out to help her up. The hand that closed around her own was strong and warm. She had always imagined his grasp would feel flaccid and cold.

She tried to pull her hand away, but he would not release it. "Let's get rid of this." He began to pick pieces of hay out of her hair. "Who knows what the help might think if they saw you so disheveled."

Eve was certain she had turned beet red. Adam appeared not to have noticed, and continued at the task. She was afraid to move or even look at him. He was just too close. She exhaled the breath she was holding, and when he finished, stepped away. When he returned to Equus, Eve reached up self-consciously to restore her hair to its proper order.

Eve lingered at the stall, fascinated, watching Adam's actions. The movements of his long fingers were steady and sure. "I never expected to see you shoeing a horse. Don't you consider that too menial a task?"

Adam did not raise his head, but continued at his labor. "If I thought it was too menial, Miss MacGregor, I wouldn't be doing it." The tone of his voice carried just enough castigation to make her feel like a child for asking.

Eve wouldn't give Adam the satisfaction of letting him know she noticed the barb. "It just surprises me that you even know how to shoe a horse."

Adam glanced up in amusement. "I am sure there are a lot of things about me that would surprise you."

"It was just a figure of speech, Adam," she rebutted.

"My father did not believe in idleness. I've worked at our lumber camp since I was a boy. You learn a lot more than how to shoe a horse." He walked over to the anvil and made a minor adjustment, then returned to the stall. "Besides, Equus takes a special shoe and doesn't allow anyone to shoe him but me."

"What kind of special shoe? Do you mean for jumping or racing?"

Adam shook his head and picked up a horseshoe lying nearby. He held it out next to the one he was working on, for Eve to compare the difference. "Equus has a hind leg slightly shorter than his other three, so I make this shoe thicker than the others. I even put a calk on the heel to keep him from slipping."

Eve examined the shoes and said in surprise, "I never noticed that before. You mean you've done this from the time he was born? You go to a lot of trouble for a horse."

"Why not? He's got spirit, intelligence, power and speed; too valuable for a trip to the butcher block. Equus deserves more." He patted Equus' neck affectionately. "Right, boy?"

Eve was amazed to discover that Adam could be compassionate. She was startled even more by his next question.

"Would you like to learn how to ride?"

"What did you say?" she asked breathlessly.

"Would you like me to teach you how to ride?" Adam repeated.

"You mean a horse?"

Adam glanced up at her, raising a brow sardonically. "What did you think I meant?"

"Are you serious, Adam? Would you really teach me? I'd love to learn. I've always wanted to learn to ride." She was so excited she had to keep herself from hugging him.

"I'll warn you in advance. I'm a hard taskmaster."

"I wouldn't recognize you if you were any other way, Adam." The eager look on her face eased the sting of the words.

"Very well, be here at seven sharp in the morning. If you're not on time, we'll forget it."

"I'll be here, I promise." Without a backward glance, Eve rushed out of the stable to tell Simone the news.

Adam paused at the job he was doing and raised his head to watch her until she disappeared from sight.

The following morning, her eagerness prompted Eve to come before the appointed time, but Adam was already at the stable. Will Higgins led out a saddled roan mare.

Eve gasped with pleasure. "She's beautiful. Is she new? I've never seen her before."

Adam took the animal's reins from the groom. "I thought it would be wise to teach you on a gentle animal."

Eve was speechless. "You mean you got her just for me?"

"I got her to make this task easy for the both of us. I don't want to see you on any of the stallions until you learn how to handle a horse properly."

Eve was too thrilled to hear what he was saying. "She's so beautiful. What's her name?" She patted the animal lovingly.

"Calliope."

"Calliope? You've named her well. She is as beautiful as a Greek Muse, but I think I'll call her Callie for short."

Sobering, she turned to Adam. In the past, she had deliberately avoided thanking him for anything; not because she was ungrateful, but because she felt certain he did not act out of generosity. However, this gift was not only generous, but thoughtful as well. It could not go unacknowledged.

"Thank you, Adam." They were not easy words for her to say.

"Don't thank me yet. She's not yours until you prove to me you can handle her. If you fail, you'll have no need for a horse."

Their glances locked over the mare's neck. "I don't intend to fail, Adam."

"Let's hope you don't, because I mean what I say."

Eve was to discover that Adam had not exaggerated; more than a taskmaster, he was a tyrant. A superb horseman himself, he would tolerate only consummate skill, from her grasp on the reins to the way she sat a saddle.

In the weeks that followed, this insistence on perfection often increased the tension between them, but Eve forced herself to maintain her composure and listen to his instructions.

Adam's business obligations took him away for long periods of time. Were it not for Simone, Eve would have been at a total loss for companionship. Riding became an obsession with her, filling in the lonely gaps created by Adam's absences.

By the time fall passed into winter, she had developed into an expert equestrienne.

CHAPTER FOUR

To celebrate Eve's seventeenth birthday, Adam had purchased tickets to the opera.

She had been looking forward to it for weeks, and to show appreciation for his thoughtful gift, had taken particular pains with her appearance that evening. She wore a gown she knew Adam especially admired.

The full skirt of the ivory satin gown was worn over a crescent-shaped bustle at the rear. Its bodice was tightly fitted with cap sleeves and a wide, off the shoulder, neckline. Black satin gloves reached to her elbows.

As she looked in the mirror, putting the final touch to her hair, she smiled, pleased at the reflected image. She took her new beaded evening purse, a present from Simone, and descended the stairs, eagerly anticipating the gala affair.

"Magnifique, ma chérie," Simone greeted in admiration. "You look so lovely."

Eve gave her an impish grin, and then quickly sobered. "Simone, why are you not ready?"

"I'm sorry, Eve, my cold has gotten the best of me." At Eve's concerned look, Simone added, "But it is really nothing, *ma chérie*. I just don't want my sneezes and coughs to interfere with the sound of the prima donna."

Eve was disappointed, but she was even more chagrined when Simone gave her a note that had just arrived by messenger. It was from Adam informing her that he would be delayed.

James and Simone watched Eve nervously pacing the floor awaiting his arrival. Finally, Eve turned to Simone in exasperation. "There's no reason why I can't go without Adam. James, will you get the carriage?"

"I don't think Adam will like it if you don't wait for him," Simone cautioned. "You know he prefers escorting you to any public function."

"I don't care, I'm going on without him. *The Marriage of Figaro* is my favorite opera. You know how much we enjoyed seeing it in Paris and I don't want to miss one note of it." Eve pulled on a full-length cloak with an ivory satin lining. The velvet mantle draped around the arms to form open hanging sleeves.

The performance of the popular Mozart opera had been sold out and the hall was filled to capacity. Briefly explaining to the doorman that she was a guest of Adam Rawlins, Eve was directed to Adam's box seats. Her entrance, unescorted, created a wave of whispers, as well as *sotto voce* comments behind raised fans.

A man, already seated in the box, rose to his feet when she entered. With a courtly bow, he clicked his heels, kissed her hand, and in a thick Russian accent introduced himself as Count Nicholas Dimitri Barshykovic. The count was slender with gray hair and sported a neatly trimmed goatee and mustache. Eve guessed his age to be in the middle fifties.

There was no sign of Adam at the end of the first act. Count Barshykovic graciously invited her to join him for a glass of wine. Eve, piqued at Adam's absence, accepted the invitation, but declined the wine in favor of a glass of cold lemonade.

The second act finished and Adam had still not arrived. The count again invited her to join him for refreshment. Speaking freely about himself, Eve discovered he was a deposed count who had come to California with Russian fur traders. The venture had proven unsuccessful, and, now destitute, he was hoping to return to his beloved homeland.

After the third act, Eve and the count remained in their seats. Eve glanced about nervously seeking the errant Adam, while the count continued to talk. Finally, he said, "While my fortunes have not been the best of late, I feel the Fates smiled on me a fortnight ago." Eve looked at him quizzically. "A fortnight ago I won the ticket for this opera in a poker game. It didn't seem like much winnings at first, but, you see, one is often fooled by the turn of the card."

The count paused to see if his remark had any effect on the young woman. It was clear to Eve that he had more than just a casual interest in her.

"Yes, it has been an excellent performance," Eve said demurely, avoiding the implication of his comment.

Undaunted by her answer, and encouraged by the fact that she was alone, the count pressed further. "I wonder, Miss MacGregor, would you do me the great honor of joining me in a carriage ride tomorrow afternoon?"

Eve, feeling bereft at Adam's disappearance on her birthday, agreed.

Adam finally appeared during the last act of the opera. He was disgruntled at the obvious familiarity Eve had developed with the Russian.

On leaving, Count Barshykovic kissed her hand. "Until tomorrow at two, my lady."

Eve was hoping Adam might have failed to hear the count's farewell to her. She wasn't that fortunate.

The following day, two o'clock came and went without any sign of the count. By three o'clock, Eve knew he wasn't coming. And she began to think she knew why.

She tramped down the stairs and confronted her nemesis in his study. "Where is Count Barshykovic?" she demanded.

Adam pulled out his pocket watch and studied

it. "By now, I would say about halfway to San Francisco, where he will catch a ship back to his Mother Russia, his wife, his children and his grandchildren. He was very grateful for my generosity. He even cried with gratitude."

Eve spun on her heel and slammed out of the room without a word. *More interference with her life. Adam was insufferable.*

Eve eventually put the incident behind her, still clinging to the belief she would meet a man and get married. Shortly before Christmas her hopes for a marriage prospect brightened when she met Richard Turner, a young surveyor who had come to California with the Fremont expedition. They spent a number of evenings together, and he had begun to speak of marriage.

But on the night before Christmas, Richard informed Eve that Adam had hired him to do some surveying in the Oregon territory. The offer was too lucrative to refuse. Naturally, the conditions would be too wild to take a wife with him.

Adam showed him to the door and watched with a smile of self-congratulation as Richard kissed Eve's cheek and told her he would never forget her.

Eve was so furious with Adam, she refused to come out of her room on Christmas day. Even Simone could not persuade her to change her mind.

To reciprocate, Adam gathered all the Christmas gifts he had bought for Eve and turned them over to a charitable institution.

Eve's only solace in her desperate situation was in riding Callie. When Adam rode with her, they rarely conversed. Eve knew that since he no longer criticized her riding form, he was satisfied with her progress.

The war with Mexico was still raging below the border. When General Scott's capture of Mexico City virtually ended the conflict, the treaty of Guadaloupe-Hidalgo in February of 1848 ceded California to the United States. The war's end brought the arrival of the American Army to Sacramento.

The city's elite gave a gala ball to raise money for the returning wounded veterans. At this event, Eve caught the attention of a young officer. Before the romance could develop further, once again Adam used his influence, making certain the lieutenant was transferred to an Eastern command.

From then on, Adam guarded her zealously, choosing to escort her to social functions himself. She was not permitted to attend them with a man of her own choice.

Adam had managed, by cunning manipulation, to keep her in relative seclusion ever since Eve returned from France. He was a determined man who always succeeded in accomplishing whatever he set out to do. Adam Rawlins had long made up his mind about his intentions for Eve's future.

However, her unescorted appearance at the opera had attracted the attention of more than one man in the audience. These socially acceptable young men from wealthy families were more likely to be tempted by Eve's flawless face and violet eyes than by any bribe Adam Rawlins had to offer. Thomas Fawnsworth was such a man.

As if Fate were the dealer in the game Adam was playing with Eve, even his power and wealth could not have worked more to his advantage than the event that occurred in March.

Peter Fawnsworth, a close business associate of Adam's, and his wife held a party to celebrate their twenty-fifth wedding anniversary. Adam, having no choice but to attend with Eve, was dismayed to observe that Thomas Fawnsworth, the couple's twenty-three-year-old son, was completely enamored with Eve.

Adam sipped a brandy while he watched Fawnsworth gaze worshipfully into Eve's violet eyes as he whirled her around the dance floor. Eve smiled brilliantly, looking up at the smitten young man as if they were the only two people in the room.

Adam was contemplating cutting in on the pair and taking her home when Peter Fawnsworth came up to him and grabbed his arm.

"Adam, my brother-in-law just rode in with the news. There's been a gold strike."

"Here in California?"

Fawnsworth nodded. "Some place near the South Fork of the American River."

Adam emitted a long, low whistle. "That's practically in our backyard."

"A guess it's a big one, too. Charley says a fellow by the name of Marshall, who works for John Sutter, found gold in the river."

"Sutter? Is that the Sutter who owns that sawmill at the fork of the Sacramento and American?" Adam asked.

Fawnsworth nodded excitedly. "Charley says Marshall discovered it near the end of January. They've kept it a secret until now. He says there's so much of it that all you have to do is bend over and pick it up."

By this time the room was buzzing with the news. Even the musicians had stopped playing to listen. The dusty, unshaven young man who brought the news became the center of attention.

"It's probably placer gold, just like that strike in '42 north of Los Angeles," one man announced.

From habit, Eve moved to Adam's side when the music stopped. She put a hand on his arm. "What's placer gold?"

"Alluvium, sediment and sand washed up in rivers and estuaries," he explained.

"This isn't just sediment," Charley King declared hotly. He untied a pouch that hung from a string around his neck and dumped some of its contents into his hand. Small golden nuggets glistened in his cupped palm.

The sight of gold electrified the crowd. In the face of such evidence, no skeptic remained.

Several of the young men clustered together, formulating plans to rush off to the gold fields.

The following morning, Thomas Fawnsworth left for the diggings along with most of the other young men in the city.

Despite this turn of events, Eve continued to believe she would meet a man who would succeed in freeing her from Adam's domination. She had this thought in mind on the night she was dressing for the Orphans' Charity Ball. Her gown of white lace over black satin was a stunning complement to her raven-black hair, caught at the nape with a spray of gardenias and hanging to the middle of her back in long, silky curls.

As was his habit lately, Adam would escort her to the ball along with Laura Raymond Kaiser.

Having tired of waiting for a proposal of marriage from Adam Rawlins, Laura Raymond had married John Kaiser, the son of one of her father's business associates. At the outbreak of the Mexican War, the idealistic young man hurried off to enlist in the American Army and was killed.

Expected by society to forsake matters of the heart during the period of mourning, his grieving widow was now in the enviable position of being able to sit back and wait patiently for Adam Rawlins' proposal of marriage. The fact that she was having an affair with him, while awaiting this offer, was for her "the icing on the cake."

Eve's heart skipped to the beat of the music as

they entered the hall. The room swarmed with women clad in colorful satins and men sporting the finest of broadcloth, evidence that the affair was attended by the cream of Sacramento society.

Even though the discovery of gold had stripped the city of all of the young men, Eve was hoping there would be a handsome and dashing young man attending, who would fulfill her dream of love and marriage. As the evening progressed, her hopes diminished. The men who asked her to dance were either middle-aged or married. There seemed to be three or four women clustered around each of the few bachelors who were there. She had no intention of trying to force herself into any one of those circles.

When one of the eligible young men finally approached her to dance, Adam was suddenly at her side, snatching Eve away from the prospective partner.

"I believe this is our dance, Eve." His manners were courtly as he led her to the dance floor. She threw a forlorn backward glance toward the young man, who was about to be converged upon by a bevy of women.

As Adam glided her smoothly around the floor, Eve became captivated by the melodious strains of a waltz. She closed her eyes, allowing herself to be swept into a world of fantasy; a world where she twirled around the floor in the arms of a handsome prince who was madly in love with her, and willing to sacrifice his throne rather than give her up.

She opened her eyes to discover Adam smiling down at her. Caught red-handed in the act of daydreaming, Eve blushed sheepishly and returned his smile.

"You're very lovely, Eve."

Adam had never complimented her before. The sincerity in the simple sentence felt like a caress. "Thank you, Adam." She didn't know what else to say to this unexpected courtesy from him. Flustered, she turned her head away.

Neither of the pair was aware of the woman observing them as they danced. Laura Kaiser's green eyes followed their movements with womanly insight, her face inscrutable. She had loved Adam Rawlins for fourteen years and knew her love was not reciprocated, clinging to the hope that one day he would marry her. In that fourteen years, Adam had never looked at her the way he was looking at Eve MacGregor at this moment. She knew now that the hope she had harbored for so many years would never come to be. When the music ended, she returned her attention to the conversation of the dowager seated beside her.

A short while later, Eve was convinced she had imagined those few moments on the dance floor. Adam appeared to have returned to his usual insufferable self, refusing to allow her to stray more than two steps from his side.

In a rare moment, while he was distracted by

a business associate, she found herself free from his watchful eye. She quickly slipped out on the patio for a breath of fresh air.

She gasped in surprise when a figure stepped out of the shadows. "Mrs. Kaiser!"

"I'm sorry, Eve, I didn't mean to startle you."

"I just wasn't expecting . . ." Despite the many occasions on which Eve had seen Laura Kaiser with Adam, she still felt uncomfortable with any of his friends.

"Were you expecting Adam?" the woman asked.

"Adam? Why would I expect Adam?" The woman's question was perplexing. Suddenly, in embarrassment, Eve realized she may have blundered into a planned rendezvous between Adam and Laura. "Oh, I'm sorry," she stammered.

"You should be, Eve MacGregor. For a while he was almost mine, you know." Laura flashed a sad smile. "But I think I always knew it would never be."

Eve didn't know what to think or say. Was Laura referring to Adam Rawlins? Had he broken off his relationship with the woman? She knew very little about Adam's personal life, and had a desire to know even less. Whatever was wrong between Adam and this woman was not meant for her ears.

"I'm sorry, Mrs. Kaiser, but I really don't understand what you're talking about."

Her mouth curving into a bemused smile, Laura Kaiser studied Eve for several seconds.

"No, I don't think you do." She then disappeared into the shadows, as mysteriously as she had appeared.

The following week Laura Raymond Kaiser sailed for Europe.

Eve wished Adam would have sailed with Laura because, other than business, he now had no distraction to keep him from interfering in her life.

Eve began grasping at straws by accepting attention from men who bored or revolted her. Often she allowed them to court her, just to annoy Adam. He would either buy them off or intimidate them into leaving. But since Adam was her legal guardian, she was helpless to prevent it.

As a result, the situation between them grew progressively worse. Eve ceased riding with Adam and joined him only for meals, or the social functions he demanded she attend.

After nearly two years, Eve found herself still unwed and virtually a prisoner, with Adam Rawlins as her gaoler. She could not make a move or speak to a friend without his discerning dark eyes observing her.

CHAPTER FIVE

"I think you are making a mistake," Simone Lisle declared. She shook her head worriedly. "You know nothing about this man. He could be just another fortune hunter."

"Of course he's a fortune hunter, Simone. Only, the fortune he's seeking is in the gold fields. Roger told me he loves me and I believe him," Eve declared fervently. "And the glorious thing about it all is Adam doesn't even know he exists. I met Roger quite by accident one day at the orphanage when he came to visit his aunt, Mrs. Sullivan, who works there."

Simone regarded the younger woman with a sad smile. She loved Eve and knew the girl was acting out of desperation. "You just met him. You don't know anything about this man. Yet, you are willing to run away with him to San Francisco."

Eve clutched Simone's hand. "As soon as I get

there I will send for you, Simone. I would take you with me tonight, but Roger has only two tickets on the stage."

"I don't like this," Simone said warily. "I wish you would wait until you knew him better."

"And have Adam find out about him? What chance would I have then?"

Eve turned back to the mirror to resume her dressing. The round violet eyes, capped with thick dark lashes, were so mesmerizing to the usual observer that often the other features of her flawless face went unheeded. A delicate rounded jaw flowed gracefully into high Celtic cheekbones. Her straight nose rested above a wide generous mouth, and a faint tinge of tawniness kept her creamy complexion from paling against her raven black hair.

Evelyn MacGregor did not see any of these details as she studied her image so intently. All she could see was *an eighteen-year-old spinster*. She turned away in despair from the offending apparition.

"What else can I do, Simone? I can't wait any longer. If I don't get married, I'll be stuck here with Adam the rest of my life. I couldn't bear that."

Simone smiled patiently. She knew how Eve felt because she had passed a similar crisis long ago in her own life. "Well, you don't want to marry just anyone, simply to escape Adam's domination."

"I thought as much at one time, but now I am beginning to wonder. The problem is, I don't get an opportunity to make the decision for myself. Adam always interferes." Eve laughed lightly. "I wouldn't doubt that he arranged the gold strike, just to get all the young men out of town."

Simone chuckled with her, enjoying the joke. Eve put her arms akimbo and shook her head in disgust. "Well, I ask you, Simone, that darn gold has been lying around for centuries. Why did they have to pick *now* to discover it? If I wasn't convinced that Adam Rawlins was in league with the devil, I would swear he was getting help from above."

"I think he is just trying to protect you from yourself," Simone said reflectively. "He has many fine qualities which you fail to recognize."

Eve twisted around in panic. "You aren't going to tell him about Roger Sullivan, are you?"

"Of course not." The Frenchwoman sighed deeply. "I should, but I won't."

Eve threw her arms around her friend. "Oh, Simone, soon we'll be away from this prison. Everything will be fine. I know it will be."

Simone returned Eve's hug, but her eyes clouded with anxiety. "I hope you are right, *chérie*." She shrugged aside her doubts and smiled. "But come, let me help you finish dressing. After all, it is a very special day when a young lady turns eighteen. This dinner is especially for you. Your guests are arriving and you are not there to greet them. You know how much that upsets Adam."

"They aren't my guests, Simone. They are *his*

guests. There isn't one person attending who is my age, or even single. And don't call him 'Mr. Adam.' It only makes him sound more imposing. That's why he can intimidate people. Everyone walks around treating him as if he were a god.''

As Eve slipped the gown over her head, her words became muffled under yards of velvet. "Well, not me." Eve's head popped out of the swirl of material. "He would love to see me grovel at his feet, thankful for any dole he hands out."

"He is very generous to you, Eve. This gown he bought you for your birthday is beautiful— and very expensive." Simone began to button the back of the dress.

"That's another thing. He even selects my clothes. I have nothing in the say of it." She began to stroke the soft velvet of the skirt, impervious to how lovely she looked in the flowing gown; the color matched the exact shade of her violet eyes. "It is beautiful, but he only bought it because he likes to show me off to his friends."

She pulled on white lace elbow-length gloves, while Simone attached an aigrette among the mass of curls on Eve's head. The delicate white plume enhanced the raven black hair that surrounded it.

"You look lovely, *chérie*," Simone said proudly as she hurried Eve out the door.

As she paused at the top of the stairway, Eve saw that the drawing room and foyer were filled with guests. She spied Adam at the foot of the stairway, dressed fastidiously in a black cutaway jacket, fitted trousers, and an embroidered waistcoat. A black silk cravat was tied neatly at his neck. *The only thing missing on that devil is a pair of horns*, Eve reflected pettishly. His sapphire eyes remained impassive as he watched her descend the stairway.

"You're late," he grumbled, accepting her hand and bringing it to his lips.

"Oh, really? I must have misunderstood what time you *ordered* me to attend." She smiled sweetly and took his arm.

Eve's eyes continually shifted to the clock as she waited impatiently for dinner to end. As usual, the conversation revolved around the gold strikes.

She was seated next to one of Adam's business associates, Arnold Kennedy. The lecherous old man had been attempting to fondle her leg under the table throughout the whole meal.

"Well, my dear, did Adam tell you about our strike?"

Eve glared at him and removed his hand from her leg. "No, Mr. Kennedy. I can't visualize you and Adam out in the hills with picks and shovels."

Kennedy broke into loud laughter, which sounded more like wheezing to Eve. "Tell me, Adam, haven't you told this dear girl about our mine?"

"I usually don't discuss my business affairs with my ward, Arnold." Eve could see that Adam was disgruntled and did not want to discuss it further.

"But it was so clever, old chap, and entirely your idea."

"Modesty, Adam?" Eve challenged.

"Not at all. I just doubt that you would be interested, Eve."

"Why don't you tell me, Mr. Kennedy." She only pursued the conversation because she knew it was irritating Adam.

"My pleasure, my dear." Arnold Kennedy looked like a blustering walrus to her. "We filed a claim in Amador County because it's rich gold country. Adam figured we should try to get to the buried ore, so our company dug a shaft five hundred feet into the ground."

"Five hundred feet deep! My Lord, man, how did you ever get the ore to the surface?" one of the men inquired.

"Genius. Sheer genius," Kennedy said. "In order to hoist the quartz, Adam designed this mammoth wheel and diverted a stream to power it hydraulically. Between the steps, the ramps, and the sluices for the structure, it took over one hundred men to build it, but the expense was worth it. We hit a mother lode, a solid vein of gold. With our operation, we're able to process tons of ore."

"Well, I guess it takes money to make money, doesn't it," Eve said sarcastically. "It's a pity all those other miners out there, with just picks and shovels, don't have the same advantage."

"The hundred men working our claim do," Adam said curtly. "They're sharing in some of the profits." He threw a scathing glare at her. "Now you know, ladies and gentlemen, why I never discuss business with my ward."

When the last guest finally departed, Eve sighed with relief and glanced anxiously at the clock. In two hours Roger Sullivan was due to arrive at the gate with a carriage.

"You have been watching the clock all evening, Eve. Are we keeping you from your bed?" Adam asked.

"I am tired, Adam, so I think I will say good night." She hurried up the stairs to her room.

The next hour passed slowly as she listened at the door for the sounds to die down in the house. When she was certain everyone had retired, she changed into a modest traveling dress and packed a few articles of clothing in a valise. She then put on her coat to await Roger's arrival.

After what seemed like hours, Eve walked over and picked up the mantel clock. Still fifteen minutes before Roger was due. She was too impatient to remain in the room and decided to wait for him at the gate. Picking up her valise, she peeked out the door. The hallway was empty, and she cautiously made her way past Adam's chamber door to the top of the stairs.

She heard the faint sound of voices below and

saw a thin shaft of light under the library door. Eve froze as she recognized Roger Sullivan's voice. "Thank you again, Mr. Rawlins, you've been very generous."

Eve shrank back as the library door opened and Adam ushered his visitor to the front door and silently let him out.

Eve raced back to her room and pushed aside the lace curtains at her bedroom window. She watched the young man below walking down the path. There was a jauntiness to his stride. Even in the dim light, she could see that it was not the step of a man devastated by heartbreak.

He climbed into a carriage without a backward glance, and she watched it move away. Still at the window, she remained motionless. Only a slow trickle of tears revealed the misery she was suffering.

Soon the carriage was enfolded by a cloak of darkness, but Eve stood mute and still until the sound of shodden hooves no longer echoed through the night.

She drew a deep breath, then expelled it in a shuddering sob. Brushing aside her tears, she shrugged off her cloak and stormed out of the bedroom and down the stairs.

Eve did not stop to knock on the library door. She yanked it open and charged into the room.

"What kept you?" Adam did not look up. His dark head remained bent over a ledger book.

"I hate you, Adam Rawlins."

"So you have reminded me on countless occasions," he replied, unperturbed. Dipping his pen into an ink horn, he continued at his task without a glance in her direction.

His indifference fueled her fury. "Will you put down that damned pen and look at me when I'm speaking to you."

Adam picked up a blotter, rolled it across the page, and closed the ledger. He glanced up with a pained expression.

"Talking? I wasn't aware you were *talking* to me, Eve. It sounded shrewishly like shouting. And how many times must I remind you that the use of profanity is unfeminine?"

Eve ignored his sarcasm. "How much did it cost you to pay off Roger Sullivan?"

His face curled into a smirk of satisfaction. "Oh, he was the cheapest of the lot. Since you met that useless wastrel while working at the Children's Home, I must insist you cease any further volunteer work there. In the future, the orphans of Sacramento will have to survive without your services."

Adam shook his head mockingly. "Tsk, tsk, tsk, I must say, Eve, your selections are becoming quite pathetic. At least the last chap had enough integrity to take two days to decide between you or the money."

Eve's hands curled into fists at her side, and her body trembled with anger. "You're the one who's pathetic. You and your warped obsession to humiliate me."

Adam's face sobered. "You're humiliating yourself by grasping at straws."

Eyes flashing, she threw her hands up in frustration. "What choice do you leave me? You've bullied or bribed every man who has ever looked at me. Why, Adam? Why do you do it?"

Adam's expression was guarded as he leaned back into the shadow of his high-backed chair. "Maybe it's because I don't think they are worthy of you."

Eve's eyes blazed with contempt. "You never cease your cruel gibes, do you? You can't resist reminding me that in your eyes, I'm nothing but 'the bastard offspring of a whore.'"

Adam shot to his feet as Eve continued to lash out. "I haven't forgotten that night. I'll never forget it. Remembering how you branded my mother a whore before she died has given me the strength to endure the pleasure you get from tormenting me."

Eve's voice quivered with emotion. "But, someday . . . someday, Adam Rawlins, I'll make you pay for it."

Forcing back a strangled sob, she ran from the room. Adam was at her side before she reached the bottom of the stairway. He grabbed her arm. "I want you to come with me for a moment, Eve."

A note of supplication in his voice succeeded in penetrating the force of her anger. She allowed him to take her arm and lead her to the portrait that hung above the fireplace in the drawing room.

"Do you see that man, Eve? In the years

you've been here, you've never asked me about him. He was my grandfather, David Rawlins."

Eve's glance rose to the strong face of the man in the portrait. She had secretly admired it from the first time she saw the painting. The eyes of the man fascinated her. The artist had captured a gleam of amusement in their sapphire depths.

"He left Virginia in 1773 and came West," Adam continued. "He was only seventeen. Not even as old as you are right now. He came alone, not knowing what he was seeking, but whatever it was, he knew he wouldn't find it in Virginia.

"So he fought Indians, Mexicans, Spaniards, and everything Nature could throw at him to get here. He found it. Anita Maria Pilar del Greco y Cortezan.

"She was only fourteen years old at the time. Her father was a Spanish don. A big landowner. A tough old bird who knew how to hold on to what he considered his own. In his society David Rawlins was an Anglo. An undesirable. No threat to him or his culture, and certainly no mate for his daughter."

Adam chuckled lightly. "But the old don hadn't reckoned on Grandfather's persistence and determination. Or maybe he saw a quality in Grandfather that made him realize he would be waging a useless struggle.

"At the outbreak of the Revolution, Grandfather announced he was returning to Virginia to help in the fight for independence. I guess the old don was gambling on time and distance being too much of a deterrent, or maybe he was hoping Grandfather would get killed in the war. Whatever his reasons, he undoubtedly believed they would never see Grandfather again, so he agreed to the marriage whenever Grandfather returned to California."

Eve glanced at Adam, surprised to see his usual sardonic expression replaced by one of pride. "He underestimated David Rawlins. Six years later, Grandfather returned to find that the woman he loved had been married off to another man. Grandfather was as patient as he was persistent. Ten years later, she became a widow and he married her. That was the beginning, not the ending."

"Adam, what is your purpose in telling me this?" Eve snapped, exasperated. She was still angry.

"My father always claimed that I had a lot of Grandfather in me," Adam replied softly.

"I'm sure there is a message in all this, but, frankly, I don't have the patience to pursue it," Eve responded. She turned away to leave.

"I would have thought that by now it was obvious to you. I intend to marry you myself, Evelyn MacGregor."

She swung back, stunned, and wondering if she had heard him correctly. Mesmerized, she could only stand there frozen, with his devil's dark eyes upon her.

Adam reached out and pulled her to him. Somehow she found a voice to force out the words. "Stop this, Adam. Please! This is wrong. You have no right to do this to me."

"I have more right than any of those other bastards you were willing to give yourself to. You belong to me, Eve. You're mine," he whispered hoarsely.

He lowered his head. His lips were firm and the pressure deepened until she was breathless. His mouth took possession of hers, forcing her lips apart. She gasped for breath, and his tongue drove into her mouth. Eve tried to push him away, but his arms closed about her like a heated vise. She struggled and attempted to cry out, but the words were forced back into her throat by his plundering tongue.

His hand slid up to her neck and down the slim column to the heaving mound of her breasts. His touch was hot—like the hand of Satan as it slipped into the top of her gown. He filled it with the fullness of her throbbing breast.

A sob escaped past her lips as his fingers began to lightly rub the aching peaks. Eve became aware of a tightening within her in response. The realization of what it meant horrified her. *Dear God, was she beginning to respond to this devil's touch?*

She tried to force the disturbing sensation out of her mind as she struggled for breath. How dare he do this to her? This was his final way of degrading her.

His mouth released hers and slid to the sensitive pulse at her throat. She gasped for breath as his hand continued stroking the sensitive peaks of her breasts.

Once again his lips closed over her own. She

could feel the mounting tension it was creating. She . couldn't understand what changes were happening to her, but she knew she had to resist.

Her body was her only possession that did not bear his mark of ownership. It was a pristine citadel that had not been prostituted by his money or domination. He was attempting to violate it, to control it like everything else he touched. She would not let him profane it.

Eve felt as if the fires of hell were swirling around her. Her mind became confused by the sensations bombarding it. Sensations from without and within—the intoxicating male smell of him, the knot at her loins which was tightening and tightening.

Adam released her and she opened her eyes. He was staring down at her. A mocking gleam in his dark eyes.

The sight of it incensed her indignation and she struck out in fury with a resounding smack to his face. "How dare you! Oh, how I hate you! I hate the very sight of you."

She saw his flush of surprise shift to an amused smirk. She turned away, but Adam grabbed her shoulders in a crushing grasp. "Tell me, Miss MacGregor, how often do you think a man can stand being told how despicable he is?" Eve cringed away, but he did not release his grasp on her. "For the past six years, you have managed by word or deed to convey that message to me every opportunity you could find."

At the sight of the dangerous look in his eyes,

Eve renewed her struggle. "But you've never hated my money, have you, Miss MacGregor, or the fancy Paris education that money bought you?"

Eve finally succeeded in shrugging out of his grasp. "I didn't ask for any Paris education. That was your idea. You sent me away to get rid of me."

He smiled at the accuracy of her insight. When she started to turn away, Adam reached out and caught a fistful of her gown, yanking her back to him. "What about these fancy clothes? Do you hate them, too?"

"I don't want them. I never asked for them. You can have your fancy clothes. You only buy them to dress me up and show me off to your friends."

His smirk was more than she could bare. She had to get away from him, but he wouldn't release his grasp of her gown. "Well, unfortunately, Miss MacGregor, nothing comes free in this world. The time has come for you to pay the piper." Having made his position clear, he released her.

Adam had never frightened her before. Even as a young girl, she had never been afraid of him. Now she found herself petrified.

"I'll never marry you. I'll kill myself before I'll let you force me into such an arrangement."

Shoving him aside, she ran from the room.

Eve was consumed with panic. Adam never issued idle threats. No matter what she said, she knew that if she remained he would somehow force her to marry him.

She had to get away. That night.

Eve woke Simone and related her plight. Without hesitation, the woman packed her bag to leave with her.

The sun was just rising as they stole out of the house and ran, as fast as their legs would carry them, down the tree-lined path. Had Eve looked back, she would have seen a shadowy figure watching from the library window.

Adam watched them disappear down the driveway. He shook his head indulgently. "You missed the whole moral of the story, didn't you, Eve? Even the old don knew when he was waging a useless struggle."

He walked to a portrait of his mother hanging on the wall and moved it aside. A small safe was concealed behind it. Adam extracted an envelope and removed the contents. His eyes hurriedly scanned the printed sheets until he found the information he was seeking. Then he folded the papers and returned them to the safe.

CHAPTER SIX

The pale blue eyes of the man behind the ticket counter remained unwavering. "I've told you a dozen times, lady. There ain't no seats on the stage. And there won't be for a good week. Everybody and his brother's headin' for the gold fields." He flipped through several sheets attached to a battered clipboard. "I've got two seats open for a week from Wednesday."

"That's too late. I have to leave now." Eve turned to Simone. "What do you think we should do?" Simone shook her head helplessly.

"Why don't you try the steamboat?" the teller suggested. He pulled a watch out of his vest pocket and studied it. "The *Senator* should be sailing in a couple of hours. It's cheaper, too. Stage costs a dollar a mile. The ship's only thirty bucks a head. In ten hours you'll be in San Francisco."

"Thank you, we will," Eve said with a grateful smile.

The man shook his head as the two women hurried off. "They ain't got a snowball's chance in hell of getting on that boat," he muttered.

The pier was a beehive of activity when Eve and Simone reached it. Crates and boxes were piled in huge stacks waiting to be loaded onto the ship that would steam down the Sacramento River to the bay of San Francisco. Although Sacramento had been originally built as a fort, it had quickly expanded into a city. Now the gold rush was making tremendous demands on the city's resources.

A crewman pointed out the captain of the *Senator* to them. His eyes followed Eve with a wolfish gleam as she threaded her way through the flurry of activity to the tall, thin man who was engrossed in barking orders to several dozen men lowering cargo into the hold of the ship. He acknowledged Eve and Simone with an impatient nod, but did not halt the operation while he listened to their request.

"It's out of the question, Miss . . ."

"MacGregor," Eve said. "And this is Mademoiselle Lisle."

"I'm sorry, ladies, but I don't have room for any more passengers."

"We don't take up very much room, Captain Grant. We'll stay on deck, or in the hold. Wherever you want us."

"I don't want you, Miss MacGregor. I don't

have a cabin available for you. And I don't have time to protect two unescorted women on my ship. You must have a damn good reason to want to get to San Francisco." He slanted a sideward frown at them. "Besides, San Francisco is no place for respectable young ladies. There's only one kind of woman heading for that town right now. I'm sure that's not what you have in mind."

Eve blushed at the suggestion. "Of course not, Captain. I have a very valid reason. I must get there."

The man shook his head. "I'm sorry, ladies. There is nothing I can do for you." He doffed his hat and walked away when a crewman called him to the pilothouse.

Eve wanted to burst into tears. It seemed as if freedom was being dangled in front of her, only to be snatched away when she reached for it. Was she a mouse and Adam Rawlins a big black cat? Any moment she expected his huge paw to slam down and catch her by the coattail.

Simone tried to comfort her. "Perhaps we should return to the house until we can reserve passage?"

"Never," Eve asserted. "I am never going back to that house. I'll think of something." She picked up her bag and began to walk away. Simone shook her head and followed her.

"Miss MacGregor."

Both women spun around upon hearing Eve's name called out. Captain Grant was walking down the gangplank, waving to them to halt. "Wait, Miss MacGregor."

Eve was a picture of hopeful expectation. She threw a promising smile at Simone as the captain approached.

"I have reconsidered your request, Miss MacGregor. Since it is so important for you and your companion to get to San Francisco, I will offer you the use of my cabin."

"Oh, thank you, Captain." Eve was too ecstatic to stop to think how unusual the offer appeared.

Simone, on the other hand, was regarding the man with a dubious frown. "What is the charge, sir?"

"Under the circumstances, I think we can forget about a charge."

"Under what circumstances, Captain Grant?" Simone was openly suspicious now. She had heard many tales of how innocent girls had been kidnapped and sold into white slavery or Chinese cribs. "Why would you offer the convenience of your cabin without a charge?"

The captain bristled uncomfortably. "Well, if you insist. Five dollars will be adequate."

Simone was not about to be appeased so easily. "The man at the stagecoach office said the charge is thirty dollars per person, Captain."

"Who is the captain of this ship? I said five dollars each is sufficient. If that isn't to your satisfaction, I suggest you return to the stagecoach office." He spun about and walked away.

Eve, who trusted everyone's motives except those of Adam Rawlins, rejected the caution of her friend. She followed him and grabbed his arm. "Whatever you say, Captain Grant. Mademoiselle Lisle is just looking out for my interests. We're both grateful to you for your generous offer and we accept it with thanks."

"As you wish, Miss MacGregor." He motioned to one of his crew. "Take the ladies' baggage to my cabin." Then he turned back to them. "I suggest you eat before we sail. It is a ten-hour trip and we don't serve food on the ship."

"That is an excellent idea," Simone agreed. "We haven't eaten breakfast." She was anxious to get Eve alone to voice her suspicions.

"We sail in an hour," the captain said curtly. He returned to supervising the loading of cargo as Simone took Eve's arm and pulled her away.

Simone's arguments fell on deaf ears. The two women returned to the ship a short while later carrying a basket with roast beef sandwiches, hard-boiled eggs, and a bottle of milk.

Soon after they boarded, the ship set sail. Simone slipped the bolt on the door into place when they entered the cabin. "I intend to keep this door firmly latched until we reach San Francisco."

Eve paid her no heed. "What if the captain needs something from his cabin?"

"He's not going to get it," Simone replied emphatically. "I think one of us should remain awake. Why don't you lie down and sleep for a while. It's a long trip and you said you've been awake all night."

Laughing, Eve shook her head. "Simone,

we're perfectly safe on this ship. You act as if Captain Grant is a pirate."

"Well, I don't understand why he changed his mind so quickly."

"Whatever the reason, I trust him," Eve said, plopping down on a chair. "So let's eat. I'm hungry."

The food tasted delicious to Eve. The whole world had taken on a rosy glow to her. She felt like a prisoner who had escaped from her gaoler.

When the initial buoyancy wore off, Eve realized how exhausted she was feeling. Relenting to Simone's insistence, she lay down on the bunk.

Despite her drowsiness, sleep did not come easy. Until now, there had been the driving urgency to get away from Adam. This was the first time, since her ordeal with him, that she had some quiet moments to reflect on the situation.

She had not told Simone the whole truth about what had happened between Adam and herself, only that they had a violent quarrel because he wanted to marry her. Why did she hesitate to tell her the whole story? She had nothing to be ashamed about. Or did she?

The biggest doubt tormenting her was her feelings at the end. True, she had resisted Adam with all her strength. But was that what she really wanted? She could not forget the sensations his touch had provoked. Was she frightened because he was kissing her? Or was it because she wanted him to?

Those moments were jumbled and confused in her mind. Hating Adam had previously been a simple emotion. Now there was another feeling—a feeling which she was not willing to weigh.

When Eve finally slept, it was the deep slumber brought on by the physical exhaustion that follows an emotional trauma.

It was dusk when Simone woke Eve. She had slept away the day, and the *Senator* had reached San Francisco.

The two women stepped eagerly onto the deck and stopped short, in shock. All the passengers were on their feet, staring silently at the grim spectacle in the harbor. Hundreds of vessels of all sizes and shapes bobbed idly on the water—a graveyard of abandoned ships.

Evening fog rolling in from the sea swirled around the eerie specter of rotting ships. Barren masts rising from their midst seemed like markers for grave sites.

"Unbelievable, isn't it?"

Eve glanced in surprise at Captain Grant, who had silently materialized beside her. She could only nod.

"The crews have abandoned them for the lure of the gold fields," Captain Grant said.

"I've never seen anything like it," Eve was finally able to mutter. "It's almost a sacrilege."

The captain nodded grimly. "Each time I make this trip, there are more of them. By next year, there will be twice as many."

"My mother and I lived here six years ago. It was just a small settlement then called Yerba Buena. There weren't five hundred people in the whole area."

"Then you know that the name of the town was changed after the war, but the gold rush changed the population. There are over forty thousand miners in the area now, and another twenty thousand people in the city. Before this madness is over, we'll probably see over a hundred thousand."

A formidable frown creased his brow. "I hope you have a reservation at a hotel. If not, I advise you and Miss Lisle to remain on board ship tonight. You won't find a hotel room."

Simone nudged Eve's leg with her own. She was convinced the captain was not to be trusted. Eve had intended on staying at a hotel, but it was obvious Captain Grant knew what he was talking about. However, she had ignored Simone's warnings until now and felt she had to respect her wishes.

"We intend to visit an old friend of my mother's."

The captain eyed her dubiously. "Well, I suggest that a couple of my crew accompany you. The city has changed drastically."

"I am sure we'll be fine, Captain Grant. I often visited there when we lived in this area."

"This whole city has changed, miss. It's pretty wild. Your mother's friend may have left the area."

"I hardly think so, Captain. I am sure the streets are still safe for any respectable woman."

"The truth is, Miss MacGregor, there are not too many respectable women who go out on these streets at night. They have the good sense to remain in their homes."

"We'll just have to take our chances, Captain," Simone quickly interjected, fearful that Eve would weaken.

"As you wish, ladies." He returned to the pilothouse to supervise the docking of the ship.

Eve and Simone retrieved their luggage from the cabin and returned to the deck, waiting to disembark. The wharf was swarming with people and color: there were Mexicans in bright serapes and wide sombreros, Chinese darting back and forth in floppy shirts and straw coolie hats, baggy-trouser miners in red flannel shirts and high boots, and well-groomed merchants in frock coats and top hats. All were watching the ship's arrival with interest. What was missing among the throng on the pier were women. There were none to be seen.

It was considerably later when the ship docked and they could disembark. The appearance of two women generated more excitement among the curious assembled there than any previous interest in whatever cargo the *Senator* might have been carrying.

Eve's eyes were drawn to a stranger leaning

against a building. He appeared to be studying her with more than casual interest. She saw that Simone had noticed the stranger also, and was watching him as well.

He appeared to be an inch or two under six feet. His skin was deeply bronzed and he had dark eyes with heavy brows. A mustache drooped around the corners of his mouth.

He straightened up and approached them. "Can I get you ladies a carriage?"

The stranger had the lean, rangy look of a man who spent a great deal of time in the saddle. Even though he spoke without a trace of any accent, Eve felt there was something foreign about his face. His nose was slightly broad and his cheekbones were high. It wasn't a handsome face; it was too chiseled, too craggy for handsomeness. And she sensed a mysterious aura about him, even a deadliness.

He wore a plain muslin shirt, dark trousers, and a buckskin vest. His hat was the wide-brimmed variety worn by the cavalry. For a moment she thought he might be in the army, until she noticed the two revolvers hanging from a gun belt at his hips. Then the realization hit her. He was a gunfighter.

"Thank you. That's very thoughtful of you, Mr. . . .?" Eve waited for him to volunteer his name.

"Montgomery. Sam Montgomery." He nodded politely and moved away.

The two women exchanged perplexed glances, but sooner than they could comment, the reticent stranger had returned with a carriage. Before she could thank him again, the man disappeared into the crowd.

As their carriage moved through the streets, Eve saw little resemblance between this boom town and the small community she grew up in as a child. Tall brick structures lined the once-deserted area around the dock. The vast expanse of barren tract, which formerly stretched between scattered buildings, was now jammed with tents, sheds, huts, and other wooden buildings. There was not an empty spot to be seen.

Loud laughter and music floated from several of the tents. The two women stole curious glances out of the carriage window as they passed by the tents, amazed to discover they were lavish gambling casinos with opulent interiors.

"Are you sure you know where we're going?" Simone asked as the carriage rambled farther away from the waterfront. The crowds had thinned, and a drunk occasionally staggered out of the shadows.

"The driver assured me he knows where Brigg's Bakery is located. Aunt Hannah lives above it. I just can't believe how much everything has changed in just six years. None of these buildings were here then. Aunt Hannah's bakery was the only building for blocks."

"Why didn't you come to live with your aunt when your mother died?" Simone asked.

"Oh, Hannah Briggs isn't my real aunt. I just

call her that because she was such a good friend of my mother's."

The carriage halted, and both girls peered out at the dark and deserted street. The driver jumped down and opened the door. "This is as close as I can get you, ladies. It rained today and the road's too muddy to try to go any farther without getting bogged down." He pointed toward a row of dingy-looking buildings on the next block. "The bakery's just up the block. Keep on the planks so you don't dirty your feet." He handed them their bags, turned the horses around, and drove off.

With resolute sighs, they picked up their bags and had not gone more than half the block when two men stepped out of the shadows, blocking the way on the narrow plank.

"What's two fine Sheilas like yerselves doin' out 'ere alone?" asked the short man with a barrel chest. His companion was taller and thinner. Each was wearing a round derby.

Eve had spent the last two years bluffing her way through confrontations with Adam Rawlins. She wasn't about to turn and run from these two.

"Please step aside, gentlemen," she said feistily.

The shorter man poked the arm of his companion. "Well, Dickie, did ya get 'er fine airs. She's a snooty one, ain't she?" The other man hooted in accord, displaying several gaping holes in the front of his mouth.

"What do you want?" Eve asked sharply.

"Dickie and me was thinkin' of givin' ya a 'elpin' 'and with them bags yer carryin'." His announcement produced another snort from his companion.

"We have no intentions of giving you our bags, so get out of the way," Eve demanded.

"Well, Sheila, me and Dickie are just gonna 'ave to take 'em then." He attempted to grab the bag Eve was carrying, while his companion did the same to Simone. The women began to scream, hanging on tenaciously to the handles of their bags as they struggled with the thieves.

The commotion attracted attention. From farther down the street, a horseman began riding toward them, firing his pistol into the air. People began to appear at doorways, drawn by the noise.

Simone lost the contest over her bag with her attacker, but Eve was still putting up a game battle. In desperation, the shorter man clenched his fist and delivered a blow to Eve's cheek. She lost her grip on the bag. It opened and the contents spilled out as she went sprawling into the mud.

"Ya bloody bitch. Ya ain't seen the last of me," he snarled. They sped away with only Simone's bag.

Eve sat up. Her head was spinning. "Are you all right, *chérie*?" Simone asked worriedly, bending over her.

Eve's vision began to clear and she cautiously tested her jaw. It was sore, but did not feel broken. Several people were clustered around them. Simone was surprised to see that the man on horseback was Sam Montgomery. Had he been following them?

"I saw who did this. It was a couple of them Sydney Ducks," one of the men in the crowd grumbled.

"Who are Sydney Ducks?" Simone asked.

"You ladies must be new here. The Ducks are those damned convicts from Australia. They tried working the fields for a while, but it was too much work for the thieving lot. So now all they do is steal and cause trouble. They all live over in Sydney Town, south of Telegraph Hill."

Sam Montgomery reached out a hand to help Eve to her feet. "Where in hell are you ladies heading for?" he grumbled to Simone.

"We're trying to find a Hannah Briggs."

"Did you say Hannah Briggs?" A heavy-set woman stepped forward out of the crowd. "I'm Hannah Briggs, or was, that is, until yesterday. Got myself married. Name's Hannah Miller now. What can I do for you?"

"Aunt Hannah. It's me, Evelyn MacGregor," Eve cried out at the sight of the woman.

The woman peered at her. "Well, land o' Goshen, Eve darling! I never would have recognized you." She grabbed the girl in a bear hug that almost cracked her ribs. "Come inside where I can get a good look at you. It's just a short way farther."

Hannah Miller put a plump arm around Eve's shoulders and led her away. The rest of the crowd returned to their houses, grumbling about damned convicts terrorizing decent folks.

Simone and Sam Montgomery remained standing alone. She smiled gratefully. "Thank you for your help, Mr. Montgomery." She began to pick up the scattered clothing.

"Let me do that," he said, stooping down to help her.

The Frenchwoman stopped in surprise. She was not used to gallantry from a strange man. Men usually ignored her. "It was you who fired the shot, wasn't it, Mr. Montgomery?"

The gunfighter nodded. "I couldn't risk trying to shoot them. I might have hit one of you."

"Thank you for your help." Simone blushed shyly and hurried away. It was difficult for her to carry on a conversation with a man. She glanced over her shoulder. Sam Montgomery had picked up Eve's bag and was following her.

By the time they reached the tiny bakery shop, Hannah Briggs had lit an oil lamp, sat Eve down at a small table in the corner, and scurried off into the kitchen.

Simone was examining Eve's bruised cheek when the woman returned carrying a basin of water and a bar of soap.

She smiled cordially at Simone. "Sit yourself down, honey. I brought some soap and water for you to clean some of that mud off you. Those damned Ducks. We ought to start stringing them up by their necks. That would put a stop to their thieving and bullying."

Her glance swung with curiosity to Sam

Montgomery, who was standing in the open doorway with Eve's bag. "What's he doing here?"

"Mr. Montgomery was nice enough to come to our help," Simone said.

Hannah Briggs regarded him with a disgruntled frown. "Put the bag in the corner and then get your carcass out of here."

Eve's eyes widened in surprise. Simone's gaze shifted downward in embarrassment at the rude remark.

"Aunt Hannah, Mr. Montgomery tried to help us. Who knows what those bullies would have done if he hadn't come to our aid?"

"I just want to ask the ladies a couple of questions," Montgomery said.

"Then get it over with and move on. I don't like half-breeds."

Eve's glance swung to him in surprise. So he was part Indian. That explained his unusual coloring.

The gunman appeared indifferent to the older woman's hostility. "Can you describe the two men?"

"Loathsome." Eve's spunky grin quickly changed into a grimace of pain. She raised a wet towel to her aching cheek.

Simone glanced timidly at him. "One was tall and thin. His name was Dickie. He was missing several of his front teeth."

"Can you tell me anything about the other? What were they wearing?"

Simone shook her head. "I think they were

wearing red shirts, but I can't be certain. It was too dark."

"The man who hit me was short and muscular," Eve volunteered. "I remember their hats. They both were wearing either black or brown derbies."

Sam nodded grimly and was out the door before they realized he was leaving.

"Please wait, Mr. Montgomery," Simone cried, and followed him. He stopped to wait for her to catch up to him. "Are you going to get the sheriff?"

Montgomery grinned sardonically. "I don't get along too well with sheriffs."

"You're not going to try to find those two men by yourself? That would be dangerous."

His reply was a negligent shrug. "That's my problem."

"But someone said those thugs have their own community. Surely you're not going there alone."

"You want your bag back, don't you?"

"Not if it means putting your life at risk. Why are you doing this, Mr. Montgomery?"

He turned and walked away without answering.

A sense of tragedy seemed to hang about the gunfighter. Simone became overpowered by melancholy as she watched the lone figure disappear into the darkness.

CHAPTER SEVEN

Hannah and Eve were sitting at the table when Simone rejoined them. The older woman was dabbing at her eyes with a towel.

"So she's been dead all these years. I might have known there was a reason she never came back to visit. Should have guessed it weren't 'cause she turned uppity." Hannah shook her head sadly. "Ah, child, your mother was a saint."

The woman's words brought a tender smile to Eve's face. Hannah blew her nose, leaned over, and patted Eve's hand. "But look at yourself, will you? What a fine lady you've become. Ah, Mary MacGregor would have been so proud of you."

"Thank you, Aunt Hannah," Eve beamed. "Now, did I understand you to say you've gotten married?"

The older woman erupted into loud laughter. "Do you believe it? Thought sure I was too ugly for any man to want to marry." She glanced quickly at Simone. "Seems like most men don't look beyond a pretty face to see what's underneath," she said gently for the plain girl's sake. Simone blushed and shifted her eyes away. "Well, women are so scarce in these parts that I got myself a husband. Charlie hit a big strike and I'm moving to Placerville tomorrow. If you'd been a day later you'd of missed me."

"Tomorrow!" Eve exclaimed. "You're going to be leaving that soon?"

"Yep. Charlie had to head back to his mine. I just came home to get some of my keepsakes."

"What about this store?" Eve asked, looking around with interest.

"I've got no use for it now."

Eve and Simone exchanged significant glances as the same thought occurred to each of them. "Would you consider selling us the building, Aunt Hannah?"

"Selling? Hell, honey, you can have it. I got no further use for it. And I don't need the money. Your ma was a good friend and I'm glad to do it." Hannah frowned momentarily. "I don't understand what you want with it, though. Thought your ma married some rich guy up North."

"She did, Aunt Hannah, but that didn't affect me. Simone and I came here to get a start. This would be ideal for us. She was a kitchen helper in France and I always helped out in the kitchen wherever Mother worked. We shouldn't have any problem operating a bakery." Eve turned excitedly to Simone. "What do you think of the idea?"

Simone was bustling with as much enthusiasm as Eve. "I think it would solve all our problems. And I love to bake."

"I don't have to tell you, you gals wouldn't have anything to worry about if you didn't take the bakery. Both of you could find a husband easy enough."

The face of Adam Rawlins flashed into Eve's mind. "A husband is the last thing I want right now, Aunt Hannah."

"What about you, Frenchie? You'll never have a better chance of finding a husband."

"I'm really not interested, Mrs. Miller," Simone replied.

"Sounds to me like it's settled then," Hannah announced. "I'll get the papers."

When she left the room, the two girls hugged each other and joined hands, twirling around and giggling gaily. This turn of events was beyond their wildest expectations. The night's previous misadventure was forgotten.

"We'll make new curtains for the windows," Simone enthused.

"And put on a fresh coat of paint," Eve added.

"I'll bake *choux puffs* and *éclairs*."

"And what's that puff pastry that tastes so good?"

"*Pâte feuilletée*," Simone responded.

"Yes, that's it. And don't forget those delicious little tarts you used to make, filled with custard and coconut."

"*Petites bouchées.*"

"Oh, Simone, my mouth waters just thinking about them."

The girls sat down to regain their breath when Hannah returned carrying a heavy metal box. She put it down on the table and plopped down in the chair.

"This here's the deed. I'll sign it over to you gals and you be sure to file it tomorrow before anyone else tries to jump the claim. Everybody's looking for land here. Don't let anybody try to scare you off. I own this, and now you will be the owners. Just file the papers to make it all legal."

Eve felt she should make another attempt to pay despite their low finances. "We insist upon paying you, Aunt Hannah. What are you asking for it?"

"I don't want your money, child. I don't need it. And besides, I kind of like the idea of you keeping the bakery going. If I sold it to strangers, they'd just make another barroom or casino out of it." Hannah knew by the determined look on Eve's face that the young girl was going to be insistent. "All right, honey. I'll take twenty-five dollars. That's what it cost me when I bought it. If you can't afford to pay me now, I'll take your marker."

Eve broke into a wide grin. "It's a deal, and we'll pay you now." She retrieved her purse from her carpetbag and counted out the necessary amount from her meager supply.

"We'll never be able to thank you enough," she exclaimed, hugging her aunt and placing a kiss on her cheek.

The older woman blustered in embarrassment. "Well, let's see about finding you someplace to sleep tonight. I must say, you're two sassy gals to think you could come to this town without any roof over your heads."

Eve's eyes danced with mischief. "I knew as long as I had my Aunt Hannah, I wouldn't have anything to worry about." The image of Adam Rawlins returned to haunt her, and her face sobered. "If only I would have thought to do the same two years ago."

The quarters above the store consisted of a cozy sitting room and a bedroom. Hannah made herself a bed on the couch and insisted on the girls taking the bedroom. When they were alone, Eve noticed a letdown in Simone's spirits.

"What's wrong, Simone? Do you think we're making a mistake?"

Dejectedly, Simone sat down on the edge of the bed. "I just remembered, I no longer have an extra stitch of clothing, or a single cent. Everything I owned was in the carpetbag that thief stole."

Eve sighed in relief. "Is that all that's bothering you? I was afraid you were having second thoughts." She got her purse and dumped its contents on the bed. "Half of everything I own is yours. We're in this together. We'll divide my clothes." She giggled delightedly. "Of course, they're all full of mud right now. But let's see how much money we have."

A careful count resulted in a total of $24.00.

"It's not much, but we'll have to make it do," Eve said confidently. She started to giggle again. "I'm sure other entrepreneurs got started with a lot less than twenty-four dollars and a carpetbag of dirty clothes."

They awoke the next morning to the sight of bright sunshine streaming into the room. Eve jumped out of bed and rushed to the window.

The street was bustling with activity. All the busy colors and shapes she had seen at the waterfront were in evidence below. The street was still muddy, but everyone picked their way along, crossing from one side to the other on planks that had been laid down for that purpose.

"Simone, you must come and see this. Isn't this an exciting city?"

Simone padded barefoot across the floor and for several seconds stared sleepily out of the window. *Oui, chérie,* but it's not exactly the Champs Élysées."

Laughing, they turned away and hurriedly dressed.

Hannah accompanied them to be certain the deed was registered properly in their names. Then, before she climbed into the stagecoach, they bade a tearful goodbye to her.

The girls did not even consider spending any

more of their precious money on carriage rides. They walked back to the bakery. The sight of the two young women created a flurry of interest wherever they passed. Men would remove their hats and, with courtly bows, step aside for them.

Eve's heart swelled with satisfaction as she entered the store. She was free. Free of Adam Rawlins forever.

An inspection of the kitchen produced an unexpected surprise. It was amazingly well equipped with pans and utensils. A well-stocked larder contained an abundance of condiments, flour and lard. There were also two full barrels of apples. However, there was neither milk nor eggs, ingredients essential to the French pastry Simone had hoped to prepare.

With her chin in her hands, she sat down despondently at the table. "Goodbye, little *éclairs* and *choux à la crème. Adieu, petites bouchées. Au revoir, pâte feuilletée.*"

Eve leaned over the table, imitating Simone's pose, so that they were eye to eye. She grinned broadly.

"But hello, apple pie!"

Simone tried to withstand the persuasive appeal of that broad grin, but lost in the attempt and ended up returning Eve's smile. "You pare the apples; I'll make the crusts."

A short while later, the small bakery was filled with the tantalizing aroma of cinnamon and baking apples.

"Do you think we should change the name of

the bakery to something other than Briggs Bakery?" Eve asked as she succeeded in paring an entire apple without breaking the peel.

"Briggs' Apple Bakery would be appropriate," Simone teased, heaping a pile of the cut-up fruit into a crust. "It looks as if apple pies are the only pastry we can afford to bake."

Eve held up the long peeling dangling between her fingers like a swirling snake. "How about The Apple Peel? It certainly fits."

"I don't understand why there are so many apples, if God intended for them to be a forbidden fruit," Simone mused.

Eve dropped the peeling she was holding and jumped to her feet. She grabbed Simone by the shoulders and shook her, dispersing a cloud of flour into the air. "The Forbidden Fruit. That's it, Simone. It's a wonderful name."

"It does have a nice ring to it," Simone reflected with a pleased smile. "The Forbidden Fruit. I like it. It even sounds a little wicked, doesn't it?"

"About as wicked as homemade apple pie can sound," Eve responded dryly.

The tinkle of the bell above the front door announced the entrance of someone in the store. "I'll see who it is." Eve stopped in the doorway at the sight of Sam Montgomery standing in the center of the room holding Simone's carpetbag.

"Who is it, Eve?" Simone peered around her, wiping her hands on a towel.

"Is this your missing bag, ma'am?" He dropped it to the floor.

"Why, yes." Simone was flabbergasted. She couldn't believe the man had succeeded in recovering the bag.

"I think you'd better check it to make sure nothing's missing."

"Did you open it, Mr. Montgomery?"

His eyes flashed resentfully. "I didn't take anything out, if that's what you're thinking."

Simone blushed and began to examine the contents of the bag. "I wasn't thinking that at all, sir." She was embarrassed to know that the young man had seen her personal underclothing. She rifled through it hurriedly, aware that his dark, brooding eyes were following her every move. She was relieved to see her purse still intact.

Simone was flustered. She avoided meeting his eyes. "I don't know how to thank you, Mr. Montgomery. Will you permit me to offer you a reward?"

"That's not necessary, ma'am. Just take better care of it in the future."

Eve had remained silent during the whole discourse. She now stepped forward with a grateful smile. "If you won't accept a reward, may we at least offer you a piece of freshly baked apple pie, Mr. Montgomery?"

"Sure smells good." He grinned. Eve was amazed to see how his rare smile transformed his appearance. He looked like a young boy.

Simone glanced up shyly and noticed a rip in the sleeve of his shirt. Her eyes widened when she saw it stained with blood. "Mr. Montgomery, did you injure your arm?"

"It's nothing, ma'am."

"It should be cleaned. Sit down and I'll tend to it at once."

"And while she's doing that, I'll cut you a piece of pie," Eve offered. However, before she could act on it, the bell tinkled again and a stranger came into the store. His wool shirt, heavy trousers, and battered hat were sure signs that he was a miner.

"May I help you?" Eve asked excitedly at the prospects of serving her first customer.

"I'll take a piece of whatever that is that smells so good, lady."

"It's apple pie, sir."

The man produced a tin plate and Eve cut him a thick wedge of the hot pie. "How much dust do I owe you?"

"Dust?"

He pulled a pouch out of his shirt. "Gold dust. How much?"

She had not considered such a development and was at a loss. "I have no idea."

"It costs a pinch for a shot of whiskey. I reckon the pie is worth more than the drink. You got a scale?" Eve looked around hopelessly, then shook her head. "Well, how about a cup then?"

Simone and Sam were listening silently to the whole exchange. Eve produced an empty cup and the miner poured some of the dust into it.

He then picked up the piece of pie and began eating it as he left the store.

Eve was speechless. She stared down at the gold dust glistening in the cup. "Remember, ma'am," Sam Montgomery cautioned, *"All that glitters is not gold."*

Simone looked at him in surprise. "Shakespeare, Mr. Montgomery?"

The gunfighter looked uneasy. "I've always leaned toward his writings."

"I don't mean to pry, Mr. Montgomery, but where did you get your education? You appear to be very literate."

The question produced a negligent shrug. "I was raised on the Texas border. My mother was an Apache. She died when I was born. My dad had been a school teacher before coming West. He made certain I learned how to read and write. I loved books. Could never get enough of them." He grinned crookedly. "But there aren't too many of them lying around in Indian camps and jailhouses."

"Is your father still alive, Mr. Montgomery?"

"As far as I know. We run into each other every now and then. The last time I saw him was about five years ago."

Simone left the room, shaking her head in disbelief, and immediately returned carrying a pan of water and a clean cloth. "Shall we check your shoulder, Mr. Montgomery?"

"It's nothing to worry about, ma'am." But he sat down and, to Simone's embarrassment, removed his shirt.

She had never had to touch a man's bare chest before and was blushing as she sponged away the blood. The half-breed had broad shoulders that sloped down into muscular arms and a smooth, powerful chest. As much as she tried to avoid glancing at him, she could not help noticing several other scars from previous injuries.

"How did you get this wound, Mr. Montgomery?" she asked as she wrapped it with some clean strips of cloth.

"From a knife," he answered succinctly.

Her glance swung to him in distress. "Did one of those hoodlums do this to you when you recovered my bag?"

"I guess so."

Simone shook her head. "I wish you would tell me why you were willing to endanger your life for us." She finished wrapping the wound, and, to her relief, he slipped into his shirt.

"I thought I was going to get a piece of that pie."

"Oh, of course." She bolted to the kitchen, flustered, and began to slice a pie. Then she dropped the knife at the sound of his voice behind her. "I'll eat it here in the kitchen. It will be better for your business."

She drew her hand up to her chest in agitation. "I didn't hear you come in."

"Most people don't, ma'am. Must be my Indian blood."

Simone's hand was shaking when she placed a cup of coffee in front of him. Sam did not fail to notice. "Sorry if I scared you."

He stood eating his pie as she returned to rolling out more pie crusts.

"Mr. Montgomery, what did you mean by your earlier remark about gold?" Eve asked, joining them.

"Just warning you to watch out for Fool's Gold."

"Fool's Gold?" she asked, perplexed.

"Iron pyrite. It looks like gold, but it's not as shiny or heavy."

Eve sighed deeply. "I guess there's a great deal we're going to have to learn about gold if we want to stay in business."

The gunfighter grinned. "I'm sure you will, ma'am, because there's sure enough of it around this city."

Much to the women's surprise, Sam Montgomery remained at the bakery the rest of the day, sitting silently at the table. When Eve wasn't waiting on customers, she managed to pare enough apples to keep ahead of Simone. Word spread rapidly on the streets, and miners began to flock to the bakery for a piece of the homemade pie.

It was dark by the time Sam Montgomery finally left.

"Strange man," Eve commented, locking the front door behind him.

"I think he's just shy," Simone disputed.

"Well, one thing is for sure," Eve declared, "nobody would be foolish enough to try to hold us up with Sam sitting at the table wearing those six-guns strapped on his hips." Her forehead creased with a frown. "Unless he's planning on robbing us himself."

"Oh, *chérie*, he's just trying to be helpful," Simone scoffed.

They sat down to count the profits for the day. The cup was filled with gold dust and their register was bulging with cash.

Eve counted the money and smiled happily. "Tomorrow we can buy some milk and eggs. I'll order a new sign painted for above the door. I think The Forbidden Fruit is going to be a success."

They went to bed that night bone-tired, but confident about the future.

CHAPTER EIGHT

As was her custom on arising, Eve looked out the bedroom window. She drew back in surprise at the sight of Sam Montgomery leaning against a building across the street.

"Simone, come here," Eve said softly.

Rubbing her eyes, Simone climbed out of bed and came to the window. "Look, there's Sam Montgomery. What do you suppose he's doing there?"

"Maybe he's hungry and is waiting for us to open," Simone suggested. There was a tenderness in her voice that Eve, in her preoccupation, failed to notice.

"But I saw him there last night just before I went to bed."

Simone was skeptical. "You aren't thinking that he was there all night, are you?"

"Well, what do you think?" Eve asked suspiciously.

"I think we should invite him to come in. Maybe he hasn't anywhere else to go. You saw how Mrs. Miller treated the poor man." Simone's eyes rested sadly on the lone figure across the street. "Others probably treat him the same way."

"Well, he's a gunfighter, Simone. You can't entirely blame people for being uncomfortable around him." Eve turned away and began to dress, but Simone remained at the window. She felt sorry for Sam Montgomery, perceiving a sensitive side to his nature that he kept concealed from people.

"I think he's not wanted because he's part Indian, not because he's a gunfighter," Simone added judiciously. "I like him and I'm indebted to him."

"I like him, too," Eve declared, her eyes brimming with laughter. "And if he's willing to wait all night for a piece of pie, I think it should be on the house."

Simone's mouth curled into a pleased smile and she began to get dressed. She threw Eve a surreptitious glance, wondering what Eve would think if she suggested he stay with them. She finally garnered enough courage to voice the thought.

"If Mr. Montgomery doesn't have anywhere to stay, could we let him sleep here?"

Eve had been splashing water on her face from a basin. She looked up, shocked, water dripping off her cheeks. "Here? Do you mean upstairs with us?" She grabbed a towel and wiped her face and hands.

Simone blushed at Eve's outrageous suggestion. "Of course not. I meant downstairs. He could sleep on the floor. He must have a bedroll or something."

"I can't believe he doesn't have a place to stay. I would think a gunfighter, if he's any good at all, could sleep anywhere he wanted to," Eve countered absently. Her thoughts had shifted to a more serious vein, the previous day's receipts and what they had to purchase with them that day.

"Then you don't mind if I suggest it to him?"

"Suggest what?" Eve asked as she bounced down the stairway.

Simone followed her to the top of the stairway and called down to her. "Suggest he sleep here."

Eve turned around and looked up at her with a wide grin. "If it doesn't bother you, partner, it sure won't bother me. You must remember, I just spent the last two years under the same roof as Adam Rawlins. Compared to that, living with a gunfighter will be like . . . apple pie." Both women erupted into giggles.

Eve unlocked the front door of the store and waved to Montgomery. He straightened up and sauntered over with the same nonchalance she remembered from the first time she had seen him at the wharf.

"Good morning, Mr. Montgomery. You're up early." If she expected an explanation, she was mistaken. He simply nodded to acknowledge her greeting. "Why don't you come in. We're just getting ready to prepare some more pies." Sam nodded and followed her.

"Morning, ma'am," he said to Simone, who was attempting to get a fire started in the stove. "I'd be happy to do that for you."

"Oh, thank you, Mr. Montgomery."

"Most people call me Sam, ma'am."

Eve's eyes sparkled with impishness. "Sam Ma'am. That's an unusual name for an Indian. Sounds Chinese to me." A smile tugged at the corners of the gunfighter's mouth, but he forced it back.

Simone was too flustered to appreciate the humor. "I insist you call me Simone." She began to busy herself by filling the coffee pot with water.

"And I'm Eve, Sam. As soon as you finish what you're doing, we've got a proposition for you."

Sam put some wood on the blaze he had started in the stove. "Won't be too long, ma'am . . . ah, Miss Eve." He closed up the top of the stove and wiped his hands on his trousers. "What proposition?"

"Simone and I were discussing the need of having a man around for protection. We wondered if you would be interested in the job. We're willing to pay you for your services."

His somber face curved slightly in an amused grin. "Most women would consider me a poor choice to protect them."

"I'm afraid we can't offer you anything but a

pallet in the kitchen as far as sleeping accommodations are concerned," Eve said regretfully.

"Are you sure the idea will sit okay with the old lady?"

"Oh, Aunt Hannah is gone. We've bought the bakery from her."

If this information came as a surprise to him, he managed to hide it behind an unflappable mien. "I've got no objection to staying, if you want me."

"Then you agree. That's wonderful," Eve exclaimed. She winked broadly at Simone as the two women exchanged pleased glances. She was beginning to feel that nothing could go wrong in her scheme of things. "What is your usual fee, Sam?"

"I'll settle for room and board if you can afford to feed an extra mouth."

"Then it's settled."

They ate a hurried breakfast, then Simone began to mix the pie crust and Eve started to peel more apples.

As the morning progressed, it soon became impossible for the supply to keep up with the demand. By midday, they were taking orders in advance. Many of the miners were reserving a half dozen pies at a time. One of the barrels of apples was empty and they were running low on flour and sugar. If they were going to fill all the orders they had taken, it would be necessary to replace the larder.

They locked up the bakery, and Simone remained behind to continue baking pies while

Eve went shopping for supplies accompanied by Sam Montgomery.

The sight of Eve walking beside the gunfighter caused many to glance askance in their direction. When they finally reached the merchant's, Sam went off to the stable to rent a horse and cart while Eve entered the store.

She couldn't believe the cost of the food. Eggs were three dollars a dozen; flour and sugar were forty and fifty cents a pound. A barrel of apples sold for $150. It didn't take long to deplete the funds from the previous day's receipts.

Eve was deep in concentration on the way home. She couldn't see the sense in spending the day struggling in the kitchen if everything they earned had to be used to pay for more supplies. There had to be a way to get around it.

Later, while they were eating their evening meal, Eve presented her proposition to Simone. "The only way we can ever make any money is to eliminate those outrageous merchant costs."

Sam was raising a fork to his mouth. His hand remained poised in midair. "Do you plan on taking up farming or stealing?" he asked drolly.

Simone recognized his logic. "Yes, Eve, how can we avoid it?"

Eve felt as if she were going to burst with excitement before she could get the words out of her mouth. "By buying directly from the farmer." She sat there, threatening to pop with pleasure, waiting for their reaction.

It was not what she anticipated. Sam and Simone exchanged perplexed glances. "What farmers, *chérie*?" Simone finally asked, fearing that perhaps the past few days had been too much for Eve. Either that, or her friend had spent too much time in the hot sun.

"There are many fruit and nut farmers in California." Eve's face was curled into a wicked but very appealing grin. "It's time I had a long talk with our friend Captain Grant."

The next evening Eve was at the wharf when *The Senator* docked. Sam stood aside waiting silently while Captain Grant listened patiently to Eve's offer. For ten percent of the profits, he agreed to bring her fresh fruit, nuts, flour and sugar on his trips up and down the coast.

Pleased with herself, Eve glowed with confidence on the way home. "One of the things I learned while sitting through those boring dinners with Adam Rawlins and his associates is never put yourself on the wrong end of the law of supply and demand. Now the next thing we have to do is buy a cow."

"A cow?" Sam was beginning to believe that nothing she said would surprise him.

Eve nodded. "We need milk and butter."

Sam's brow rose derisively. "Have you ever milked a cow?" He was damned sure he wasn't going to do it. There was a limit to what he would do for them. He was a gunfighter, not a farmer.

"I can learn," Eve said confidently.

"And where do you intend to keep a cow?"

Her eyes twinkled mischievously. "In the shed with the chickens."

Sam struggled momentarily with her response before she saw the light dawn in his eyes. "Eggs?"

"Exactly." Her smile was too appealing to resist and he returned a lopsided grin. "We'll get on it first thing tomorrow morning."

By the end of the week they had converted half of the shed in the rear to a stall and the other half to a chicken coop. After a disastrous attempt at milking, resulting in Eve ending up on her backside in the dust, she began to pay a young boy a dollar a day to sweep out the shed and milk the cow.

The day finally dawned when Eve stood out on the street, her eyes glowing with pride. A sign in the shape of a bright red apple, bearing the name The Forbidden Fruit, was hung above the door. A fresh coat of white paint and ruffled curtains at the window had refurbished the building so that it looked as pleasing as it smelled.

A short time after the opening of *The Forbidden Fruit*, construction of a gambling casino began across the street. For weeks wagons would arrive daily, loaded down with crates containing crystal chandeliers, tables, chairs, and bolts of red carpet. Like everyone else in town, Eve and Simone watched the progress of the building with interest. It was completed in record time, and the name The Original Sin was painted across its facade.

The excitement on the day of the grand opening of The Original Sin was eclipsed because the bakery was offering custard-filled éclairs for the first time. To a passerby, it might have seemed like a run on a bank. People lined up the length of the block, waiting to purchase the rare pastry.

Simone and Eve had stayed up the previous night preparing and baking the *chou* pastry, fashioning the dough into hundreds of miniature cylinders. While Simone then prepared the tasty custard with which to fill them, Eve cooked the chocolate icing to spread on the tops.

From sunrise to sunset, a steady stream of hungry miners, many of whom had never tasted chocolate eclairs before, flowed into the store. That night, two exhausted women collapsed into their bed. The "Closed" sign remained on the door the following day.

Both welcomed the much-needed rest. Eve awoke at noon, to the sound of shouting in the street. Two men, rolling about in the dust, were exchanging blows. The fight, which had begun in the casino, had spilled over into the street.

It was the first of many such occurrences. By the week's end, Eve had just about lost her patience with the commotion and noisy din from the establishment.

To add to the aggravation, many of the drunks who left the casino would often stagger into the bakery. The two women would have been helpless to handle some of the situations, were it not for the presence of Sam Montgomery. However, he had begun to spend less and less time with them. So on most occasions, they were forced to get rid of the disturbing element themselves.

"Mrs. Mahoney told me he's very handsome," Simone said one night as they were finishing washing the pots and pans.

Tongue-in cheek, Eve asked, "Who's very handsome?" She was certain Simone was going to bring up the subject of Sam Montgomery.

"The owner of The Original Sin," Simone answered. "Mrs. Mahoney saw him yesterday when he arrived. She said he's tall and handsome."

"What does Sam say? He's over there enough."

"I'd never ask him such a thing as that," Simone said, blushing. "Besides, you know as well as I, Sam wouldn't tell us. He's very reticent and not the type to carry gossip." She wiped her hands on her apron and dumped the pan of soap and water into a bucket.

"Well, I think I'll ask him the next time I see him. All he can do is give me his usual noncommittal shrug." Eve raised a hand to stifle a yawn. "I'm going to bed. What about you?"

"I'll be up shortly. I just want to set some dough for tomorrow morning. I'll try not to wake you when I come to bed," Simone added.

Eve halted at the bottom stair and smiled at her. "You never do, Simone. You're the most considerate person I've ever known. I swear I don't deserve a friend like you."

Simone lowered her head in embarrassment and proceeded to stir vigorously the batter she was mixing.

In the bedroom, Eve paused at the window and glanced in disgust at the casino across the street. It was Friday night and the place was in full swing. The tinkle of a piano, combined with raucous voices, floated across to her in a clamorous cacophony.

Two drunken cowboys, shouting and laughing, staggered out of the swinging doors. One of them drew his pistol and fired several shots into the air. The other meant to follow suit, but tripped and fell just as he discharged his gun.

The stray bullet shattered the front window of the bakery. Eve heard Simone's scream and went racing down the stairway. The woman was hunched down on the floor. She was pale and trembling, her eyes wide with alarm, when Eve reached her.

"Who's shooting at us?" Simone gulped out in fright.

Eve helped Simone to her feet and gathered the frightened woman in her arms. "It's just some drunken cowboys. Are you hurt?"

"No, it just frightened me," Simone said, relieved to find out they were not under attack.

"Sit down, while I check the damage in the other room." Eve lit the oil lamp and set it on the counter. The floor was covered with shards of glass. She unlocked the front door and stormed out on the street, but there was no sign of the two men responsible.

"Damn!" she grumbled, and returned to the store. At the sight of Simone sitting at the table looking forlorn and confused, Eve's heart swelled with concern for her friend. "You get to bed right now. I am not taking no for an answer. I'll clean up this mess."

"But I still have the dough to set for tomorrow," Simone protested.

Eve would abide no argument as she led Simone to the stairs. "I can finish that. Get to bed."

She took a broom and made short work of sweeping up the glass. The gaping hole left the store accessible to anyone passing by. She was glad she had deposited the receipts at the bank earlier that day. "Where are you, Sam Montgomery, when we could really use you?" she grumbled.

Eve blew out the lamp and returned to the kitchen to vent her anger on the crust. With every roll of the pin, her anger increased. Someone should have to pay for the damages, she fumed to herself. If not the cowboys, then the owner of the damned saloon where they got drunk in the first place.

The more Eve thought about it, the more she was convinced she was right. And there was no time like the present to do something about it.

She wiped the flour from her hands and threw aside her apron. Eve strode purposefully across the street to The Original Sin and pushed past the swinging doors. The room was packed with an assortment of miners, mountain men, mule-teers, and plain drifters in every size, shape, and nationality.

All activity and conversation halted at the sight of her standing in the doorway. Everyone seemed to sense that the small bundle of deter-mination meant trouble.

At the sight of all the faces turned to her, Eve's courage began to falter. She told herself she had come that far and must not turn back now. She took a deep breath and headed for the long mahogany bar that stretched the length of one wall.

A wide swath opened for her as people step-ped aside for her to pass. The bartender eyed her with interest when she stopped at the bar.

"I would like to speak to the proprietor."

"You looking for a job, honey?" he drawled with mocking humor. It was obvious to all that she didn't belong in such an establishment and he was attempting to get a laugh at her expense.

Eve was mad, not amused. "Are you the proprietor or just the buffoon hired to do the entertaining?"

The haughty angle of her dark head coupled with the icy disdain in the violet eyes quickly convinced him that he bore the brunt of the humor. His ego was bruised at being bested by this slip of a woman.

"He's upstairs." Disgruntled, he nodded toward a wide stairway covered with thick red carpeting.

With a determined stride, Eve headed for the stairway. She didn't glance at Sam Montgomery, who was standing alone at the end of the bar.

At the foot of the stairway a beefy bouncer of gargantuan proportions blocked her path. "That's far enough, lady. Nobody goes upstairs without the boss's say-so."

"Let her pass," Sam said.

The man glanced belligerently at Sam. The gunfighter was leaning casually against the bar. "Keep out of things that don't concern you, Montgomery."

"I just made this my concern."

The bouncer had heard enough about Sam's prowess with a gun to be cautious. "You gonna draw that iron you're wearing to make me?"

Sam's unwavering gaze remained fixed on the man. "I don't think I'll have to."

The hapless bouncer hesitated for several seconds, torn between pride and caution. The tension in the room was so taut, that something had to give. He finally stepped aside for Eve to pass.

Eve had held her breath throughout the whole exchange. She didn't want to get Sam involved, especially in a gunfight. She was beginning to feel foolish about the whole thing. What was she doing here in this casino and at this time of night? Why hadn't she at least waited until morning to resolve it?

Too late to back down, especially with everyone watching her, she climbed the stairway and paused at the sight of several closed doors.

Instinct led her to a door at the end of the hallway.

Eve opened the door and stepped into the room. A man was sitting behind a desk. She gasped with shock when he raised his head.

"Well, Eve, I see you're still barging into rooms without waiting to be invited."

CHAPTER NINE

"You!" she gasped.

Eve could not believe her eyes. Speechless, she stared into the face of the man she never expected to see again. Blood throbbed at her temples and ears as she struggled with the shock. She closed the door and leaned back against it, her trembling spine in great need of support.

Adam Rawlins rose to his feet and stepped around the desk. Eve felt like an animal snared in a trap as, mesmerized, she watched him approach. His presence was overpowering, dominating the thoughts and impressions swirling through her head. With bizarre awareness, she found herself not focusing on what he was doing here, but rather how handsome he looked. *Had he always been so handsome?*

Adam stopped before her. His dark eyes hungrily devoured every facet of her face before he reached out to caress her cheek. In a husky whisper he murmured a counterpart to the very thoughts that were ravaging her mind.

"I had almost forgotten how beautiful you are."

His touch was warm, unbearably disturbing. Too provocative to cringe from. Her skin tingled beneath the light touch of his fingertips and she shivered with a new resurgence of trembling.

Eve forced words out of a throat that suddenly felt parched. "What are you doing here, Adam?"

"Can't you guess, Eve?" There was no mockery in his eyes—only undisguised desire.

His hand slid from her cheek to cradle the back of her neck, drawing her to him. And then he lowered his head.

Eve fought hopelessly to resist the persuasive arousal of the kiss, but the first touch of his lips recaptured a similar moment between them. A moment whose impact she had tried to convince herself had been more imagined than factual. Other men had kissed her, caressed her. None but Adam had ever succeeded in provoking a response. Now it was happening again, and to her horror, it excited her.

Eve struggled in vain with logic, telling herself to resist the temptation of his lips. She hated this man. He was horrid. Repulsive. Her flesh should be shrinking beneath his touch, yet she felt her breast swelling, filling the hand that had slid to caress it as the kiss deepened.

Her arms encircled his neck as he crushed her against the firm length of his body. Logic told her she should be recoiling from the nearness of his body, but logic could not reckon with the thrill of the solid warmth pressed against her—too arousing to reject. Her lips parted beneath the firm pressure of his, to allow his tongue to slip into her mouth, creating erotic sensations exquisitely irresistible.

For several seconds after his lips released hers, Eve remained motionless in his arms, savoring the effects of his kiss. She slowly opened her eyes, hindered by lids weighted with passion. Adam's dark eyes were fixed on her with self-satisfaction swirling in their sapphire depths.

"Are you ready to come back to where you belong, Eve?"

She felt a blush sweep over her, knowing that her response to his kiss had fueled his smugness. Yet she refused to admit it aloud to him or herself. "What game are you playing with me now, Adam?"

Irritation flashed on his handsome face. Adam grasped her shoulders. He wanted to shake her. To shake some sense into that obstinate, beautiful head of hers. "Maybe they were games in the past, Eve. But the games ended with that kiss."

Eve was too confused to be able to explain anything she was thinking or feeling at the moment, especially with her body and mouth still tingling with the touch and taste of him. She reverted to a familiar litany until she could sort it all out in her mind.

"I hate you, Adam. I've hated you from the moment I saw you. How many times must I tell you that?"

Adam leaned forward, propping a hand on the door at each side of her head. His warm breath ruffled the hair at her ear in a whisper. "I once believed that, Eve, but your response to my kisses tells me different." He dipped his head toward her. "So tell me again, lovely lady, how much you hate me."

She turned her head aside to avoid the descent of his mouth. Adam's lips brushed a tantalizing trail along her cheek. Her traitorous body trembled with renewed desire as she fought the temptation to mold herself against the lithe body only inches from her. She could feel the warmth of it, as if it were wrapped around her.

Eve forced herself to shove him away and raised her head in defiance of his physical intimidation. "Think what you want, Adam. You always have. But I'm not returning to Sacramento with you, so you might as well drop this ridiculous farce."

Her violet eyes flashed scornfully. "Adam Rawlins operating a gambling casino! Who's running the mighty Rawlins Empire in your absence?" she scoffed. "I suggest you go back to where you belong."

Unperturbed by her sarcasm, he raised his hand and gently wiped a smudge of flour off her cheek. "I see you're wearing kitchen flour for face powder and Eau de Cinnamon for perfume these days."

"And loving every moment of it, you supercilious snob," she lashed out.

His words had stung her as much as anything he had ever said to her. His obvious appreciation of her beauty had always been a secret satisfaction to her in the past. That, and her spirit, were the only two weapons she had ever possessed to use against him.

Adam chuckled in amusement and pulled her into his arms, burying his face in the thickness of her hair. "My darling Eve, I'm not trying to sound contemptuous or snobbish. You belong dressed in silk and velvet, not cotton aprons." His hands slid caressingly down her spine. "And you belong here in my arms, in my bed. Soft. Desirable. Not in a kitchen, up to your elbows in flour. Why won't you admit it?"

His husky murmur was lulling her into a complacent languor. This was the side of Adam she feared the most. An exciting, dangerous side. More lethal than the steely-eyed adversary who had always confronted her.

She found herself weakening, tempted by the thought of how good it would feel to seek the sanctuary his arms were offering and to surrender to the promising fulfillment of his kisses. To forget the past.

Adam drew her tighter into his embrace. "I was wrong in driving you away. In letting you go. What I said and did in the past was a mistake.

In the beginning I refused to admit my true feelings for you. I became caught in a web of my own making."

His look was intense as he gazed down at her. "I even admit that I didn't always have your interests at heart. I acted out of jealousy when I lured your suitors away from you. It was a mistake, because it only made you hate me more. But there was one thing I never understood until the night before you left Sacramento. How it all began—the real reason for your early hatred of me."

He reached out a hand, tipping her chin to force her to meet his gaze. "Do you think I'm going to allow a few foolish words, spoken long ago in anger, to keep me from having you?" His voice was rough with emotion. The steely gleam in his eyes was a familiar one. How often had she faced it before?

Her eyes were wide with fright. Fright of her own emotions and the traitorous doubts he aroused within her. In panic, she wrenched herself out of his arms. "Well, they weren't foolish words to me. I'll never forget them."

How could she have felt so tempted and momentarily forgotten that this was Adam Rawlins, the man who had cursed her mother's name, had plagued her for years? Adam Rawlins, her nemesis, the devil incarnate.

She had vowed vengeance upon him.

"Go back to where you came from, Adam. Where you belong. Leave me alone," she cried out frantically. She groped for the door knob, but Adam reached out and closed his hand around it, preventing her exit.

"You're just postponing the inevitable, Eve." There was no mockery or censure in his eyes. Just complete confidence. She had to escape the threat his nearness imposed. She opened the door and fled down the hall.

Adam followed her to the top of the stairway. Her agitation was written across her face as she rushed past Sam Montgomery. His glance swung to Adam Rawlins, who was grimly watching her hasty departure. The two men's eyes locked for a brief moment, then Sam turned and followed Eve through the swinging doors.

Eve tramped across the street and into the shop. She plopped down into a chair, and her fingers began to tap a nervous staccato on the table top. *How dare he follow her to San Francisco?*

Eve jumped to her feet in alarm when the door opened. At the sight of Sam Montgomery, she sat down in relief.

"What happened to the window?"

"The window?" The distraction of seeing Adam again had obliterated her purpose in going to The Original Sin. There still was that problem to resolve. "Oh, a drunken cowboy smashed it with a stray bullet."

Eve sat steeping in frustration while Sam walked over to examine the window more closely. Long, jagged pieces of glass remained hanging on the frame. "That was my reason for going over there to begin with. Damn that Adam Rawlins!"

Sam sat down at the table and shoved his hat to the back of his head. "What has Rawlins got to do with it?"

The question fueled her righteous indignation. "He's the one who's making money by getting those men liquored up, isn't he? Well then, he should pay for the damage they do as a result of it."

"Did he refuse to pay for the window?" There was a trace of a grin on his face. "Is that what got your dander up?"

Eve sprang to her feet. "No, the man was so insufferable, I forgot to tell him about the window." She marched toward the kitchen. "Do you want a cup of coffee?" she asked over her shoulder.

"None for me." Sam got to his feet and followed her. "I'll talk to Rawlins in the morning. I'm sure he'll pay for a new window. In the meantime, I'll stay here tonight, so you gals won't have anything to worry about. Where is Simone?"

"She was so shook up by the bullet through the window that I sent her to bed. She was in the kitchen when it happened. Simone could easily have been wounded, or even killed. That's why I was so angry."

Sam's jaw hardened. "This town's no place for two women on their own. And the way it's growing, it's going to get a lot worse before it gets better. Why don't you both go back to where you belong, before something serious happens to one of you?"

Go back to where you belong. Adam's very words. Why couldn't anyone believe she was capable of taking care of herself? "You sound just like Adam Rawlins. He gave me the same advice."

"It's good advice, Eve. You ought to listen to it for your own good."

"Except Adam Rawlins doesn't have my interests at heart. He's . . ." she faltered, unable to tell him the full story.

"Just what is there between you two anyway?" Sam asked with uncharacteristic curiosity.

Her eyes flashed with resentment. "Adam Rawlins is my legal guardian. His father married my mother six years ago. They died in an accident on their honeymoon."

Sam expelled a long, low whistle. "So that's it. Things are beginning to make more sense."

"Things? What things?" Eve asked. She waited with a perplexed frown.

The gunfighter turned away, an obscure expression masking his face. *Damn, he's as exasperating as Adam,* she found herself thinking as she watched Sam retrieve his bedroll from the corner. Eve knew it would be useless to pursue the question further. "Good night, Sam," she grumbled and climbed the stairs.

Sleep was an elusive thief, snatching up the hours of the night as it escaped her pursuing grasp. Finally, fearing she would disturb

Simone, Eve rose and went to the window. All was quiet on the street below. The Original Sin loomed in spectral murkiness.

Still brooding, Eve stared at the darkened structure. *Where was he? Was he watching her this very moment from the shadows of one of the windows?* She stepped back furtively, guiltily.

An indefinable shudder swept her spine.

The prison walls had risen around her once again.

CHAPTER TEN

Eve woke with a start to an empty bed. It was dawn by the time she had finally fallen asleep, but she knew that was a poor excuse for allowing Simone to handle the work load alone.

She sniffed the air appreciatively. The fragrant aroma of baking cinnamon rolls drifted up from below, a further testimony of her malingering. Wracked with a feeling of guilt, Eve hurriedly dressed and groomed herself, then rushed down the stairs. She drew up in surprise at the sight of Simone sitting at the table chatting casually with Adam Rawlins.

Adam picked up a cup of steaming coffee. Simone leaned over and said something that caused him to break into an amused chuckle. He looked so totally relaxed that Eve was swept by a wave of annoyance.

"What a cozy scene," she snapped. Ignoring

Adam intentionally, she threw Simone a glance bordering on resentment. "Why didn't you wake me?"

"I thought you needed the rest, *chérie*." Simone looked none the worse for her heavy load of work. In fact, there was a sparkle in her eyes. Eve couldn't believe that Adam Rawlins was responsible for it.

"Good morning, Eve," Adam said amicably. "I was certain that if I waited long enough, you would finally get out of bed."

Eve bristled under his greeting. The remark was so typical of Adam—a restrained graciousness coupled with an underlying censure.

"And I knew the moment I opened my eyes, the day was starting wrong for me," she gritted through an artificial smile. "Seeing you here, Adam, convinces me I was right." He acknowledged her taunt with a grin.

"However," she continued, "I do have something to discuss with you. There is a small matter of our front window, which was broken by one of the drunkards who frequents your establishment." She swung her hand with a theatrical flourish toward the window to corroborate the point, then drew up dumbfounded at the sight of the shiny new glass sparkling in the sunshine.

Adam smiled broadly. Not smugly. Not triumphantly. Just broadly. The look of it was enough to infuriate her. Oh, how she wanted to smash the smile off his arrogant face.

"It would appear you slept quite soundly, Eve. I hope it wasn't because you had a restless night." Amusement gleamed in his dark eyes.

He knows, she lamented to herself. *Damn him. That disciple of the devil knows I was awake all night thinking about him. Now he's laughing at me.*

Her glare of antagonism did nothing to bridle the pleasure he was relishing at the moment. Adam pulled out a chair for her. "Sit down, Eve, and join us."

Simone was aware of the undercurrent between the two and tried to ease the tension. "Mr. Rawlins was kind enough to replace the broken window."

"Simone, didn't we just reach an agreement that you would call me Adam?" he scolded with a charming smile.

Blushing, Simone buried her face in her cup. "Oh, of course—Adam."

Eve sat down in disgust. She had never been fooled by Adam's ability to captivate people with a deceiving charm. *He could charm the skin off a snake, but Simone, of all people, should be wise to such a ruse,* she thought.

"I am amazed how you were able to get such quick action," Simone continued as Adam filled Eve's cup.

"Mr. Rawlins' money usually gets him immediate results," Eve declared sarcastically. She began to nibble on one of the fresh rolls.

Simone wisely elected to excuse herself and got to her feet. "It's time to take the rolls out of the oven. Sam has been working on the shed in the back, and he's probably thirsty, so I think I should take him something to drink. Thank you again, Mr. . . . ah, Adam, for the window."

After Simone's departure, there was an awkward silence between them. Eve could feel Adam's eyes on her, but she deliberately avoided making eye contact with him. She heard Simone go outside and knew that if she had any common sense at all herself, she would follow suit. She was uncertain what was causing her to remain, other than a need to prove to Adam she was not intimidated by him.

"Miss MacGregor, as adorable as I find that pout, either you wipe it off this instant or I'm going to kiss it off."

It was too much of a challenge for Eve to ignore. She faced him defiantly. "I would like to see you try. Sam Montgomery is outside. All I have to do is call for help. It would give me the greatest of pleasure to watch him put a bullet right between those devil's eyes of yours."

Adam threw back his head with a burst of laughter. "I don't doubt you would enjoy it." Eve couldn't help smiling. Adam's charm was contagious.

The expression on his face shifted from amusement to longing. "But the idea is much too tempting to resist." He pushed back his chair and slowly rose to his feet.

Eve laughed nervously, her heartbeat quickening in her chest. "You're serious, aren't you, Adam? You don't believe I'll do it."

Adam's hands were on her shoulders, drawing her to her feet. He lowered his head, his mouth hovering a breath above her own. "You'd better start screaming, Miss MacGregor, because you're about to be thoroughly kissed."

Eve could feel herself drawn into the mesmerizing effects of his nearness, his touch. Her senses became heightened to the scent of him, the rousing, masculine combination of part bay, part shaving soap—part male. The female in her responded to it.

Excitement coursed through her, drowning any reservations in the wake of the passion it generated. Breathless, she waited for his next move.

"Put your arms around me, Eve." He breathed the words into her mouth.

Trembling, she slid her arms around his neck. At the feel of his arms enfolding her, she parted her lips with a groan of surrender. If he didn't kiss her at once, she felt as if she would explode from the expectation building within her.

Unable to prolong the agonizing moment, he claimed her mouth in a deep, lingering kiss that made her lose herself in its depths. There was no awareness of time or space. No awareness of anything except exquisite sensation and a driving urgency to savor and prolong it.

When he released her, for several seconds his heavy-lidded gaze studied the mounting uneasiness in her eyes. "Where are you going to bolt to now, Eve? Is there anyplace else to run to?"

Her arms dropped limply to her sides. "Damn you, Adam. When will your torture of me end?" There was as much plea as anger in the question.

Adam grasped her chin in his hand, his long fingers crushing her cheeks. For the breathless span of several seconds he stared down into her troubled face with just an edge of resentment in his eyes. "It's a double-edged sword, Eve."

He bent down and pressed an angry kiss to her lips, then turned and disappeared through the front door.

Simone had been glad for an excuse to escape outside and leave Eve and Adam to their bickering. Sam was busy repairing the damage to the shed caused by a recent storm. The building was in a decrepit state, repaired several times since they had decided to put it to use. To Simone it seemed obvious that the best approach would be to tear it down and build a new one.

He was on the roof of the small building and had removed his shirt. A sheen of perspiration glistened on his bronzed chest and shoulders.

"I thought you would be thirsty, so I've brought you a glass of lemonade," she called up to him. "Would you rather have coffee?"

"Lemonade is fine." He put aside the hammer and jumped down, reaching for his shirt. "That's real thoughtful of you, Simone." Thirstily, he drank the liquid, then slumped down on the ground, leaning back against a wooden crate. "I could use another one, if you don't mind." Sam held up his glass and Simone refilled it from the pitcher she was carrying.

A silence developed between them, but it was more companionable than awkward.

"I see you've almost finished the shed. That's good. All this pounding is keeping the chickens from laying," she said with a good-natured smile.

"Well, I can't make any promises. I never tried to earn my keep as a carpenter."

Her glance shifted to his gun belt hanging from a peg just a few feet away. "Have you always been a gunfighter, Sam?"

"Not always. I scouted for the army during the Mexican War. When it was over, they wanted me to scout against my own people, the Apache. I refused, so they kicked me out of the army." His white teeth flashed against his bronzed face. "I once even served as a town marshall, but the challenge of outdrawing a half-breed marshall brought every drifter and two-bit gunslinger in the territory into the town. Got to be too much for the townfolks, so they asked me to move on."

Her eyes mirrored her sympathy. *He's never been given the chance to be anything but an outcast*, she thought sadly.

Having revealed more about himself than was normal, Sam closed his eyes as if to nap, ending the discussion.

Simone waited for several moments, hoping to pursue the conversation. There was so much mystery to Sam. When it appeared he wasn't going to volunteer any more information about himself, she rose and left him.

Sam opened his eyes and watched her disappear into the house. The look on his face remained inscrutable.

Eve had just regained her composure after Adam's departure when the bell tinkled and she looked up, fearing that Adam had returned.

The tall and thin man who entered was dressed in a plaid shirt and dust-covered trousers. A battered hat sat on a full head of hair as white as the snowy beard that covered his lower face.

"Something sure smells good," he said, sniffing the air. Merriment twinkled in his blue eyes. "Don't think I've smelled anything this good since I left Virginia."

"They're freshly baked cinnamon rolls." The man looked down on his luck, but Eve had found that appearances were often deceiving in this town. Assuming that he meant to make a purchase, she started to reach for one.

"Didn't come to buy, ma'am. I was told I might find Sam Montgomery here."

Eve now regarded the stranger with much closer interest. It was clear to her that he wasn't a gunfighter. "Are you a friend of Sam's?"

The man snatched the hat off his head and nodded politely. "The name's Bailey Montgomery. Sam is my son."

"You're Sam's father! It's a pleasure to meet you, Mr. Montgomery. I'm Evelyn MacGregor."

He was taken by surprise at the sight of her welcoming smile. The mention of Sam usually caused a negative reaction in people.

"I don't mean to bother you, Miss MacGregor. If you will tell me where I can find my boy, I'll be getting out of your way."

Eve wouldn't consider it. She took his arm and led him over to the table. "Nonsense, you just sit here, Mr. Montgomery, and have a cup of coffee and one of these freshly baked cinnamon rolls. I'll get Sam. I think he's in the back."

Eve poured the old man a cup of coffee and put a plate of rolls on the table. "I'll be back in a moment."

Simone was just entering the rear door and Eve whispered, "Sam's father is in the store."

"His father!" Simone exclaimed, shocked.

"Why don't you go and keep him company while I get Sam."

"No, you keep him company. I'll get Sam," Simone replied. She knew she was not adept at carrying on conversations with strangers and hurried out the door before Eve could say another word.

Sam had just risen to his feet when Simone returned. "Sam, Eve just told me your father is waiting for you in the store."

If the announcement surprised him, he did not show it. He strapped on his gun belt and followed her.

Bailey Montgomery had just finished his second cinnamon roll. He jumped to his feet when Sam came through the door. The old man embraced his son, slapping him several times on the back and shoulders to disguise the emotion he was feeling.

Eve and Simone remained in the kitchen to allow the two men a private reunion. Sam, with his usual reticence, stoically accepted the old man's enthusiastic embrace with a glint of pleasure in his dark eyes.

When a steady stream of customers prevented the two men from having any privacy, they left the bakery and walked over to The Original Sin.

Eve was kept too busy for further reflection on her dilemma over Adam, but an obscure image of him skittered and cavorted on the edges of her mind, frolicking with her thoughts throughout the day.

Sam and his father returned in the evening. Bailey was leading a mule with a saddle pack and blanket strapped to the animal's back. That night, after the women retired, both men stretched out their bedrolls on the kitchen floor.

CHAPTER ELEVEN

Sunday was a lazy day because the bakery was closed on the Sabbath. Eve was in the habit of doing the ledgers while Simone prepared the shopping lists for the forthcoming week. The rest of the day was occupied with lesser chores.

When Eve and Simone returned from church, they were pleasantly surprised to discover that Bailey Montgomery had swept and mopped the kitchen and store for them. He was now cleaning out the shed.

"The job is yours if you want it, Bailey," Eve offered later as they sat around the table with Sam eating lunch.

"Well, I plan on only being around long enough to get a grubstake," the old man declared. "But I'm willing to help out any way I can."

"We're willing to pay you for your services," Eve said. "It would be a relief not to have to do those tasks ourselves. But what is this about a grubstake?''

Bailey's eyes lit up with a glow of excitement. ''I've found it. This time, I've found it for sure.''

Sam snorted and tipped back his chair, balancing on the back legs as he leaned against the wall.

The two girls exchanged perplexed frowns. ''Found what, Mr. Montgomery?'' Simone asked with curiosity.

''The mother lode,'' Bailey declared awesomely. His eyes swept the faces of the three people in expectation.

He was disappointed when Eve frowned in disgust. ''Are you talking about a gold mine?'' Since arriving in San Francisco, she had seen hundreds of these would-be millionaires who had come to strike it rich only to end up destitute and often derelict.

Bailey was not about to be put down. ''This isn't just another gold mine. I'm telling you, I've found a mother lode. The gold is there. I can feel it in my bones. Only it took all my money to file my claim, so as soon as I get enough for a grubstake, I'm heading back to work it.''

A thought was beginning to take shape in her mind. ''Well, how much of a grubstake do you need?'' Eve asked, now intrigued.

''I've already got old Socrates, so I don't need a mule. It'll take several hundred dollars for food and supplies. Sam's giving me half of it, and when I get the rest, I'm heading back.''

Once again the two women exchanged

glances, knowing full well what the other was thinking. "We'll give you the other half, Bailey," Eve offered.

Bailey's head jerked up in surprise, renewed hope glimmering in his eyes. "I'm not asking for a handout, miss. I'm willing to work until I get it."

Eve held out little hope that Bailey Montgomery would actually strike gold, but having lived the last few years clinging to the hope of escaping Adam's domination, she was not about to discourage an old man's dreams.

"Then we'll consider it a loan," she suggested. "You can pay it back to us when you make your strike."

Bailey shook his head adamantly. "I don't ask for loans unless I can put something up in return." A sudden thought crossed his mind and his eyes gleamed with inspiration. "Tell you what I'll do, I'll sign over a part interest in the mine to you gals, and a part to Sam as well. We'll all be partners. The mine will belong to the four of us." His blue eyes glowed with merriment. "There will be plenty of gold to go around."

"Then it's a deal. Tomorrow I'll go to the bank and get you the money. I don't have that much here, or I would give it to you now," Eve said.

"And Sam and I will go and refile the claim so that all our names are on it," Bailey declared.

The old man's enthusiasm was infectious, and Eve jumped to her feet exuberantly. "I think we should all celebrate this new business venture.

Just think, Simone, now we own a bakery and part of a gold mine."

Keeping with the spirit of the moment, Simone rose and headed for the kitchen. "I think we have a bottle of wine somewhere. I'll look for it, and you get the cups, Eve."

They were toasting the new venture when Adam Rawlins entered the front door. His brow rose inquisitively at the sight of their raised cups. "This looks like a celebration."

Disgruntled, Eve lowered her arm. "It is. We heard you just left town."

"Eve!" Simone scolded. "You know that isn't true." She shook her head indulgently at her friend. "Will you join us, Adam?" She got him a cup and Sam filled it with wine.

"Just what are we celebrating?" Adam asked.

"Bailey's filed a claim on what he *thinks* is going to be a mother lode," Sam explained. It was obvious he was still skeptical about the whole thing.

"There's no thinking about it," the old man declared defensively. "I know there's pure color there."

Adam raised his cup in the air. "Well, then, I'll drink to that."

Eve glanced askance at him. "I thought you would, Adam. I've never known you to turn down a toast when the prospect of money is involved."

"Why don't you all come over to The Original Sin and we can celebrate properly," Adam suggested, ignoring Eve's barb.

"I am not in the habit of frequenting saloons," she added disgustedly. "But if the rest of you want to go, don't let me stop you."

Simone intervened immediately. "This isn't a celebration. We haven't struck gold yet. We're just toasting the partnership."

"If that's the case, perhaps you won't mind if I steal Eve away for a few hours." Adam turned to her with a winning smile. "I thought we could go riding."

It was an underhanded offer and Adam knew it. Long ago he had perceived that the one thing Eve enjoyed doing in his company was to go riding. In the past two years he had shown patience and expertise in teaching her how to properly handle a mount. His efforts had not been wasted. She had developed into an expert equestrienne.

Eve struggled with his invitation. *Damn him! He knows how much I love to ride,* she fretted. The offer was too tempting to resist. After all, as long as she was on a horse she'd be safe from Adam's advances. Against all measure of common sense, she agreed.

After they departed, Bailey went out to the shed to check his mule. Sam seemed to have retreated into one of his silent moods, so Simone collected the cups and proceeded to wash them.

Just as she finished, the front door opened. The man who entered was short and very distinguished looking. Dressed neatly in gray trousers and frock coat, he appeared to be in his early fifties. At the sight of Simone, he removed his black beaver hat, nodding politely.

"Reverend Williams, what a surprise."

"I hope I am not intruding, Miss Lisle." He glanced disapprovingly in Sam's direction.

"Of course not. Please come in and sit down. Reverend Williams, I would like you to meet Mr. Montgomery." Sam nodded to acknowledge the introduction, but neither man extended a hand.

"May I offer you a cup of tea or coffee? I'm sorry, we haven't any fresh bakery, but we don't do any baking on Sundays."

"Coffee is fine, Miss Lisle."

The man sat down at the same table as Sam, who once again tipped back his chair and leaned against the wall. Simone poured the preacher a cup of coffee and joined them.

For a moment, the trio sat in awkward silence, the shy Simone having difficulty initiating conversation with the stranger, the stuffy preacher being annoyed with the presence of the half-breed, and the inscrutable Sam sullenly regarding the preacher.

Finally, Simone managed to speak. "I am sure Eve will regret missing your call, Reverend Williams."

The man smiled stiffly and once again glanced nervously at Sam. "As a matter of fact, Miss Lisle, I did not come to see Miss MacGregor. I came to see you."

"Me!" Simone was astounded. "What for?"

"It's a private matter, Miss Lisle. Perhaps I can come back at a more convenient time."

Sam's chair banged to the floor as he got to his feet. "That's not necessary. I was just leaving."

Simone was at once mystified and irritated. She had no idea what the minister's purpose was in calling, but resented the fact that he was driving Sam away.

Reverend Williams waited for Sam to leave. When he was certain Sam had left the building, he turned back to her. "If I'm not mistaken, isn't that fellow Sam Montgomery, the gunfighter?"

Simone nodded. "Mr. Montgomery has been very protective of Eve and me."

Disapproval was written on his face. "There have been rumors among my parishioners regarding Mr. Montgomery's presence here. You understand, I am not questioning *your* virtue." He cleared his throat. "There has even been talk that he spends the night."

Simone bristled at the unfair assumption. Eve's virtue was being challenged because she was beautiful, and her own virtue was above reproach because she wasn't.

"The rumors are correct, Reverend Williams. Mr. Montgomery does spend the night here, and he sleeps on the kitchen floor. Miss MacGregor and I share the only bed." Innately shy, Simone blushed at revealing such an intimacy to him. A well-brought-up woman would never mention a bedroom in mixed company.

"Why . . . Reverend Williams, we were warned by people of this very city that it is not safe for two unprotected females. We hired Sam as a protective measure."

"Nevertheless, Miss Lisle, such an arrangement should be discouraged. The presence of a half-breed gunslinger in your household is neither an acceptable nor appropriate protective measure."

Simone Lisle, although a docile, self-effacing woman her whole life, would nevertheless defend without hesitation those who had captured her loyalty. She refused to listen to this man malign Sam Montgomery.

"Your objection is ill-advised, sir. Mr. Montgomery's conduct toward Miss MacGregor and me has always been above reproach. If that was your purpose for this visit, I will mention your displeasure to Miss MacGregor." Simone rose to her feet to end the conversation.

"Well, actually, Miss Lisle, that was not the purpose for my call. Please sit down so I can discuss it further with you."

Simone already had as much of the good reverend as she could tolerate. However, she was too much of a lady to order a man of the cloth out of the store. She sat down and waited for him to continue with whatever he had come to say.

"As you may have heard, Miss Lisle, I lost my wife ten years ago. The past years have been lonely ones for me. I have missed the comforts and gentility a woman brings into a man's life. I have often considered the feasibility of someday remarrying. However, the prospects have been limited."

Simone thought he sounded as if he were

delivering a sermon. The preacher must have sensed what was going through her mind, because he smiled as if to soften the message. "The arrival of two genteel women such as Miss MacGregor and yourself has given me a new perspective. Therefore, I am willing to overlook this unfavorable association with that notorious outlaw and consider marriage."

Simone would have felt sympathy for the man if he wasn't such an overbearing ass. Good Lord, did the man actually believe Eve would consider marrying him, when her beauty and intelligence could attract any man she wanted? One such man being Adam Rawlins, who was not only handsome, but wealthy as well.

"I think you will have to address this to Miss MacGregor herself, Reverend Williams. I'm hardly in a position to speak for her."

The minister looked perplexed. "You do not understand, Miss Lisle. I'm not referring to Miss MacGregor. I've already spoken to her guardian, who has informed me he intends to wed her himself." Swelling with vainglory, he intoned pompously, "I am willing to marry you."

Simone stared at him aghast. Although unaccustomed to proposals of marriage, she longed to be loved. To feel cherished. And more important, she knew how much love she was capable of returning to the man who was willing to give his heart to her.

But this man's proposition was humiliating. Did he really think she was so desperate to wed that she would accept such an insensitive proposal of marriage? Did people ever stop to think that homely women also had feelings? And dignity, as well. She had encountered this kind of tactlessness her whole life and should have been hardened to the heartache—but it always hurt.

With as much composure as she could muster, Simone rose to her feet. "Thank you, Reverend Williams, for your offer, but I am not considering marriage at this time."

"Do you realize what I am offering you, Miss Lisle?" the pastor sputtered. "Security. A respected place in the community as my wife. When, ever again, will you have such an opportunity?"

"I am sure I never will, Reverend Williams, but I must still refuse. My concern is not for what you are offering, as much as your reason for offering it. I am sure that in time there will be other women arriving in San Francisco, one of whom will be appreciative of your proposal."

Simone opened the door to show him out. "Now if you'll excuse me, I have work to do."

The preacher had not expected Simone to refuse him and was put out by her rejection. "I'll not ask you again, Miss Lisle. I have my pride, you know."

"I do, too, Reverend Williams."

She closed the door.

Sam Montgomery was outside leaning against the building. He did not fail to overhear their exchange at the doorway. Whatever transpired between them had left the preacher in a huff. Sam glanced in the window and saw Simone wipe a tear from her eye.

The slight hardening of the gunfighter's jaw was barely perceptible. He crossed the street and walked through the door of The Original Sin.

Adam led Eve to a nearby stable. As soon as they entered, Eve was greeted by a familiar snort. The horse in one of the stalls lifted its head with agitation and began pawing the ground to be freed.

"Callie!"

Eve rushed to the stall and hugged the horse, burying her cheek against the mare's velvety neck. Overcome with emotion, a combination of tears and laughter bubbled from her throat.

A loud snicker from the adjoining stall announced Callie's stable mate. "Equus!" Eve squealed with pleasure. The stallion tossed its proud head in greeting.

Eve turned to Adam, tears brimming in her eyes. "When did you bring them here?"

"They arrived this morning. I'm sure they're both ready for some exercise."

Within minutes, Eve gave Callie the rein and let the mare run as soon as they got to open country. This was what she enjoyed the most, racing across the countryside at a full gallop.

The wind billowed her skirt around her legs

and tugged at her hair until the long silky strands, freed from their restraint, flowed behind her in a shiny black stream.

The rolling verdant valley lay in tranquil contrast to the cloying congested city. Even the air smelled fresher to Eve. Her face glowed with exhilaration. This was a freedom like no other. The perfect marriage—a coupling of mind and spirit. In her pleasure of the moment, the figure galloping at her side was forgotten.

Adam made no attempt to intrude on her sanctum. He had often seen her like this. The first occasion had been when she was only sixteen. He knew then that he had to have her. To possess her. It was at that moment that he had made the decision to wed her.

Eve finally reined up beside a flowing stream and slid off the mare. She held the reins to let Callie dip her head and lap the water. Adam dismounted to allow Equus to do the same.

When the animals had drunk their fill, he took the reins of the horses and tied them to the shrubbery that lined the river bank. Eve was still flushed with exhilaration.

The urge to kiss her became an ache in his groin, but he knew that to kiss her would be a mistake. She was not ready for him. She would have to want the moment as much as he.

This was the fantasy that obsessed him—to possess her and drive into her at a moment like this when her body was still energized with the wild abandonment coursing through her.

Eve knelt down and drank from the stream. She looked up at him and smiled, her lips moist with water. His desire for her surged into lust. Knowing how easily he could arouse that smoldering passion in her, he was tempted to try.

Once, it had been easy to conceal his need for her, until the night he had lost his control and kissed her. Now remembering the taste of her, the feel of her in his arms, Adam again felt his control slipping away and feared that the revealing bulge in his trousers might be evident to her.

To check his raging desire, Adam wandered out into the middle of the stream. He removed his hat, filled it, then dumped the contents over his head. The water ran down his face and saturated his shirt. The shock of the cold water produced the desired effect on his bulging manhood.

When he returned to the river bank, Eve had settled down in the shade of a tree and was watching him cautiously.

"Thank you, Adam."

"What are you thanking me for?" he asked. These were the first words they had spoken from the time they left the city.

"For bringing Callie to me."

He frowned grimly. "I must insist that you don't ride her unless I accompany you. It's too dangerous out here."

"Adam, the gesture was a thoughtful one. Please don't spoil it all by resorting to your usual nasty officiousness."

He plopped down beside her, tossing her an

apple he had taken from his saddlebags. "Now who's the one being nasty?"

Eve laughed lightly and bit into the piece of fruit. "You're right. I'm sorry. That was a left-handed compliment, wasn't it?"

They settled into a comfortable silence, unusual for them. Eve watched him as he chewed on the apple. Finally she shook her head.

"I just can't get used to seeing you like this. You're so out of character. What are you doing here, sitting under a tree munching an apple, Adam?"

He smiled crookedly. "I thought you didn't want to argue, so why bring up the subject? Especially when you know the answer as well as I do, Eve."

"Then you're wasting your time going through all this trouble. It won't get you anything in the end, because I'm not going to marry you, Adam."

Amusement gleamed in his eyes. Tossing the apple core aside, he rose to his feet and reached down to help her. "Would you like to make a wager on that?"

A pleasant warmth spread through her as his hand closed around hers. He pulled her to her feet, and for a few seconds their gazes locked. Eve saw the familiar glint of confidence in Adam's eyes. She met it with a new-born confidence of her own. She was no longer intimidated by him. He wanted her to the point of losing his control. This had been in shocking evidence just a few moments ago at the stream.

The knowledge gave her an added edge she never had before. His cool and calculating control was beginning to slip.

While the misgivings of the past were too deep-rooted to be forgotten, for the moment they were shoved aside to meet a newer and greater challenge. Their private conflict had become a battle of the sexes.

The gauntlet had been tossed. Once again the battle lines were drawn between them—two seasoned campaigners who had met often in combat and knew one another's strengths and weaknesses.

CHAPTER TWELVE

The following morning when she went downstairs, Eve found a note Adam had slipped under the door informing her he was returning to Sacramento on business, and, under no circumstances, was she to ride Callie in his absence.

Eve snorted her derision. *Adam, above all others, was aware she was not a child. It was so typical of him to issue orders as if she were.* She crumpled the letter in disgust and tossed it into the stove.

The bakery was busy as usual, so Eve put all thoughts of Adam aside. As the day wore on, she noticed that Simone was uncommonly quiet and withdrawn.

During a brief afternoon lull, Eve's concern led to inquiry. "Aren't you feeling well, Simone?" To Eve's surprise, Simone sat down and began to cry.

Eve rushed to her. "What is it, Simone? Are you feeling ill?"

The woman shook her head and dried her tears on her apron. "No. Forgive me."

Eve couldn't bear to see her friend weeping. She loved Simone like a sister. "What is it, dear?" Her young face was etched with distress as she gathered Simone into her arms.

In the past five years Simone had been Eve's strength and support. Now it was Eve who provided comfort and strength for her best friend.

"While you were gone yesterday, Reverend Williams paid me a visit," Simone began haltingly.

"And?" Eve asked, kneeling down on her knees at Simone's feet. "What did he want? I'm sure it was something other than a donation for the new church." She regretted the remark as soon as she said it. Simone was too upset for her to be flippant.

"He said there are rumors about Sam staying here. Apparently, the Holy Reverend Williams and his good congregation disapprove of him, and the fact that Sam stays here overnight . . ." Simone groped for words, unable to complete the insinuation made by the minister.

"People will always find something to gossip about, but if it bothers you, Simone, we can ask Sam to leave."

Simone grabbed her hand in panic. "No, I don't want him to leave."

"Well then, don't let them upset you. What do we care what some scandalmonger has to say?"

"I don't want to go back to that church, Eve." Her eyes and voice were laced with desperation.

Eve sensed there was more to the story than Simone was telling her. "If we don't go back, Simone, people will think we're running away. Is there something more you aren't telling me?" she asked gently.

"Reverend Williams asked me to marry him." She shifted her eyes guiltily to peer at Eve.

For a few seconds after Simone's announcement, Eve sat stunned. The thought of Simone marrying and leaving her was devastating. Then her happiness for Simone burst within her in a joyous outpouring. Tears of happiness streaked her cheeks as she hugged her.

"I'm so happy for you." Eve drew back with a false frown. "But why didn't you tell me? I thought that Sam . . ." She shook the thought aside. "Well, I never suspected for a moment that you and Reverend Williams were in love."

At the look on Simone's face, any further words of congratulations died in her throat. "There is something you haven't told me, isn't there?" she asked, rising to her feet.

Simone nodded. "I refused his offer. It was degrading. He only made it because he's desperate for a wife."

Simone was composed now. It was Eve who became upset. Her spirits plummeted. "You mean the two of you aren't in love?"

"Of course not. I don't even like the pompous idiot. *C'est un âne bâté!*" Having called the man a perfect ass, Simone dismissed the subject of Reverend Williams.

Eve was the picture of desolation as she sank into a chair. "We're a real pair, aren't we. It seems the only men we can attract are the ones we don't want."

Simone smiled sadly. "That is true. But you, *chérie*, are a fool, if you'll forgive me for saying so."

Eve knew Simone was referring to her attitude about Adam. He had the woman completely duped. Simone never saw the side of Adam that she did.

Eve was saved from replying when Sam came into the room. "The shed's finished. Do you want to take a look at it?" He saw their grave expressions and realized he had interrupted a serious conversation. "It can wait until later."

As he turned to leave, Simone jumped to her feet. "I want to see it." She followed him out.

Eve watched the two of them crossing the yard together, then sadly shook her head and returned to the store.

Toward dusk, Eve grabbed two apples and slipped away with a promise to Simone to be back soon. The short walk to the stable was refreshing after a long day of being cooped up at the bakery.

Callie and Equus were glad to see her, snatching up the apples offered them. Eve spent several relaxing moments with her mare before returning to the store.

The next day when she had a free moment, she returned to the stable and opened Callie's stall. The blacksmith who operated the stable stopped her at once. "I'm sorry, Miss MacGregor, but Mr. Rawlins gave me strict instructions that you're not to ride the mare."

Eve was incensed. Callie was her horse. How dare Adam humiliate her like this? He made everyone a party to his domination of her.

She threw the blacksmith a disgruntled glance. "I'm just going to exercise her. Callie's used to a lot more exercise than she's getting."

"Good idea," the man agreed and handed her a bit and rein. "Take her out in the corral in the back."

Eve walked the horse several times around the fenced-in yard, then did the same to Equus. The black stallion had long grown accustomed to her and had gentled to her touch. Each day thereafter, when the opportunity presented itself, Eve would hurry to the stable and exercise the horses.

Adam had been gone for almost two weeks when Eve approached the stable one afternoon to discover there was no sign of the blacksmith. She was about to begin her daily ritual with the horses, when she was hit with a streak of rebellion. *Why not go riding?* she asked herself. *Why live her life according to the Gospel of St. Adam?*

She put a bit and saddle on Callie and led the mare through the gate.

*   *   *

Adam headed straight for the bakery as soon as he returned from Sacramento. He patted his coat pocket and felt the bulge of the document he had kept concealed in the safe for the past six years. The time had come to show it to Eve.

He felt a sense of foreboding at the sight of the "Closed" sign on the door. When he entered, the stricken look on Simone's face confirmed his fears. "Something's happened to Eve?"

Simone nodded. "Sam and Bailey are out looking for her now." Adam felt a tightening in his chest as Simone continued, "She left for the stable about three hours ago. She's been going there every day to exercise the horses. When she didn't return, Sam went there to look for her. He said the mare was gone, too. So he and Bailey rode out to try to find her."

"Did they say which direction they were heading?"

Simone nodded, dabbing at her swollen eyes. "Bailey said he'd take the road south, and Sam headed toward the mountains."

Adam was out of the door immediately, stopping only long enough at The Original Sin to change his coat and strap on his gun belt. After saddling Equus, he took the route he had previously ridden with Eve, hoping she might have followed the familiar path.

Adam rode hard, cursing himself for being foolish enough to bring Callie to San Francisco. He knew how obstinate and headstrong Eve could be at times. If anything happened to her, he would be responsible.

As he neared the stream where he and Eve had once halted, his anxiety escalated at the sight of Callie tied to some brush. Glancing around desperately, he spied Eve sitting on the ground nearby with her knees tucked under her chin.

His first reaction was one of overwhelming relief. For several seconds he could only sit motionless, trying to check the trembling that was sweeping over his body. Then his relief turned to anger. Blind anger.

He galloped over to her and jumped down before the horse had come to a halt. Deep in thought, Eve had been unaware of his approach until he suddenly was upon her.

Adam yanked Eve to her feet, his eyes blazing with fury. She had never seen him so angry. Adam's customary forte had always been a guise of cool control.

"What do you think you're doing?" he shouted, shaking her until she feared her teeth would rattle. "I gave you explicit orders not to ride that horse unless I was with you."

"I'm capable of handling a horse without any help from you," she flared defiantly.

"Do you have any idea what could happen to you out here alone? There are wild animals, bandits—every manner of low life in the territory crawling around these hills. You're a fool, Eve. A headstrong, irresponsible little fool. You never stop to think about anyone's interests but your own."

"I'm not hurting anything or anyone, so take

your hands off me," she blazed, her innate spunkiness surfacing to challenge him.

"Are you so sure? What about Simone? She's half out of her mind worrying about you. Sam and Bailey are out riding around these hills looking for you. Maybe you haven't noticed, Miss MacGregor, but it's getting dark. Lord knows what they might run into."

Eve was beginning to see the folly of her impetuous act. It was a mistake to ride out alone. She hadn't stopped to consider the dangers. As much as she hated to admit it to Adam, she mumbled an apology. "I'm sorry. It was thoughtless of me."

"Well, you're going to pay the price for that thoughtlessness. I'm taking Callie away from you. I'll ship her back to Sacramento in the morning."

Eve was willing to admit she had been thoughtless and inconsiderate, but he was going too far. What she did was her business. She was not accountable to him. "Oh no, you won't. Callie is my horse. We made a bargain."

It was a mistake. Her defiance only rekindled his anger. "I don't give a damn about any bargain. I gave you orders not to ride that horse. If you can't be trusted, then Goddammit, I'll shoot the horse."

Adam drew his pistol and stormed off toward the tethered animal. Eve was horrified. She ran after him and grabbed his arm to stop him. "Don't kill her! Please don't kill her, Adam. I swear to you, I won't do it again." Tears rolled down her cheeks. Sobbing, she sank to her knees, burying her face in her hands.

Adam stood motionless above her, fighting for control. He eased the pistol back into the holster at his hip. He raised his hands to discover they were shaking. Finally, unable to bear the pitiful sound of her crying, he grasped her shoulders and raised her to her feet.

"Why do we do this to each other, Eve?"

The hoarse plea caused her to lift her head and look into a pair of dark eyes as tormented as her own. For a breathless moment she thought he was going to kiss her. And, in some kind of bizarre reckoning, Eve realized she wanted him to. Adam's jaw shifted into a grim line, then he lifted her onto her saddle and climbed onto Equus.

They rode back to the city in silence.

It was pitch black when they arrived at the bakery. After Eve dismounted, Adam took Callie's reins and rode away. Her guilt resurfaced when she saw Simone. Adam had not exaggerated. The poor woman was in a state of near hysteria. There was no word from either Sam or Bailey, and she had been pacing the floor since Adam's departure.

Eve had just succeeded in calming Simone when Sam returned. Bailey followed shortly behind. Eve apologized to the two men for putting them to such trouble, then retired for the night.

However, her troubled thoughts kept her awake. She feigned sleep when Simone came to bed, because she wasn't ready to talk about her conflicting feelings toward Adam.

He was foremost in her thoughts. The anguish in his eyes was still vivid in her mind. *Why do we do this to each other?* echoed again and again in her head.

What was this love-hate emotion between them? Out there tonight she had wanted him to kiss her. It was not imagined, but real. So real that her body still throbbed with the ache of it. What power or spell did the man have over her to cause this confusing sensation? Until she faced it, and conquered it, she would never be free of him. As long as his touch excited her, she would be at his mercy.

Eve closed her eyes in torment, trying to force his image out of her mind. But it was in vain. She remembered the excitement of his kisses, could feel the taste of them on her lips. Her nipples grew taut with arousal and she bolted to her feet in panic.

Damn you, Adam. Why did you come here? Why after all this time does the touch of you, the scent of you, the very sight of you drive me to distraction?

Strange, how just a few short weeks ago she had welcomed that very same challenge with confidence. Had she naively believed she could withstand those temptations and come out the victor? *No one wins any bout with him,* she thought sardonically. *Adam always comes out the champion.*

Yet, tonight she had sensed he found no

satisfaction in that victory. *Why do we do this to each other?*

Could it be that his torment was equal to her own? Could he be agonizing with the same misgivings this very moment?

Eve walked to the window. The Original Sin was in darkness except for a dim light gleaming in the casino. It was a beacon to a lost ship tossing aimlessly on a sea of turmoil.

Eve donned her robe and slippers.

Except for a man sweeping the floor, the casino was deserted. He opened the door at her knock. Eve crossed in a trancelike state to the red carpeted stairway. The man made no effort to stop her, but stared dumbfounded as she climbed the stairs. She was drawn to the door at the end of the darkened hall. Eve stepped into the room and closed the door behind her. A single lamp reflected dimly on the dark hair of the man sitting with his head buried in his hands.

Adam raised his head at the sound of the door closing. For several seconds his eyes locked with hers. She could feel the blood coursing through her body as he rose to his feet and walked toward her. His eyes never wavered from her own.

The curve of his mouth was barely perceptible. She didn't have to speak. Offer an explanation. He knew her purpose for being there, as well as she.

Adam swooped her into his arms and carried her to the adjoining room. When he lowered her, her legs were trembling so much that she thought she would collapse. The instant her feet touched the floor, he pulled her into his arms, engulfing her in an interminable kiss. Spinning and twisting helplessly, Eve was drawn deeper and deeper into the depths of a swirling eddy.

When he released the tie of her robe, Eve closed her eyes, her long dark lashes thick against her cheeks. He pressed a kiss to each closed lid. The heady masculine smell of him began permeating her senses.

Adam slipped the robe off her shoulders. His eyes clung hungrily to the sight of the thin lawn gown molded to the thrust of her breasts and sleek lines of her body. Overpowered by the scent of him, she had to reach out to touch him. Her fingers caressed the corded column of his neck. She could feel the tautness that held his body in check as she slid her hand into the dark thickness of his hair. Its texture tantalized her fingertips. Lowering his head, Adam pressed light kisses to the sensitive hollow behind her ear. His fingers lightly glazed her cheek and slid down to her chin, tipping her face to his. He nibbled at her mouth, his tongue conducting darting forays to extract the response he was seeking.

Satisfied, his hand moved to her hips, pressing her against the intimate proof of his arousal. Eve responded with a breathless gasp when he began to release the buttons of her gown. His hand felt firm and warm. Cupping her breast through the thin garment, he slid his hand down her body in a slow, tantalizing exploration.

Eve continued to be swept along in a torrent of long-suppressed desire as Adam lightly traced the outline of her mouth with his tongue. Her hunger for him was becoming unbearable and she began communicating this passion with her body in a mounting, pulsating response.

With a motion as smooth as the satin of her skin, Adam lowered the gown off her shoulders. As he slipped the garment past her breasts, his hands swept them caressingly.

His name became a sensuous purr on her lips when his mouth slid lazily to the cleavage of her breasts, capturing one of the mounds in the cup of a hand. His thumb played with the taut peak, until he dipped his head and let his tongue toy with the hardened nipple. Eve's breath became wracking gasps when his mouth closed around it in an exquisitely rapturous suckling, wrenching a groan from her throat. Her hands dug into the thickness of his hair, forcing his head to its quivering twin.

Adam moved his hand across the smooth plane of her stomach, pushing the gown past her hips. Soundlessly, it fell in a heap to the floor. His eyes devoured her nakedness in a smoldering feast, and she trembled as he began to yank impatiently at the buttons of his shirt. In seconds he divested himself of his clothing, returning to press against her and filling his hands with her rounded cheeks.

She began to lose her hold on reality with no idea how much longer she could endure the erotic torture of his strong fingers splayed across the sensitive nerve ends of her buttocks and spine. Her head reeled with dizziness. Her trembling legs were barely able to support her.

Adam pressed his hands more tightly into her silky flesh, catching his breath in an expectant gasp when, helplessly, she reached out and found the inside of his muscular thigh. Her fingers began to trace a tantalizing trail to his swollen warmth. Smothering a groan against her mouth, he swept her up in his arms and carried her to the bed.

His naked body pressed against her. What had been a preliminary probing earlier erupted into ultimate exploration now that his hands and mouth had greater and freer access to her body.

To gain release from the exquisite torture, Eve pleaded for mercy. "Please, Adam, I can't take any more," she cried mindlessly, her body arching against the sensory moistness of his mouth closing around the taut peak of her breast.

Adam raised his head to stare down at her. Her black hair was spread in dishevelment on the pillow. He watched the changing expression in her passion-laden eyes as he stroked the throbbing, aching apex of her womanhood until she writhed helplessly in wild abandon. The sight of her inflamed his lust. His tongue traced her swollen lips, then plunged into the parted moistness that opened in invitation.

Eve responded instinctively. Her tongue

danced erotically across the roof of his mouth and he pulled away, muffling a groan into the thickness of her hair. Her arms slid to embrace him and her fingers began to sweep the long length of his spine as she hugged his steely strength against her own rounded curves.

Adam continued to explore her in a relentless erotic probe. He had been waiting too long for this moment and was forcing himself to exercise control until he could familiarize his hands and mouth with every crevice and hollow of her body.

Once again her body shuddered, this time under the intense sensation of his tongue. She felt driven to the brink of madness when he began to nibble the tender flesh of her inner thigh, until he reached the pulsating nucleus of her being.

"Please . . . please . . ." she groaned incessantly in heaving gasps, unaware that her own restless hands in their convulsive sweeps were raining havoc on his body. She sobbed in a quivering breath when Adam raised himself and thrust into her, rupturing the thin membrane.

Eve cried out. In those final, mindless moments she forgot the conversations with her school chums in Paris, the stories of the pain and bleeding that accompanied this moment. She writhed beneath him, trying to dislodge him.

"Don't, Eve. Don't struggle," Adam cautioned. "You'll just make it hurt worse."

He began to move slowly in and out until the

pain was replaced by a new sensation, an exquisite feeling building toward eruption. The tempo and force of his thrusts increased until his name escaped her lips in a blissful cry that shattered the last vestige of his control.

In the long moments it took to restore her breathing to a contained rhythm, Eve's chest ached from the throbbing of her heart. She finally raised her head and stared down into the dark luster of his eyes.

Adam smiled tenderly as he reached up to cup her face in the strength of his hands. He buried his fingers in the silken thickness of her hair. "I knew it would be like this."

Her eyes misted as she gazed at him. "I don't understand what's happening to me. It frightens me."

Adam rolled over, pinning her to the bed with his weight, and studied her face intently. "It wouldn't if you didn't fight it so hard. You're mine, Eve. You'll always be mine." He leaned down, gently kissing her swollen lips, then lay back again, cradling her head against his chest. Within seconds, his steady breathing disclosed to her that he had dropped off to sleep.

Eve lay awake in his arms, doubts plaguing her mind. How had this happened? Was Adam right? Did this night truly seal the bond between them once and for all?

What had just passed between them was the most incredible sensation she had ever experienced. Nothing she had ever done had given her such intense satisfaction.

Was it all sexual? Would Adam demand it of her again? And having experienced it, would she want to refuse? Was she no more than just another of his conquests?

Eve rose to her feet and quickly donned her gown and robe. She slipped quietly out of the room.

Adam opened his eyes when Eve left the bed. He didn't try to stop her from leaving. He knew she would rebel if he tried to demand any more from her now. He was willing to wait because he was aware of one thing which, in her naivete, she had not recognized. Eve was in love with him. He had known enough women in the past to realize that Eve could never have responded as totally and uninhibitedly if she were not in love with him. He just had to give her the time to arrive at that conclusion herself.

Adam smiled confidently, then rolled over and fell back to sleep.

CHAPTER THIRTEEN

It had rained during the night and the street was a quagmire. The sun, however, was a red ball in the sky when Eve hopped across the planks on the road and slipped into The Forbidden Fruit. Simone was dressed, sitting at the table sipping a cup of coffee. Much to Eve's relief, there was no sign of Sam or Bailey.

She got a cup and sat down opposite Simone, savoring the steaming brew in silence. She could feel Simone watching her.

Eve raised her eyes and peered at Simone over the rim of the cup. Finally, no longer able to contain herself, she blurted out, "I gave myself to him, Simone. I threw myself at him like a cheap whore."

Simone flinched at Eve's harsh assessment. Then, surmising the situation, she said kindly, "You gave yourself like a woman in love. Why are you angry, *chérie?*"

"I'm uncertain how I feel. Yesterday I was convinced that I hated Adam Rawlins, and today I know what it's like to be in his arms." She slammed the cup down on the table and coffee splashed out. Several drops splattered on her hand, but she was impervious to them. Simone leaned over and brushed them off when Eve failed to do so.

Eve buried her head in her hands. "I just wish I could understand it all." She raised her head with anguished eyes. "Is it possible to love and hate a man at the same time?"

"I am afraid you are asking the wrong person, *chérie*. I haven't had much experience with men. But my heart tells me Adam loves you very much." Simone clasped Eve's hand and squeezed it reassuringly.

"I wish my heart would tell me as much," Eve replied with a woeful sigh.

"It would, if you would only allow it to."

"Adam said the same thing to me." A smile briefly crossed her face as she mused over the familiar advice. A frown quickly followed as she continued, "I'm afraid, Simone. There's too much of the past to try to forget. I'm afraid I will regret trusting Adam."

"Isn't trust the real meaning of love? If I loved a man, I would listen to my heart and have faith in him. What does your heart tell you, *chérie*?"

Eve smiled warmly and pressed the hand holding hers. "My heart tells me I love him."

"Then listen to it. If your heart is ready to trust Adam, then you must have the same faith.

Let yourself believe in him and put aside the grievances of the past."

Before Eve could allow herself to entertain any further misgivings, Simone rose to her feet. "It is a good thing the bakery is closed today because I think you should go upstairs and get some rest."

Eve stood up and hugged her. "Oh, Simone, I love you. What would I ever do without you?"

Tears glistened in their eyes as they held one another in a bond of love. Then Eve climbed the stairway and sank into the bed. Her thoughts were on Adam as she succumbed to slumber.

It was noon when Eve awoke. Bright sunlight streamed through the window. She lay savoring the pleasure of the quiet moment, her thoughts on Adam. Her love for him seemed to be intertwined with the glowing warmth of the day.

Rising to her feet, she decided she wanted a bath and hurried downstairs. There was no sign of Simone. Eve put several large kettles of water on to boil. Then she pulled out the tub and towels for her bath.

She carried the steaming kettles up the stairs. It was an arduous task, which the two women always did together, but Eve was too uncomfortable to wait.

When she finally lowered herself into the hot water, she knew it was worth the effort. The soothing water was a succor to her spirits and body. Eve surrendered to the pure enjoyment of the bath. She remained in the water until it began to cool, then climbed out refreshed and relaxed.

Eve had drained the tub and was dressed by the time Simone returned, glowing with excitement. "I have been shopping with Bailey and Sam. Bailey's leaving tomorrow for his mine, so I am going to cook a grand meal tonight. I invited Adam to join us. I hope you don't mind, *ma chérie?*"

Eve felt her heart quicken at the mention of Adam's name. "Of course I don't mind. Where did you meet Adam?"

"He came looking for you earlier this morning, but left without disturbing you." It brought a smile to Eve's face.

"Well, what can I do to help you with the dinner?" Eve said enthusiastically. "I'm going to be sorry to see Bailey leave. I enjoyed having him around."

"I did too," Simone agreed. She began unpacking several bags of groceries. "That's why I want to make dinner as elegant as possible. I'll cook the meal and you can set the table. Let's have candlelight and wine."

Eve looked perplexed. "The wine is easy enough, but where am I going to get candle holders?"

"That is your problem," she declared, shooing Eve away. "Now out of the kitchen. You mustn't disturb the *chef de cuisine*. She has much work to do."

Eve hesitated outside the door of the bakery, trying to decide whether or not she should go over to see Adam. Would he think she was chasing after him? After all, she had just left him that morning.

Simone did say that he'd been looking for her earlier. Perhaps she could use that as an excuse, so as not to appear to be running after him.

As if reading her thoughts, Adam came out of The Original Sin. She watched his approach as he moved from one plank to another with an effortless stride.

Adam came into the store and bent down, kissing her lightly. "You're looking very beautiful today, Miss MacGregor."

"It must be because I'm in love," she said smiling, with a lingering glance at his dark eyes. "I understand you will be joining us for dinner tonight."

Adam nodded and took her arm. "How about helping me select a going-away gift for Bailey, or are you too busy?"

"Simone has just ejected me from the kitchen, so my time is free. I would love to go with you. I haven't shopped for anything other than groceries since I came to San Francisco."

It seemed strange to Eve to be strolling down the street hand in hand with Adam. If anyone would have suggested such a thing a week earlier, she would have laughed.

When they reached Market Street, both sides of the avenue were lined with people. A German brass band came parading down the street. "What's the occasion?" Eve shouted, trying to be heard above the oom-pah-pah of the tuba.

"The circus, lady," a grizzled miner next to them announced.

"Oh, of course, I forgot all about it."

The street was not completely dry from the recent rain, and the boots and trousers of the band got splattered with every downbeat of the music. Adam leaned down and whispered in her ear, "It looks like they oomed when they should have pah-pahed."

Eve covered her mouth as she began giggling uncontrollably. Adam's carefree mien was a side of him she never suspected. Studying the handsome profile, now softened with pleasure, she couldn't help but wonder how their relationship might have changed had he revealed it sooner.

"Oh, I wish Simone were here to see this," Eve exclaimed as a contingent of Chinesemen walked by, each holding onto strings attached to odd-shaped kites soaring overhead in the breeze.

They were followed by a colorful paper dragon. Its huge head and bulging eyes made it look as if it could breathe fire. The fearsome serpent weaved from one side of the street to the other as it was maneuvered by a dozen pair of human legs. The dragon stopped before Eve and emitted a loud snort, with smoke pouring out of its nose. Eve screamed and buried her head against Adam's chest, much to the amusement of the spectators around her.

Coming down the street next were the two hand-drawn and hand-pumped fire wagons of the city of San Francisco. Each was preceded by two young torch bearers. One of the wagons, which had been imported from the Hawaiian Islands, had long passed its usefulness. The other had formerly been used by President Van Buren to water his gardens in New York. Although it was pitifully inadequate for fighting fires, the volunteer firemen who pulled it walked tall and proud.

In the passing parade, the clop of the wagons gave way to the lilting strings of Mexican lutes as a group of strolling musicians in colorful serapes and wide sombreros walked past.

The miners clapped and hooted their approval at an aggregation of ladies-of-the-night. Their painted faces and daring gowns drew more applause as the women waved and called out to familiar faces in the crowd. Adam's tall form drew the attention of many of the ladies, and he joined in the spirit of the day by returning their greetings. Some of their more daring offers brought a blush to his normally controlled features.

The crowd quieted temporarily when a uniformed group calling themselves The Hounds marched past. Remnants of a regiment from New York, this gang of ruffians had come to California during the Mexican War. After the war ended, they set up headquarters in San Francisco and became bounty hunters, tracking deserting sailors. From there, they had graduated to bullying and robbery.

At the tail end of the parade, having just

arrived from Panama, appeared that which all were waiting anxiously to see. The George Rowe Olympic Circus had come to town.

A male and female midget each carried a sign announcing the times of the performances. The antics of the clowns and jugglers as they marched by delighted the crowd.

A cage rolled past with a sprawled tiger peering through iron bars, followed by a lumbering elephant with a woman in pink tights waving to the spectators.

"Do you want to go see the circus?" Adam asked her as soon as the final cage passed. The crowd had begun to disperse, most of the people moving toward the circus site on Kearney Street.

"I would love to, if we have time after finding Bailey a gift."

They continued to stroll along the street, peering into store windows. They stopped at a jeweler for Adam to buy Bailey a pocket watch, then moved on to a mercantile store that offered everything from nails to women's silk stockings. Adam purchased Bailey a small volume of the recently published *David Copperfield* by England's popular author, Charles Dickens. Eve got Bailey a tin of pipe tobacco, to enjoy on his lonely nights.

After leaving the store, Adam pulled her aside and tied a purple ribbon in her hair. He stepped back to admire it as she smiled up at him. "I couldn't resist buying it; it matches your eyes perfectly." He bent down and kissed her, oblivious to the men who passed them with envious grins.

Hand in hand they hurried over to Kearney Street, arriving just in time for the first performance. The ring master drew the audience's attention to a man balanced perilously over their heads on a wire strung between two poles.

Eve found herself holding her breath and clutching Adam's hand as the daring young man inched himself cautiously, foot over foot, along the narrow wire.

The audience, which had waited anxiously, broke into a round of applause when he safely reached the opposite pole. They then watched a lion tamer, with top hat and black whip, climb into the cage with the beasts.

Eve's favorite performer was the bare-back rider, standing upright on a galloping horse as it circled the ring. She and Adam sipped lemonade and chewed on fresh taffy, laughing at the clowns' escapades or jugglers manipulating three and four apples at a time. One of them tossed a bright red apple to Eve with a roguish wink.

Eve stopped at the booth of a fortune teller and was told she was going to come into great wealth.

"Does that mean you're going to agree to marry me?" Adam asked hopefully.

"Of course not," Eve teased, her eyes flashing merrily. "It means that Bailey is going to strike gold and make me rich."

"Is that really important to you, Eve?" Adam asked soberly.

For several seconds she remained silent, gazing into his somber eyes. "Being rich? Yes. But only to the extent of making me independent. Then I'll marry you, Adam."

When the clouded sky threatened rain, they returned to the bakery. Adam left her at the door, with a promise of returning that evening for dinner.

Simone was still busily occupied in the kitchen and wanted no intervention. Since she hadn't visited Callie earlier, Eve grabbed two apples and departed laughing. She was radiant with happiness, jumping from one plank to another as lightly as a gazelle. Strangers' heads turned in her direction at the appealing sight of her as she passed them with a smile or a wave.

The smile left her face when she reached the stable and discovered the two empty stalls. She dashed to the back in the hope that Mr. Granger, the blacksmith, had them in the corral. He was there, but there was no sign of the two horses.

"Mr. Granger, where are Callie and Equus?"

The man doffed his hat. "Why, Mr. Rawlins had them shipped home this morning."

Eve couldn't believe that Adam would carry through his threat and take Callie away from her. Especially after last night. *Hadn't it meant anything to him? Why am I fool enough to believe in him?*

The ache in her chest became a sob in her throat as she ran back to The Original Sin.

CHAPTER FOURTEEN

Adam was sitting on his bed holding his head in his hands when she burst into the room. He was bewildered when she began to lash out at him accusingly. "How could you, Adam? How could you do it to me?"

Adam attempted to spring to his feet, but fell back clutching his head. "What are you talking about, Eve?"

"Callie. I'm talking about Callie. What pleasure do you get out of hurting me so?"

"For God's sake, Eve, will you get a hold on yourself and let me explain?"

Eve was too angry to listen. All her doubts about him had once again manifested themselves. "I don't want to hear any more of your explanations. You threatened to take Callie from me, and the mighty Adam Rawlins doesn't make idle threats, does he? I, of all people, should know that."

A telltale muscle began to jump in Adam's cheek as he tried to suppress his anger by closing his eyes and lying back on the bed. Eve continued to berate him. "I thought last night might have meant something to you. I was a fool to think you could ever change."

Adam was hurting and getting more irritated by the minute. "Can't we discuss this later, Eve? I've got a terrible headache. I just threw out a drunken miner and he hit me on the head with the handle of his pick."

"You're lucky it wasn't me, or I might have been tempted to use the other end of the pick."

Despite the pain in his head, Adam couldn't help chuckling. Eve looked so angry that she probably meant it. "You're right about one thing, Eve. I haven't changed. I never make bargains or compromises in bed. You wasted your time, if that was your reason for coming here last night," he chided lightly. "In fact, there is a name for women who strike that kind of bargain, but I would hesitate to use it."

Adam had meant it to be a mild reprimand, just to try to curb her anger. It backfired, because he had touched on the very issue plaguing her conscience. "How dare you? What do you think I am? I came here last night because, for a foolish moment, I believed I loved you. That is what's bothering me. I trusted you and let you play me for a fool."

"No, Eve, I'm the fool for thinking you will ever grow up. You aren't bothered because you let me make love to you last night. You wanted it as much as I did. What's really bothering you is that you enjoyed it. That's the reason for this display of righteous indignation. Your conscience is bothering you, Miss MacGregor. Last night in my arms you were all woman. So start acting like one and drop these childish tantrums."

At the sight of her looking so wounded and vulnerable, he added sadly, "It would be a pleasant change in our relationship, Eve, if just once, when you are in doubt, you would *ask* instead of *accuse*."

Eve crossed her arms across her breast and glared at him. "You needn't concern yourself about our relationship, Adam, because there won't be any in the future."

"Eve, I intended to tell you about Callie earlier, but you were asleep. Granger said she bruised her front leg and started favoring it, so I shipped her back for Will to check it out and tend to it. I sent Equus to keep her calmed down on the trip back. She gets too riled up if he's not around. I didn't send her back to punish you."

Adam didn't have to be a doctor to know the real basis for her actions. Eve had been just twelve years old when she lost her mother, the only person in the world who loved her. She had to blame someone for that loss. He had been that someone. Adam's tone gentled. "Eve, I'm not responsible for your mother's death. You have to stop blaming me for it."

She gasped, her eyes swinging to his as he continued. "I regret that I was not kind to your mother. I acted as childish and immature as you have been. I was wrong in not allowing myself to know Mary MacGregor. But I didn't kill her. I also regret that I was angry with my father for marrying your mother. I wish I would have told him how much I loved him. But I'm not responsible for his death either. I can't change the past. And I can't keep paying for my mistakes. You've got to let go of them, Eve."

There was neither plea nor anger in his voice; there was only a desperate need for understanding. "I love you. I want to marry you. Why must you doubt me? I don't know what other assurance I can give you of my love for you."

Eve went limp. All the anger drained from her body leaving her floundering in a sea of guilt and shame. She wanted to disappear through the floor—anything to escape—as she realized the truth of his words. Adam's rejection of her mother and his domination of her were the basis for every doubt and suspicion she harbored toward him. She conveniently pulled them out of a sack whenever it served her purpose.

"I suppose it won't help to say I'm sorry," she said contritely.

"It's always a good place to start." He was fighting a need to take her in his arms.

"I am sorry, Adam." Eve walked over and stood above him. "I need time, Adam. You must understand that."

She turned to leave. Adam reached out, grabbing her hand before she could move. She waited above the bed, looking down at him, surprised to see supplication in his eyes. He looked like a wounded deer.

"Let's go home, Eve?"

It was hard to withstand the plea. Was that what she wanted? If she went with him now, she would be going back with a great deal unsettled between them. Adam had allowed her to leave once, but she knew he would never do it again. This time, she would be his completely, bound by much greater ties than ever before.

Adam watched her struggle, waiting hopefully for her answer. Eve could see there was pain in his dark eyes. The eyes she once foolishly had thought of as merciless. Was she wrong about other things as well? If she had misjudged Adam's motives and actions, perhaps her own were just as questionable.

She had to have time to determine the truth before she would be able to give him an answer. "Right now, Adam, my home is here in San Francisco."

When she started to move away, he pulled her back. Off balance, she fell across him. Adam rolled her over and she found herself pinned beneath him. He raised his head, tenderly cupping her cheek in his hand, worshiping her with his gaze. "That's not true and you know it. You belong with me. How many ways can I say I love you, Eve? Why are you afraid to admit that you love me?" he whispered in a husky entreaty. He lowered his mouth to hers.

Eve had intended to resist him, but the pressure of his warm lips sparked an emotion that was hard to acknowledge to herself, or him—her desire for him. The first time he kissed her had awakened her to that reality. Adam's very touch, his nearness, the scent of him, all excited her. Now, in his arms, bombarded by these very temptations, her blood felt like molten lava, flowing through her veins igniting a response.

"Eve, Eve," Adam murmured in hoarse whispers, burying his face in her hair. She had responded. It was not imagined.

He drew back to gaze down into her shimmering violet eyes. There was a naked passion in their depths, and her luscious mouth parted to accept his. All the signs were visible, telling him what he wanted to believe. Still he needed more of an assurance before daring to venture farther. Although the rein he was holding on his control was a tenuous one, there was still time to halt. In a few seconds he would be beyond checking his passion.

"You're going to have to say it to me, Eve. You're going to have to say it," he repeated in a hoarse plea.

She knew she was like a moth dancing with the danger of the flame, but the mounting urgency within her drove her to dare the Mephisto waltz.

"Make love to me, Adam," she sighed in a smothered groan, slipping her arms around his neck to force the return of his provocative lips.

Their mouths moved on one another's. Each began seeking, savoring the taste of the other in repeated kisses. Adam's hand was shaking as he began releasing the buttons on her gown. Eve lay trembling, held motionless by the dark smoldering eyes locked with her own. Groping for the hem of her gown, he slid it hastily up the length of her. His hands left a heated swath in their wake, moving past the swell of her hips to the curve of her breast. When he attempted to raise the gown over her head, his sudden wince of pain snapped her out of the eroticism that had kept her immobilized. She sat up abruptly.

"Your head, Adam. You're hurting yourself."

"It doesn't matter." The ache in his loin was far greater than that in his head.

Eve gently pushed him away. Adam fell back on the bed in despair, flinging his arm over his eyes. He needed her. How much longer could he bear that pain?

"Let me look at your head, Adam."

"I said it was fine," he grumbled. *Christ! Don't touch me or I'll snap.*

His nerve ends jumped beneath the sudden slide of her fingers into his hair. "Damn it, I said I was fine. For God's sake, Eve, take your hands off me or I'll end up raping—" The words died in his throat when he lowered his arm and opened his eyes.

Eve was kneeling. She had removed her gown. Adam's startled gaze swung to her naked breasts. He attempted to moisten his lips, which suddenly felt parched from the heat of his surging desire. When his passion-laden eyes shifted to her face, he saw she was watching him with a seductive smile. Adam sucked in a breath as she continued to slide a hand down the plane of his chest to his stomach and legs. She helped him to remove the trousers that covered them.

He was erect and throbbing.

Eve sensed her power over him. He was vulnerable and defenseless. This new awareness inflamed her own passion. She dipped her head, sliding her tongue across his chest. She could feel the increased pounding of his heart beneath her lips. He was at her mercy. Her nemesis was helpless beneath her fingertips, powerless to prevent whatever vindication she sought.

The sudden role reversal made her heady with power, inflaming her boldness. Her head fell back, her slim legs straddling his hips, and she sucked for breath in ragged gasps when she mounted his shaft.

Adam's response was instinctive. With a feral growl he pulled her to him, his mouth finding her thrusting breasts.

Eve buried her hands in the thick texture of his hair, basking in the throes of ecstasy. The tempo of their movements increased to a frenzy as his mouth voraciously gorged the sensitive peaks of her breasts, sending exquisite tremors up and down her spine. Her mane of raven hair flared around her shoulders in glorious dishevelment as Eve flung back her head in wanton abandonment and rode him—wildly, uninhibitedly, exuberantly.

When he began to erupt beneath her in surging convulsions, her cry of fulfillment was a blend of rapture and triumph.

Eve's heart was pounding so rapidly she thought it would burst. Fighting to restore her breathing, she was surprised to discover she was coated with a fine film of perspiration. Her eyelids felt heavy with it as she raised them slowly.

Adam's dark eyes were fixed on her face. There was bemusement in their depths. Eve guessed the reason for it. She slipped off him, reached for her gown, and pulled it over her head. He remained lying silently, as if waiting for her to speak. He, too, was glistening with perspiration.

"You're going to get a chill lying around like that." She pulled up the blanket to cover him.

Eve leaned over to adjust it and Adam grasped her shoulders, pulling her down to him. "Are we even now?" he asked.

She was surprised to see his expression dissolve into anguish. "Why, Eve? Even the bed is a battlefield, isn't it?"

She met his gaze without contrition. "I don't know what you're talking about."

"Like hell you don't."

Her eyes flared accusingly. "Well, who started this war, Adam?"

Adam's hands dropped from her shoulders. "War? Why must it be a war? I wanted us to make love, Eve. I wanted to show you how much I love you."

There was sadness and a bit of hopelessness in his voice. "In the past months I've cursed myself endlessly for my actions. I kept telling myself I could somehow convince you to forget the past. I wanted you to let me love you, Eve. I never wanted war."

Somehow, what had just happened between them had succeeded in creating a sense of futility that all her past denials had failed to accomplish. This time she was the one responsible for drawing a battlefield between them.

"I can't deny that I'm to blame for what just happened between us, Adam. I guess I was shocked to discover my power over you. For six years you have intimidated me. Suddenly you were helpless, completely at my mercy."

"I've always been at your mercy." He swung his head to her and she saw the full measure of despair he was suffering. "But I'm not blaming you. I understand why you did it, Eve."

Adam got up and grabbed his robe off a nearby chair. He went to the window and stood staring out. She felt a painful ache in her chest at the desolate slump of his shoulders. Her long-awaited triumph had a bitter taste.

Her heart quickened with a resurgence of hope. Maybe the act had served a purpose. Maybe it was a catharsis they both needed to purge them emotionally.

Eve got out of the bed and walked over to him. She stopped behind him, sliding her arms around his waist.

"The moment doesn't have to be lost, Adam. I do want you to hold me. I want you to make love to me."

Adam turned to her. The sadness in his eyes had turned to wariness. "I don't think you actually know what you want, Eve."

A glimmer of impishness sparkled in her eyes. "You still insist upon doing my thinking for me, don't you, Adam Rawlins? Do you believe I would throw myself at you like this if I didn't know what I was doing?" Her mouth curved into a seductive smile as she moved closer, rising up on her toes to slide her arms around his neck. "I think we've hurt one another enough for one night."

Before him stood the woman he had sought with desperation. The greatest obsession in his life. Was it possible there could still be hope for them? Adam cupped her face in his hands. Uncertain, he studied the face looking up into his, trying to probe the depths of her eyes. "Whatever your motives, Evelyn MacGregor, it's a tempting offer."

Satisfied with what he saw in the violet eyes meeting his own, Adam pulled her into his arms, burying his face in the perfumed silk of her hair. "Oh, Lord," he groaned, pressing her warmth against him. "I have dreamed of this moment for so long."

His lips took hers tenderly, almost hesitantly, as if he were still fearful of rejection. Eve's mouth parted under his and any further hesitation was incinerated by the fire that began to rage through him as that longed-for warmth molded itself to him.

His mouth and invading tongue possessed hers completely until, breathless, they were forced to part. Adam covered her face with gentle kisses, returning to claim her lips.

The hands he had fought to control for so long were now caressing messages of love. Fired with impatience, he swept the gown off her shoulders and it dropped to the floor.

Eve stood naked, trembling with passion as his mouth slid in a moist trail to her breasts. His name became a sensuous purr on her lips, then quickly changed to pleasant gasps when his tongue began to toy with one of the hardened nipples. She threaded her fingers through the thickness of his dark hair, pressing his head to her heaving breasts.

He willingly obliged her demands and closed his mouth around one of the swollen peaks, then turned his attention to its mate. Raising his head, he slipped a warm hand up the column of her neck, tilting her chin to meet his smoldering gaze.

"This is how I always dreamed you would be. How I wanted you."

The sound of his husky voice excited her more, and she curved into him, her body pressing against the hardened plane of him and the heated evidence of his arousal.

Eve raised her head and lifted her long lashes.

Her violet eyes were laden with sexuality. "I want you, Adam," she sighed against his mouth.

He had waited a lifetime to hear those words.

Sliding her hands down the furry mat of his chest, Eve released the tie of his robe. He slowed his actions to allow her to slip it off him. Oblivious to her own naked loveliness, her hands and fingertips tingled from just the feel of him.

Adam's breath was ragged as he allowed her this examination, until urgency forced him to lift her into his arms. He carried her to the bed.

Eve was beneath him now, in the circle of his arms. With loving exploration he traced the delicate line of her jaw with his tongue to the hollow of her ear. His breath ruffled her hair as he murmured his love for her, sensuously probing the interior with his tongue.

Her spine began to tremble with shivering tremors and she pressed against the inflexible weight holding her down. He reclaimed her quivering lips, increasing in demand as the hot poker of his tongue set her aflame. It was too exquisite to bear a moment longer.

A groan slipped through his lips when her fingers glazed the lean surface of his stomach, seeking his throbbing tumescence. She found him, returning his love in velvet strokes. Adam covered her eyes and face with kisses, rasping husky expressions of love and encouragement.

He rolled onto his back, his hands tangled in her hair as he pulled her to him in a bruising kiss. This time there was no dueling between them. Only the need and urgency to love and pleasure each other. Entwined, they rolled back until she was beneath him.

Adam nibbled a trail down the slim column of her neck, his hand sliding to part her thighs. Eve began swirling in an erotic sea of sensation. He stopped his descent to toy with the tips of her breasts, then continued his downward slide to the pulsating core of her being.

His hand cupped around it. She became senseless with ecstasy, mindlessly arching her hips into the tantalizing touch. She began shuddering with paroxysms, her clutching hands ravishing his body—grasping, caressing, searching.

He then entered the velvet softness, raising his head to reclaim her mouth as his tongue plunged into the honeyed chamber. Her arms wrapped his neck and she clung to him.

"This is the way it should be . . . can always be between us," he whispered.

"Yes. Yes. Yes," she groaned, as the tempo of his thrusts increased. Once again her body began convulsing, this time in rhythm with his. Her wondrous sob of "Adam" was smothered under the demanding pressure of his mouth.

It took several moments before speech was possible. Several moments of just holding, savoring the feel of one another. Adam smiled tenderly and brushed aside the strands of hair clinging to her cheek.

"I love you." He lowered his head and lightly brushed her lips, then lay back with a contented smile.

Eve's eyes misted as she lay in his arms. She loved him, too. She couldn't deny it to herself any longer. If there was any hope for a future together, she had to face that reality, because it outweighed any grievances of the past.

"I love you, too, Adam."

They dozed in one another's arms until Eve was jolted to wakefulness by a nagging conscience. She shot up.

"The candle holders!"

"What are you talking about?" Adam asked drowsily.

"I promised Simone I would find some candle holders."

Adam yawned and pulled her back down into his arms. "I think there must be some around here someplace. Why does she need candle holders?" He was fully awake now.

"She wants this farewell dinner for Bailey to be very elegant."

Adam rolled over and pinned her beneath him. He dipped his head and began to nibble a trail to the cleavage of her breasts. "I must go, Adam. I have to help with dinner," she protested weakly.

Adam raised his head. The sapphire depths of his dark eyes were gleaming with devilishness. "I like my dessert before dinner." He grinned wickedly, and lowered his head.

* * *

By the time Eve left The Original Sin, Adam had found a tablecloth and candle holders. He promised to bring the wine as his contribution to the dinner.

Simone's expertise in the kitchen was never in greater evidence. She had prepared a white onion soup, chicken fricassee and rice, garnished with baked croutons. Dessert was chocolate molds filled with a rich custard.

"I just bet this dinner cost us our profits for a week, but it was worth every cent of it," Eve said when they all sat back fully sated.

Bailey grinned his appreciation. "I'm going to have to remember this meal for a long time. Especially when I'm on a steady diet of beans and salt pork in the next year."

Simone blushed under the praise and glanced shyly at Sam. He nodded in agreement, but said nothing. Adam raised his wine glass. "My compliments to the chef. Any time you want to open a restaurant, Simone, I'll be glad to back you."

The conversation had turned to the very issue Eve had been considering. "This morning when I was struggling with the tub for my bath, I was thinking along similar lines. Why don't we enlarge the building by adding more living quarters and possibly a small restaurant or tea room?"

"It would be nice to expand our living quarters," Simone agreed.

"Remodeling can be quite costly, Eve. Lumber is going for a dollar a board foot, and even unskilled labor is getting ten to twelve dollars a day," Adam cautioned.

"I don't care. Since Simone has no objections, I'm going to the bank tomorrow and see if I can borrow the money. Besides," she added gaily, "when Bailey strikes gold, we'll all be rich and we can easily pay it back."

The remark triggered an outbreak of laughter. Sam glanced over and saw that Adam had not joined in the merriment.

CHAPTER FIFTEEN

Bailey left at sunrise the following morning. Before departing, he drew a map for Sam pinpointing the location of the mine.

Eve, determined to pursue her plans for the building, waited anxiously for the bank to open. Hiram Pendergast, the bank president, listened politely to her request. He then advised her of the risks involved for two single women attempting to operate a business without male protection. It was an argument she had heard often. Pendergast agreed to present her request to the loan committee.

That evening she dined with Adam in his quarters at the casino. When they finished, he told her he would be leaving the following morning for Sacramento and would not return until the end of the week.

"The Eagle Theatre Company is coming to

town next Saturday. Edwin Booth is appearing in *Hamlet*. Would you like to attend?"

Eve was ecstatic. "I haven't seen a play since I left France."

Adam took her in his arms and pressed a light kiss to her lips. "Do you want me to have Clara pack some of your gowns? I can bring them back with me." His hands caressed her shoulders. "I haven't seen you in anything except the same two gowns since I came to San Francisco."

"And you won't, until we rebuild. I haven't any room for extra clothing."

Adam frowned. She had seen the expression often enough to know that something serious was bothering him. "Eve, why don't you forget this rebuilding? Marry me and come back to Sacramento."

"I won't do that, Adam. I enjoy what I'm doing. Besides, it would defeat my purpose in coming here. I want to be independent of you."

"Is that so important to you now?" he asked. "I don't know how much longer I can keep running back and forth. Poor Richard Graves has been carrying most of the burden."

"Adam, I'm not ready for marriage. I know you're neglecting your business. If you must, go back to Sacramento. I'll come to visit you whenever I can." Eve knew she was hurting him, but she wasn't ready to relinquish her dream. She needed more time before making such a commitment to him.

"No. I won't consider such an arrangement. When you return to my house, it will be as my wife. That is our home. Some day our children will be born there. I'll not turn it into a trysting place. I want a wife, Eve, not a mistress." The look on his face was uncompromising.

She stepped away from him. "You never should have come to San Francisco and built a gambling casino. I didn't ask you to, Adam. Please don't make me feel guilty about it."

"How else was I to see you, Eve? Besides, it's proven to be a very profitable investment. Graves is attempting to find an honest man to run it for me."

"That would have been a good job for Bailey," Eve reflected, thankful that the conversation had shifted to a safer subject.

"Honey, Bailey is the kind of man who must be free to seek an El Dorado, Ophir, or whatever other pipe dream he's pursuing at the moment. He's Jason in search of the Golden Fleece. Tying him down would be like clipping the wings off a bird." His face sobered. "I have something I must tell you about Bailey."

Eve saw his change of mood and returned to his embrace, slipping her arms around his neck. "Let's not spend our last evening together arguing or discussing Bailey Montgomery."

Adam relaxed and began to nuzzle her neck. "Are you sure you don't want me to bring you back one or two gowns, at least?"

Eve drew back and looked up at him with an adorable pout. "Why do I have the feeling you don't like this gown I'm wearing?"

He grinned, the smile carrying to his eyes. His

hands felt warm and provocative as he began to slide the dress down her shoulders. "It's a very lovely gown, my dear, but I like it better off you," he whispered huskily, before his mouth lowered to cover hers.

"I have to find a new dress just to surprise him," Eve said as she and Simone stared at the dress in the shop window the following day. The gown was black satin and heavily bedecked with ribbons and ruffles.

"Everything we've seen looks like it was made for a . . . lady of the night."

"You mean a whore. Go ahead, Simone, say it. I know that's what I'll look like when I put it on," Eve said despondently. "But it's the only gown we've seen that has potential. Maybe with a few alterations I could make it work."

Simone regarded the dress again with a dubious frown. "I don't know, *chérie*. It's rather gaudy, don't you think?"

"Simone, I'm desperate. We can tone it down. At least it's not red like most of the others we've looked at. It's the best of the lot."

Eve took her hand and pulled her into the store. The merchant's brow raised in surprise when Eve informed him she was purchasing the gown. She bought a pair of black hose, lace mitts, and jeweled pumps as accessories. Simone selected a white plume for Eve's hair, convincing her it was a necessary expense.

Once within the private walls of the bakery,

Eve put on the dress. "This will have to go for sure," Simone announced, snipping off tiers of black chiffon and velvet ribbon. She then removed the ruffle of white tulle that bordered the hem and front slit of the gown. Two shoulder straps of the same fabric met a similar fate.

The dress was bereft of ornamentation. The satin, strapless gown clung to Eve's voluptuous curves like a glove. She gasped at the sight of it. "I can't wear this in public. It's shocking."

Several yards of chiffon lay in a heap on the floor. Simone put the iron on the top of the stove to heat, while Eve applied a needle and thread to the chiffon. Within minutes, the flimsy material was ready for pressing. Simone tacked it to the top of the gown, setting it wide off Eve's shoulders in a Bertha flounce. The effect was stunning.

"I'll brush your hair to the top of your head, and with the elbow-length mitts and the plume, you'll look ravishing, *chérie*."

Eve regarded her image warily. "Do you think I'll look too scandalous without a bustle?"

"I think you'll be the envy of every woman there," Simone assured her. "You'll probably start a fashion trend."

"I doubt that," Eve scoffed. "Are you certain you won't come with us, Simone? Adam did say the invitation includes you, too."

"No. No, *chérie*. You and Adam enjoy yourselves. Sam is going to teach me a card game called Monte."

"I'm afraid he's beginning to corrupt you." Eve giggled. "Perhaps, I should stay home and supervise."

The following Saturday night, Eve took careful pains dressing for her date with Adam. Simone had pinned her hair to the top of her head and attached the white plume. A carved cameo that had belonged to her mother was tied around her neck on a black velvet ribbon. She looked sleek and sophisticated.

"I'll show you," she threatened, lightly dabbing several drops of her meager supply of French perfume behind each ear. "Eau de Cinnamon, indeed!" She added a spot at the pulse of her neck. "See how you like this, Mr. Rawlins."

Eve grabbed a white shawl and tossed it lightly over one arm. She turned back to the mirror for a final inspection. Her heart was pounding with excitement and her violet eyes were sparkling with anticipation. She hadn't seen Adam for five days and felt as if she were going on her first date. She hurried down the stairway.

She found Simone and Sam seated in the kitchen. "How do I look?" she asked, twirling around for their inspection.

"You look beautiful, *chérie*." Simone beamed approvingly. It had been a long time since she had seen Eve dressed so elegantly. She thought Eve had never looked lovelier, glowing with an inner quality that Simone had not seen before.

Sam stared in open admiration. There was no

question the woman was beautiful. He was glad he wasn't in Rawlins' boots. The poor man would have his work cut out for him tonight just keeping his hands off her. "Are you sure you won't need a bodyguard tonight?"

"No. I should have no problem. I'll be with Adam."

"That's what I mean," Sam said dryly.

Eve blushed when she grasped his meaning. Adam entered the store at that moment. He froze in his tracks at the sight of her and let out a long, low whistle. It added to her crimson coloring.

"I thought you weren't wearing any red tonight, *chérie*." Simone teased.

"If the three of you don't stop, I'm going to refuse to go," she warned.

"Does that mean I could have you to myself all evening?" Adam piped wickedly.

"It certainly does not," she warned. "It means that I'll turn around and go right up those stairs for the rest of the night."

"Then, by all means, your arm, my lady." He tucked her hand in the crook of his arm. As they departed, he turned around and winked at Simone. "Don't wait up for her. I think it's going to be a very late evening."

The smile lingered on Simone's face after their departure. Sam sat secretly admiring it. He knew she had no idea how much her happiness for others enhanced her own features. He felt the tug at his heart that Simone always generated. He realized his feelings for her were becoming too complicated. He soon would have to think about moving on.

Sam Montgomery was a phlegmatic man by nature. The accident of his birth had forced him to traverse through life as an outsider, remaining impassive and indifferent to those around him.

An acquired skill with a six-gun had earned him a niche in a hypocritical society, which courted this skill while treating him as an outcast because he was a half-breed. This did not disturb him. Sam was a realist and never wasted time or remorse on something that was out of his grasp.

Yet, this woman's gentle ways had dug a deep hole in his heart.

Simone crossed to the table and began mixing dough. "I never see you dress up in a fancy gown."

Simone flushed, unable to meet his steady gaze. "A woman like me has no need for fancy gowns," she said in a tone much lighter than she was feeling. What remained unsaid was that she had no man to dress up for.

She was afraid to look at him. Afraid that his probing stare would read the emotion she had fought to conceal. She was in love with him. She knew that this fact would embarrass him. It would drive him away and she would lose these moments she had with him.

"What do you mean 'a woman like you'?"

"Oh, that's just a phrase," she said quickly.

She threw him a covert glance, afraid she had already said too much.

"I still don't understand what you mean by it," Sam persisted.

"Oh, Sam, there's nothing wrong with your eyesight. You can't make a cream puff out of sour dough."

"There you go, mouse, putting yourself down again. You've got more to offer a man than any woman I've ever met. Someday the right man will come along and see it."

The right man, she thought. *But not you, Sam, is that what you're trying to tell me?* Her heart felt as if it would burst. *Oh, Lord,* she thought with misery, *he's guessed how I feel and is trying to be kind.*

"Why did you call me mouse just now?"

"It suits you. You remind me of a mouse in the desert. Tiny and scared of everything around it. Darting and scurrying about in the shadows, just trying to survive. Preyed upon by eagle and reptile alike."

Simone looked up with a sad smile. "That's not true, Sam. People have always been good to me, and I haven't encountered too many reptiles in my life." She smiled shyly, "And as for eagles . . . well, they do cast splendid shadows."

She forced a light tone to her voice and popped a pastry sheet into the oven. "As soon as these cookies bake, I want you to try one. I think I used too much salt."

"I'm going to have to think about moving on. If I keep testing your bakery, I'll get so fat that I soon won't be able to climb on a horse." They smiled at each other, but both knew there was a deeper meaning behind their casual words.

The stage for the evening's performance of *Hamlet* was set up in the far end of El Dorado, San Francisco's most lavish gambling casino.

James McCabe, one of the owners of the opulent structure, recognized Adam on sight. "Mr. Rawlins," McCabe greeted, shaking Adam's hand. "How is our competition doing? I was impressed with your establishment when I looked it over."

"I don't think The Original Sin poses too much of a threat to you, McCabe," Adam replied, looking around at the mammoth building. "But the liquor's good and we do offer an honest game."

"You aren't implying I don't, are you, Rawlins?" McCabe gibed good-naturedly. The man's attention swung to Eve.

"My betrothed, Evelyn MacGregor," Adam offered at the man's obvious interest.

McCabe kissed her hand and introduced them to Irene McCready, who was standing at his side. The woman appeared to know Adam, but merely acknowledged the introduction with a nod of her head before regarding Eve's gown with avid interest. Much to the irritation of both women, McCabe's eyes continued to wander in Eve's direction.

Eve was uncomfortable under the man's lascivious stare. She was relieved when Adam took her arm and moved away.

"What an unusual couple," she whispered.

Adam lowered his head and said softly, "You have just met one of San Francisco's most famous, or infamous, couples. McCabe is a gambler and Irene McCready is his mistress. She operates a very high-class bordello, probably the finest in San Francisco. It's just around the corner."

Eve glanced up with more than a casual interest. "You appear to be quite knowledgeable about Mrs. McCready. Should I be jealous?"

Adam laughed lightly. "My dear Eve, whatever I might have done in the past is past. You are the one consuming love in my life." He put his arm around her shoulder and steered her to their seats.

Eve sat engrossed during the performance. Edwin Booth was a dynamic actor with superb stage presence. During the intermission they were joined by Hiram Pendergast and his wife. Eve was concerned that her daring gown might be an embarrassment to Adam. To her relief, the banker's wife greeted her cordially and complimented her on the dress. Eve was able to relax from then on. During a brief moment while Adam was engaged in conversation with his wife, Pendergast leaned down and informed Eve that her loan request had been approved.

She returned to her seat exhilarated by the news. For the rest of the performance her mind drifted from the play to her future plans for The Forbidden Fruit.

Adam's love-making that night was passionate and wild. The long separation had taken its toll on him. Eve returned to the bakery at dawn, troubled by the awareness that it was becoming more and more difficult to leave him.

CHAPTER SIXTEEN

The small wooden building next to The Forbidden Fruit was owned by a German couple named Bacher. They had come to California in '48, but Fritz Bacher's declining health had changed their minds about remaining, so they were returning to their native country. When Eve heard the news, she approached the couple and they agreed to sell her their property for $20,000. At the price land was selling for, it was a reasonable request. It required increasing her note at the bank, but the transaction was completed and now a much greater expansion of the bakery was possible.

The price of brick was too costly for consideration, so a wooden structure quickly took shape. Since Adam was in Sacramento during most of the remodeling, Eve and Simone were able to use his sleeping quarters in the casino until their own were completed. This arrangement, they were sure, must have caused great distress among Reverend Williams and his pious flock. But then, it did give the good people something to think about.

It was a joyous day for the women when they were able to move into their own bedrooms. Each of them had a large comfortable room on the second floor, linked by a shared bathroom. Adam's gift to them arrived the week before they opened. It was a large bathtub, which he had personally engineered. Attached to the tub were a pump and hose leading to a water tank in the kitchen, which was heated by a stove. Thus they would be able to bathe without carrying buckets of water upstairs, and also have hot water available for bath or kitchen use at any time. A drain emptied the tub and carried the waste water to a cistern in the back of the building.

Eve was the first to test the new appliance, and she sat luxuriating in its warmth, blessing the day Adam Rawlins was born.

It was decided between them that Simone would have exclusive authority over the bakery. Two young daughters of a Swedish family on the block were hired to assist her. Eve took the responsibility of operating the tiny tea room, which offered coffee, tea and fresh bakery to its customers.

When The Forbidden Fruit reopened, a steady stream of people came and went throughout the day.

Eve drew up in surprise when a short man

wearing a black derby entered the tea room. She gasped in recognition. It was the same rogue who had struck her in the face and attempted to steal her luggage on the night she arrived in San Francisco.

She looked helplessly about for Sam, but there was no sign of him. The man was just as surprised when he recognized Eve, and disappeared through the door before she could cry out for help.

For a while, Eve fretted over this unexpected encounter, but as the day wore on, she was too busy to give the incident much thought.

That evening both women were totally exhausted. Adam insisted they dine with him rather than attempt to cook for themselves. Sam joined them for dinner, but Eve found herself too weary to enjoy herself. For the past several weeks she had found herself tiring easily, attributing her fatigue to the effort of remodeling. She excused herself, and Adam walked her back to the bakery. They shared a lingering kiss at her doorway, and he returned to the casino.

After Adam disappeared through the door of The Original Sin, a figure stepped out of the shadows. The round derby on the man's head cast an eerie shadow on the side of the building as he moved stealthily in the dim moonlight to the rear of the bakery.

In the throes of terror, Eve awakened abruptly to find herself in the midst of a hellish inferno. Gray smoke swirled around her, and she froze at the sound of crackling flames consuming the stairway, creeping toward her room.

She screamed in fright, sucking smoke into her lungs, which caused her to double over in a seizure of coughing. Tears flowed from her stinging eyes. Clutching at her chest, Eve staggered to her feet. Gripped by panic, she stumbled toward the open window, trying to escape the flames licking at the bedroom door.

Halfway to the window, she sank to the floor, overcome by the searing smoke that filled her lungs. She lay unconscious as the door burst into a sheet of flame.

Smoke drifted into The Original Sin when a frantic figure burst through the doorway shouting, "Fire! The bakery's on fire!"

Pandemonium broke out in the crowded casino as people scrambled to get to the door. Adam jumped to his feet in panic, Eve's safety foremost in his mind. Not knowing if she was still in the bakery, Adam fought his way through the crowd to get to the street. Sam tried to follow, struggling to keep Simone on her feet in the crowd shoving and yelling to get out of the door.

Adam paused in horror at the sight of the bakery. The entire bottom floor of *The Forbidden Fruit* was engulfed in flames. Fiery sparks flashed in the dark smoke rising above the burning building.

Chaos reigned on the street. Frightened and squalling children were being herded out of their homes. As he crossed the street, Adam bodily encountered people running in all directions. Frantically, he looked around for Eve, but there was no sign of her.

"Get a bucket brigade going," Adam shouted when he spied his bartender. Men quickly lined up and began passing buckets of water from a nearby cistern.

"Have you seen Eve?" Simone cried, clutching Adam's arm when she and Sam reached his side.

Adam shook his head. "She's not on the street. She must still be in there." He charged into the entrance of the adjoining building.

"Oh God, no," Simone sobbed, burying her head in Sam's chest.

People screamed and ducked for cover when the glass windows in the bakery blew out from the heat, spewing shards of glass over the turmoil below.

Sam shoved Simone back into the casino. "Stay inside, but get out quick if the fire jumps the street." He ran to find Adam.

As the fire engine arrived, the clang of a fire bell added to the noise of the screaming and shouting already in progress. The small, hand-drawn machine was barely adequate. The firemen hurriedly set up the hose and pump to draw water from nearby cisterns.

Men climbed out of upstairs windows of nearby buildings to reach the roofs to soak them with water. It was clear the bakery was lost, but an effort was made to save the adjacent buildings. A strong wind blowing from the northeast fanned the flames, but it kept the fire confined to one side of the street.

Sam, having grabbed an axe and rope from the engine, followed Adam, who had already reached the burning roof of the bakery by leaping from the adjoining building. He had pulled burning timbers off the area above Eve's bedroom with his bare hands. Sam joined him and quickly chopped a hole large enough to slip through.

"Eve, can you hear me?" Adam shouted frantically through the opening. He stared in horror at the orange glow flickering through the billowing smoke below.

Sam anchored a rope to the cupola on the roof while Adam shouted for help to one of the fire fighters on the adjacent roof. "Hand me one of those buckets."

"You two crazy fools get off that roof before it collapses," the man shouted back.

"For Christ's sake, will you give me the God-damned bucket!"

The man relinquished the bucket to Adam as Sam returned and dropped the end of the rope through the hole in the roof. Then removing the bandanna from around his neck, he dunked it into the water and handed it to Adam. "Here, put this over your nose so you can breathe."

Adam quickly tied the wet scarf around his face, and Sam dumped the bucket of water over Adam's head.

Adam slithered down the rope Sam had lowered into the room. The door and wall were blazing and the room was so full of smoke he could barely see. He got down on his knees and started crawling toward the bed, until he bumped into a heap on the floor near the window.

"Oh God, baby," he moaned aloud, lifting Eve's unconscious body into his arms.

He made short work of tying the rope under Eve's arms, and Sam hauled her up to the roof, then quickly untied her and lowered the rope for Adam.

"Get her away before the roof goes," Adam shouted to him. He could have saved his much needed breath, because Sam had already picked up Eve and was carrying her to the adjoining roof.

Adam thought his lungs would burst in the few seconds it took him to tie the rope under his arms. He began raising himself hand over hand up the rope.

The rafters began collapsing around him as he climbed. He was nearing the top when a large portion of the roof gave way, pulling him down with it. One of the burning timbers hit his head, knocking him unconscious.

The small cupola was burning but had not collapsed, so Adam's body was dangling by the rope in the gaping hole of the roof.

Sam spun around at the sound of the falling timbers. Handing Eve to one of the men, he leaped back onto the blazing roof and began to laboriously raise the rope holding Adam's unconscious body. Sparks flew around Sam, and the smell of singed hair irritated his nostrils. He realized his own hair was burning.

One of the more courageous fire fighters saw his plight and leaped over to help him. They had just succeeded in dragging Adam's body to the adjoining building when the remaining roof of The Forbidden Fruit collapsed. The entire building appeared to erupt into a gargantuan flame, then toppled to the ground. The sound rent the soul of the horrified Simone, who was watching, not knowing if the people she loved were engulfed in the flames.

One more building was destroyed and two damaged before the fire was extinguished. Mercifully, no one was killed. Several of the firemen inhaled excessive smoke, but Adam was the worst casualty. He had suffered a concussion, his ribs were badly bruised, and his hands were burned from the timbers he had pulled off the roof.

Eve was physically unscathed. Once fresh air replaced the smoke that had filled her lungs, she regained consciousness. Sam's injuries were treated with unguent, applied with tender care by Simone.

The bakery was reduced to ashes, but Adam was alive. That was the primary thought in Eve's mind as she sat at his bedside throughout the night waiting for him to regain consciousness. In her concern for him, her own near tragedy was forgotten.

The odor of smoke still hung in the air the following day as Eve stood at Adam's window, gazing sorrowfully at the charred heap of wood and smoldering ashes.

The rumor on the street was that the fire had been set deliberately. Gunnar Swensen had been out walking his dog and glimpsed a figure running away from the rear of the bakery just before the outbreak of the fire.

Overcome with frustration, Eve slammed down the window to shut out the offending smell. But she knew the odor of the burnt wood would remain with her for a long time to come. Her hopes for independence had burned along with The Forbidden Fruit.

She turned to discover that Adam's eyes were open and gazing at her. She glowed with love as she smiled at him, then walked to his bedside.

Adam extended his hand, heavily swathed in gauze, and she clasped it gently between her own. She brought it to her lips and tenderly kissed it, then pressed it against her cheek. Tears were trickling down her face when she laid it on the quilt.

"Then you are alive," Adam murmured softly. He closed his eyes as if in pain. "There were moments when I thought I was dreaming. I could smell the fragrance of you and I thought I was imagining it."

"You mean Eau of Cinnamon," Eve teased lovingly, stroking his brow.

Adam opened his eyes and the sapphire depths were fraught with the intensity of the emotion he was feeling. "No, Eau of Eve."

For a breathless moment their eyes locked.

There was an intimacy in the moment greater than any they had ever shared in bed. He reached out a hand to her, then, frustrated, was forced to let it drop back onto the bed. "I wish I could feel you. Hold you in my arms. Oh God, Eve, I thought I had lost you." The anguish in his eyes was more than she could bear.

Adam closed his eyes again. Eve could see he was slipping away, but only into slumber. Her love for him swelled into a throbbing ache in her heart.

She pulled aside the quilt and climbed in beside him. Gathering him in her arms, she cradled his head to her breast like a mother with her child.

"Then let me hold you, my darling," she crooned softly, and pressed a kiss to his brow.

CHAPTER SEVENTEEN

Adam Rawlins and Evelyn MacGregor were married the following morning. The urgent and irresistible pleas of the heretofore invincible Adam, flat on his back after a bout with death, had made it impossible for Eve to refuse the proposal of her life-saving hero.

Besides, she loved him.

The unorthodox nuptials, however, convinced her that the concussion he had sustained must surely be affecting his judgment.

The wedding of one of California's wealthiest entrepreneurs was held in a bedroom above a gambling casino.

The bride was beautiful, blushing—and barefoot. She wore a white dimity nightgown trimmed in lace, with a paisley shawl around her shoulders.

Complementing her elegance, the groom was

handsome, pallid, and indisposed. He wore a brown flannel robe trimmed in leather, with a fresh dressing of white gauze adorning his head and gracing his hands.

The invited guests were limited to a French cook's assistant and a notorious half-breed gunfighter.

And the marriage was performed by a devout man of the cloth, a vociferous disciple of God's love for the merest fallen sparrow, who did nothing to attempt to disguise his contempt for the whole affair.

But to the two people who became man and wife that day, it was the most beautiful wedding ever celebrated.

"Do you regret we didn't wait, so you could get married in a fancy gown?" Adam asked later, as he and Eve sat in bed toasting the event with the one glass of wine permitted by the doctor.

Eve couldn't resist teasing him. "No, my beloved. I regret I didn't marry a man who could wait until I had *some* gown. Any gown, or at least a pair of shoes."

Adam chuckled and put his arm around her, drawing her to his side. "Any gown is a silly thing to a man desperate to claim the woman he almost lost. And as for having no shoes, my love, get used to that idea, because I intend to keep you pregnant and barefoot."

Eve smiled to herself. He didn't realize how close his banter bordered on the suspicion she had been harboring since missing her monthly flow. A suspicion she hadn't expressed even to

Simone. Eve shoved the thought aside and kissed his cheek.

"Most men would wait to get married until they could stand on their feet. I think you're still affected by the blow to your head, Adam Rawlins." She put her hand to his brow. "You're even feverish, and I think you better lie down now. You've had too much excitement for one day."

Adam lay back obediently and closed his eyes. "I'm sorry, honey. I promise you I'll make it up to you as soon as I'm back in shape." He was asleep instantly.

On the day after they were married, the first quarrel between the newlyweds erupted when Eve informed Adam that she was going to rebuild the bakery.

He sat up in bed with an explosive motion. "Like hell you are! You're my wife now, Eve. You are coming home with me."

"Will you please calm down, Adam?" Eve cautioned worriedly. "You're getting too excited. It's only going to make your condition worse."

Adam saw red. His condition was not his immediate concern in light of Eve's newest rebellion. "How do you expect me to remain calm when my wife has just informed me she doesn't intend to live in my house? Is that your idea of marriage?"

Eve was suddenly confronted with a fact of life that had not occurred to her until this moment. As Adam's wife, she had new responsibilities. "I guess I didn't have time yesterday to think about giving up the bakery and going back to Sacramento. You were so insistent . . . and you saved my life . . . and I was grateful . . ."

"Grateful! My God, are you saying you married me out of gratitude?"

"No, of course not," Eve said emphatically. "I love you, Adam. It's just that we got married before we took time to discuss a few details."

"Details! A man expects his wife to live with him. I took it for granted when you agreed to become my wife that at least you intended to return to Sacramento with me." His temple was beginning to throb with pain, forcing him to lie back. The rift loomed as the latest of Eve's incomprehensible obstacles to harmony between them, but at the moment he was too weak to argue.

She was relieved to drop the subject. He needed rest. As she lovingly placed the blanket over him, the new Mrs. Rawlins reflected on Evelyn MacGregor's need to revise her plans.

When Simone returned from shopping several hours later, Eve was finally able to shed Adam's shirt for conventional feminine clothing.

As each day passed, Adam regained his strength. By the end of the week he was on his feet and almost fully recovered from his injuries. Upon removing the bandages, the doctor reported that Adam's hands had not been burned as seriously as originally believed. Although still stiff and sore when he flexed them, they were healing.

There had been no further discussion about the bakery. Brooding in silence when he thought about Eve's plan, Adam avoided the subject, while he searched for a way to peacefully resolve the situation.

Eve waited until dinner a few nights later to make her suggestion for solving the quandary. Adam and Simone were seated at the table waiting for her when Eve sat down. "I was hoping Sam would be joining us." He was an integral player in her stratagem. "I haven't seen too much of him lately," she added.

Simone cast her a nervous glance. "I'm afraid he's out looking for that Sydney Duck you saw the day of the fire. He's convinced that's the man who started the fire."

"I hope Sam's not foolish enough to try anything alone. We can get the law to handle this," Adam declared. "I wish he would have told me what he intended to do. I would have stopped him."

Simone's voice trailed off to a worried sigh. "The last time he went to that Sydney Town, he came back with a knife wound."

Eve reached across the table and patted her hand reassuringly. "Oh, Sam can take care of himself, Simone. But while we are on the subject of that fire, what do you think about the idea of rebuilding the bakery? We own the land. Once the debris is cleaned away, we could put up a new building."

Adam shook his head in a hopeless gesture. "Simone, maybe I can talk some sense to you. Wouldn't you like to forget all that hard work and come back to Sacramento? There will always be a home for you with us."

Simone, who had always tried to avoid being in the middle of an argument, now found herself the arbiter between two people for whom she deeply cared. A fair person by nature, she could see the merits of each side. "I understand why Eve feels the way she does, Adam. The bakery can make money. We've proven that. Were it not for the fire, we wouldn't have a problem."

"What guarantee do you have that there won't be another fire? Especially in this city," Adam argued.

"If there is, we could just rebuild again," Eve responded with tongue in cheek, playing devil's advocate.

Having mulled over the idea of Eve rebuilding the bakery for several days, Adam had at last decided on a compromise to ensure wedded bliss. "All right, you win," he said unexpectedly. Eve's eyes opened in disbelief. "But any wife of mine stays under my watchful eye."

Eve and Simone looked at each other quizzically and then returned their attention to Adam. He smiled broadly and continued his announcement. "We'll build a house here and I'll move my office to San Francisco."

Eve squealed with pleasure and flung herself in his lap, slipping her arms around his neck.

"Do you mean that, Adam? Would you really do that for me?" Tears were glistening in her eyes.

Adam tried to maintain a stern facade, but it was too difficult with her sitting on his lap. "How else am I ever going to see my wife?" He kissed her lightly. "But I want one thing understood. You work the bakery only when I'm gone. When I'm home, I want you home with me. I don't want my wife off somewhere serving coffee and tea to other men."

Much to Adam's surprise, Eve shook her head, apparently rejecting the idea. "Damn it, Eve, I just offered to move lock, stock, and barrel. Can't you ever compromise?"

She smiled secretly, savoring the decision she had reached earlier that week. "You are right about my responsibilities, Adam. As your wife, my duty is to be with you."

Adam eyed her in mock suspicion and then nodded in approval. "A noble sentiment, madam," he gibed, forcing back a grin of amusement. He sensed that she was bursting with a pent-up enthusiasm.

"You told me this casino was a good financial investment, didn't you?" He nodded again, this time warily. "And you also told me that you are looking for an honest man to operate The Original Sin, but you haven't found him yet, have you?" Adam slowly shook his head from side to side in an exaggerated gesture indicating his wish for her to get to the point.

"Well, Mr. Adam Rawlins, beloved husband

and esteemed businessman without equal, The Forbidden Fruit is also a good financial investment, but whereas your casino is in need of an honest manager, my bakery is not. *I* have already found an honest man to run my establishment. Only, *he* is a *she*, and that *she* is not me," she declared with a saucy toss of dark curls.

Adam was beginning to grasp her train of thought. "How about it, Simone?" Eve asked. "You could operate The Forbidden Fruit. We could hire a baker and you could manage the whole operation."

Simone, delighted to be a participant in the evolving events, and secretly wishing she could stay in San Francisco, replied instantly. "I'd love it, chérie."

Eve turned back to Adam, smiling impishly. "Well, what do you think of the idea? Is that compromise enough for you?"

Laughing, Adam hugged her tighter in his embrace. "I can't believe it. That's a wonderful idea, honey." He kissed her lightly. "For the time being, though, I think you both should take a well-deserved rest. You can't go on living above a casino, and you both need additional clothing, so come back to Sacramento until the bakery's rebuilt. I'm taking command here, ladies. Tomorrow we sail for home."

He leaned down and kissed Eve again. "And I don't want to hear of any more compromises— or arguments," he added, at the sight of her changing expression.

Eve had no intention of giving him an argument. The idea was too practical and appealing to resist. They had worked hard since coming to San Francisco—Simone more than herself. A good rest in the luxury of a home again, being waited upon, would do them both good. But Eve wondered if Simone was willing to leave Sam. She doubted that Sam would be willing to tag along with them to Sacramento. The question of how to keep Simone and Sam together had set her thinking.

Adam's brow arched at her hesitation. "I don't suppose my bride would consider anything as insignificant as a honeymoon?"

Adam's question provided the answer she needed. "I'd love it, Adam," she said excitedly, jumping to her feet. Then hopefully she added, "Now would be a good time to go, wouldn't it?"

Simone, happy for her friends and eager to begin her new venture, enthusiastically encouraged the proposal. "I think that's an excellent idea. You go on your honeymoon, and don't worry about the bakery. I can handle all the arrangements for rebuilding."

"It's not too much to ask of you, is it, Simone? Especially if Sam were there to help?" Eve smiled with pleasure. The pieces had fallen into place.

"Oh no, *ma chérie*, I insist you go."

Adam, unaware of Eve's matchmaking, was so pleased that Eve had consented to a honeymoon without an argument that he did not suspect she had an ulterior motive. "Then it's agreed that we'll all go back to Sacramento. For now, Sam can oversee the construction of the building, and by the time we get back from our honeymoon, Simone will have it all decorated."

Eve was suddenly struck with a vagrant thought. "What if Sam won't agree to the idea? I won't consider allowing Simone to come back here alone."

"Let me handle Sam," Adam said confidently. "We'll find out as soon as he gets back."

The impatient rapping at the door was an ominous response to Adam's remark. He opened the door to Billy Chambers, the casino's bouncer. The man was breathless from running.

"Thought you'd want to know, Mr. Rawlins, there's a mob over on Kearney and Commercial gettin' ready to string up Sam Montgomery." The cup Simone was holding slipped through her fingers and smashed on the floor.

"My God, what for?" Adam asked, shocked.

"I guess he shot some guy."

"Did anyone send for the sheriff?"

"I don't think so. There ain't too many folks who care if they string up a half-breed."

"Get Ben and bring your rifles," Adam ordered. Billy left hurriedly to obey the command. Adam flinched in pain as he strapped on his heavy gun belt. Then, momentarily flexing his sore hands, he grabbed his rifle and headed for the door. He drew up sharply when Eve and Simone followed on his heels.

"Oh no. You women stay here. There's nothing you can do. Lynch mobs are ugly, and you'll just get in the way."

Eve glanced at Simone. The look on the distraught woman's face wrenched at her heart. "We can't stay here not knowing what's happening, Adam."

"Damn it, Eve, I don't have time to argue." He dashed down the stairway without a backward glance.

"We must go to him." Simone's distress was evident.

Eve clasped Simone's hand. "I know, dear. I don't care what Adam says. We're going."

The mob had assembled outside a warehouse on Kearney and Commercial. Among the jeering crowd on the street was a large contingent of Sydney Ducks. Although this gang of hoodlums was hated by one and all, for the moment, local grievances were set aside in a common bigotry toward Indians.

One of the Ducks, a tall, skinny man with two missing front teeth, was trying to whip the crowd into a frenzy. "Let's string up the murderin' 'alf-breed now," he shouted.

The crowd hooted their approval, and a rope conveniently appeared from their midst. It was quickly tied into a noose and tossed over the projecting arm of a block and tackle, used for hoisting large crates.

Sam was backed against the wall of a building, hedged in by the crowd. A drawn pistol in each hand discouraged the mob from rushing him at the moment.

Adam, accompanied by his two confederates,

elbowed their way through the assembled swarm. A path appeared as some of the crowd assumed the three men were going to finish the deed which they were too cowardly to attempt.

They vocalized their disappointment with nasty shouts and jeers when Adam turned on them with a raised rifle. His two companions followed suit. The sight of five gun barrels quieted the mob, which backed up collectively.

"Now, what in hell is going on here?" Adam demanded. His very presence exuded a no-nonsense authority.

"Tell him, Dickie. Tell him what that bastard did to Alfie," one of the Ducks shouted.

"That breed gunfighter killed poor Alfie. He didn't have a chance," cried out the thin man known as Dickie.

"What's your side of the story, Sam?" Adam's eyes never wavered from the crowd.

"I came looking for him. When I found him, the two of them pulled their knives and jumped me. I've got a cut to prove it."

"He's lying," Dickie shouted. "I never laid me eyes on 'im till he shot Alfie."

"That's a lie. I beat the hell out of that skinny bastard a few months ago," Sam declared calmly.

Adam had no doubts that Sam had found, and killed, the man who started the fire. The object now was to make the crowd aware of it. "You said you were looking for this Alfie. What did you want with him?"

Sam was becoming impatient. "To find out if he started the fire at the bakery."

"He's lying through his rotten Indian face," Dickie cried out. "Alfie didn't start no fire." He pointed a bony finger at Sam. "He's the one what burned down the bakery."

A chorus of angry shouts swept the crowd as the other Sydney Ducks supported their cohort. Arson was a crime much worse than murder to most of the assemblage, because a fire out of control ravages the whole city. The mob surged forward again, reaffirming with damning accusations the demand for a lynching.

Just then Eve and Simone arrived on the scene, their worst fears confirmed as they heard the angry jeers of the mob. By the macabre glow of torches held aloft by some of the crowd, they saw the lifeless body of Alfie lying on the street. The black derby had rolled off his head and now lay trampled.

In spite of her panic, Eve was quick to recall the face of the man. "That's him. That's the man who struck me and tried to rob me. He was in the bakery the day of the fire," she cried out.

Her shouts attracted the mob's attention. Surprised, she saw Reverend Williams among the angry faces.

The man known as Dickie moved up to the front of the crowd. "Don't pay her no mind. That black-headed bitch is the half-breed's whore."

The blow Adam dealt him with his rifle butt knocked him to the ground, breaking his jaw.

"You've got just ten seconds to apologize to my wife, you bastard, before you end up next to your friend." The petrified man was holding his broken jaw, blubbering with pain and fright. Adam stood above him, his eyes blazing with fury.

"What's going on here?"

Adam glanced at the man who had just arrived. He walked with a slight limp and stood almost head to head with Adam when he moved to Adam's side. Eve clasped Simone's hand in relief to see that the sheriff had arrived before more blood was shed.

"This mob wants to lynch Sam Montgomery for killing the man who burned down The Forbidden Fruit, sheriff."

His glance swung to Sam, who was still standing with both pistols drawn. "You kill that man, Montgomery?" Sam nodded. "Well, holster that iron before anybody else is killed."

Sam Montgomery was a desperate man facing a lynch mob. He wasn't about to give up without a fight. "You don't think I'm going to stand here and let these bastards hang me, do you?"

The sheriff was an honest man, doing an insurmountable job in the fastest-growing, most sin-infested city in the world, but he did not hold his job by being a man who backed down easily in an argument.

"There's not going to be any hanging until I hear all the facts."

He was saved any further argument with Sam when Hilge Swensen, whose daughters worked at the bakery, stepped forward breathless from running. Her arm was around the shoulders of a tow-headed boy. "Sheriff Flanders, my boy has something to tell you."

"What is it, son?"

Nine-year-old Gunnar Swensen's blue eyes were round with excitement. "That's him, sheriff," he declared in a reedy voice, pointing to the corpse. "That's the man I saw sneaking away from the bakery the night of the fire."

"You're sure, son?" the sheriff asked kindly. "It's much too serious to make a mistake."

"Yes, sir," the youngster said earnestly. "I was out walking Bowser and got a good look at him that night 'cause there was a full moon."

"Well, Montgomery, you can put your guns away. Seems you saved the city the cost of hanging him. But in the future, I'm the law and order around here." The sheriff's craggy face creased into a frown. "And I don't want any more killings." Sam hesitated, then slipped the pistols into their holsters.

"Fun's over, folks. I'm ordering you all to get back to where you belong," Sheriff Flanders shouted.

The disgruntled crowd began to disperse, displeased because they had been deprived of their sport for the night. "Get out of here. I'll get the man to a doctor," the sheriff ordered as several of the Ducks in the crowd tried to help Dickie to his feet.

Adam was not appeased so easily. "I have some unfinished business with your friend there, sheriff. I haven't forgotten he insulted my wife."

"Please, Adam. It doesn't matter," Eve pleaded, tugging at the sleeve of his shirt. "I'm just relieved it's all over and you and Sam are safe."

"Forget it, Rawlins," the sheriff declared. "The next time the man's able to open his mouth, he'll think twice before calling respectable women names."

"I told you ladies there were nasty rumors about you among the good people of the city," Reverend Williams snickered, sliding up beside them. "Now do you believe me?"

Eve regarded the man with haughty disdain. "Really, Reverend Williams? I didn't notice any *good people* among that crowd. Present company included." She spun on her heel and stormed away.

"Hey, firebrand, wait up," Adam called after her. He caught up with Eve and slipped an arm around her shoulder. "Haven't we had enough excitement for one night?"

Eve threw a backward glance at Sam and Simone, who were trailing a short distance behind. "I don't understand why there has to be so much hatred toward Sam just because he's part Indian. He hasn't hurt any of these people."

Adam pulled her closer to his side as they strolled along. "Don't expect me to explain human nature. My wise old grandfather often declared that the only thing to understand about human nature is that you can't change it."

"And that Reverend Williams is such a hypo-crite," she fumed. "No wonder the city's getting so lawless, if he's an example of religious leader-ship."

"Honey, he's just one pastor. Don't judge all of them because of one man's actions."

Eve had finally cooled down by the time they arrived back at the casino, then immediately received another shock, along with Adam and Simone, when Sam announced that he would be leaving San Francisco. "I guess it's time I move on. I've stuck around the town long enough."

"We were hoping you would come with us to Sacramento," Eve said, disappointed.

Sam shook his head. He knew that all of their lives were becoming too entwined. He would always bring trouble to these people. "I'm used to fighting my own battles, folks."

Adam understood his meaning and recog-nized the pride and dignity in the man. "Where are you planning on going, Sam?"

"Maybe I'll try to find Bailey and see how he's doing."

Simone had not said a word during the whole conversation. Eve couldn't bear to look at her. She knew how much her friend was suffering. "I wish you would reconsider, Sam," she asked hopefully. "We were hoping you would give Simone a hand in the rebuilding arrangements for The Forbidden Fruit while Adam and I go on a honeymoon."

Sam shook his head. "No, I'll be pulling out in a couple of days. If you gals had any sense, you would forget building that bakery and go back to Sacramento."

"I've been trying to convince them of the same thing," Adam agreed.

Simone rose to her feet with a false smile that looked painted on her face. She knew if she didn't get out of there immediately, she would break down in front of all of them. "All this excitement has given me a terrible headache. I think I'll retire. Whatever is decided is fine with me." She almost ran out of the room. There was an awkward silence after Simone's departure. Sam made an excuse and followed suit.

Eve was tormented now with a multitude of doubts. Maybe it would be wiser to forget about rebuilding the bakery. Perhaps the smartest thing to do would be to sell the property and pay off the bank, then return to Sacramento. It would make Adam happier, as well.

In retrospect, she saw how her attempt to escape Adam's domination had failed totally. Not only was she now married to him, Simone was forced to pay the price for the whole self-indulgent move. Eve felt that the look on Simone's face when she ran from the room would haunt her forever.

As she undressed for bed, Eve sighed with guilt, knowing she was responsible for Simone's future unhappiness. Somehow there had to be a way to make it all up to the most loyal friend she would ever have.

CHAPTER EIGHTEEN

After leaving Adam's office, Sam walked down the hallway, pausing outside of Simone's room when he heard the sound of weeping from within. He raised his hand to rap, hesitated, then lowered his arm. Frowning, he walked away.

The casino below was bustling with business-as-usual activity. In this city of constant change, last week's fire was ancient history.

Sam ordered a shot of whiskey. The astringent liquid felt like acid as he gulped it down. Repeatedly, his eyes looked up to the top of the stairway, drawn by a force he was battling to resist. He was haunted by the memory of Simone's stricken face in the mob that night.

He ordered another drink, consumed it in one gulp, and slammed down the glass. He strode back up the stairway. This time there was no hesitation as he rapped on the door.

"Who is it?" Simone's voice was still quaking with sobs.

"Simone, it's Sam."

"Just a moment," she replied. He still didn't know what he was doing there. It was a mistake.

Simone opened the door a crack. Her eyes, which usually were narrowed with a near-sighted squint, were almost swollen shut from crying. "What is it, Sam? Is something wrong?"

"May I come in, Simone? I would like to talk to you."

She stepped aside and turned her back to wipe away the evidence of tears. Sam entered and closed the door behind him.

Simone blushed nervously. This was the first time he had ever been in her room. Even at the bakery, he never once had entered their living quarters. "I'm sorry, but I can't offer you a seat except on the bed."

"That's okay. I can stand." He was feeling awkward. He sensed she was, too. He had never felt this way with her before. She had seemed like a kindred spirit to him, and now that they were parting, he regretted this feeling of uneasiness between them.

"I've decided to pull out tomorrow and I wanted to say goodbye to you privately."

"I didn't think you were leaving so soon." She couldn't bear to look at him without making a fool of herself, so she turned away again.

Sam shifted his feet nervously. "I guess you'll be heading back to Sacramento with Eve and Adam." Simone nodded, and wiped away a tear.

She turned around to face him, bravely attempting a smile. It was futile. One look at him and her chin started to tremble as she struggled to contain her tears.

"I'll miss you, Sam. I hope you'll take care of yourself." Her voice broke off in a sob.

Sam remained staring at her, fighting the urge to take her in his arms. "I'm going to miss you, too." Unable to stop himself, he reached out and cupped her cheeks in his hands. His thumbs brushed aside the tears trickling down her face. "Are these tears for me, mouse?"

Simone nodded and shifted her eyes downward, too embarrassed to look at him. "Please don't look away." He lifted up her chin, forcing her anguished eyes to meet the despair in his own. "No woman has ever shed tears for me." Sam dipped his head, capturing one of the teardrops with his tongue. "Now we share the same heartache."

Her face softened with a smile. "It's a beautiful gesture. Did you learn it from your mother's people?"

The soft smile and the nearness of her toppled his control of steel. "Forgive me? I have no right," he pleaded in a smothered groan as he lowered his head and kissed her.

Simone had never known a lover, had never been kissed by a man. She responded with a spontaneous release of longing that had been held in check from the moment their lives had touched. She was pale when they broke apart, shaken by the intensity of the kiss.

Sam's dark brown eyes, guarded in the past, were now bare with remorse. "I tried to warn you, mouse. I tried to tell you how vulnerable you are to the reptiles of this world. I had no right to kiss you, but I couldn't ride away without being honest with you."

Simone could no longer restrain the words in her heart. Her face transformed to radiance. "I love you, Sam."

"Mouse," he sighed sadly, gathering her in his arms. Her hair was a soft cushion as he laid his cheek against her head. "Tell me to get out of here before I hurt you even more."

"You'd never hurt me, Sam. I know that. My heart tells me so."

Sam pulled away and grasped her shoulders in a strong grip. "You don't understand. I can't offer you anything. I'm a half-breed. There can never be a life for us. There's noplace we can go and be accepted. We wouldn't even be able to find a clergyman willing to marry us."

"I don't care, Sam," she cried desperately. "I want to go with you. Be with you. Nothing else matters to me as long as we're together."

She wrapped her arms around his neck, but he forced them down. "You don't know what you're saying. You have no idea what it would be like. People will scorn you as much as they do me."

Simone's heart became heavy with pain, fearing her happiness would be short-lived. She was losing him. "I don't care what people say. I only care about you. You're the only person that matters to me, Sam."

"You have Eve, mouse. You have her friendship to lean on."

"And I'll always have it. But we both have our own lives to live. I want to spend mine with you." She looked up at him pleading. "Eve has a husband now. I'll only be in the way. I know I'm uncomely, Sam—"

Before she could finish, he stopped her with a kiss. The sharp planes of his face softened with tenderness as his love gleamed undisguised in the depths of his eyes.

"What have I told you about putting yourself down, mouse? Next you'll be telling me I deserve more than *a woman like you*."

"No, you deserve to be loved, Sam, and no other woman could love you as much as I do."

Sam's reservations were crushed by a need greater than the practical arguments he was offering. With a stifled groan, he pulled her into his arms. Their lips met again, and again, as their love, long held in check, flared into flames, creating an urgency that went beyond the limitations of a kiss.

"Oh God, mouse," he whispered huskily as he began to slide the gown off her shoulders, "if they haven't found a reason to hang me up to now, I'm sure giving them the excuse they're looking for."

* * *

Eve was ecstatic the following morning when Simone related the events of the previous evening. She hugged her tightly. "Oh, Simone, I'm so happy for you. I've known for a long time how you felt about him."

"Sam warned me that it's not going to be easy. People won't accept us, and we'll always be treated as outcasts."

"You know Adam and I don't feel that way. Come with us to Sacramento. Or if you want, you and Sam can stay here and run the bakery."

"Sam wants us to leave here. He said he wants to find Bailey and then we'll move on."

"Move on to where, Simone?" Eve asked, alarmed. "I thought you would be coming to Sacramento."

"Maybe someday we will, *chérie*," Simone replied with a brave smile. "Sam is getting supplies now. We will be leaving as soon as he returns."

Eve tried to hide her distress with a practical suggestion. "Wait until I return. I'm going to the bank to sell the land we own."

"That's not necessary," Simone protested.

"Promise me you'll wait until I get back?"

"Of course. We would never leave without saying goodbye."

Eve hugged her again with tears smarting her eyes. "I know you love Sam, but are you certain this is what you want? Your life will be so hard. Why won't you try to persuade him to come to Sacramento? Things could be so different."

Simone reached out and clasped her hand. "I

am going to do whatever Sam decides. Be happy for me, *chérie?*"

On the brink of tears, Eve hugged her again. "Oh, I am, dear. I just hate to say goodbye." She turned and sped away before bursting into tears.

The Bank of San Francisco did not vary in appearance from the other banks in the community. Four teller cages lined part of a wall, with a huge vault holding a fortune in gold standing behind them. It was bustling with activity when Eve entered, as miners stood in line waiting to deposit cash or gold dust.

After being informed that Hiram Pendergast would return shortly, Eve sat down to wait for him. Her thoughts immediately shifted to Simone and Sam. As much as she worried about her friend's future, she couldn't help being happy for Simone. There weren't two people more deserving of happiness than Simone and Sam. She knew they would work it out somehow.

"Mrs. Rawlins?" Deep in thought, it took her a few seconds to respond to the unfamiliar term of address. "I beg your pardon, Mrs. Rawlins."

Eve glanced up to discover a bespectacled young man whom she had never met. "I'm Gerald Pendergast. I understand you are waiting for my father. I'm sorry, he isn't here at the moment. Can I be of help?"

Eve smiled nervously, but her smile was enough to dazzle the young man. "I have some urgent business to discuss with Mr. Pendergast."

"Perhaps I can help you. Why don't you step into my office?"

Gerald Pendergast was the epitome of courtliness as he showed her to his small office. Once assured she was comfortable, he sat down behind the large desk.

Eve thought he seemed more apprehensive than she. "Have you always been with the bank, Mr. Pendergast? I don't remember seeing you here before."

Pendergast blushed. "Actually, this is my first day serving customers. I recently returned from the East Coast after completing my studies at Harvard University."

"Well, congratulations, that is quite an accomplishment. Your father must be very proud of you."

The young man preened with pleasure and seemed to relax. "Is there something I can get for you, Mrs. Rawlins? Perhaps a glass of water?"

"Nothing at all," Eve began, then changed her mind. "Well, actually, there is. I would like to know the balance I owe on my note with the bank."

Gerald Pendergast looked confused. He was a person who prided himself on thoroughly researching a project before approaching it. Thus he had already carefully gone over all the accounts to familiarize himself with the bank's business transactions, and the name of Eve Rawlins was not in his memory.

"Are you referring to a checking account?"

Eve shook her head. "No, I'm interested in knowing the amount remaining on the money I borrowed to expand my bakery."

Pendergast, with the self-assurance of youth, was certain he was not mistaken. He had a photographic memory, could visualize every account, and her name was not among them. However, to appease her, he left the room and returned shortly with a ledger.

"Just as I thought, Mrs. Rawlins, we do not show any open note bearing your name."

Eve remained undaunted. "As much as I would like that to be true, Mr. Pendergast, I'm afraid it is not the case. Perhaps it is listed under the name of my business."

"Of course, that must be it," he replied in relief. "What is the name of your establishment?"

"The Forbidden Fruit. It's a bakery."

His face dropped in disappointment because he had no recollection of that name either. However, he went through the motions of running his finger down the list of entries in the ledger before shaking his head.

Eve was momentarily perplexed, then suddenly smiled with comprehension. "Oh, how silly of me. I've just recently wed. The loan would be under my maiden name, Evelyn MacGregor."

He shook his head, frowning with certainty. "There is no MacGregor, Mrs. Rawlins."

Exasperated, Eve leaned over and perused the column. No account appeared pertaining to her or the bakery.

Gerald Pendergast began to wonder if this beautiful young woman was in the wrong bank. "Mrs. Rawlins, are you sure you took out a loan from this bank? There are several other—"

"Of course I'm sure. I dealt personally with Hiram Pendergast," Eve said emphatically.

"There obviously is some kind of misunderstanding, Mrs. Rawlins." Self-conscious about his first day on the job, he began to suspect that one of his friends had set this woman up to make him the brunt of a practical joke. Gerald Pendergast did not see the humor in it.

The woman was so beautiful, too, he thought with a resentful glance at the exquisite face watching him intently. The color of her violet eyes with their dark, thick lashes reminded him of purple pansies. They were the most beautiful eyes he had ever seen.

Her beauty was probably the reason she had been chosen for this stunt, he reasoned. Well, two could play the game, he thought smugly.

Pendergast leaned over the desk with a lecherous leer. "Perhaps we could discuss this problem at a more convenient location? Your room, for instance? I'm sure your fee will be enough to cancel any . . . open balance."

Eve's eyes widened in shock at his words. How dare this brazen young man make such a proposition? Why, she was a married woman and this pimply-faced dimwit had barely reached puberty. If she wasn't so insulted, it would be laughable.

She was about to tell him to go and wash out his mouth when the door burst open and Hiram Pendergast rushed into the room.

"Miss MacGregor . . . ah, Mrs. Rawlins, I was told you were waiting. I hope my son has kept you entertained in my absence. He's just back from law school, you know."

Still fuming with indignation, Eve cast a disgruntled glare at the young man. "Entertained is hardly the word, Mr. Pendergast. Are you so sure he spent his time out East attending a school of law?"

The banker sensed something was amiss and cast a wary glance at his son. The young man blanched, realizing in horror that Mrs. Rawlins was not a part of a practical joke. He had just insulted one of the bank's clients.

Hiram Pendergast became tense with apprehension. Good heavens, the woman was the wife of Adam Rawlins! If his half-brained son had said or done anything to reveal the truth of her loan, there was no telling what Rawlins might do in anger. The man's wealth and power were phenomenal.

"Do come into my office, Mrs. Rawlins. I am sure you will be more comfortable."

Eve felt tremendously uncomfortable at the moment. She had come to the bank merely to conduct a business transaction, but the elder

Pendergast was treating her as if she were royalty. Something was amiss. The manner in which Hiram Pendergast shuffled and hovered about only increased her suspicions.

Once seated behind his desk, the banker smiled sympathetically. "I heard about your fire. What an unfortunate disaster."

"Then you can guess my purpose in coming here today, Mr. Pendergast. I was just asking your son about the balance of the note I have with you, but there doesn't seem to be any record of it."

His smile flickered to a sickly grin. "Nonsense, there must be some mistake."

"I saw the ledger myself, sir. Why isn't my note listed with the others?"

When Hiram Pendergast drew out a handkerchief and began to dab at the perspiration dotting his brow, Eve felt she was on to something. Eve was no fool, and it was clear that the man's agitation was due to much more than an oversight on the books. As she waited for him to answer, her eyes never left his face.

"Exactly what is going on here?" she demanded when no reply ensued.

He seemed to collapse like a deflated balloon into his chair. "I suggest you . . . ask . . . your husband." His halting speech sounded his defeat.

Eve's heart made a leap into her stomach. "What has my husband got to do with it?"

Pendergast saw no way he could avoid telling

the truth to the determined woman. He chastised himself for being so negligent in forgetting to warn his son about the transaction. He feared he had made a dangerous enemy of Adam Rawlins.

Hiram Pendergast began to wring his hands. "When you applied for a loan to expand your bakery, the bank committee felt it would be too risky to lend money to two young women, so they turned down your application."

"I don't understand," Eve said perplexed. "I signed a note, and you gave me money."

Pendergast cleared his throat. "Well, you see, Mrs. Rawlins, the bank didn't exactly—"

Guessing the truth, Eve interrupted him. "Are you saying Adam Rawlins backed the loan for me?"

The banker had no choice but to give her the details of the whole conspiracy. "Somehow Mr. Rawlins heard about the committee's decision and approached me with a proposition. If I agreed to make it appear that the bank was giving you the loan, he would put up the money in addition to making a very large deposit in our bank."

Pendergast looked apologetic at the sight of Eve's stunned expression. "Try to understand, Mrs. Rawlins, your husband is a very influential man. I didn't want to make an enemy of him. When he explained you were betrothed to him and would be uncomfortable taking the money from him, I saw no reason not to comply with his request. After all, the whole ruse was just to avoid further embarrassment for you.''

Eve felt numb, her face was impassive. She sat without an outward expression of her raging turmoil. "I understand your position perfectly, Mr. Pendergast," she said calmly. "I would like to know now whether the bank is interested in purchasing the property I own."

The banker's eyes gleamed at the prospect of acquiring the excellent site. "Of course, we would not hesitate to purchase that piece of property, if the price was reasonable, of course."

"I would like to transact the sale as quickly as possible. The deed was burned in the fire, but it is a matter of public record." Eve reached into her reticule. "Miss Lisle is the co-owner and I have here her power of attorney to sell the land."

"Of course, I understand. I'll have my son draw up the papers immediately."

Within minutes they had reached a compromise. Stoically, Eve signed the papers. Her mind, numbed by Adam's latest act of betrayal, seemed apart from her body.

She left the bank and returned to the casino. When she entered The Original Sin, Billy Chambers nodded politely. "Good afternoon, Mrs. Rawlins." In her trancelike state Eve did not acknowledge him. She continued up the stairs.

Adam rose to his feet as she entered the room. The look in her eyes wiped the welcoming smile off his face. Eve opened her purse, pulled out the cash she had just received at the bank, and laid it down on the desk in front of him.

She turned to leave but didn't get any farther than the doorway before Adam's hands clamped down on her shoulders and spun her around to face him.

"What is this all about, Eve?" he asked, perplexed.

She brushed his hands aside. "If it takes me the rest of my life, I'm going to pay you the interest on your investment, Adam."

Eve turned, but he stepped in front of her to block her exit. "For God's sake, Eve, will you tell me what you're talking about?" He tried to take her in his arms, but met the same resistance as she brushed his hands aside.

"The bank note, Adam."

His face lit up in comprehension. "Oh, that damned note. I'd forgotten all about it. I don't want your money, Eve."

"And I never wanted yours, Adam. When will you realize that?"

She stepped past him to leave, but his arm hooked around her beneath her breast, drawing her back against the length of him. She stood stiffly in his arms. Adam lowered his head, resting his cheek against the silky thickness of her hair.

"Eve, love, what does it matter about the money? What's mine is yours. I knew the bakery was important to you. I was only trying to help."

Eve drew a shuddering breath and allowed herself to lean back and relax against him.

"Then why did you lie to me, Adam? Why did you resort to lies and deceit?"

His lips slid in a moist trail to her ear, causing the hair on her arms to stand on end. "Because if you knew it came from me, you never would have taken the money. I love you, Eve, and I didn't want to see you hurt."

"There are many ways people can be hurt, Adam. When will you understand that it hurts when I don't have control of my life?"

Adam released her at a knock on the door. When he opened it, Eve slipped past Billy Chambers as he entered. She returned to their room, devastated by Adam's latest deception.

His discarded jacket was lying on the bed and Eve moved it aside. Then, thinking the better of it, she carried it over to the armoire. A thick envelope fell out of the pocket and she bent down to pick up the contents scattered on the floor.

Eve's attention was drawn to the name of Allan Pinkerton Detective Agency written across the top of one of the sheets. Intrigued, she sat down on the bed and began to read.

Long after she finished reading, the document remained hanging limply in her hand. Eve sat staring into space, numbed by the horror of disbelief. What might have been a joyous moment under different circumstances was transformed into a nightmare by yet another deception.

She had attempted to put aside the grievances of the past in response to Adam's plea. But the letter from the detective agency, evidence of his latest betrayal, was too great to forgive.

There was no other course open to her. Eve packed her few pieces of clothing and went to find Sam and Simone.

To her relief, she found them in Simone's room. Both were prepared for the heartache of having to say goodbye, but were taken by surprise at her unexpected request.

"May I go with you?"

Eve offered no explanation at their startled looks. "Please don't ask me to explain right now. I want to go with you."

The look on Eve's face was enough to convince Simone of the gravity of the situation. She reached out to her. Drowning in despair, Eve grasped her hand as if it were a life line. "What about Adam, *chérie*?"

"He lied to me again, Simone." She shook her head hopelessly. "It's all a sham. Adam lied to me again."

Sam recognized Eve's tendency to grasp only partial truths in dealing with Adam. Although reticent, he felt compelled to speak, asking guardedly, "Have you listened to his whole side of the story?"

"His side is a repeated litany I've become tired of hearing, Sam. Adam will never change. My only hope to be free of him is Bailey's gold mine. I know it's grasping at straws, but I'm desperate enough to try it."

Simone's reaction was instinctive. She turned imploringly to Sam. He grimaced, then shrugged his shoulders. "I hope you know what you're doing, Eve. You're welcome to come with us, but I think you should hear Adam out."

"I will, Sam. I'll listen to his excuses for the last time."

As soon as Billy Chambers departed, Adam hurried to their bedroom. Eve was sitting on the edge of the bed. Adam was shocked by the change in her appearance. There was no longer a flush of anger on her face or the gleam of fiery rage in her eyes. She was pale, as if the blood had been drained from her body. Her eyes were soporific, lusterless, as if she had been drugged.

"My God, sweetheart, what's wrong? Are you ill?"

"No, Adam. You're the one who's ill." Eve laid the envelope down on the bed beside her. Adam recognized it at once, and his eyes sought hers in panic.

"How dare you, Adam! How dare you deny me this knowledge for the past six years." Color began to return to her cheeks in the force of her indignation. "Who do you think you are? What gives you the right to play God with other people's lives?"

"I wanted to tell you, Eve. I tried to tell you several times."

"Oh, please, spare me your excuses. I don't want to hear them. You had six years to tell me. For six years, you have denied me my blood. When did you intend to tell me, Adam? When were you going to let me know that Bailey

Montgomery is my father, and I have a half-brother by the name of Sam?"

She shook her head, still unable to believe he would stoop to such perfidy.

Desperately, he groped for words. "I don't know . . . maybe, I was never going to tell you. For some reason, something kept me from it."

"I know the reason, Adam. If I had had a legal parent, I would no longer have been under your thumb. I wouldn't have had to suffer your domination and interference in my life."

"You're wrong, Eve. That was never my reason. I knew that Bailey Montgomery was a drifter. I hoped your paths would never cross, but when he showed up right here in San Francisco, I knew I had to tell you the truth about him. I delayed, trying to spare you from being hurt."

"Spare me from being hurt!" Eve scoffed in outrageous indignation. "Adam, hurt is being twelve years old and losing the only person you love. Hurt is being betrayed by the one man you love. You don't have to explain to me what hurt is. You taught it to me."

"I know my judgment was wrong, Eve. I should have told you the whole story when you returned from France," he admitted contritely.

"Oh, no, why should you!" she exclaimed, outraged. "Why should you tell me that it wasn't necessary to live any longer under your tyranny? Why should you tell me that I have a father who could give me the love I needed so badly?"

"Because you don't have a father who can offer you that kind of love. You have a father who is a dreamer—a drifter who has hurt every woman that has ever loved him. Your mother. Sam's mother. Bailey Montgomery is a likable, irascible old man, but he isn't a father. He could never meet the demands of that role. Ask Sam. He's more qualified than anyone to answer."

"Only *I* am qualified to answer," she flared back. "Only *I* know what I'm looking for, what I would ask of him. Neither you nor Sam are qualified to make that judgment for me." Tears were streaking her cheeks.

"You had no right, Adam. No right to deny me my own flesh and blood." Eve was sobbing openly now, unable to check her tears.

Adam took her in his arms, trying to comfort her. "Eve, I thought Bailey would never enter your life. As for Sam? He's a gunfighter living on borrowed time. I didn't want to bring them into your life, just to see your anguish when you lost them."

He pleaded for her understanding. "When I met them . . . and grew to know and like them . . . I knew I had to tell you. I no longer could deny you your birthright. Why do you think I brought Pinkerton's report to San Francisco, Eve? If you never believe another word I say, I beg you to believe that I intended to tell you the truth. I love you. I never wanted to hurt you."

Eve stirred in his arms and looked up at him. Tears of heartache glistened in her eyes. For a breathless span of time she studied the face above hers etched with concern—and love for her.

Yes, she knew Adam loved her. But, his love was too protective. A possessiveness that would ultimately destroy her.

She reached up and tenderly caressed his cheek. Despite everything, she loved him as well. Too much had passed between them. Their love-hate relationship had left feelings too deep to deny. That was what made leaving him so much harder. Whatever the future held for her, there would always be a part of her that belonged to him.

But a lasting love had to be built on a foundation of trust. Not lies, deceit, or manipulation.

Adam cupped her cheeks in his hands and smiled down at her. "I know you're upset right now, honey. I'll leave you so you can rest. Later we'll sit down and talk it all out. There isn't anything else, sweetheart. No more surprises. No more secrets. You know everything now."

Eve rose up and kissed him. A bittersweet kiss—sweetened with the tenderness of love, saddened by the pain of farewell.

She smiled at him through her tears, her heart an unbearable ache in her chest.

"Goodbye, Adam."

CHAPTER NINETEEN

After Eve departed, Adam remained in his office staring pensively into space. He knew this latest rift between them was not just another misunderstanding that could be brushed aside with a kiss. Eve was deeply hurt. No matter what she said in the passion of their love-making, her doubts about him had only been suppressed. How could he win her complete trust? How would he ever get her to accept his actions without the suspicion of an ulterior motive?

Rightfully, he admitted, she did have cause to be hurt. But even when his decisions were wrong, why couldn't she recognize that he usually had her interests at heart? Somehow there had to be a way to break down that wall of distrust that stood between them. Until he did, there would always be these argumentative scenes corroding their love.

Adam grimaced. He was running out of time.

Whatever he did, it would have to be soon if he was going to succeed in persuading her to return with him to Sacramento tomorrow.

He knew it would be wiser to allow Eve to work it out for herself rather than approaching her now, but the thought of her trying to cope with her heartache was too hard to handle.

He returned to their bedroom but there was no sign of her. Adam walked down the hallway to Simone's room, certain Eve would be there with her. After several raps, he turned away in irritation. "Damn! Where in hell could they disappear to so quickly?" he grumbled.

Adam returned to his office and leaned out the window in the hope of spying them on the street. There was no sign of the two women.

He paused briefly, his eyes drawn to the empty spot where The Forbidden Fruit had once stood. The grim evidence of the disaster reminded him how close he had come to losing her forever, a reminder which reinforced the senselessness of their foolish quarrels.

Any hope for pursuing his hunt for Eve faded when a carriage stopped below. His secretary, Richard Graves, stepped out of the conveyance, followed by a stranger. The man reached up to assist a woman. From Adam's vantage point, she appeared quite young. She was tall and slim, and her face was hidden by the wide brim of a hat lavishly adorned with feathers. She glanced up, and he could see she was lovely. For a few seconds their eyes met. A spark of interest flared in the depths of her green eyes. Then her wide, sensuous mouth curved into a barely perceptible smile, before she returned her attention to the man assisting her.

He stood slightly shorter than the woman and appeared to be about twenty years her senior. Hatless, he had a full head of dark hair generously streaked with silver.

Adam stepped away from the window, forced to put aside his concern for Eve to attend to the business at hand, a recommendation of his secretary.

Because he needed reliable men to help him manage his diverse business interests, Adam considered himself fortunate to have had the services of Richard Graves as his secretary.

Graves was an Englishman by birth, an American by preference. He had come to North America in 1821 to serve in the English embassy in Mexico. In May of 1823, when the Emperor Iturbide fled the country during a revolution, Graves decided he had had enough of foreign entanglements and left. Instead of returning to England, he traveled up the West Coast and by chance met Daniel Rawlins, who hired him immediately.

Intensely loyal to the Rawlins family, the shy, self-effacing young man had never married, and now at the age of fifty-five had devoted the last twenty-six years faithfully serving their interests. Adam trusted his judgment and competence unequivocally.

Soon after Graves introduced them, Adam

was impressed with Peter Woodward, the man Graves had recommended to take over the running of The Original Sin. However, Adam was dismayed at Woodward's taste in women, if the lady with the green eyes was an example. The lady, Lily Cavanaugh, was too sensually aware of herself. She flirted openly with Adam, using the obvious body signals he had been receiving from women ever since he was sixteen. That is, most women. Not Eve, he mused wistfully, allowing his thoughts to drift. Eve had an innate sensuousness which she wore as guilelessly as her innocence.

A short while later, when he had an opportunity to be alone with Graves, he expressed his concern that Woodward's ability to judge people was questionable. Graves had no such skepticism. The secretary had done his usual thorough investigation, and had found nothing shady about Woodward's associates or past life.

"Miss Cavanaugh is just a passing fancy, Adam. Woodward says she has an appealing singing voice." Adam's brow rose dubiously, and Graves could not help grinning. "You see, he is looking out for our interests already. Besides, I doubt the lady will stay around long. The El Dorado will be too much of a lure to her."

"All right, Richard. I bow to your judgment," Adam conceded. "Besides, I like the man," he added, swatting Graves on the shoulder. "I think you made a good choice."

"Well, now that we have that business settled, I've been anticipating seeing Eve. Where can I find her?"

Adam was chagrined. "Oh, God, Richard, I've forgotten to tell you the news. Eve and I were married a week ago."

Graves grinned broadly, pumping Adam's hand enthusiastically. "Congratulations, Eve's a wonderful girl."

For the past several years, Richard Graves had watched with amusement the byplay between the two young people. Although Adam Rawlins had tried to conceal his true feelings for Eve MacGregor, his secretary had always suspected the truth. When a man as busy as Adam neglected his business to build a San Francisco gambling casino across the street from a particular bakery, Richard's suspicions had been confirmed.

"Well, where is the blushing bride hiding herself?"

Despite the seriousness of the situation, Adam could not help erupting into laughter. "Hiding is the word for it. I wish I knew the answer to that question myself. She's off somewhere with Simone Lisle. At the moment, she is very angry with me. Sit down, Richard, and I'll tell you the whole story."

When Adam finished relating the events of the previous week, Graves walked to the window and viewed the remains of the bakery. "My God, man, you both could have perished in that fire."

"The important thing is that we didn't, Richard. The problem now is that not only did Eve find out that I financed the expansion of the bakery, but also the truth about her father."

Richard shook his head sadly. "I hate to say I told you so, Adam, but I knew Eve would be upset when she found out. I never understood why you weren't honest with her from the beginning."

Adam sat slumped on the edge of his desk, the picture of despair. "I wish I would have listened to you, but after waiting so long, I thought that by the time I told her the whole story, we would be married. Then it wouldn't matter." He grinned wryly. "I was half-right, anyway."

"You should have told her about Bailey Montgomery years ago, Adam," Graves said solemnly.

Adam felt totally deflated. He closed his eyes, reminded of the hopeless situation in which he now found himself. "I know that. Believe me, I intended to. I even started to tell her once, but Eve stopped me before I could finish. Now she's so hurt that I question if she'll ever forgive me."

Adam opened his eyes. Richard's face mirrored his sympathy for Adam. "How could I mess up everything so miserably, Richard?"

"Maybe if you both sit down and thoroughly talk it out, she will understand. I think the greatest problem has been that she found these things out herself, Adam. Perhaps if you had been honest with her, she would have accepted them."

Troubled, Adam rose to his feet. "You don't have to tell me that, Richard. I couldn't blame Eve if she never spoke to me again."

When the two women hadn't returned by nightfall, Adam began to pace the floor. Hoping he had somehow missed them, he returned to Simone's room. When his rapping failed to produce any result, Adam opened the door and peered inside. The room was empty. Too empty. His eyes swept the room and his suspicions increased. Nothing there was Simone's. The few personal belongings she owned were now gone. He bolted to their bedroom. Eve's things were missing as well. The significance of it left him in a cold sweat.

Adam hurried out of the casino and encountered Hilge Swensen outside her home. She told him Eve and Simone had been there earlier that day. They had bought some trousers and shirts belonging to her fourteen-year-old son. Adam thanked her, then, with his heart in his throat, raced down to the stable. The blacksmith confirmed his worst fears. Sam Montgomery had bought three horses from him. *The two women had ridden off with Sam.*

Adam was swept with panic. How could Sam have betrayed him like this? He wanted to search in all directions at once. Which way would they have gone?

Adam racked his brain, trying to recall bits and pieces of conversation. Last night Sam had said he was going to try to find his father. Adam cursed himself for not paying closer attention to Bailey's ramblings about his mine.

Devastated, Adam raised a clenched fist into the air. "Damn you, Eve! Damn you for being such a hot-headed, impetuous little fool." And his heart cried out, "Oh, God, baby, where are you?"

By the time Adam returned to The Original Sin he had regained his composure. He knew if he was going to succeed in finding Eve he couldn't allow his emotions to muddy up his reasoning.

He knew Bailey had filed a claim at the assay office which would give him the general location of the mine. He would check it out in the morning. Then, if he had to, he would hire every detective he could find in California. With his reputation, Sam Montgomery could not go unnoticed. Traveling with two women, even if they were dressed as boys, should make him easier to follow.

Adam stepped beside Graves and Woodward, who were at the bar. All the patrons in the casino were standing in rapt attention listening to Lily Cavanaugh singing. Woodward had not been wrong, Adam thought grudgingly, the woman did have a way with a song. He listened for a few minutes longer, then motioned to Graves to join him upstairs.

As he was climbing the stairway, Lily finished her song and the room exploded with applause and whistles. Adam stopped on the stairs and looked back at her. Lily's eyes were on him, and she smiled smugly. For several seconds his dark eyes remained locked with hers, then he turned and continued up the stairway.

Graves was shocked and worried when he heard the news about Eve. He agreed that Adam's plan to trace her was the best possible course to pursue. "I'll contact Allan Pinkerton as soon as we get back to Sacramento. He's a superb detective. If anyone can find Eve, he can," Richard declared positively, trying to bolster Adam's spirits.

But both men knew that it was impossible to find anyone in the gold fields who didn't want to be found.

"This changes my plans. I won't be returning to Sacramento with you. I'll stay here for the time being and contact other detective agencies. If I get lucky, maybe I'll even find out something from miners coming in from the diggings. You do the same in Sacramento," Adam said glumly.

He spent a sleepless night, tossing and turning in torment. The bed was too much of a reminder of the passionate hours he had shared with Eve. He finally got up and returned to his desk.

The following morning Adam received very little satisfaction from his visit to the assay office. Bailey's claim was located in the diggings near the Tuolumme River. However, the area was vague because so many rivers twisted and turned in a confusion of channels and canyons.

He again met with discouraging results when he spoke to miners who had just arrived in the city. None remembered seeing a man and two young women.

"There must be something more that I can do," Adam said later that evening as he and Graves sat in his office.

To Graves the poor man looked desperate. "You've done everything you can do right now, Adam." Rising to his feet, Richard patted Adam's shoulder. "I suggest you try now to get some sleep."

Adam remained at his desk after Graves left. Trying to put Eve out of his mind was an impossibility. The same questions flashed through his mind over and over again. *Where could she be? Did she need him as much as he did her? Did she even miss him?*

A shadow at the door caused him to look up. Lily Cavanaugh was in the open doorway, leaning back against the jamb.

"Are you lost, Miss Cavanaugh?" Adam asked irritably, settling back in his chair.

"You look lonely. I thought you might like some company." The woman had a low, husky voice that seemed to curl around each word she spoke. The dress she wore displayed her legs generously to her knee. Long and slender, they reminded him of Eve's—except that Eve had a dimple in each knee that he could not resist kissing. Unconsciously his hands curled into fists just thinking about it.

"I heard a delightful rumor that your wife ran out on you." Lily sauntered over to his desk. "I think it would be a shame if a man like you would have to sleep all alone." Lily sat down on his lap and slid her arms around his neck.

"I think it would be a greater shame if Pete Woodward would have to sleep alone. Don't you, Miss Cavanaugh?"

"One man's loss is another man's gain," she murmured in a throaty sigh. Lily dipped her head, her lips hovering above his. "I can be any kind of woman you want me to be, Adam Rawlins," she whispered intimately before her lips covered his.

Her mouth moved on his with erotic expertise. Her tongue parted his lips, conducting darted, heated forays into his mouth. The kiss was enticing in his pent-up need for Eve.

Lily raised her head with a seductive smile. "Did you like that, Adam?"

His smile did not carry to his eyes. "Oh, you're good, Lily. Damned good. I see you know how to use that mouth of yours for considerably more than just singing."

She slid her hand into his shirt. "And wait until you see what it can do to the rest of you," she purred salaciously. "You'll be the one who's singing."

"I think not, Lily," Adam said icily, forcing her away. "You see, once you've tasted the finest wine, it's impossible to swallow a cheap barroom variety."

Adam rose to his feet, practically dumping her on the floor. "I suggest you stick to singing, Miss

Cavanaugh. That is all you were hired to do. Close the door on your way out."

Three days later Lily Cavanaugh moved out of The Original Sin, bag and baggage. Adam, standing at the bar with Richard Graves and Peter Woodward, watched her depart in a flurry of feathers and swinging hips.

Woodward accepted her leaving with an impassive shrug. "She says she's got a job singing at the El Dorado. I wish her luck."

Adam uttered a hump of amusement. "I think she's going to need it. Jim McCabe has a roving eye. As soon as she tries to practice her *singing* on him, she's likely to lose a lot of that pretty blonde hair. Irene McCready has been known to be rough on the competition."

An idea had been formulating in the back of Adam's mind since he met Woodward. The one reservation he had been harboring was now erased with the departure of Lily Cavanaugh. "How would you like to buy The Original Sin, Pete?"

Peter Woodward laughed in amusement. "I couldn't accumulate that kind of money in the rest of my lifetime."

"What if we work out an arrangement. Let's say ten percent of the profits each month until you pay it off."

Uncertain whether Adam was serious, Woodward appeared nonplused. Richard Graves knew Adam too well not to know he wasn't joking. "I haven't any further use for a gambling casino."

"You are serious, aren't you?" Woodward asked, astonished. "Are you saying you're willing to sell out without any front money?"

"Why not? Besides, it's a good way to keep you honest. There would be no point in skimming off the top. The more profit, the greater my ten percent. The greater my ten percent, the quicker you own it. Simple economics."

Adam put down his drink and turned to Graves. "Richard, why don't you work out whatever details you want to with him. Draw up the papers and I'll sign them when I get back."

Adam left the two men staring after him. Graves, he knew, would think him out of his mind. Adam headed for the wharf in the hope of finding someone who might have seen Eve.

He returned several hours later, discouraged that his search had produced no results. Graves had drawn up the papers and the transaction for the sale of the casino was completed.

The three men stood toasting the arrangement, when Billy Chambers rapped at the door. He hung back in the entrance, as if afraid to enter the room.

"Come on in and join us, Billy. You've got a new boss. Mr. Woodward has just purchased The Original Sin."

The big man shuffled in and nodded nervously. "Congratulations, Mr. Woodward." He turned back to Adam sheepishly. "I'm sorry, boss . . . ah, Mr. Rawlins, but I forgot to give you this in all the excitement of the past couple days." He handed Adam a wrinkled envelope. "Sam Montgomery dropped it off the morning he left town."

Adam slammed down his glass. His eyes were wild with fury. "You mean you've had this for almost a week!"

Woodward had witnessed men in uncontrollable rages and he feared Rawlins would do something violent to the man if he didn't get him out of the room. He wisely stepped between them. "Come along, Billy. I need you below." Chambers didn't need any further encouragement as Woodward rushed him out of the room.

Adam's hands were shaking as he ripped open the envelope. It contained a single sheet of paper. He scanned it quickly and broke into a wide grin. "Bless you, Sam Montgomery."

"What is it, Adam?" Graves leaned over the desk to read it.

"A map, Richard. It's a map leading to Bailey Montgomery's mine. Sam has drawn the exact route he'll be taking. I take back all the nasty thoughts I had about him these past few days. He knew I'd follow." Adam was practically dancing around the room in elation. "I love you, Sam," he shouted joyously.

"Thank goodness, Adam. It's the breakthrough we've been hoping for. We can send riders after them at once."

"Riders?" Adam scoffed. "Eve would never come back that way. I'm going after her myself. I'm her husband, you know." He grinned like a mischievous young boy. "If she's too stubborn to listen to reasoning, legally I can hogtie her and drag her back."

He shook his head in disbelief. "Damn Chambers! Now they've got a five-day head start on me. I'll leave at dawn."

"You're being as impetuous as Eve. What about your business, Adam?" Richard asked, trying to remind him of the impractical action he was taking. "I am sure we could get Eve to return through legal channels, if necessary."

"Richard, Eve is my wife. I have to find her. You're as capable of running the business as I am. I trust your judgment completely."

Richard sighed in resignation. "I knew it would be useless to try to dissuade you, Adam, but I thought I should try." There was more affection than censure in his tone.

Adam spent the remaining daylight hours acquiring a mule and packing it with supplies. Graves accompanied him to the stable early the following morning. Adam was wearing a buckskin shirt and trousers and a cowboy's wide-brimmed felt hat, its high crown shoved to the back of his head. Even more incongruous to the usual appearance of Adam Rawlins were the rifle in his hand and the colt revolver in the gun belt strapped to his hips.

Adam wore them all with the same casual flair he did his impeccably tailored clothing.

He slipped his rifle into a sheath on the saddle and turned back to Graves, handing him a sealed envelope. "Just in case I don't make it back, I've written some final instructions."

Richard nodded gravely. Adam gave him another envelope. It was the one from the Pinkerton Agency. Graves looked up quizzically when he recognized it. "I don't want to carry this with me. I don't know what might happen on the trail. I wouldn't want this information to fall into the wrong hands."

"I understand, Adam."

Adam reached out to shake his hand. Richard clasped it tightly, then pulled him into his arms and embraced him. "Good luck, son." There was grave concern in the older man's eyes as Adam mounted his horse.

The sun was a faint glow on the horizon when Adam rode out of the city.

CHAPTER TWENTY

Since Simone had never ridden a horse, their progress was slow and by the time they made camp that evening she was in intense pain. Remembering her own aches and pains the first time she had ridden a horse, Eve would not allow Simone to lift a hand to help with the chores. She prepared the evening meal alone, while Sam pitched the tent.

The tent was small, just large enough to sleep two people. It wasn't until Sam bedded down outside that Eve realized, by tagging along with them, she was keeping the two lovers apart. Before they retired, Eve took the opportunity to apologize while rubbing unguent on Simone's aching body. "I'm truly sorry, Simone. I didn't stop to think that I would be intruding on you and Sam."

Simone, as usual, was selfless. "Nonsense,

chérie. We are your friends. You're not intruding."

Eve sighed as she reflected on Simone's thoughtfulness. Neither Simone nor Sam had brought up the subject of Adam. Whatever problem Eve was having with him, they did not want to pry; they merely wanted to help her. "My being here is keeping you . . . *apart.*" The slightly accentuated last word adequately conveyed the reason for Eve's apology.

Simone blushed as she grasped the meaning of Eve's concern. First she giggled and then, with a shy smile, managed to say, "I'm aching so much, it is of no matter." The smile faded. Simone looked up at Eve, her eyes filled with admiration. "We want you with us, *chérie,*" she said sincerely, and then reiterated, "We are your friends."

At this moment Eve desperately wanted to tell Simone that she and Sam were far more than just friends to Eve. *Sam is my brother, Simone.* The simple truth, which she could not utter, raced through her mind. Eve hugged her in gratitude. "I love you, Simone. You and Sam are such good friends to me. Better than I deserve. Do lie down now and try to sleep if you can. I remember how sore I was the first time I rode a horse. Believe me, your aches and pains will soon disappear."

It didn't take long for Simone to fall asleep. Eve was not so fortunate. She lay awake for hours thinking about Adam. Her heart was aching because she loved him and she missed him. Just one day away from him and the temptation to forgive him, to go riding back to him, was overwhelming.

Eve knew her own ache would not pass as swiftly as Simone's.

The following morning, Simone found it impossible to climb on a horse. Sam tied the horses to the mule and they all walked. The only inland roads were occasional cattle paths, so their progress was slower than on the previous day, but the journey was much easier on Simone.

Eve found herself studying Sam with serious regard, trying to discern any resemblance between them. It was a strange feeling to realize she had a brother. He was so close, and yet he did not know.

She had no idea how to tell Sam the truth. She decided she had to wait until they found Bailey and then tell them both at the same time.

The thought of having a father was just as startling to her. She could hardly wait to see Bailey again, and wondered if it would please him to find out that she was his daughter. Until she told them all, Eve knew she would be just as guilty as Adam was for keeping the information a secret.

Adam. The harder she tried to put him out of her mind, the more she thought about him. At times she felt as if her heart would burst, just from the ache of missing him.

That evening they pitched their tent at the junction of the Sacramento and San Joaquin Rivers. As a result of the slow journey, they were only about thirty-five miles from San Francisco. Sam couldn't have been more pleased. He knew Adam Rawlins would have no trouble following them. And he was certain Adam *would* follow them because he, Sam, was a good judge of character. Sam Montgomery, gunfighter, often had to depend upon keen insight to stay alive, and this time his intuition told him that Adam's arrival on the scene was imminent.

The next day, before he climbed on the barge that would ferry them across the river, Sam took one final backward look, hoping for a sign of Adam. He refused to believe that Adam Rawlins would not come after Eve.

For the next five days, they crossed countless streams that snaked through the dense forests of evergreen and oak. They passed miners squatting in the shallow cold waters as they panned for gold with flat-bottom tin pans.

Preferring to remain anonymous, Sam avoided spending time with the miners they encountered. However, the two women always attracted attention. They waved to the miners in passing, and on occasion Sam would let them take the time to share a cup of coffee or a plate of beans.

Most of the miners were concerned about the welfare of the women. Time and again they were warned to look out for wounded grizzlies, renegade Indians, or the legendary bandit leader, Joaquin Murieta.

After their third warning about the man, Simone asked Sam one night, "Who is this Joaquin Murieta?"

He shrugged negligently. "He's a Mexican bandit."

"Is the man as dangerous as they're saying?"

"I guess it depends on who's doing the talking. To some people he's a folk hero, a Robin Hood. I'm not as worried about Murieta as I am about wounded grizzlies and renegade Indians."

When the terrain permitted, they rode, but most of the time they walked. It was blazing hot during the day and cool at night. They passed through dense forests abounding with elk, and boulder-strewn canyons where nothing moved except an occasional lizard scurrying beneath a rock. They bruised themselves stumbling over loose rocks, choked on the dust from dry river beds, bathed in frigid mountain streams—and fell into their sleeping bags every night with aching legs and blistered feet.

The snow-capped peaks of the Sierra Nevadas towered over them. Their destination was somewhere in the dark line of timber that fringed the imposing slopes.

By this time, Eve was certain she was carrying Adam's child. She did not tell Sam and Simone. If Sam knew, he would make them turn around and go back to San Francisco. It would be another secret to keep until they found Bailey. She often awoke with a queasy stomach, but she knew the discomfort would pass.

Bailey's map showed a trail parallel to the Tuolumme River leading to the town of Sonora. Sam promised that when they reached the town they would stop overnight to replenish their provisions. The prospects of a hot bath and a bed were incentive enough to keep moving.

When they finally rode into Sonora, the two women thought they had entered a different world. The town had an exotic and festive air. Groups of Mexicans sat on brightly colored serapes spread out on the ground, talking and gambling beneath lighted tapers that lined the streets.

Gaming tables lined each side of the street covered with gold and crescent cloths. Miners, accompanied by scantily dressed women, crowded around these tables playing three-card monte, faro, and a popular French card game, vingt-et-un, which the miners called twenty-one. A clamorous din of guitars, fiddles, and Mexican flutes rose above the shouting and laughing of the revelers.

The hungry travelers eyed the many tables loaded with cakes, pies, hot meats, and cooling beverages which had been packed in snow from the mountains.

They dismounted before a wooden structure with "Miners Hotel" painted on a sign above the front door. At the sight of a drunken miner being pulled into a tent by a half-dressed woman, Eve turned to Simone with a disdainful look. "Do you think this is Sodom or Gomorrah?"

"I suspect one side of the street is Sodom, *chérie*, and the other is Gomorrah," Simone scoffed.

Eve's eyes flashed mischievously as she leaned over and whispered in Simone's ear. "I can't wait to explore it, can you?" The remark set off a siege of giggles between them.

Sam knew the women were curious and eager to investigate the town. Before Eve could even suggest it, he informed them of his intentions. "I hope you gals aren't getting any ideas. I'm putting you in a room and I want you to stay there."

"And just what will you be doing, Sam Montgomery, while we're tucked safely away in bed for the night?" Eve teased. She winked at Simone.

"Sleeping on the floor right beside you," Sam sighed.

"Can't we look around for a little while?" Eve cajoled, with a backward glance at activities in the street.

"Inside, ladies," Sam declared, placing a firm hand on each back.

Eve and Simone shared the same tub of water to save money and time, while Sam went to stable the horses and get them some food. When he returned, they were both clean and refreshed.

After they had finished their meal, Sam, true to his word, made himself a pallet on the floor. When Eve's steady breathing indicated she was asleep, Simone climbed out of the bed and moved to the pallet.

"Sam, if you want to go and play some monte, go ahead," she whispered.

He reached up and clasped her hand. "There isn't anything in this town that interests me as much as you, mouse." He pulled her down beside him and held her in his arms until they both fell asleep.

When they stepped outside the following morning, the town was bathed in sunlight. The dawning of another day had not seemed to diminish the activities of the previous night. The noise had not abated, and the gambling was still in full operation.

Eve and Simone strolled among the crowd and confusion, absorbing all the sights and sounds with rapt interest. Watchdog Sam trailed behind.

"I can't believe the number of women in this town," Simone commented as they passed several Mexican women with children in tow. "I haven't seen this many since I came to California."

"This town was originally settled by immigrants from the Mexican state of Sonora," Sam explained. "They brought their families . . . or other assorted . . . ladies with them," he drawled.

Eve grabbed Simone's arm excitedly. "Look at those houses. I wouldn't believe it if I didn't see it with my own eyes."

Most of the dwellings were three-sided with fronts opening on the street. Unlike the crudely erected shanties and stark tents of the other mining towns, vivid colors decorated the simple structures. Bowers of green branches and vines interwoven with brilliantly colored pieces of silk and cotton, along with colorful scarfs, shawls, and serapes, hung from the sides and overhanging roofs of the modest dwellings.

Eve stopped to admire a garden patch in full bloom. "This is really an enchanting place, Sam. What a shame it has to be spoiled by all the gambling and carousing."

"I suspect that's only on weekends, Eve, when the miners come to town. It's probably just a sleepy community during the rest of the week."

They had completed their circle of the town and found themselves again in front of the Miners Hotel. "I guess we better go and stock up on as many provisions as we can afford. I'm afraid our cash is running low."

"You mean we haven't enough for supplies?" Simone asked, surprised.

Sam grinned. "I was thinking of selling your horse. You don't seem to enjoy riding it anyway. I could take the money we have left and play some three-card monte. But there's always the chance I might lose it all."

Thinking of the bank money she had given Adam in anger, Eve regretted the foolish deed.

She should have kept some of it, or at least have given some to Simone. Staring deep in thought, Eve pondered their pressing need for supplies. Suddenly her eyes focused on a poster tacked to the hotel door. It was the solution to their predicament.

With a cocky grin she pointed to the sign and read the message aloud. "'Horse race today. One o'clock. Entrance fee $100. Winner take all.' I know a way we can make some money. Let's take the money we have and enter the race."

Sam shook his head. "I'd have just as good of a chance at monte as I would in a horse race. My horse just isn't racing stock."

"I'm not talking about you racing; I'm talking about me," Eve declared.

When Sam turned to Simone for an opinion, she shrugged and said, "Eve can ride, there's no doubt about that."

Sam was dubious about the idea. "This isn't going to be a steeplechase or a pleasant romp through the fields, Eve. It could be rough."

"Sam, look at the sign. The route is only two miles long. Heck, in a two-mile race, I could probably beat Pegasus." She grinned confidently. "You know as well as I do, those men outweigh me by at least fifty pounds, and they might be even more weighted down if they're fool enough to wear heavy gun belts.

"And I can't believe anyone would even have a fast horse in these mountains. So if I break in front, no one will be able to catch me."

She glanced hopefully at him. "The odds are much better than if you tried to beat some slick card dealer."

Sam was still reluctant. "If the horse stumbled, you could break your fool neck."

"That roan I've been riding is as surefooted as a mule," Eve said excitedly, sensing Sam's capitulation.

Sam did not want Eve to put herself in a dangerous situation, but he realized the possibility of the outcome: she could win if she stayed ahead of the pack.

"Well, it's against my better judgment, but let me sign you up. If they don't see your size until the race, maybe it will give you an edge."

Both women squealed with pleasure. To his startled embarrassment, they hugged and kissed him, dismantling his stoic composure.

CHAPTER TWENTY-ONE

Many of the drinkers and card players had temporarily ceased their sporting and stood among the town's women and children who had assembled at the starting line to watch the event. Judges had been strung out along the winding two-mile route to keep the narrow trail free from anyone who might stray upon it during the race.

Eve took her place among the ten riders who had entered the event. She was dressed like a man, and her hair was securely pinned up underneath the ten-gallon hat she had borrowed from Sam. It was obvious that she was the smallest rider, but the fact that she was a woman went undetected.

Nervously, Eve glanced to her left at the rider holding the reins of a black gelding. The man outweighed her by at least a hundred pounds, and as Eve anticipated, he was wearing a heavy gun belt. But she knew this was the horse her roan would have to beat. Her aplomb had faded at first sight of the magnificent-looking animal. Adam had told her once that a gelding was a strong horse that could carry a heavy load for a long distance. The rider's weight would not be a problem to the horse.

I had to open my mouth about Pegasus, she reflected in self-reproach. *I wonder if that gelding will sprout wings when we get under way.*

Eve knew she must break out ahead or the race was lost. If the gelding got the lead, there would be no passing it on the narrow trail.

"Riders, shank leather," the starter called out. As the other contenders swung their legs over their saddles, Eve stopped to pat the roan's neck. "I know we can do it, boy," she whispered, trying to bolster her own confidence as well as that of the horse. She climbed into the saddle and waved at Sam and Simone standing quietly among the spectators.

The crowd hushed when the starter raised his pistol. At the sound of the blast the spectators roared as the horses bolted forward, while an assortment of mangy dogs took up the dust in yapping pursuit.

The first part of the race was a straight stretch, a simple matter of speed. Then the riders were required to cross a stream, climb up a steep hill, follow the trail that circled the town, and then repeat the entire route.

Eve got off to a slight lead, with the gelding at her heels. By the time she splashed across the stream, her lead had narrowed. She gave the roan full rein as they climbed the hill. The trail was narrow and she sensed the gelding's breath at her back. As they started their descent, she checked the reins to keep the horse's head up so that it wouldn't stumble.

By now, the race had turned into a two-horse contest. They were rapidly closing in on a fallen tree that had been dragged on the course as an obstacle. Eve didn't slow the horse's stride, urging it on with a slight pressure of her knees. The roan leaped over the tree as if it had wings.

Unfortunately, the gelding followed suit. The trail widened when it reached the town, and the riders galloped through it amid the cheers and shouts of the enthusiastic crowd. With half of the race to go, the two horses were now neck and neck. Water sprayed like a fountain as the horses splashed across the stream. To win Eve had to reach the top of the hill before the gelding, so that she would be leading when she hit the jump again.

With a powerful surge, the black horse crested the hill ahead of her. She was blocked out. There was little hope for her now, unless the black horse stumbled. At the speed of the chase, a spill would be fatal to rider and horse.

Eve took a desperate measure to descend the hill. She turned the roan off the beaten path, propelling them down the treacherously steep slope.

The crowd saw the daring maneuver and gasped. "That darn fool girl is going to break her neck," Sam grumbled to Simone, who clutched his hand and held her breath.

Rocks and dust skittered and flew as Eve descended the steep hill at a full gallop, until the roan virtually slid part of the way with its hind legs almost doubled. Eve's legs gripped the sides of the animal, checking the reins tightly to keep the roan's head from drooping. She was calling on every skill Adam had taught her to keep a horse on foot and herself in the saddle.

The roan and the gelding reached the bottom of the hill with Eve slightly ahead as they turned and headed for the finish line. Her daring maneuver had won the support of the crowd. They yelled encouragement as the spunky little horse cleared the final jump. Eve leaned low over its neck, the roan stretched out and sped across the finish line to the cheers of the spectators.

Eve had no sooner dismounted than Sam was at her side. "That trick was the most foolhardy thing I have ever seen," he snarled through gritted teeth. "You could have broken your neck."

Eve was too breathless and excited to do anything except pant and smile. Simone, practically in tears, hugged her. The man who had ridden the gelding began pumping her hand with enthusiasm. As she pulled off her hat, he discovered he had been bested by a female, and was flabbergasted.

"I tell you, little lady, that was the best race I ever rode in. It's a pleasure to shake your hand."

Eve could only beam with pride when the

judges presented her with the thousand dollars in prize money. Sam was still scowling when she handed it over to him.

The horse race had been scheduled as a brief diversion in the morning, and the main entertainment for the weekend had been planned for the afternoon. For weeks, posters had been circulated in all the nearest towns announcing the event.

On the floor of a box canyon near the outskirts of the town, an arena surrounded by a fence had been erected. Overlooking the arena, tiered rows of seats on each wall of the canyon offered security to the spectators who had spent five dollars for an admission ticket. Newly arrived miners, willing to squander the gold they had scrapped and grubbed from the earth, offered as much as two ounces of the valuable metal to obtain front row seats. Eve, who had captured the heart of the town with her spirited race, was given the seat of honor at the event.

The focus of this extraordinary interest was a contest pitting a fighting bull against a grizzly bear.

"You are not going to enjoy it," Sam warned.

Still flushed with victory, Eve would not bide his warning. "How can I refuse them, Sam? They mean well." Against Sam's better judgment, he and Simone accompanied her.

Many of the town's enterprising citizens had moved their colorful canvas tents and booths to the site to hawk tamales, tortillas, and various selections of the tasty Mexican confection, marzipan.

Whiskey, selling for a dollar a shot, was generously consumed by the rowdy spectators. A band offered musical accompaniment to the carnival atmosphere.

A huge bear, weighing at least fourteen hundred pounds, was tethered by a twenty-foot chain at the center of the arena. A ferocious-looking bull was then driven into the canyon. The animal seemed to pause like a boxer in the ring sizing up its adversary. Raising a cloud of dust as it pawed the earth, the bull lowered its head and powerful shoulders, preparing to charge.

At the sight of the bull, the bear sat down and braced for battle in a hole several inches deep, which it had scooped out with its paw. To pull its opponents close to the ground, where they would be trapped by its lethal jaws and crushing arms, was a bear's favorite battle maneuver.

The bull attacked, trying to hook its horns into the bear, which would enable it to toss the grizzly into the air. The bear dodged the bull's rush but was dislodged from its seat. The bear turned to face the next charge.

Eve had seen all she wanted to of the struggle, and she regretted she had not heeded Sam's warning. Blistering hot air was rising from the canyon floor, swirling around her head in an encompassing veil of heat and grit from the battle. She was beginning to feel faint.

For the second foray, the bull lowered its head

even more, its snorting nostrils raising dust as it charged. The grizzly's jaws clamped down on the side of the bull's head, and its forelegs locked around its body.

For several moments the beasts thrashed mightily in a death struggle. When they separated, half of the bull's face was in shreds; one eye had been ripped from the socket.

Revolted, Eve turned away. She put her hand to her mouth to force back the bile that had risen to her throat. Simone buried her head in Sam's chest.

The spectators around them were on their feet, shouting and cheering. None appeared repulsed by either the sight or the concept of the carnage. Eve couldn't believe that the same crowd that earlier had cheered her game victory now screamed for blood and gore.

Blinded by its own blood, the bull stumbled and fell. The contest was over. Instantly, the bear lunged at the animal, and once again the roar of approval from the crowd shattered the air.

The bear was quickly caged, and Eve thought that was the end to the horrid affair. To her extreme distress, it was not. She was to become the center of attention. In the manner of a triumphant matador, the impresario approached her.

He bowed before her with a dramatic flourish. Then he extended the award of honor. Eve stared in horror at the severed tail of the bull dangling from his outstretched hand.

Sky and earth began to whirl around her head. Eve groped helplessly for Sam and fainted.

When Eve opened her eyes, she was lying in the shadow of a tall pine. Simone was on bended knees beside her, fanning her with a straw fan given to her by one of the Mexican women. There was no sign of Sam.

"Don't tell me I fainted?" Eve asked feebly.

Simone smiled tenderly. "*Oui, chérie*, and what a fright you gave us."

Eve sat up with a sheepish grin. "I should have listened to Sam. I guess it was too much sun and that horrible bloody tail hanging in front of my face." She shuddered in revulsion.

"I think it is something more, *chérie*," Simone added with a wise smile. She sat down beside Eve.

Eve's face curved with a culpable grin. "I can't fool you, can I? I wanted to tell you, Simone, but I didn't want Sam to know. If he knew I was pregnant, he never would have agreed to bringing me along."

"That is for certain," Simone scolded. Then she added soulfully, "*Chérie*, you belong with your husband."

Eve saw Sam approaching, carrying a glass. She clutched her friend's hands in desperation. "Please, Simone, I beg you not to tell Sam. He will make me go back to San Francisco and there's something I must do first."

Unaware of Eve's desire to spend time with

the father and brother she had never known, Simone assumed that Eve still had an obsession to be independent of Adam. She shook her head in disapproval. "In your condition, you belong with Adam."

Seeing her plan slipping away, Eve was unable to hide her heartbreak. Her eyes welled with tears. Simone's heart was too tender to withstand the sight of Eve's distress. She kissed her hand lovingly. "Very well, *chérie*, I promise."

Quickly Eve wiped away her tears before Sam reached them. He handed her a glass of fruit juice. The cool liquid helped to refresh her, and soon Eve felt she had recovered. "In the future, Sam Montgomery, I promise to take your advice about everything. I'm sincerely sorry for all the trouble I've caused you."

Sam grinned shyly. "I'm glad you're okay. Do you feel well enough to make it back to the hotel?"

"Of course. I'm fine now."

To prove her point, Eve rose quickly to her feet. Simone linked her arm through Eve's. "Just the same, *ma chérie*, I think we should walk together."

In the concealment of the trees higher on the hill, a man stood watching the three people. His wide sombrero made the man's head appear too large for his short, portly body. In a swarthy face disfigured by pockmarks, dark, beady eyes glittered with malevolence. A heavy, drooping mustache curved around the ends of a mouth more accustomed to wearing a sneer than a smile. The man appeared to have a quality of evil, causing people to fear him on sight. His thin lips curled into a sinister snarl. "So, we meet again, *amigo*."

He slowly descended the hill.

Once Sam had the women safely ensconced in their room, he went to check the horses and mules. When he left the stable, he stopped abruptly at the sight of the figure lounging against the wall.

"*Holá, amigo.*"

"Morales." Sam disguised his surprise at seeing this face from the past as he said flippantly, "I'm surprised to see you're still alive. I thought someone would have shot you by now."

The man grinned broadly, exposing a perfect set of teeth in the otherwise flawed face. "I thought the same of you, *amigo*."

Sam looked about expectantly. He knew Morales was never far from his gang of cutthroats. Guessing Sam's thoughts, the Mexican leader laughed aloud, "My *hombres* are in the mountains, *amigo*. I did not want to cause attention. The army has been pursuing us for weeks."

"Then I suggest you return to your men, Morales, while you are still able to walk."

At the veiled threat, the bandit leader slowly straightened his stance and casually walked toward his horse. "I see you are traveling with two *gringas, amigo*."

Sam had hoped the man thought he was traveling alone. To get even with him, Sam knew

Morales would not hesitate to harm the women.

"They hired my gun arm to take them to their father." Sam shrugged lazily. "It's just another job to me."

Morales swung onto his horse. "That could be quite dangerous, even for you, *amigo*." He halted his horse in front of Sam and glared down at him. "*Hasta luego, amigo*." The promise to meet again was more threatening than felicitous.

Sam watched the bandit ride away, wishing he were as capable of shooting a man in the back as he knew Morales was. Sam hurried back to the hotel. He wanted to get Eve and Simone out of town before Morales could join up with his band.

As he entered their room, he said bluntly, "Eve, are you well enough to travel?"

"Of course, Sam."

"Then we'll leave as soon as it gets dark."

Both women sensed by his manner that something was seriously wrong, and his reticence meant he had no intention of telling them what it was. Since they respected his judgment, neither questioned his reason. Wordlessly they packed their saddlebags while Sam pulled out Bailey's map and studied it carefully. Traveling at night in the mountains was almost impossible. He hoped they could get out of town in the dark without being sighted. If Morales intended to follow, he would have difficulty picking up their trail.

The streets of Sonora were still ablaze with candles as the three figures stole furtively from the back door of the hotel. Hugging the shadows, they moved to the stable where the horses were saddled and waiting.

They led their horses along the narrow trail until they reached the stream, then veered eastward, climbing higher into the mountains.

In the darkness, the trail was treacherous. Often, one or another horse would fall or slide. Finally, for the safety of themselves and the animals, Sam called a halt. In fear it would attract attention, he didn't want to build a fire, so they bedded down in a cold camp.

Tired, shivering, and exhausted, the women fell asleep. They were fearful of the unknown, but had steadfast belief in Sam. Alert to each sound in the night, he remained awake.

At dawn Sam stole away to a higher rise to study the terrain. He sighted wisps of smoke rising from several different sites, but it was impossible to determine whether they were the camps of miners or Morales.

Rather then risk a fire, they ate dried beef and drank cold water. "I want you girls to study this map," Sam announced as he spread it open before them. "Here is Sonora and we're about here." He traced the route with a finger. "Bailey shows a cabin right here." He pointed to the location and paused, allowing the women to absorb the details. "We should reach it by nightfall. From there, it looks like a couple more days to reach the mine."

"What are we running away from, Sam?" Eve

asked, unable to restrain her curiosity any longer.

Sam sighed and sat back. "I might as well tell you. Yesterday in Sonora I saw a man by the name of Juan Morales. He's a renegade and I know his band is around somewhere."

"Why would they bother to rob us when there's so many miners around with gold?"

Sam did not want to alarm the women further by revealing the dreadful truth: Morales was a coldblooded killer with a penchant for raping white women.

"He has a grudge against me."

"Why?" Eve pursued, with a nervous glance at Simone.

"We once rode together under Murieta."

"Joaquin Murieta!" Eve exclaimed, shocked. The warnings they had received from miners leaped to her mind.

At Simone's gasp of surprise, Sam looked at her and said defensively, "Don't believe everything you've heard about Murieta. Half of the bandits in California, Mexican and American alike, are riding around claiming to be him." To add credence to his argument, Sam added, "Murieta threw Morales out of his band when he heard about it."

"Heard about what, Sam?"

"I shot Morales's brother when I found them raping a woman. I should have killed that bastard, too, but he wasn't armed." Sam's face was set in a grim line, remembering the incident.

"When Murieta heard about it, he warned Morales he would hang him up for the buzzards if their paths ever crossed again."

Eve now understood Sam's reason for being so secretive. "So you think this Morales is following you to get his revenge."

"I *know* he is," Sam said emphatically. "And his method is to see his victim squirm, so the bastard showed his face in Sonora knowing I wouldn't take him on until you two were safe."

"Why didn't you just have him arrested in Sonora?" Simone asked.

"If I had tried that, Morales could claim I rode with Murieta. You saw yourself how some people react to that name. Some think he's a God, and others the devil himself."

Sam rose to his feet. "We'd better move on. I think we've given Morales the slip. He had no way of knowing where we were headed."

They rode all morning, nervously looking back over their shoulders from time to time. By midday, when there was no sign they were being followed, all three were able to ease their vigilance.

CHAPTER TWENTY-TWO

By the time they reached it that evening, the cabin was a welcomed sight to the hungry and weary travelers. As soon as they forced open the weather-jammed door, they were startled by unexpected guests. There was a frantic fluttering of wings as several birds flew out through a hole in the rear wall of the cabin. At the same time, several tiny critters scurried across their feet and out the door.

While Sam and Simone drove away the intruders, Eve scanned the decrepit cabin. She wondered how long the dismal shelter had been unoccupied as she went over to examine the hole in the wall. Apparently a couple of loose logs had become dislodged. One teetered askew to the ledge of the opening, and the other was lying on a debris-scattered cot beneath the gaping hole. Eve put a knee on the cot, leaned out, and quickly drew back in alarm. "My goodness, there's nothing there."

Coming over to see what had caused her fright, Sam saw that the back wall of the cabin overhung the face of a cliff, a sheer drop of at least forty feet.

After he put the logs back into place, Sam went to gather wood for a fire. By the time he returned, Eve and Simone had swept the cabin, cleared out the cobwebs, and cleaned off the leaves and dirt that had accumulated on the meager furniture. Sam got the fire going while Simone and Eve unpacked enough supplies to prepare a meal.

Within a short time the aroma of perking coffee blended with the savory smell of the beef-and-onion-filled tortillas bubbling in a skillet on the hearth. Now the humble dwelling was not only habitable, it had been transformed by the glow of the fire and the expertise of the resident French chef.

The meal was the best they had eaten since leaving San Francisco. "I'm a much better cook when I'm under a roof," Simone offered in explanation after Sam and Eve had heaped praises upon her. They finished off their dinner with tasty pieces of marzipan.

Since the cot could sleep only one, Eve and Simone insisted that Sam use the bed for the night. They would sleep on a pallet in front of the warm fireplace.

"I haven't slept in enough beds in my life to

know how to be comfortable in one," Sam protested.

"It's only a cot, Sam," Eve responded. Reluctantly, Sam gave in and lay down.

While he slept, Simone lay studying the beloved figure. She realized that Sam had not been teasing. Raised in an Indian camp, and drifting from one place to another as an adult, it was unlikely he had spent many nights in a bed.

She yearned for the opportunity to keep house for him. To cook his meals each day while he . . . Her thoughts drifted. *What would he be doing?* She couldn't see him content spending his life behind a plow like her father. Nor could she visualize him behind a desk engrossed in the task of building financial empires like Adam Rawlins.

What would be Sam's niche? Not a lawman, she thought hopefully. It was too dangerous; she would not be able to bear the worry. Men who lived by the sword, died by the sword.

Simone's face suddenly lit up as she visualized Sam atop a horse herding horses and cows. *A ranch*, she thought with relief. *Sam could become a rancher*.

She yawned and closed her eyes in contentment. Tomorrow she would think of a name for the ranch.

Eve, too, was wrestling with her own thoughts. She wondered if the ache for Adam would ever leave her. She recalled the sight of him stretched out by the stream, laughing up at her as he chewed on an apple. How long would it be before such tender moments ceased to haunt her?

Sam awoke abruptly and sat up. He had slept through the night without stirring. Light was now shining through the cracks in the cabin. A quick glance showed him that Simone and Eve were still sound asleep. He was proud of the two women. They had been real troopers through the whole trip. They both were exhausted but neither had uttered a word of complaint.

He quietly left the cabin to get fresh water from the river. By the time he finished watering the horses and mule, Eve and Simone were awake.

After a breakfast of oatmeal and dried peaches, they packed their saddlebags. Sam saddled the horses, waiting for them to finish washing the pots and pans. Returning to the cabin, he suddenly felt edgy, anxious to get moving.

"All right, we're through," Eve announced, shoving the coffee pot into the pack.

"I'll bring up the mule." Sam stepped outside.

Eve stopped to glance around the cabin for one last inspection. "Did we miss anything?"

"I think not, *chérie*," Simone said lightly.

When they stepped out of the cabin, Sam was standing motionless with a pistol in each hand, his eyes fixed on the hill in front of the cabin. It was lined with at least a dozen men with raised weapons waiting for a sign from their leader.

"You tell your men to lower their iron, Morales, or my first shot is going right between your eyes," Sam shouted.

Juan Morales smiled nervously at the sight of Sam's drawn pistols aimed at his head. "Hey, *amigo*, is this a way to act with an old friend?" he cajoled.

"Get back into the cabin," Sam ordered brusquely to Eve and Simone. They responded immediately as Sam cautiously began to back up toward the door. "Close the shutters, and keep away from the window and the door." His gaze never wavered from the sinister figure standing on the hill.

"Why don't you and your men ride away, Morales, while you're still able?" Sam's threat brought an outburst of laughter from the band.

"*Silencio!*" Morales barked. He knew Sam Montgomery did not issue idle threats, and now regretted the decision to take Sam alive; he should have shot him down the moment Montgomery stepped outside. The idea of inflicting a slow, painful death to this hated enemy had been too appealing to the sadistic renegade.

When Sam heard the shutters slam shut, he threw himself through the cabin door. A fusillade of bullets smacked into the wall. "Stay down," he ordered, kicking the door shut and jamming a bar across it. In a low crouch, he hurried over to the bunk and quickly pulled away the loose logs in the wall. "You've got to get out of here."

"But how?" Eve asked breathlessly. Although

the firing had stopped, her heart was pounding furiously.

"Come out, *amigo*," the bandit leader called out. "We'll have a drink together for old times and then you can ride away. All we want is the women."

Sam grabbed the lariats used to tie the packs on the mule, which were still clutched in Simone's hand. He began knotting the ends of the ropes together. "How do I know you won't kill me?" he yelled to Morales as he anchored the rope to the bunk and dropped the loose end through the hole in the wall.

"Kill you? Why would I kill you, *amigo*? We're old friends." His voice betrayed his words.

Inside the cabin Sam issued final orders to Eve and Simone. "Listen carefully. When you get to the bottom, head into the trees. Find a hiding place and stay put. They'll never figure you went out through the back because of the cliff, and it would be risky for them to waste time looking for you up here."

What he left unsaid was that there was about to be a gunfight, the shots would attract attention, and the gang would hastily depart once they saw the women were not in the cabin. "After you hear them ride away, head west. You'll cross the trail heading back to Sonora."

Outside, Morales was getting impatient. "Why should you die, *amigo*, for the sake of two white *putas* who think they're too good to spread their legs for you? You know none of these *gringas* like half-breeds any more than they like Mexicans."

"Get going," Sam said to the women. "I'll stall them as long as I can."

Simone's eyes widened with panic as the significance of his plan penetrated her fright. "Stall them? You can't stay behind, they'll kill you."

"You've got to get into the trees before . . . before the firing stops, or they'll spot you." Sam checked the chambers of his pistols and then slid them back into the holsters. "Okay, get going! They're not going to wait much longer."

The tears ran down Simone's cheeks as she flung herself into his arms, sobbing against his chest. "No, I'm not going."

Sam tipped up her chin and tenderly smiled down into her eyes. "You're the best thing that ever happened to me, mouse."

"Don't make me go, Sam. I'm begging you. I love you. I can't leave you."

"Why can't you come with us, Sam?" Eve pleaded, wiping her own eyes on her sleeve.

"There isn't time. Your only hope is if they don't know where you are. They'll be coming through the door in a few minutes if I don't get out there. Do you want them to see the hole and the rope?"

In her anxiety, Simone could not consider her own welfare. "Then let them rape us, as long as they don't kill you."

Sam drew a shuddering breath. "There are at least a dozen of those bastards out there and they are animals. You'd both be dead before they all finished with you."

As if to augment Sam's statement, another chilling warning sounded from Morales. "My men are getting restless, Sam. Many have been a long time without a woman."

Sam leaned down and kissed Simone, then gazed for several seconds into her upturned face, now streaked with tears. "You're beautiful, mouse." He kissed her swiftly. "Get her out of here, Eve."

Eve took Simone's arm. "Come on, honey. I won't leave without you."

Simone was choked with heartache as they forced her to crawl through the hole. Still sobbing, she began to lower herself on the rope. Eve waited anxiously until Simone was halfway down. Her eyes were brimming again with tears when she stole a final look at Sam. This was her brother about to die for them! She should have told him; she dared not in these final moments together.

Eve leaned over and kissed his cheek. "God bless you, Sam. I love you."

He nodded. "One favor, Eve. Go back to Rawlins."

"I will, Sam. And I promise you that I will always take care of Simone."

Sam nodded in gratitude. "Get going, Eve." He went to the window and opened the shutter a crack as Eve began to lower herself down the rope. "Hey, Morales. How can I be sure you won't gun me down if I come out?"

Trying to convince Sam of his sincerity, the

bandit leader cautiously stepped out from behind the rock. "Have we not ridden together, *amigo*?"

"Yeah, we've ridden together, Morales. But I heard that you've sworn to cut out my heart and eat it for killing Diego."

He closed the shutter and hurried back to peer through the hole. Eve had reached the foot of the cliff. Sam quickly freed the rope from the cot, threw it out the hole, and shoved the logs back in place. They needed a few more minutes. Just a few more minutes.

"That was just in the heat of anger," Morales called out. "You killed my brother in a fair fight."

"That's right, Morales. I let Diego draw on me first. I've been thinking about your offer. These women aren't paying me enough to die for them. You get my horse up to this cabin and I'll come out."

The smile remained fixed on the bandit leader's face, but his eyes glinted with anger. He was looking forward to killing the half-breed. He hated Indians as much as he hated the *gringos*. "Don't you trust Juan Morales?"

"Sure, I trust you, Morales, as long as I'm facing you."

Morales' jaw hardened and his eyes gleamed with fury. He turned to one of his men crouched nearby. "Take the breed his horse. When he comes out, shoot him."

"But, *jefe*, he could kill me first."

"I will kill you quicker if you don't move," he growled.

The luckless man slunk away to where the horses were tethered, as the bandits began to step out from their hiding places. All were anxious to get to the women.

Sam watched the Mexican approach with the horse. He figured the women should have reached the cover of the trees by now. Morales was still standing confidently by the rock. Sam drew his pistols and stepped through the door. Immediate blasts of fire followed.

The hapless fool had gotten himself between Sam and the line of fire. Sam's horse and the bandit leading it, toppled to the ground, struck by a hail of bullets from behind. Sam dove for cover behind the fallen horse, but not before a bullet struck his leg. His first shot knocked the sombrero off the head of Morales, but the bandit leader succeeded in scrambling for safety behind the boulder. Sam emptied his pistols into the bandits closest to him.

His rifle was in the scabbard on the dead horse. Sam pulled it free, but took a bullet in his left shoulder. He was able to pick off two more with the rifle as they scattered for cover. The whole exchange had taken only thirty seconds.

He reloaded his pistols while the bandits regrouped. Bleeding from his shoulder and leg, Sam knew his position was vulnerable if they rushed him from all three sides.

There were at least four men on the ground, but he knew that when the remaining men charged, he wouldn't have a chance of getting all of them.

As he expected, they came at him from three directions. Sam began firing as rapidly as possible with both pistols. Two more of the bandits went down. His guns were empty when a bullet struck his head.

Eve's hands were stinging from rope burns. She blew on them to try to soothe them. "Come on, Simone, we must hurry." She grimaced with pain when she clasped Simone's hand to run into the cover of the trees.

Simone was weeping openly and stumbled along behind her. Eve had to fight to keep the brokenhearted woman on her feet. She would have liked to stop to comfort her, but there wasn't time to stop. Sam had emphasized the importance of getting as far away as possible.

Once in the cover of the thick pines and oaks that lined the mountains, Eve stopped to try and get her bearings. Sam said to head west. *Damn it, which direction was west*? Eve had no idea which way to go, so she tugged at Simone's hand and they continued their flight.

The first sound of gunfire reverberated through the mountains like the crack of lightning. Simone froze in her tracks with a cry of despair. She dropped to her knees and buried her face in her hands. Eve could not contain her own tears and knelt down beside her, gathering her in her arms. She rocked her back and forth, but there were no words of comfort to offer her.

The repeated sound of the gunfire seemed to go on endlessly. As long as it continued, Eve knew Sam was alive. Simone's body jumped and recoiled at the sound of each blast.

Suddenly, all was still. The deafening silence closed around them in a suffocating mantle. Simone raised her head in anguish. "No! No!" she cried aloud.

Eve tried not to succumb to her friend's despair. "Come on, honey, we must go on. We owe it to Sam."

She pulled Simone to her feet and for several seconds looked about hopelessly. Then clasping Simone's hand, she began to run.

They had not gone far when Eve stumbled over a rock and fell. She rose to her feet, clutching her ankle in pain. "Damn!" The pain intensified when she attempted to put any weight on the foot.

Eve slumped down and leaned back against an oak tree. "Simone, I've hurt my ankle. I'll have to rest it. Go on without me and I'll catch up with you."

Eve's predicament had a calming effect on Simone's shattered emotions. "I'm not going on without you. I won't leave you, *chérie*."

"Well, we can't stay here. We're too much in the open. If those bandits figure out where we've gone, they'll follow." Eve looked around for some place to hide. Except for the trees, there was nothing insight. *The trees are our only refuge*.

She glanced above at the overhanging branches and sat up suddenly as a solution became apparent. "The tree. We'll climb the tree and hide in the branches."

Simone, the taller of the two, tried to reach the lowest branch. It was out of her grasp. After several unsuccessful attempts at jumping to reach it, she gave up. "I'm afraid it's too high."

"What if I stood on your shoulders?"

"It might work, *chérie*."

Eve slipped off her boots and Simone knelt down. Using the trunk of the tree for support, Eve climbed on Simone's shoulders. Her sore ankle was throbbing, but she managed to stand on it long enough for her fingers to reach the branch. She got a firm hold on the limb and pulled herself up.

Simone handed up her boots. She anchored them firmly in a bough and reached to help Simone.

Eve lifted as Simone braced her feet against the trunk and climbed. "I'm glad you're so light," Eve huffed breathlessly when Simone was firmly entrenched beside her. "As soon as I get my breath, we'll go higher so they can't see us." As much as she would have preferred to stay barefoot, Eve put on her boots. Her ankle was tender but the injury did not seem to be serious. They worked their way higher up the tree.

"How will we ever get down?" Simone asked, peering below them. The ground appeared so far away.

"We'll figure something out," Eve reassured her.

They had firmly anchored themselves onto a

solid limb when the sound of gunfire split the air. It startled them, and they clung to each other.

Simone's eyes opened wide with renewed hope. "Is that coming from the cabin?"

"I can't tell." Eve listened as more shots were fired in rapid succession.

"What do you suppose it means? Do you think Sam is still alive?"

She shook her head hopelessly and reached for Simone's hand.

Like condemned felons awaiting a firing squad, they remained silent, lost in the gloomy abyss of their thoughts. Two women, each yearning for just one last moment—one last opportunity, to reach out and caress the face of the man they loved.

CHAPTER TWENTY-THREE

When his eyes opened, Sam was lying on the ground at Morales' feet in excruciating pain. His head felt as if it were on fire.

The bandit leader's eyes blazed with hate and his mouth slashed into a snarl. "So, you are not dead, *amigo*. I am glad I am not robbed of the pleasure of killing you myself. I shall see that you die screaming, but not until you have the pleasure to see how well we take care of your women."

A couple of men came out of the cabin shaking their heads in disbelief. "The women are not there, *jefe*."

Morales was wild with fury. "*Imposibilé*. They are hiding. Look for a trap door in the floor, you fools." He glared down at Sam. "Where are the women?"

Sam gritted his teeth in pain as Morales

kicked his wounded leg. For several seconds he hovered on the brink of unconsciousness.

When a second search failed to produce the women, the bandit leader raged out of control. "You crazy idiots! There is only one door. One window. Did you see them leave? No! They are there!"

He lashed back in fury at Sam. "Tie him to a tree. He'll tell me or I'll cut out his tongue."

Two of the outlaws grabbed Sam by the arms, dragging him on his stomach. Yanking him to his feet, and wrenching his arms behind him, they tied him to a nearby tree.

Morales advanced on him with a drawn knife. "Now, *amigo*, tell me where those women are."

Sam raised his head, focusing his eyes on the face of his crazed captor. Morales' extreme wrath at losing the quarry brought a grin of victory to Sam's tortured face. "Where you can't get them, Morales."

With a malevolent snarl, the bandit leader grabbed a fistful of Sam's hair and yanked his head. "Hold him. Hold his head. I want his tongue." Two of the bandits grabbed Sam's head and forced his mouth open as Morales raised his knife.

His hand froze in midair as a shot rang out. The bandit leader's eyes widened in astonishment. The knife dropped to the ground, his arm remaining upright, until suddenly he pitched forward. He was dead before he hit the ground.

The two men holding Sam's head released their grip and turned to run. A second shot rang out. One man fell to the ground. Still running, the other dropped cold when a third blast knocked him off his feet.

The remaining three bandits broke for their horses with a barrage of bullets kicking up the dust at their heels as they rode off in a flurry of flying hooves.

Cautiously, Adam Rawlins stepped out from a nearby concealment.

After making certain the three men were dead, he rushed over to Sam. Adam flinched when he saw the blood dripping down from Sam's head wound and the saturated shirt and trouser leg. The wounded man was barely conscious. He held on to Sam as he cut the ropes that bound him.

"Jesus, Sam, can you make it to the cabin?"

The wounded man's strength was waning rapidly from the loss of blood, but with Adam's help he struggled the few feet to the cabin, collapsing on the floor.

"What happened to the girls?" Adam asked frantically when he discovered they weren't in the cabin.

"Hiding . . . trees at foot . . . of cliff," Sam muttered, before losing consciousness.

Adam quickly cut apart a blanket and made a compress to stop the bleeding in Sam's shoulder. He wrapped another one around the man's leg and head. After covering him, he couldn't do any more at the moment. *He had to find Eve and Simone.*

Despite a disregard for caution, Adam lost

precious time as he skidded recklessly down the steep hill. Once at the bottom, he stopped to think which way they might have gone. It could have been any direction. Common sense told him, west. Then he remembered that Sam said they were hiding. But where?

Adam cupped his hands to his mouth. "Eve! Simone!" His shouts got no response. After going a short distance he called out louder. "Eeeve . . . Simooone . . . Can you hear me? It's Adam."

He swung around in relief at the plaintive cry of "Adam" coming from his left. When he called out again, the reply sounded nearer. Eve's voice was guiding him in the right direction, but he still could not see them.

"Eve, where the hell are you?" Adam shouted.

"Look up. We're up here." She peered down at him incredulously. "Is it really you, Adam?"

Adam looked up and saw the two women sitting on the tree limb. "Thank God you're both safe."

"I don't think we can get down," Eve replied.

Adam shook his head in disbelief. "How did you get up there?"

"I stood on Simone's shoulders and then helped her to climb up."

"Hold on to the branch, swing your legs down, then let go. I'll catch you. But be careful. Get a good hold on the branch," he cautioned. Simone asked anxiously, "Sam? Did you find Sam?" At Adam's nod, she asked softly, "Is he alive?"

"He was when I left him, but I don't know for how long."

"I'm coming down," Simone cried without hesitation, lowering herself as directed and dropping into his arms. As soon as her feet touched the ground, she raced back toward the cabin.

Eve followed her lead and dropped into Adam's arms. He didn't release her. She clung to him with her arms around his neck, laughing and crying as she buried her head against his chest.

"You're safe now, sweetheart," Adam crooned, covering her face with quick kisses.

Eve raised her head and for a breathless moment their eyes locked in an age-old message of love. Then Adam kissed her passionately. Forgotten was the terror she had just endured, her reason for leaving him, her concern for Sam—everything except how much she needed this man. All she remembered was that, in her moment of hopelessness, she had yearned for one final glimpse of him.

"Thank God you're not harmed," he murmured huskily. "We'll talk later, we must get back to Sam." He reluctantly lowered her to the ground. Eve winced, and he clasped her shoulders in alarm. "Are you hurt?"

"Just my ankle. It's not serious. I think I sprained it."

Adam picked her up and carried her in his arms. He hurried through the trees.

"Adam, how bad is Sam?"

"I can't say. He's lost a lot of blood. I don't know if he'll make it."

"He was so courageous. Simone is in love with him, and her heart will break if she loses him."

Further conversation was impossible. It took all his breath and energy to scale the hill. The heat of the sun made the climb all the more difficult. When he reached the top, Adam was breathless and was forced to put her down.

Eve leaned her head against his chest, and as her eyes closed in weariness, he picked her up and carried her to the door of the cabin. Adam put her down gently, but Eve was startled by the pain in her ankle. Then, repelled, her eyes opened wide at the sight of the dead horse in front of the door. "Good God," she gasped. "Sam's horse, too." Adam hurriedly drew her into the cabin and closed the door.

When they entered, Simone was kneeling by Sam. She looked up at them with tears in her eyes. "He's unconscious. What can we do for him, Adam? Please, please don't let him die."

Adam knelt down to check Sam's breathing, then rose to his feet. "The first thing we must do is cut away his clothes and determine the extent of his wounds. We'll need some hot water. Get some boiling while I get my horse. I have medical supplies in my pack."

After he disappeared through the door, Eve kneeled beside Simone. She put her arm around her friend's shoulder. "He'll pull through, honey. I know he will. Sam's strong."

Simone's chin quivered as she tried to return Eve's smile. "But look at him, Eve. There's so much blood. He's so pale." She stroked his forehead and leaned down, placing a light kiss on his lips.

Eve gave her another reassuring hug and rose to her feet. She limped to the fireplace. "I'll get the water boiling." Simone got up slowly and began to remove Sam's boots.

Adam returned, leading their horses as well as his own. He brought in all their packs. Simone dug through hers and grabbed a slip to rip up for bandages.

She sponged the blood off Sam's face and head as Adam cut away the bloody clothing. They were relieved to see that the bullet had only grazed Sam's scalp, but the wound had caused a great deal of bleeding.

The bullet that struck his leg had left an ugly gash, but had not lodged in the flesh or broken a bone. It too had bled profusely.

The wound to his shoulder was more serious. The bullet was still entrenched and would have to be removed.

"He's too weak and he's lost too much blood to try and get that bullet out now," Adam cautioned. "We've stopped the bleeding, so if he can hang on, there's a good chance he can make it. The only thing we can do is keep him warm and pray that he has the strength to stay alive. He must not get chilled. We'll watch him in shifts through the night."

"That won't be necessary. I'll stay with him,"

Simone insisted. Adam nodded, sensing her anxiety. He knew it would be useless to argue with her.

Since there was nothing else she could do for Sam, Eve occupied herself by making a pot of coffee and frying salt pork and beans.

Simone accepted a cup of hot coffee, but declined the plate of food. She stayed at Sam's side, keeping a bedside vigil.

"What happened to the bandits?" Eve asked when Adam was able to wrap her ankle. When he finished, the two of them sat down on the floor in front of the fireplace to eat their meal.

"They took off. They won't be back."

They sat in silence for several minutes until Eve asked, "How did you know where to find us?"

"This cabin is on the map to Bailey Montgomery's mine."

"You mean you have a copy of the map to Bailey's claim?"

"Sam left me a copy."

Eve frowned, confused. "Why would Sam leave you a copy of the map to Bailey's mine?"

Adam shrugged his shoulders. "Why wouldn't he? It was a perfectly logical thing to do. He knows I have more than a casual interest in you." Adam put aside his plate. "I've got to tend to the horses and get more wood for the fire."

Eve began to clean the dishes. By the time Adam returned, she had put the cabin in as orderly fashion as possible and had made a soft pallet in front of the fire. "Simone, won't you just lie down in the bunk for a few moments? I will watch Sam."

"No. You and Adam go to sleep."

"Eve is right, Simone. There's nothing more anyone can do for him right now. Why don't you lie down and try to get just a couple hours of rest?"

"I will later, Adam. I know I couldn't sleep right now."

Since nothing would be gained by insisting, Adam lay down on the pallet. "Come on, honey, get some rest."

Eve sat down reluctantly beside him. "I feel guilty about going to sleep while Simone sits up watching Sam."

"Eve, it's something she must do. She can't help it. You said yourself, she's in love with him."

Eve lay back and Adam put an arm around her, gathering her to his side. She curled against him. "Oh God, Adam, I hope he makes it," she whispered.

Adam watched a slight smile dance across her face. "What can you find to smile about at a time like this?"

"Sam's in love with Simone, too," she whispered softly to him. "Isn't that wonderful."

"It will be, if he pulls through. Otherwise, it's going to be tragic."

"He's going to make it. I know he will," she said emphatically, resting her head on his chest.

Eve was drifting into the mellow state that comes just before slumber. She thought of the baby she was carrying. "I have something to tell you, Adam. We'll talk in the morning," she sighed, surrendering to sleep.

Eve awoke just before dawn and sat up. There was no sign of Adam. Simone had finally fallen asleep, curled up next to Sam. Eve got up to cover her and check Sam. Simone had a blanket firmly tucked around him.

She stepped outside in search of Adam and, by the dim light of the moon, moved skittishly to get around the dead horse, which was frozen in rigor mortis, blocking the front of the cabin door.

Eve made a big circle around the animal and continued a few yards when she stopped, squinting at what appeared to be a hump on the ground before her. She moved cautiously to it and bent over the strange form.

In horror, her eyes riveted on the grizzly sight of a dead man. Revolted, she quickly backed away from the corpse, and in the haste of panic tumbled backwards—over another body.

Eve clamped a hand over her mouth to stifle her scream and scrambled to her feet. Sweeping the area, her eyes spotted more of the grim shapes lying about. She sped back to the cabin.

She was trembling uncontrollably and forcing back the bitter taste of bile in her throat. Shortly later Adam came in carrying his rifle. At the sight of her stricken face, he looked in alarm at Sam. "Is it Sam? Is he . . . ?"

Eve shook her head. "No . . . no, it's not Sam."

Adam gathered her into his arms. "What is it, sweetheart?"

Eve closed her eyes momentarily, savoring the protective safety of his arms. Adam's arms. Strange how they had become a haven to her. He stroked her head as if she were a child. "Tell me, Eve. What is it?"

The words came in ragged release. "I went to look for you . . . and I saw . . . more than . . . a dead horse. Bodies . . . dead bodies . . . everywhere. And I . . . fell over one, Adam."

He hugged her tighter and pressed his cheek against her head. "Oh, God, Eve. Why didn't you just call out to me? I was looking for scavengers I heard prowling around out there."

She burrowed deeper against his chest. "So many bodies . . ."

"It's okay, baby. Remember, there was a gunfight here."

Eve began to relax in the comfort of his arms. "I know, I wasn't thinking. It was just a sudden shock." She looked up at him in anguish. "There's so many of them."

Adam's gaze was warm with understanding. "But, thank God, love, one of them isn't Sam."

Simone awoke and sat up groggily. "What's wrong, Eve?"

Adam dropped his arms, releasing her. "Nothing, Simone, she just had a nightmare. Go back to sleep."

Simone placed a hand on Sam's brow. "Sam's warm, but he doesn't feel feverish." She slipped her arm across his chest and laid down her head.

Eve returned to the pallet and watched as Adam piled more wood on the fire. "Go back to sleep," he said. "It will soon be dawn. We need more wood." He left the cabin.

Staring into the fire, Eve rested her head on her propped-up knees. Sleep was out of the question. Adam was right. The day had been nothing but a nightmare. Hopefully, it would soon be over.

Her gaze swung to the woodpile, and quizzically she raised her head. Adam had filled the woodpile before he went to sleep, and there was still plenty remaining.

When the scraping sound began outside, Eve knew it came from a spade, not an axe. Unable to believe the bizarre events that had unfolded, she remained motionless, staring into the fire and listening to the steady rhythm of the spade.

CHAPTER TWENTY-FOUR

In the morning, the only sign of the gunfight was the wounded man lying in the cabin. Adam had worked throughout the night digging a hole out of sight of the cabin to bury the bodies. He even had hitched up a team and dragged away the carcass of the dead horse.

Eve stepped outside in the bright light of the sun and saw no evidence of the previous day's slaughter. She strolled down to the river that flowed near the cabin, and knelt down on the bank to fill the bucket. When she finished, she stopped to splash some water on her face.

Icy and pure, the stream originated in the snowy peaks above. She dipped her head and drank deeply of the invigorating liquid.

"Don't swallow too much cold water at one time or you'll get a stomach ache."

She looked up, surprised to find Adam standing above her. He had been sleeping when she left the cabin.

"That's what I missed most in these past weeks, my darling. Your standing over me with a list of dos and don'ts. Sam isn't half the taskmaster you are."

Adam chuckled warmly and reached down a hand to pull her to her feet. "I thought you might have missed this as well, because I sure as hell did." He gathered her in his arms and his head dipped, his mouth claiming hers.

Eve slipped her arms around his neck and clung to him, returning his kiss with all the pent-up passion she had struggled to suppress the past weeks.

"I guess I missed that, too," she acknowledged with a throaty sigh.

Adam kissed her again, his hands sweeping her spine in a familiar route as the kiss deepened. When it ended, she remained clinging to him, her arms around his neck. "Oh, Eve," he sighed deeply, "running off into these hills was the damndest, most stupid, headstrong thing you've ever done."

"Regardless, my love, it doesn't change the fact that your actions were just as irresponsible."

"I know, honey, and I'm not proud of them. Sometimes people allow themselves to get squeezed into a corner, when actually a door was open to them all along."

Still not relinquishing her hold around his neck, Eve grinned up at him. "That sounds very profound, Adam, but I'm afraid it's much too early in the morning for me to decipher its meaning. Are you saying you make life more difficult than it has to be?"

Her arms slid off his shoulders and Eve sat down, leaning back against the trunk of a huge oak. Adam lowered himself beside her. "Just because I love you and can't bear to live without you does not exonerate your guilt. You were wrong, Adam. You had no right to deny me the truth about my father and brother."

"I'm not disputing that, Eve. But I did have a reason for denying you that truth."

"I've heard so many of your reasons, I have a hard time blindly accepting your judgment. I want to decide for myself."

"And if I swear to you, by all that's holy to me, that I will never deceive you again, will you believe me, and not go running off in the blink of an eye?"

For several moments she gazed into his eyes, seeking the truth of his words. "I believe you, Adam."

"And your promise?"

"I'm sorry. I can't make such a promise now."

"I see." Adam turned away displeased.

"Once Sam is back on his feet—"

"Honey, face the fact that Sam may not pull through this. He's been shot up pretty bad."

"I know he's going to make it. I believe that everything happens for a reason, Adam. A divine purpose." She reached out and clasped his hand between her own.

"If I wouldn't have left Sacramento, Simone would never have met Sam. However, that might not have altered the fact that Sam would have been here yesterday when those bandits attacked. But, *I did* leave Sacramento; she *did* meet Sam. Then, if I wouldn't have come here with them, Simone would have stayed with Sam yesterday, so they both would be dead today. And why? Because *you wouldn't have followed me to appear on the scene to save them*. Do you see what I mean?"

Eve raised a pointed finger to emphasize her meaning. "That is why I am now convinced that Sam will pull through. If he died there would have been no purpose to all that has preceded." She sat back with a pleased smile, convinced of her own logic.

"My beloved wife, that is the most simplistic interpretation of destiny that I have ever heard. You have entirely closed your mind to allow for modifying ingredients which change the whole scenario."

Adam held up his hand to cut her off when Eve started to interrupt. "But since you do believe that fate makes all things attributable, then obviously my lying to you has to be part of the divine purpose."

Now Adam sat back smugly, certain that Eve had backed herself into the corner he had just squeezed out of. He tried not to smile as he watched her expressive face struggling with his theory.

Finally, Eve's face contorted into an adorable frown, and she jumped up. "Well, that's just the confusing part that I have yet to figure out."

Suppressing his amusement, Adam shook his head indulgently and rose to his feet, picking up the water bucket. He slung his arm around her shoulders as they strolled back to the cabin.

When they entered they saw that Sam had regained consciousness. Simone was holding up his head, trying to get him to swallow water. His eyes met Adam's in unspoken appreciation. "So, I didn't imagine it." Then with a feeble grin, he added, "I thought you would never show up. Where in hell were you?"

Adam was relieved that Sam was strong enough to banter. "Listen, partner, I might have missed the start of the ball, but at least I was on my feet for the last waltz."

He leaned down. "How are you feeling, Sam?"

"Like I've been run over by a herd of buffalo. My head feels bigger than my body, and, God . . . I think somebody stoked a fire in my shoulder."

"The bullet is still there, Sam."

Their eyes met in understanding of the ordeal ahead. "Then let's get it over with."

"You've lost a lot of blood. You should get some of your strength back first."

"I'm not going to get any stronger with a damned bullet sucking my strength. Now's as good a time as any."

Adam nodded grimly. "Well then, we'll need boiling water. Meantime, get some hot coffee down you."

Adam nodded to Eve, and while she set two pots to boil, he rummaged through his saddlebags and pulled out a bottle of whiskey.

Sam was sitting up with his back against the wall, sipping from the mug of coffee Simone held to his mouth. Adam handed her the bottle, and she started to pour the liquor into the cup.

"Just give me the bottle, mouse," Sam said impatiently.

"No, *bien-amié*, you drink the coffee first," she ordered firmly. He complied, but finally she relinquished the bottle when she was satisfied he would consume no more coffee.

Eve watched them from across the room while she waited for the water to boil. She busied herself tearing the rest of Simone's petticoat into strips for bandages.

When the water was ready, Adam poured some into a basin. "Did you bring along any kind of scissors?" he asked. Eve shook her head.

"Then we'll have to use my Bowie." Her eyes widened with astonishment when he reached to his hip and unsheathed a lethal steel knife, over a foot long. "Here, sterilize the blade."

She grasped the handle gingerly, amazed that Adam owned such a weapon, and dropped it into the boiling water.

Adam lathered his hands and scrubbed them assiduously. Staring into the steaming vessel, she broke the awesome silence. "Do you actually . . . use this, Adam?"

"No, I only carry it because it came with the trousers," he said drolly, trying to ease the tension. "It's only a knife, Eve. You can't get along without one in these mountains."

Still disconcerted, she shook her head. "It surprises me you would have such a thing."

Adam leaned over in a whisper. "You'll find out I have more surprises the next time I get you alone in a bed."

Blushing, she looked up to him in shocked indignation. His brow crooked suggestively; he gave her a devilish grin, turned, and walked away.

Sam had consumed practically the whole bottle of whiskey by the time Adam knelt beside him. "I sought . . . an Injun cudn't hold . . . his likker." Sam's slurred speech and the outlandish smile on his face told the whole story.

Despite her anxiety, Simone's glance shifted to Adam's, and she could not stifle a smile.

"It must be your white blood, Sam," Adam agreed.

Sam took another swallow. "I su . . . shur whish . . . you'd did thsh . . . win I wuz uncon . . . unconshish."

"I think you're going to be, very shortly, Sam." Adam winked at Simone.

Eve came over and waited to hand Adam the knife. Simone took the bottle out of Sam's hand. Adam braced himself for the job ahead, and when he leaned over Sam, there was no longer any levity in his eyes.

He did manage to say, "You know how the saying goes, Sam. This is going to hurt me, more than it does you."

Sam cocked an eye at the distressed face of his beloved. He picked up her hand and squeezed it. "No, itsh gonna hert moush the mosht." His eyes closed and his head slumped down on his chest. Mercifully, he had passed out.

Simone gently laid him back down on the pallet and with trembling fingers, lifted the bloody compress off his shoulder.

The wound was wide. The rifle bullet had torn away a great deal of Sam's flesh. Trying to locate the bullet, Adam probed the opening with the point of the blade. After he found it and withdrew the knife, blood surged from the wound. Eve wiped it away, so he could continue. Once again Adam inserted the blade and pried at the bullet to dislodge it. Finally, after several attempts, he was able to force the piece of metal to the mouth of the wound. Using the blade and his fingers, Adam lifted it out.

After checking to be certain all the bits of material from Sam's shirt were flushed from the wound, he nodded to Simone. She poured the remaining whiskey into the wound, then Adam pressed a compress to Sam's shoulder to stem the flow of blood.

Adam leaned back on his heels. "I think this needs some stitches to keep it from opening." He arched his brow in vague suggestion.

"Which one of you ladies want the pleasure of sewing him up?"

Eve picked up the needle and thread. "My hands are clean. I'll do it."

The slender steel rod slipped through her fingers several times as she plied the needle making tiny, neat stitches to join together the torn skin.

Finally, Eve raised her head and smiled at Simone, who had followed her every move without making a sound. The women's eyes met in understanding, before Simone's face curved into a smile of relief.

The monstrous task was lovingly completed.

Several hours passed. Adam finally convinced Simone that Sam was not unconscious but sleeping off the affects of the whiskey. Although he was still feverish, there was no delirium.

In her concern for Sam, Simone had not eaten and had barely slept for two days. After much cajoling, Eve lured Simone away from Sam's bedside by telling her Sam would be hungry when he awoke.

From the first time Simone sifted flour into a batter, she had enjoyed the culinary arts. The kitchen was a sanctuary to her, a playground to test her skill, which in her heart put her on a par with the girl who had the prettiest face. The challenge of a new recipe generated as much excitement for Simone as a new dress or expensive bauble would do for her peers.

Then Sam Montgomery entered her life. To

demonstrate this skill for him gave cooking an entire new purpose and definition—it became a labor of love.

The reminder that Sam would awake, with a need for this mastery, transformed the timid, demure Mademoiselle Simone Lisle into an agitated, bold, aggressive woman with a mission.

"Adam, go out and shoot a deer," she barked in a crisp command.

Poor Adam, who had just brought a cup of coffee to his mouth, choked and spilled most of the hot liquid down the front of his shirt. "Go out and shoot a deer! My dear Simone, one does not just step out the door and 'shoot a deer.' You have to track one first. They aren't standing around, waiting to be shot."

"How long will that take?" she asked impatiently.

Adam shrugged negligently. "Maybe two or three weeks."

Simone began a rapid fire of French that even Eve couldn't follow. The woman finally slowed her tirade when Adam offered a suggestion.

"How about a couple of trout?"

"*Oui*, that is the answer." She quickly reorganized her course of action and attacked it with fervor.

Simone whisked, skimmed, stirred and sautéed at a speed that left Eve with her mouth agape. Puffs of flour rose into the air in the wake of Simone's feverish pitch. Although Adam was able to produce only one fish, the trout was scraped and filleted with lightning speed. In the evening when Sam awoke, a royal feast was awaiting.

He was too hung over to eat.

This could have been disheartening to a woman of lesser mettle, but not to Simone Lisle. Relief at having her beloved alive and awake outshone any disappointment she felt when he spurned her love's long labor due to a hangover. Besides, she would prepare the whole meal the next day when he would be feeling better.

She returned to her bedside vigil.

That evening, Eve and Adam, prepared to eat a meager meal of beans and salt pork, were treated to a savory onion soup and a baked trout served with a tasty *velouté* sauce.

By the next morning Sam appeared to be on the road to recovery. He ate some hot broth and drank a cup of coffee. Simone's tension subsided along with Sam's fever. When Eve glanced in their direction at midday, she discovered the two of them sleeping contentedly side by side.

Smiling, she stepped outside. She was feeling completely relaxed for the first time since the shooting. She wandered down to Adam, who was sitting near the river bank under a large oak.

"They're both sleeping like babies," she said lightly.

Engrossed in thought, he smiled up at her and rose to his feet. The two of them began to stroll aimlessly. Adam felt there was no better time to express the thoughts that weighed heavily on his mind.

"Eve, as soon as Sam recovers, I would like for us to return to Sacramento."

Eve had anticipated this declaration from the time of Adam's appearance. She stopped and turned to him.

"Adam, don't you understand what it means to me to discover that I have a father? I have to talk to him. Tell him my feelings about it. I haven't even told Sam that I'm his sister, because I wanted to tell them together."

She grasped his hand, her eyes pleading for understanding. "I've come this far, Adam. Please don't make me turn back now."

Adam gathered her into his arms. "I understand, honey, but as soon as you tell them, we will return to Sacramento."

Eve's smile was radiant as she looked up at him. "Oh, Eve. Eve," he whispered huskily. No longer able to deny his needs, he lowered his head.

His lips closed hungrily over hers as their mouths moved on one another's—seeking . . . finding . . . savoring the sweetness. The joining of their lips was a catalyst that set dual fires raging through their bodies. Her arms slipped around his neck, and her soft round contours pressed against the hard muscular length of him.

He rained kiss upon kiss on her mouth, her face, her eyes, until his insistent lips became demanding and the smoldering fires of the past weeks flared into flame. The urgency of their kisses lifted them to a state where time or space were of no consequence; love was the only essential.

They sank to the ground, and with frenzied movements clothing was cast aside, and her rigid breasts thrust upward to meet his descending mouth. When his fingers found the heated honeycomb of her being, Eve groaned, and her body writhed uncontrollably.

"Adam," she whimpered in convulsive sobs, reaching to find him. Her fingers began to arouse him to such rapture that he was unable to discern ecstasy from agony.

He entered her and the tempo of their waltz quickened to a shattering, resounding culmination.

CHAPTER TWENTY-FIVE

After a week of Simone's loving care, Sam was strong enough to travel. Before they left, Adam chopped and stacked a pile of firewood for the next weary travelers who might seek refuge in the cabin.

"I wonder who built the cabin," Eve reflected with a backward glance as they began to ride away.

Adam shrugged, relieved to be under way. He had grown restless in the long delay. "Probably some miner who had a claim nearby."

Eve's eyes widened in surprise. "You mean we might have been sitting on top of a gold mine all this time?"

"I doubt that," Adam scoffed. "The miner would still be around."

"Unless he's dead," Simone intoned with a worried glance at Sam.

That evening they camped in a grove of tall sequoia trees overlooking a vast canyon. As she stood beholding the sight, Eve found herself overwhelmed by the magnitude of the spectacle. The lofty, snow-capped pinnacle of the majestic mountain range rose above them to touch the blue sky. On the opposite wall a magnificent waterfall plunged abruptly down the mile-deep canyon into the river below, where its rushing waters had carved out a spectacular gorge flanked by giant sequoias, sugar pines, and white fir.

When Adam came seeking her, he found Eve sitting in solemn reverence. She took his hand and pulled him down beside her, and in the twilight splendor of the panorama, Eve told him of the child she was carrying.

Simone started to approach the couple, but drew back at the sight of Adam sitting with his arm around Eve. Her face softened into a smile, and Simone's womanly intuition sensed that Eve had chosen this moment to tell Adam about the baby. She returned to the campfire and smiled down lovingly at Sam, unaware of the tears misting her eyes.

Now, aware of her condition, Adam was more solicitous of Eve than ever. He watched her zealously in the following day and a half that it took to reach the mine.

Bailey Montgomery greeted them joyously, although astounded by the appearance of all four of them. The older man did not appear to notice anything unusual about the lengthy embrace Eve bestowed upon him.

After the formality of greetings was exchanged, Adam and Sam wasted no time in examining Bailey's setup. The mine sat at the foot of a rocky crag dotted with scattered shrubs of manzanita and an occasional fir tree. He had fashioned a crude wooden cradle in the nearby river to strain the dirt and gravel he mined.

His efforts had produced several ounces of the precious metal, but the process of digging and scraping the hard quartz, then toting it to the water, was a slow and laborious procedure. By his own admission, most of the gold he produced had been panned directly from the river.

After a thorough examination of this arduous process, Adam finally shook his head. "I'm afraid you're not going to get rich very quickly, Bailey."

Bailey refused to accept such an assumption. "I haven't hit the mother lode, but it's here. I'll reach it soon."

Adam had no intention of arguing with the old man; what Bailey Montgomery did was his own business. Adam was sure the residual would never be worth the back-breaking labor it would take to obtain the gold dust. He hoped Sam and Simone would not waste time and fruitless hope by going along with the old man's scheme. He could hope he was mistaken. He cared about all of them, but the decision was theirs to make.

His concern was for Eve and their unborn baby. As soon as she told all of them what she had come to say, he would take her home.

Eve had been watching Adam closely, and any expectations for sudden wealth died at the sight of him turning and walking away. She had been hoping in her heart for a miracle, no longer for her own sake, but for Simone and Sam. Her future was secure with Adam, but she could not help worrying about what would become of Simone and Sam, drifting from one place to another, unless . . . *unless Sam could be persuaded to return to Sacramento with them. Would having a sister convince him to do so?* The moment had arrived for her announcement.

Eve smiled to herself and took a deep breath. "I want all of you to sit down. I have something important to tell you."

Curious, they all gathered around Bailey's small campfire to listen to Eve's announcement. Adam, suspecting what she was about to say, listened with mixed emotions.

"The first thing I want to say is how grateful I am to Sam and Simone for allowing me to accompany them here. Neither of you questioned my motives nor expected explanations I wasn't ready to offer." She smiled affectionately at them. "You are the dearest friends one could ever hope to have and I love you both."

Eve turned to Adam with love gleaming in her eyes. "Secondly, I want to thank my husband for allowing me to complete this trip. I know my coming here was against his better judgment, but he knew how important it was for me to do so. I love you very much, Adam.''

Adam acknowledged the citation with a slight nod of his head, but the speech was baffling to the others. They waited patiently for Eve to continue.

''The reason it was important for me to continue this journey was because I have finally learned the true identity of my father.'' Smiling through her tears, Eve looked at Bailey. ''I'm your daughter, Bailey.''

Sam had been leaning negligently against a tree. Shocked, he straightened up, and his startled glance swung to Adam for confirmation. He read the truth in the grim line on Adam's face. Simone was too astonished by the revelation to even move.

Uncertain whether Eve was serious or playing a joke, Bailey sat with a bemused grin. Eve flung her arms around him and kissed his cheek. ''Mary MacGregor was my mother, Bailey.''

Tears of happiness were streaking Eve's cheeks as she gazed into Bailey's face. He returned her embrace, but his confusion was obvious to all present, except Eve. The old man shook his head. ''I'm not sure I understand what you're saying, girl.''

Eve was still too emotionally engulfed to sense the real confusion behind the question. ''Father, Mary MacGregor was my mother.''

Bailey's baffled expression remained unchanged, and Eve stood in the circle of his arms, smiling as she awaited the anticipated reaction. It never came. Slowly, realization began to sink in and her arms dropped from his shoulders. She looked at him, stunned. "You don't remember my mother, do you?"

Bailey's face was set in a culpable grin as he shook his head. "I'm sorry, girl. Ah . . . when . . . where . . . ?"

Adam could no longer stand and watch another moment of Eve's agony. He stepped forward and put his hands on her shoulders. "The year was 1830 near Yerba Buena. Mary MacGregor was a Scottish immigrant who had just arrived in this country," he declared in a clipped voice.

"A Scottish girl you say." The old man's face suddenly lit up with comprehension. "Now I remember. Yes, a Scottish girl with black hair—"

"And the blue eyes of a saint," Eve uttered sadly. She turned away and walked to the river.

Bailey turned hopelessly toward the three people staring impassively at him like a jury. "I didn't remember. . . . It was a long time ago. . . . I never knew . . ."

"Nobody's blaming you, Bailey," Adam said stiffly.

The old man bent down and reached for his pick. He was the picture of dejection as he returned to his mine.

Simone started to rise to go to comfort Eve, but Sam stopped her with a restraining hand. Adam was already headed toward the river. "Let him handle this, mouse."

Adam walked up behind Eve and slipped his arms around her waist, drawing her back against him. She leaned into the comforting wall of strength and his arms enfolded her like a protective mantle. He dipped his head and kissed her cheek. "Are you all right, sweetheart?"

Eve closed her eyes as his mouth slipped to her neck to place a light kiss behind her ear. "Yes, I'm fine now." She drew a shuddering breath. "You knew this would happen, didn't you?"

Adam rested his cheek against the top of her head. "I suspected it. Don't judge him too harshly, honey. Bailey's a free spirit. The world needs his kind, too."

Smiling gratefully, Eve turned in his arms. "And what kind of spirit are you, Adam?"

Sensing that her mood was beginning to lighten, Adam grinned down at her. "Oh, I'm just a stodgy old businessman of twenty-nine."

"Stodgy!" Eve's face perked up in protest. "I never once thought of you as *stodgy*, Adam Rawlins. Stubborn, yes, but you are never dull or uninteresting. Furthermore, my darling husband, you are only twenty-eight. Your birthday isn't until—." She broke off her sentence, her expressive face shifting from initial shock to dismay. "Oh, Adam, today is your birthday and I don't have a gift to give you." Eve raised up and kissed him. "Happy birthday, darling." She smiled up at him with loving tenderness.

Adam gathered her closer and gazed down

into the beauty of her upturned face. "You're giving me the only gift I need, my beloved. Your beautiful, beautiful smile."

That night the atmosphere around the camp-fire was a relaxed and happy one as they cele-brated Adam's birthday. With Eve's spirits restored, the tension had eased. She had re-signed herself to accepting the idea that an apathetic father was better than no father at all. She even managed to convey to Bailey, with a pat on the shoulder and an apologetic smile, that all was forgiven. Once Adam and Sam pitched separate tents, a weary but contented group finally retired for the night.

When Eve awoke the next morning, Adam was not beside her. She poked her head out of the tent and there was no sign of him. Dressing hurriedly, she scampered outside.

Adam had managed to scale the crag and was peering over the top in concentration. Eve cupped her hands to her mouth and called to him. "Adam, what are you doing up there?"

He smiled and waved. "Good morning. Stay where you are. I'll be right down."

The others were all at the fire by the time Adam reached the bottom of the cliff. His excite-ment was apparent when he sat down and accepted the mug of coffee Eve handed him. "I think I've figured it out."

Four sets of eyes swung in his direction with curiosity. Finally, Eve voiced the question that was on all their minds. "Figured what out?"

"Where Bailey will find the lode, if there is one."

Bailey Montgomery's eyebrows knit together in a frown. "You know something I don't, son?"

Adam now appeared composed. "Bailey, you told us most of the gold you've gotten was panned out of the river, and you figured it was carried downstream."

The old man nodded toward the flowing water. "Yeah. I even followed it for a while. Man by the name of Jenkins has staked a claim about a mile up from here."

"Has he found very much gold?"

Bailey shrugged. "Says not, or at least he's not saying so if he has."

"What's all this leading up to, Adam?" Sam asked. "Are you suggesting Bailey stop digging and go back to panning the river?"

Adam shook his head. "No, I'm not suggesting he quit digging. I just think he's digging in the wrong spot. I don't believe the gold Bailey got out of the river was washed downstream. I think it came from simple erosion right above our heads." They all raised their heads to look at the overhanging ledge Adam pointed to above them. "Your lode's up there, Bailey, somewhere at the top of that crag."

Eve smiled at him with pleasure and pride. Adam winked at her over the top of his cup, leaned back, and took a deep swallow of the coffee. The others remained staring up at the ledge.

"Short of blasting, how in holy hell could a

person ever get the ore down from there?" Bailey asked. "The hill's too steep to tote anything up or down it."

Adam nodded in agreement. "I've been giving that some thought. There is a way it can be done."

"Well tell us, son, don't just play cat-and-mouse with us," Bailey declared impatiently.

Adam pointed above to a tall pine tree standing near the edge of the ledge. "What if we could rig a pulley with a projecting arm to that pine tree up there. We could swing the arm and lower buckets of ore over the edge and down."

Sam shoved his hat to the back of his head. "Sure would beat toting those buckets down the hill."

Bailey still had reservations. "Where are we going to get a pulley and whatever else is needed to rig what you're suggesting?"

Adam's glance swept the campsite. "What do you have around here that's made of iron?"

Bailey shook his head. "Can't say I've got too much. There's a perforated sheet of iron on the bottom of the cradle." His face twisted in concentration. "Oh yeah, I've got a pry bar made of iron."

Adam's thoughts were already racing. "Do you have an axe?" Bailey nodded. "A hammer and nails?"

"Of course," the miner replied. "How else would I shore up the walls of the mine?"

Adam picked up a stick and began to sketch in the dirt. They all crowded around to peer over his shoulder with avid interest. He glanced up at Bailey. "How far is it to the nearest town?"

Bailey took off his hat and scratched his head. "Can't tell you in miles, but it's about a four-hour ride."

Adam returned to his sketching and finally threw down the stick. "I can't see any way around it. I guess I'll have to go into town."

"Tell me what you need and I'll go," Sam offered. "My shoulder's still too sore to do any heavy lifting right now, but I can run errands."

"That's a good idea," Adam agreed, jumping to his feet. "I'll get the tree sheared off and the post set while you're gone. I'll need a pulley, some hooks, and a couple of eye bolts. Also, get chain if you can find some. If not, we'll make do with rope. And, Sam, bring a couple more buckets, we can always use them."

Sam nodded. "I'll get moving right away. Bailey, draw me a map how to get to this town."

Within minutes Sam was mounted and ready to leave. Adam stopped to converse quietly with him, then pressed some bills into his hand.

"What can we do to help, Adam?" Eve inquired, as soon as Sam had ridden off.

"There's nothing right now. When Sam returns, there'll be plenty to do. Why don't you two women try to catch a couple of fish for supper. Bailey, you can begin to carve out some crude steps to make the climb to the top easier," he asserted in a crisp order.

Adam grabbed an axe to prepare to scale the

craggy hill. Eve stood with her hands on her hips as he walked away. "That's the Adam Rawlins I know and love," she lamented. She turned back to Bailey and Simone. "Well, I guess we've all got our orders for the day." She grinned at Simone. "Looks like we're goin' fishin'."

CHAPTER TWENTY-SIX

Adam spent the rest of the morning stripping the lower twelve feet of the tree of anything that would create an obstacle to the shaft he was devising. He selected a sturdy six-foot limb from the branches he removed to be used as the projecting arm needed for the operation. Adam trimmed it clean, and when he was satisfied with the end result, he joined Bailey to help carve out crude steps up the face of the hill. They succeeded in creating a rough stairway to simplify the steep climb. As a safety precaution, Adam drove several long stakes into the ground and ran a guide rope along the side of the steps to grab in an emergency.

Eve and Simone kept themselves just as busy. After abandoning an unsuccessful attempt at fishing, they devoted their energies to doing the laundry. The two women washed every stitch of clothing in the camp. Flannel shirts, cotton trousers, dimity petticoats, and lace-edged drawers were stretched out on shrubs and bushes, or hung from ropes strung between the trees.

All was in waiting at sundown when Sam rumbled into camp pulling a wagon behind him. The sight was a surprise to all except Adam.

"What is the wagon for?" Eve questioned of Adam. "I can't believe you're so optimistic you plan on hauling away the gold in it."

"Your carriage awaits, my lady," Adam announced with a sweeping bow. "You are not going to do any more horseback riding until after the baby is born," he added in a decisive declaration.

Eve regarded the conveyance with a jaundiced glare. "I hate riding in a wagon."

However, Adam was not about to wilt under the scorching glower. "Not as much as I do, my love, and I'm the one who has to drive it," Adam reminded her.

Further argument on the subject was prevented by Sam's hapless disclosure. "No pulley. No eye bolts. No chain. All I could get in the whole damned town were some buckets, a couple spikes, and a few hooks. Are they any good to us now?"

Adam was not happy with this unexpected setback. He frowned in thought. "The chain is no disaster, we can always use rope. The problem is I need a pulley and a set of eye bolts for the arm." His sweeping glance fell on Eve's tethered horse. Suddenly his face brightened. "Of course! Why didn't I think of it sooner. I'll take the shoes off the roan. Eve won't be riding it anyway."

"Oh no, not my horse!" Eve protested.

"It's only temporary. We can always shoe the damned horse again," Adam announced. "Aren't you the one who wants to find gold?"

"I'm sorry, old boy, but we all must make sacrifices," Eve sighed later, standing like a protective mother with her arms around the horse's neck as she watched Adam remove the animal's shoes.

Long into the night he toiled at the hot fire, hammering and forging the metal shoes into new shapes. Gradually, one by one, the others strayed back to their tents until only Eve remained. She sat engrossed, hugging her knees to her chin and watching Adam's every move with fascination.

When he dropped a piece of the hot metal into a bucket of water, the cold liquid spat and sizzled, forcing a chuckle from her throat.

At the infectious sound Adam glanced up quizzically to meet the amusement dancing in her violet eyes. "I notice that water reacts to you the same way that I often do."

His warm chuckle brought a silent sigh of pleasure from her. "At times you do have a tendency to hiss like an angry cat."

"I thought cats purred," she challenged playfully.

Adam's eyes gleamed roguishly in the glow

from the fire. "They purr real pretty if you stroke them right."

Eve did not fail to miss the intimate innuendo. She blushed and rose to her feet. "I think it's time I go to bed."

"I think so, too. You're beginning to divert the smithy's thoughts from the important task at hand."

He reached into the bucket and removed the cooled piece of metal. The shoe had been forged into a small round wheel with a grooved rim. Adam smiled with satisfaction as he studied the pulley. "This is going to work."

"Thank you, Adam," Eve said softly. He looked bewildered, so she added, "For helping my family."

He grinned crookedly. "I'm only doing it because I always wanted a rich wife."

Eve smiled tenderly, aware of how lightly he regarded his own accomplishments. "I'm sure that had to be the reason why you insisted upon marrying me." Her eyes clouded and the smile left her face. "Adam, are you that certain the lode is up there?"

He looked almost boyish in his intensity. "I've always depended on my gut instincts in business matters, Eve. It's up there."

She raised up on her toes to kiss his cheek. "I hope you're right. Good night, Adam."

The day dawned with Adam ready to assemble the mechanism.

He had shaped two metal rings and interlinked them. As Sam attached one of the rings to the end of the six-foot arm, Adam hooked the pulley to the other end. With Sam and Bailey holding up the long arm, Adam attached the second ring to the tree trunk at a spot above his head.

The two main pieces were in place now and the worst of the job was over. As a necessary support, Adam grabbed a rope he had tied to the unattached end of the projecting arm and wrapped it securely around the tree about twelve feet above the ground. The long arm could now be easily swung back and forth as if on a hinge.

A lengthy guide rope was then wound around a hook, anchored at arm's level in the trunk of the tree. The loose end of the rope was threaded through the pulley and then tied to the handle of a bucket, which Bailey had filled with ore awaiting the trial run.

Adam unwound the rope that was wrapped around the hook, swung the arm out over the rim of the ledge, and released the tension on the rope. Effortlessly, the bucket lowered to the ground without displacing an ounce of the contents.

Bailey emitted a whoop of victory, and a grinning Sam shook Adam's hand. Adam smiled with bemusement. "I'm always amazed. It's one of mankind's most primitive devices, but it's effective."

Below at the foot of the crag, Eve and Simone

had thrown their arms around each other and were cavorting gaily in a circle.

Their gaiety was quickly diminished when the task of screening the dirt and gravel fell to them. With only Bailey's cradle and a flat pan as implements, the chore was a grueling one; both devices were back-breaking and slow.

By day's end Eve's back was aching so badly she could not sleep. Adam, who had worked through the previous night, slept unaware of her plight.

The following morning when he saw her clutch at her back in pain, Adam cursed himself for being ten times a fool. He squared his chin grimly and set about constructing a simple sluice to alleviate the wracking drudgery for the two women.

Sam assisted him in building the long trough used for separating the ore. They each framed-in a twelve-foot section of wood, nailing narrow bars crosswise every half a foot along the bottom of the section. When the two parts were completed, Adam joined them together and they placed the sluice in the river.

The continuous flow of water running through the contrivance flushed away the dirt, and the heavier gold particles were caught by the bars where they lay on the bottom of the box, shining and sparkling like yellow sand. Eve and Simone found this process to be much easier on them and their backs than the cradle or pan.

That is, what gold dust there was to be found.

A three-day effort by five people produced a total of two ounces, for a value of $24. It was disheartening to all of them, especially Adam, who had been convinced about his theory of where to find the gold.

After another two days with similar results, Adam decided to abandon the project. He voiced his decision to Sam as they stood leaning on their picks during a brief rest. Both men were bare-chested, perspiration gleaming on their shoulders and arms. "I told Eve I'm taking her home. We'll be leaving at the end of the week."

Sam nodded. "I've been thinking along the same lines. Leave Bailey to his mine. He can get enough out of here to keep himself in grub. Maybe we'll ride along with you to Stockton."

Adam removed his hat and wiped the sweat off his brow. "That should make Eve happy. She doesn't want to leave any of you. Have you thought about coming to Sacramento, Sam?"

The gunfighter shook his head. "Cities and me don't agree."

Adam continued to earnestly pursue the topic. "I own some good grazing land near the Oregon border. It would make a good spread. Are you interested?"

"Nope. Not interested in anything I can't afford."

"I'm not talking charity, Sam. You work the spread and we'll split the profits fifty-fifty."

Sam was not an easy man to wheedle. He

laughed and shook his head again, declining the offer. "Sure sounds like charity to me."

Adam knew that Sam Montgomery was a proud man. He would not be able to change his mind. "I hate to see you go, Sam. You're a good man to have around." He kicked a rock in frustration. "Damn it! I feel like it's my fault. I would have staked my life we'd find gold up here." He slammed his pick into the ground. Chagrined by his childish outburst, Adam yanked out the pick and started to leave to return to the digging.

"Holy Christ!" Adam turned to see what had caused the exclamation. Sam was staring at the hole Adam had just made with the point of the pick. A golden nugget the size of a melon seed sparkled in the sun.

Without a word, both men knelt down and began to scrape away the surrounding earth with their picks. Their excitement mounted as a narrow golden vein appeared before them. Crawling along, they scraped out a line parallel to the golden streak until it disappeared at the edge of the cliff.

On hands and knees the two men looked at each other with wide grins. Then Sam rose to his feet and emitted a long, shrill whistle.

Below, Eve and Simone raised their heads, shading their eyes to look up at him. "We've found it! We've found the lode!" Sam shouted, waving his hat in the air.

Bailey Montgomery sat below in the sparse

shade of a manzanita shrub. Tears shone in the old miner's eyes as he looked up at the two excited figures on the ledge above.

Any further talk of leaving was forgotten in the face of this latest discovery. Even Adam was not immune to the gold fever that struck all of them. The previous heartless drudgery now took on a shiny new aspect.

A golden shine.

Driven by urgency to pluck the precious mineral out of the ground, they all worked at a punishing pace. By evening, when they were no longer able to see by torchlight, the five people had amassed a hundred ounces of gold.

The following morning the task was resumed with the same intensity. Hot meals were abandoned for a quick snatch of a day-old biscuit or a fast chew on a slice of dried beef.

Adam finally refused to allow Eve to continue and called a halt to the exhausting grind. By then, the mine had produced over fifteen hundred ounces of gold—$18,000 for a week's effort. They decided to bank the gold, so after packing up one of the mules, Bailey and Sam departed for town.

Pulverizing the ore was becoming a problem, so Adam turned his attention toward devising a contraption to speed up the process.

Eve and Simone took advantage of the hot and sunny day to bathe themselves and wash their hair. For the first time in months they both felt free from pressure and worry, able to relax and enjoy each other's company. They laughed and giggled, cavorting like children in the water.

"We have not eaten a decent meal in a week," Simone declared later as she braided her damp hair. "There are still some dried peaches left, I think I will bake a pie."

Eve had different thoughts. "Why don't we try our luck again at fishing? Baked trout would certainly be a pleasant change."

Simone turned up her nose at the suggestion. "Fishing was very boring, *chérie*, but I will try for an hour, then we will just have to settle for a hot pot of beans—"

". . . with salt pork." Eve grimaced.

When they trooped past Adam with poles in hand, he stopped his labor and regarded them with pessimism. "We are going to catch dinner," Eve responded saucily to his skeptical look.

"I hope it's more successful than your last attempt," he gibed with a wry grin.

Eve's bravado quickly dissipated when she was forced to bait the fishing hook. "This is disgusting," she shuddered as she impaled the squirming worm on the hook.

Simone was equally squeamish. "If I lose this worm, I'm not baiting the hook again. Sam spears the fish; we should learn how to fish that way."

After five minutes without a sign of a nibble, Eve glanced grumbling at the sluice. "I think that box is driving all the fish away." She waded further upstream away from the campsite.

Simone followed with less confidence. Finally they found a comfortable spot and sat down on the river bank, letting their poles dangle in the water.

The conversation drifted lazily into the topic of the baby.

"Are you hoping for a boy or a girl?" Simone's face was softened by a wandering thought of how wonderful it would be to have Sam's baby.

"I would like one of each," Eve reflected with a whimsical smile. "Do you think I would be lucky enough to have twins?"

A sudden jerk on her line prevented any further flights of fancy. "I've caught one," Eve squealed with excitement. She pulled in her catch and a big trout dangled from the line.

All of the excitement of success was crushed at the sight of the fish floundering helpless on the ground. The two women stared appalled until the fish ceased thrashing. Their eyes shifted to one another. Repugnance was mirrored on both their faces.

"What should I do with it now?" Eve asked, sickened.

Simone shrugged. "I guess you unhook it."

Clearly abashed, Eve drew back, almost dropping the pole she still grasped in her hand. "I can't. I can't bear to do that."

"If you don't, how can you catch another fish, *chérie*?" Simone asked, with a logic she wasn't feeling.

"I never realized before how brutal the whole

thing is." Eve's face contorted in distaste. "I don't like fishing."

Unable to force herself to unhook it, Eve reached down and gingerly picked up the fish by the tail. When she glanced in revulsion at Simone, the woman was staring transfixed past Eve's shoulder. Eve swung around to see what had caused the woman's alarm. A grizzly bear had come out of the trees and lumbered into the water. Having arrived upwind from them, the bear appeared to be unaware of the two women.

The appalling scene at Sonora flashed through Eve's mind. She screamed at the top of her voice. Emitting a low growl, the bear raised its head and began to lumber toward them. Horrified, Eve reacted by using the first weapon within reach. She threw the fish at the bear, hitting the animal in the face. Then, screaming like a banshee, she grabbed Simone's hand and the two women bolted.

Distracted by the scent of the very thing it had come seeking, the bear snatched up the fish.

Absorbed in his newest project, Adam had been unaware the women had strayed so far until he heard the sound of their screams. He swung around startled, then grabbed his rifle and raced along the river bank in the direction of their cries. Eve and Simone came dashing toward him as if the hounds of hell were yapping at their heels.

After listening to their tale of terror, he quickly dispatched them to camp and cautiously

approached the area the girls had just abandoned. The bear was plodding off into the trees
with the fish in its mouth and the pole dragging
behind. Daring not to leave the women unprotected, Adam returned to camp.

Later, when Sam and Bailey returned, the
three men alternated guard duty throughout the
night in the event the bear would return and
wander into their camp. The following morning
Adam and Sam tracked the bear until it became
obvious the animal had left the area.

The incident convinced Adam that Eve had to
learn how to use a pistol for her own safety. His
efforts met with little success. Eve could no
longer stomach the thought of even catching a
fish, much less point a pistol with the intent to
kill. She was uncooperative in the attempt, and
after about fifteen minutes, Adam lost his patience with her. "You're being immature, Eve.
No one should be in these mountains without
knowing how to fire a pistol." He stormed away
angrily.

They now could return all their efforts toward
mining the gold. In Sam's and Bailey's absence,
Adam had rigged a crude grinding mill. Two
abrasive stones crushed the ore, propelled by a
mule hitched to an axle and driven around in a
circle.

In the beginning the mine was producing
about three hundred ounces of gold a day. After
a month of steady mining, the precious mineral
supply was practically exhausted, but they had

mined another $150,000 worth of gold dust, flakes, or nuggets.

They dared not keep such a large quantity of gold on hand, so another trip to town was necessary. In her condition, Eve preferred to remain in camp resting, instead of making the trip joggled about in the wagon, which was the only thing Adam would allow her to ride. Naturally, Adam would not consider leaving her. This time Simone decided to accompany Sam to town.

"Don't expect us back tonight," Sam declared as they rode off leading the mule.

Watching their departure, Adam decided that with Eve now six months pregnant, they could no longer delay their return to Sacramento. He made up his mind that they would leave as soon as the couple returned, no matter how much Eve protested.

CHAPTER TWENTY-SEVEN

Paddy was typical of the many mining towns that had sprung up in the gold fields. It stood on a narrow gulch near the rich diggings of the Tuolumme River.

The town started after Ian and Fiona Campbell came to California from a small village in the Grampian Mountains of Scotland. They soon got lucky and made a moderate strike. When news of their good fortune spread, other miners converged on the area. Being of frugal and judicious stock, the Campbells had taken their newly acquired assets and opened a mercantile store. Fiona operated the store while Ian continued to work his claim. She took in more gold daily than Ian could pan.

Cabins and shacks sprang up around them, and soon the Campbells expanded their store to include a saloon, then a hotel. They named the sprawling settlement Paddockhaugh after their native village in Scotland. However, the miners got into the habit of abbreviating the name to Paddy, so that when the boundaries were officially registered, Paddockhaugh was founded simply as Paddy.

By the time Ian's mine ran out, the town boasted the services of a doctor, blacksmith, pharmacist, minister, and even a bank. Tents and shanties still constituted many of the town's houses and businesses, but the settlement of Paddy had blossomed into a full-fledged community.

The small town attracted its typical share of prospectors, gamblers, renegades, and drunken drifters—immigrants and native Americans alike, with resulting clashes of ethnic cultures and prejudices. But they were Argonauts all in search of the pot of gold at the end of the rainbow, and they used whatever methods it took to obtain it.

As Sam and Simone neared the outskirts of the town, she reined up in shock. "Oh, dear God. Those poor men."

The cause of her dismay was the sight of two Chinamen hanging by their long queues on the back of their heads from a rope strung between two trees. Several drunken ruffians were enjoying themselves by pushing the two men back and forth as if they were children on a swing. The poor Orientals struggled to ease their torture, much to the further amusement of their tormentors.

Sam dismounted and pulled out his knife.

"Hey, what are you doing?" one of the men grumbled. He was a tall, heavy-set man, built like a bull, with an unkempt black beard covering his face. Sam recognized the man as Jake Bledsoe, a horse trader with a notorious reputation for dishonesty.

"Fun's over, Bledsoe." Sam sliced the rope and the Chinamen dropped to the ground. They quickly freed themselves and scurried away without looking back.

"Keep your nose out of things that don't concern you, Montgomery," Bledsoe snarled, and he staggered to his tethered horse. The rest of his motley companions followed.

Simone was shaking with relief when the men rode away in a cloud of swirling dust. "Who were those men, Sam?"

"Just some troublemakers, mouse."

"I wonder what those Chinamen did to them?"

"Probably nothing. Bullies pick on people who can't fight back. Bledsoe is the worst kind."

Simone shuddered in revulsion, shaking her head in disbelief. "I don't understand how they get away with it. Doesn't anyone try to stop it?"

"Men like Bledsoe always play with the odds in their favor, mouse." Sam swung into his saddle. "Let's get going. A hot bath and a clean bed are waiting just for us."

Simone put the unpleasant incident aside and allowed her thoughts to dwell on the bath she was going to enjoy as soon as they deposited the gold.

When they had finished at the bank, Sam registered them at the hotel, then left Simone to her bath. He took the horses and mule to the stable.

The first person he saw there was Jake Bledsoe. This time the scoundrel was negotiating the sale of a dapple-gray mare. Sam began to unsaddle their horses in the next stall. The buyer of the horse handed Bledsoe a wad of bills, then turned and saw Sam.

"Senor Sam," he called out with pleasure.

"Rico? Rico Estaban!" Sam was astounded. The two men shook hands. Enrico Estaban was the son of a Spanish don for whom Sam had once worked near Los Angeles, when the man's ranch was terrorized by Mexican bandits. *"Como esta usted, amigo?"*

The two men began to converse rapidly in Spanish to the obvious displeasure of Bledsoe. He stormed away impatiently without giving Estaban his change or a bill of sale.

"And how is the don?"

"Not well, Sam. But he still rides each day."

Sam nodded in understanding, visualizing the proud, obstinate old man. "What brings you this far north, Rico? You're a long way from home."

"I've come seeking my brother Pedro. He and Father quarreled when Pedro left to search for gold." The young man's eyes clouded. "And now Father is not so good. I wanted to bring Pedro home." He paused, his gaze distant in thought, and then continued. "Worst luck, a grizzly killed my horse so I came here to get another."

"I gather you didn't find Pedro."

"That is right, Senor Sam. It is useless. I return home in the morning."

"I'll keep my eyes open, Rico. If I happen to see him, I'll give him your message."

The two men continued to chat for a short while, then shook hands and parted. When Sam returned to the hotel, Simone had just finished her bath. He took advantage of the warm water and climbed into the tub. By the time he shaved and Simone washed her hair, it was time for supper.

Rather than join the rowdy miners below, they ate a quiet meal in their room. That night, for the first time since leaving San Francisco, Sam and Simone found themselves alone in a room with the comforts of a bed. He made tender love to her throughout the night.

No one is aware of the true essence of a man's character as much as the woman who sleeps with him. Simone marveled at how this man, who had such a latent potential for violence, could be so gentle when he took her in his arms.

The following morning Simone and Sam were purchasing supplies in Campbell's when the Scotsman's nine-year-old son rushed breathlessly into the room. "Hey, Pa, Jake Bledsoe is getting ready to hang some greaser he claims stole a horse from him."

"Oh dear," Fiona groaned. "Why can't that horrible man leave this town alone? What are we going to do, Ian?"

"Nothin'. I nay be daft enough to try to stop him," her husband replied.

"Don't you have a sheriff?" Sam asked.

Campbell shook his head. "The mon left months ago." Aware of the gunslinger's reputation, he frowned at Sam with hostility. "It's nay your business, mister. We donna want any trouble here in Paddy."

"What do you call a hanging?" Sam scoffed. He peered out of the window and straightened up in alarm. "My God, it's Rico Estaban! That man is no horse thief. You've got to stop it."

"No mon here can stop Bledsoe an' his gang," Campbell declared.

"You'd let that bastard hang an innocent man!" Sam hurled the accusation and swiftly moved to the doorway.

Simone grabbed his arm to restrain him. "It's the town's responsibility, Sam. There's too many of them. Please stay out of it."

Sam's set jaw relaxed, and, smiling down at her, he confessed, "I probably could have a year ago, mouse, but falling in love develops a conscience in a man."

For a brief moment Simone stared into the warmth of his brown eyes. Eyes that Sam kept masked from the world to conceal the soul of the man behind them. She knew that nothing she could say would stop him from going out on the street.

Simone returned his smile. The empathy they had always shared flowed between them. "You have always been a man of conscience, Sam." She lowered her arm and released him.

Once outside, he joined the crowd that had gathered by a huge oak tree. They stood silently, their eyes transfixed as a noose was tossed over a limb of the tree. Hands tied behind his back, the victim was dragged to the site by Bledsoe and five eager henchmen. The startled mare veered as they hoisted Estaban onto the saddle.

"What did the man do, Bledsoe?" Sam challenged.

"He stole this mare from me," Bledsoe snarled.

"You mean the one he's sitting on?" Sam asked, with a nod toward the dapple-gray.

"That's right. Had the nerve to try and ride out on a stolen horse in full daylight."

"I paid him for the horse," Estaban cried out.

"Oh yeah, then where's the bill of sale? Any of you can search him. He ain't got none, 'cause he stole the horse from me, I tell ya."

"You're lying, Bledsoe. I saw him pay you for that horse myself," Sam declared.

The daring accusation brought shocked gasps and ominous murmurs from the crowd. Everyone waited for Bledsoe's reaction.

Bledsoe glared at Sam. "You calling me a liar, Montgomery?"

"That's what I'm doing, Bledsoe." Sam stepped forward.

"This thief's a friend of yours. I heard you talking together in that greaser lingo. I'm telling you . . . you're working in cahoots."

"And I'm telling *you*, he paid. And there was no bill of sale. Let him go, Bledsoe," Sam ordered calmly.

"No such thing, Montgomery. We're hanging him right now. We don't want his kind in this town. Them greasers in Sonora will be fair warned to stay there."

"I said, let him go," Sam repeated in a voice crackling with impatience.

"Don't try anything stupid, Montgomery, you ain't got a chance against all of us," the bully smirked confidently. "Look around, none of these people care what happens to any damned greaser. They want 'em all outta here, same as I do. There ain't nobody here gonna help you."

Sam's eyes swept the crowd. He knew the man was right. Whether or not these people approved of the man's actions, none of them would put his life on the line to stop Jake Bledsoe.

"What the hell's wrong with you people? Don't you see you're all as guilty as Bledsoe? Yesterday it was a Chinaman. Today a Spanish-American."

"You calling this greaser an American?" Bledsoe jeered.

"You're damned right, he's an American. Born right here in California." Sam turned back to the crowd. "Who's he gonna hang tomorrow?"

Bledsoe sneered mockingly. "I was kind of thinking the next scum we rid this town of . . . oughta be a half-breed."

"Anytime you're feeling lucky, Bledsoe, go ahead and try." The warning was charged with a lethal intensity.

Sam's eyes swept the ring of faces. "You all had a stake in building this town. Are you going to let Bledsoe take it away from you?"

Although Sam could see many of the people nodding in agreement with him, no one by word or deed dared to back him up. His eyes stopped to rest on Ian Campbell. Sheepishly, the Scotsman dropped his head and, taking his wife's hand, headed back to his store.

Knowing Sam was waging a hopeless cause, Bledsoe laughed confidently. "Tell you what I'm gonna do for you, Montgomery. Since you seem so damned anxious to die for this greaser, I'll let him go and put you in his place." Now certain of his power over the people, he did not hesitate to add, "I ain't had a chance to hang an Indian in months."

Instantly the gap widened between Sam and the crowd. Sam's code of honor would never allow him to back down from the direct challenge; a gunfight was inevitable.

Sam knew it would happen before he stepped out on the street. He cursed himself for being foolish enough to believe anyone would help him. "If there's going to be a hanging, Bledsoe, you're not going to be alive to see it."

Bledsoe and his accomplices spread apart; six against one.

Then, for seconds, no sound was heard. Suddenly a voice rent the silence. "Ye'll nay be hangin' any mon in this town, Mister Bledsoe." Ian Campbell stood on the street with a raised rifle pointed toward the six.

Clarence Edmund, the town's banker, stepped out of the crowd with pistol in hand. He took a place next to Sam. Two miners silently moved up beside them. Now there were five against six, enough for the crowd to find a voice, and they began chanting in support.

The banker raised his hand to silence the din. "I think what the man is saying makes sense, Bledsoe. This town is open to any law-abiding man," Edmund declared.

Bledsoe glared angrily at Sam. Faced now with greater odds against him, he snarled at one of his minions to release Estaban.

The tension was dispelled at last. The crowd began to disperse, and Simone rushed into Sam's arms. Seizing the opportunity, Bledsoe drew his weapon and fired. Sam shoved Simone aside, his pistol clearing the holster in a lightning flash. Bledsoe fell to the ground with a bullet through his heart, but not before a red stain appeared on Sam's shoulder.

Minus their leader, the other gang members had no stomach for a fight. They threw up their hands in surrender and were quickly seized by some of the citizens.

Later, at the doctor's office, Simone was relieved to hear that Sam's shoulder had suffered only a surface wound, but the sight of the blood was enough to extract a grimace from her. "It seems like ever since I met you, Sam, I've been cleansing your wounds." She washed away the blood while the doctor prepared to stitch the gash in Sam's flesh.

Sam grinned at her, an appealing smile that transformed his face from gunfighter to boy. "Now, if you could only cook a halfway decent meal, I might be willing to marry you." Their eyes met wishfully.

"Well, I thought the way things were going there for a while, I'd be sewing up a lot more people than you. Don't have to tell you this is going to hurt, son," the doctor cautioned as he began to ply the needle.

Later, as Sam and Simone sat talking to the Campbells and Clarence Edmund, Sam learned the extent of Simone's misery during his confrontation with Bledsoe.

"You owe this little lady something, Sam," Edmund informed him. "Ian told me he had to wrestle the shotgun out of her hands. She was going to go out on the street and help you out."

"Aye. Twas wha' gave me the courage to do it meself," Campbell grumbled good-naturedly.

Simone blushed to the roots of her hair. She had hoped Sam would never have to know. Her would-be bravery had nothing to do with a cause or conscience. She simply wanted to die with him, because she had no reason to live without him.

Sam sat silently studying her. Simone finally

garnered enough courage to look at him. She knew he could read her thoughts.

He reached over and squeezed Simone's hand, overwhelmed by a need to touch her. This woman's love was like a soothing balm that healed every ache, every injustice he had ever suffered. "You have no idea how much I owe her," he replied pensively.

At that moment Enrico Estaban entered the room with hat in hand. "I came to thank you, Senor Sam. You saved my life. I and my family are forever in your debt."

Gratitude was a sentiment Sam had not learned to deal with. Smiling in embarrassment, he shook the young man's hand. *"Vaya con Dios,* Rico."

"This town owes you something too, Sam," Edmund declared after Estaban's departure. "You made us look at ourselves today and stand up to be counted. It was about time and we are forever in your debt. We would like to find a way of thanking you."

"I nay suppose ye want the job o' sheriff?" the canny Scotsman offered.

"No, thank you," Sam said with a laugh and a sideward grin at Simone. She exhaled a sigh of relief. "There is a way of thanking me, if you mean it." Sam's eyes remained locked with Simone's. "Miss Lisle and I would like to be married. I understand there's a minister in this town."

"Married, ye say?" Ian Campbell exclaimed.

"Weel, I mus' say the town owes ye that, lad. And a bonnie weddin' 'twill be, wi' all o' Paddy attendin'."

Simone's heart swelled with happiness as she smiled at Sam. It was decided, on the spot, that the wedding would take place the following Saturday.

Later, when they rode out of town, each had a kindled hope for their future together.

CHAPTER TWENTY-EIGHT

Simone was the most nervous about the wedding, but Eve was a close second. It seemed to her as if Saturday would never arrive. Bright and early on the morning of the wedding, Eve had her yellow gown and slippers, along with a change of clothing for Adam, all packed as they waited for him to hitch up the wagon.

Bailey was not abandoning his digging to go into Paddy for the ceremony. As happy as he was for Sam and Simone, he considered the rite useless and, worse, a hypocrisy.

He did not understand why people thought a clergyman had some mystical power to declare a couple husband and wife. A man and woman could only do that in their hearts. The clergyman's declaration was as meaningful as a soothsayer proclaiming that the sun will rise in the morning and set at night.

In Bailey's eyes, Sam and Simone had been

married long ago; likely it happened the first moment they looked at one another. He felt that nothing uttered before a minister could make them more so.

What irony, Bailey thought cynically, that this pair felt compelled to follow the dictates of the very society that had excluded them both. The brotherhood of hypocrites had eternally branded them misfits, merely for accidents of birth: Sam for being a half-breed, Simone for her uncomeliness.

Bailey wanted no part of that lunacy. He had run from society his whole life. Yet, he knew that by following an unshackled path, he had dodged commitment as well.

I am the real misfit, Bailey reflected. He had never been able to make any kind of a commitment, not to Sam, not to Eve, not to Mary MacGregor. Not even to Sarita. A smile softened his craggy face as he recalled the gentle Indian maiden who had died giving birth to his son.

Yes, he was the real misfit, Bailey told himself as he watched the wagon ramble away. But he was too old to change his ways, he thought with a sigh. Besides, he had no such intentions.

Ian Campbell had been true to his word. When the bridal party arrived in Paddy, the town was arrayed for a royal wedding. The Chinese populace, grateful for Sam's intervention with Jake Bledsoe in their behalf, had devoted their talents to making brightly painted lanterns, which were strung along the narrow main street and bedecked the wooden dance floor erected in the center of the town.

Red, white and blue bunting adorned the store fronts. American flags, California flags, and foreign flags of several nations fluttered from roof tops, tents, and crudely erected posts.

Two rooms in the hotel had been reserved for the wedding party. Simone and Eve were whisked away to one while Sam and Adam withdrew to the other.

When they entered the room, Simone burst into tears at the sight that greeted her. A beautiful wedding gown was neatly laid out on the bed awaiting her arrival. Fiona Campbell had provided a bolt of white dotted Swiss organdy, and several of the women had spent the week designing and sewing the creation.

The bodice was fitted with short cap sleeves and a high round collar trimmed in lace. Numerous petticoats had been amassed to wear under the three-tiered full skirt with a bottom tier, edged in lace, made longer in back to trail behind in a fetching train.

In honor of the occasion, a cherished pair of white, elbow-length, lace mitts had been retrieved from the chest in which they had been so carefully packed away, and now rested beside the gown.

The town's prostitute had even made a contribution to the trousseau. She had donated a white transparent peignoir for the wedding night, which had just arrived from Sonora by way of the latest pack-mule delivery.

While Simone bathed, Eve pressed her own yellow gown. She took a bath and washed her hair, brushing the black silken strands until they shone. Then pulling the long hair off her face, she tied it back with a yellow satin ribbon. The end result was that Eve looked like a sixteen-year-old. A *pregnant sixteen-year-old*, Eve thought as she studied her silhouette in the mirror.

Eve took special pains with Simone's hair, sweeping it to the top of her head in a loose bun, with a white satin bow tucked at the back of the crown. When they stopped for a final inspection in the mirror, tears glistened in Eve's eyes as she looked at Simone. "You look beautiful, dear."

The long months in the hot sun had enhanced Simone's appearance. Her face and arms had deepened into a flattering bronze, and her previously lusterless hair had lightened to an appealing tawniness streaked with gold. Coupled with the radiance of a bride on her wedding day, Eve's praise was not hyperbole.

"Oh, *chérie*, this is the happiest day of my life." Simone smiled through her tears as she and Eve stood with their arms around each other's waist gazing into the mirror.

"Now, I'll go down and tell them you're ready. You wait here until I come back to get you." Eve kissed Simone on the cheek and hurried from the room.

* * *

The whole town was assembled to witness the nuptials. Out on the street, Ian Campbell orchestrated the activities until the bride would appear. Even the saloon, normally packed to the rafters, was empty except for a couple of stragglers at the end of the bar and three strangers seated at a corner table.

Adam and Clarence Edmund dragged Sam into the saloon for a final farewell toast to his carefree bachelor days. They forced him to suffer the usual humorous remarks reserved for nervous bachelors.

The good-natured banter was shattered by an unfamiliar voice. "How come yer servin' that redskin liquor?"

The laughter died in their throats. Adam and the banker swung around in surprise. The question had come from one of the strangers at the corner table.

Adam recognized the man's shirt as being part of the uniform worn by the San Francisco Hounds. The outraged citizenry had run the gang out of the city when their terrorism had finally led to the rape and murder of a woman.

Sensing trouble, the two stragglers moved away from the end of the bar. Sam's jaw hardened into a grim line, all the jocundity erased from his face. He did not turn around from his place midway at the bar. Slowly he lowered his arm and placed his glass down on the bar. "Fill it up."

Adam shifted uneasily; he and Sam had abandoned their gun belts for the wedding. The bartender's eyes glanced nervously to the corner table as he picked up the whiskey bottle and refilled Sam's glass.

A chair crashed to the floor as the stranger rose to his feet. "I ain't interested in drinking in the same room as a damned redskin."

"We don't want any trouble, mister," Clarence Edmund said tensely. "We're celebrating with our friend here. It's his wedding day, so why don't you just relax."

"That injun's what?"

"As I said, our friend is getting married today. The whole town is celebrating, and you're welcome to join us if you'd like."

The invitation brought a roar of laughter. "You hear that, boys? We're invited to dance at the redskin's wedding. Don't think I know all those steps they whoop and holler to. I think the redskin should show us how it's done." He drew his pistol and aimed at Sam's back. "Hey, redskin, turn around when I'm talking to you."

Sam put down his glass and slowly turned around. His expression was inscrutable. "Are you talking to me?"

"Ain't talking to the wall. You heard what I said. Start kicking up your moccasins, boy, or you ain't gonna have any feet left."

"The man's unarmed," Adam declared.

"He's soon gonna be unfooted, too." That brought another hoot of laughter from his cohorts. Sam turned back to the bar, ignoring the man's threats.

Adam knew that the man intended to carry out his threat. Rushing the bastard was the only way out. Desperately, he looked around for something he could use as a weapon or shield. To his horror, he saw Eve enter the saloon from the hotel lobby.

A few moments before, Eve had come down the stairs looking for Adam and Sam. When she saw the lobby was deserted she glanced into the adjoining saloon. Immediately, she spied Adam. Eve sensed something was wrong just by the way he was standing.

When she overheard some of the conversation, her suspicion was confirmed. The situation was urgent, leaving her no time to go and get help. Knowing that Ian Campbell kept a pistol behind the desk for protection, she frantically rifled the drawers and shelves. Her search ended quickly as she opened a loosely tied box of old records and spied the concealed weapon.

Eve snatched it up, checked the chamber for bullets, and released the safety catch. Now she regretted not having taken Adam's advice to learn how to aim and fire one of the damned things. Somehow, she had to get the weapon to Sam.

Concealing the gun in the folds of her gown, Eve entered the saloon and stopped at the end of the bar, just as the man fired.

The floor beneath Sam's feet splintered. "Let's see you dance, injun," the bully shouted, enjoying the sport.

"Sam!" Eve cried out, and sent the pistol

spinning down the bar. Sam grabbed the pistol and swung around before the startled gunman could get off another shot. Sam's bullet ripped a hole in his hand and the bully's gun careened to the floor.

Quickly, Adam recovered the fallen gun. Drawing weapons, the other hoodlums started to rise, then stopped in the face of two squarely aimed pistols, and without saying a word retreated to their seats.

The look in Sam's eyes was deadly as he glared at the injured man. "My wedding day is no time for killing, so you're getting off easy. Next time you won't be so lucky."

"Okay, you heard the man. Get on your horses and ride fast," Adam ordered.

Attracted by the sound of the gun shots, people began to converge on the scene. With hanging heads and belligerent scowls, the three men left the saloon, one holding his bloody hand. "We don't want to see you in our town again," Clarence Edmund warned as they climbed on their horses.

The instant she heard the gun shots, Simone was sure that Sam was involved. Frantically, she rushed out of her room and down the stairway. She pushed through the crowd into the saloon and collapsed into Sam's arms with sobs of relief when she found him unharmed.

The commotion subsided and the wedding was delayed in order for Adam and Sam to calm down the two shaken and trembling women they loved. Within a short time, Ian Campbell had the proceedings back on schedule and the bridal couple was standing before the minister.

Sam's gaze was steady as he took Simone's hand and declared, "I, Samuel Montgomery, take this woman as my wedded wife . . ."

Eve's happiness for Simone was evidenced in the joyous smile she turned on her husband when Adam reached over and squeezed her hand.

Standing silently, Fiona Campbell dabbed at her eyes, recalling the same moment at her own wedding in Paddockhaugh. Beside her, Ian fidgeted with his stiff collar and glanced at the sky. He smiled in satisfaction; there wasn't a cloud to dampen the painstaking arrangements he had organized for the day.

Any in the gathered assemblage who pondered misgivings for the future of this marriage between the half-breed and the French woman found their doubts difficult to sustain in the glowing evidence of Simone's love, as she smiled up at Sam and stated her vows unfalteringly.

The sun was high in the sky when the valley resounded with cheers and shouts as the minister pronounced the couple man and wife and Sam kissed his bride.

Throughout the afternoon, the atmosphere of a country fair prevailed. There were a dozen games to test one's luck and skill, from cards to horseback racing and target shooting. All the games were enjoyed in the spirit of good sportsmanship, with neither charge nor prize attendant.

Many of the curious had heard of Sam's expertise with a six-gun. Throughout the afternoon, he was beseeched to participate in the shooting competition but declined, claiming a sore trigger finger as an excuse.

Tossing rings over whiskey bottles was an easy challenge for Adam's sure eye and steady hand. Equally as successful, Eve guessed under which of the three shells the illusive pea was hiding. They stood with Sam as he chuckled with pleasure watching Simone display her skill at three-card monte, due to his patient hours of tutelage.

Because of her condition, Eve passed up the fun of a three-legged sack race to watch Adam and Sam thoroughly trounced by a set of twelve-year-old twins. Adam grumbled good-naturedly, "The race wasn't fair. It's common knowledge that twins think alike."

"Well, I suppose you could say it's a case of the right foot knowing what the left foot is doing," Eve quipped.

If one were keeping tabs, Eve had the edge in wins over Adam. And he knew it. As they walked along, he spied apples floating in a tub of water. Immediately he challenged her to a match. A crowd gathered in amusement as Adam and Eve vied for the apple.

Their faces dipped into the water as they poised over the tub with their arms behind their backs. Each attempted to snare a bobbing piece of the fruit with their teeth. At one time Adam succeeded in raising an apple almost fully out of the water, only to have it slide through his lips and splash back into the tub, sending up a spray of water that spattered his face.

Finally, with hair and face dripping with water, Adam raised his head with his jaws clamped around a big red apple. Eve was waiting for him, casually holding the apple she had succeeded in plucking out of the tub with her teeth.

Laughing with good humor, Adam dried off the water trickling down his face. "The only thing this proves is that your mouth is bigger than mine."

"Not so, my beloved husband. Who was the one doing all the trumpeting earlier? A pity there's no contest for the losingest braggart; you could win easily." With a saucy backward smile, she moved on.

As soon as the sun set, the dancing began. Every miner claimed a dance with the bride. The wooden planks of the floor rumbled with the sound of trampling and stomping feet. Since Sam, the groom, did not know how to dance, he stood back, smiling with delight as he watched his bride glide and hop around the floor in an endless variety of folk dances.

Because of the delicacy of her condition, Eve limited her activity on the dance floor. Exhausted after several dances, she abandoned the exertion for the lure of a nearby bench. She was relieved to rest her tired feet and watched with pleasure as Adam whirled Simone around the floor.

There was not a soul present who was not waiting for the food to be set out. The town could not boast of more than a dozen women, but each had done the work of twice her number to help prepare the wedding feast. Many of the men had also contributed their skills.

Pots, pans, platters and plates in all sizes and shapes were brought out and set on tables. The mixed culture of the town was evidenced by the great assortment of international cuisine. There was a platter of roast beef, so tender it could be cut with a fork, surrounded by English Yorkshire pudding piping hot from the oven. A Dresden china bowl held a Scottish haggis.

Trays of delicacies were there for sampling. Small round balls of Mexican wedding cakes, Danish lemon bread, Norwegian lefse, German kuchen, Scottish scones, and French crepes. Not to be ignored were several American apple pies and a Viennese Sacher torte with its equally scrumptious chocolate frosting.

Eve and Adam wandered the street, stopping at the various tables to sample the wares. They feasted on savory tamales wrapped in dried corn husks called hojas. But having eaten nothing but beef for months, Eve passed up more of the many varieties of the meat to sample a sautéed chicken coated in a mixture of sugar and cornstarch.

"This is delicious," she enthused to the smiling Chinaman who was serving the dish. "What do you call this?"

He continued smiling broadly, bobbing his head politely. "Thankee, missee. Thankee."

"The name?" Eve repeated, pointing to the plate. "What is its name?"

"Name? Oh, name," he smiled in comprehension. "Name Cantonee chickee." Once again his head bobbed up and down with a big smile. "Thankee, missee."

"Thank you." Eve backed away, her head unconsciously mimicking his up-and-down motion. "Thank you. Thank you very much. It's delicious."

She returned to Adam's side, who had stopped to sample a toad-in-the-hole, which, according to the Australian who had prepared them, was the name for the little round sausage ball Adam had just popped into his mouth.

"Adam, you should try some of this Cantonese chicken, it's delicious," Eve advised with her mouth full of the tasty mixture.

"What is it?" he asked, preoccupied with deciding whether or not to have another one of the sausage balls.

" 'Cantonee chickee,' " she responded humorously, consuming another bite.

Adam's brow arched in amusement. "Will you repeat that, please?"

Eve raised her head and pursed her lips to punctiliously form the words, "Cantonee chickee."

She now had his complete concentration. He

lowered his head over hers in rapt attention. "Again, please?"

Eve laughed playfully, then once again rounded her lips together. "Cantonee—"

His mouth cut off the rest. When he drew away, Adam's dark eyes gleamed suggestively. "You're right. It's delicious."

"Adam Rawlins, I can't believe you would kiss me right out here in front of everyone."

He took her in his arms, and this time the kiss lingered. "Do you believe it now?" he asked huskily.

"Adam, you're embarrassing me." The sparkle in her eyes failed to match the censure of her words. "I think we better move on."

Hand in hand, they continued strolling past the tables, stopping to enjoy the taste of a nutty mincemeat abounding with currants and raisins. As scrumptious as it appeared, Eve passed up the chocolate torte and settled for several bites of the piece of apple pie that Adam was chomping. They chewed on pieces of pineapple, the juice running down their chins, and laughed like children.

Finally, unable to consume another bite, they returned to the dance floor. Eve looked around for the bridal couple, but there was no sign of them.

"I don't see Simone and Sam. I wonder where they are?"

"Wisely retired to their room, if Sam is as smart as I think he is. And that, my young wife, is exactly where we are going right now."

"But the evening is still young," Eve protested, hanging back.

"Exactly, so let's not waste any more of it out here." He grasped her hand and headed for the hotel.

Once at the top of the stairs Adam stopped, studying the two closed doors. "Which room do you think the newlyweds are in?" Eve pointed confidently to the room where she had dressed earlier.

"What makes you think that's the one?" Adam asked, still doubtful.

"Because logically, it's the bridal room. The wedding dress was in there and so was a peignoir."

"I think you may have a point." Still not totally convinced, Adam tiptoed to the opposite door and cautiously turned the knob. The door creaked as he opened it a crack. He stopped and glanced at Eve indecisively.

Shaking her head at all his precaution, she smiled confidently and shoved open the door.

To Adam's relief the room was empty. He grabbed her hand and yanked her into the room.

"That was smart, Eve. Just what would you have done if they would have been—" He cut off his words and turned away to lock the door.

"If they would have been . . . sleeping?" she innocently completed the question.

Smiling fondly at him, she was amused at the inconsistency of men. It seemed, either by threats or promises in whispered innuendos, that they walked around preoccupied with thoughts of sex. They postured and pranced, boasting to each other of their prowess, attributes, and expertise. Propriety was often forsaken to fondle or fornicate a prostitute in the presence of one another.

But, with the woman they loved—they insisted on privacy.

Then dignity, modesty, and respect were required—and the need for sensitive intimacy, shared by the lovers alone, was essential.

Adam sat down on a chair and began struggling to pull off a boot. "Who in hell sleeps on their wedding night?"

"We did, my beloved husband." She got down on her knees and pulled off his other boot.

She had bested him once again. He leaned back and sighed in defeat. "I am considered an intelligent adult. I can't understand why I put up with this."

Eve sidled into his lap and slipped her arms around his neck, gazing at him through lowered lids. "And why do you think you put up with it?"

With a crooked grin, Adam gathered her into his arms. His mouth hovered in an intoxicating invitation above hers. "You're flirting with me now, Evelyn MacGregor Rawlins, I hope you're prepared to pay the consequences."

The male scent of him was an aphrodisiac. At first his lips were playful, exploratory, but she responded too instinctively to sustain the mood. Within seconds the kiss became demanding as their mutual desire ignited a flame of urgency.

Breathless, they pulled apart. Adam tightened

his hold on her, sliding his lips to the sensitive hollow of her throat. In response, she burrowed deeper against him, feeling the pounding of his heart against her own.

Smothering a groan, Adam reclaimed her lips. The kiss intensified, his tongue probing the moist sweetness of her mouth, sending erotic tremors the length of her spine. He held her in the cradle of his arm and stroked her back in tantalizing sweeps, until his hand slid around to caress the fullness of her breast. Seeking release from the sensation raging rampantly through her, Eve moaned, leaning into the warmth of his touch. His heated arousal pressed against her as he began to open the buttons of her gown.

Her head fell back in the throes of passion, and she struggled for breath in ragged gasps, forcing back a strangled sob when his mouth lowered to claim a hardened peak of her breast. Eve slid her fingers into the rich texture of his dark hair and pressed his head into the quivering fullness.

Effortlessly, Adam lifted her and carried her to the bed. Clothing was cast carelessly aside in their haste as leisurely exploration quickly gave way to the demand of urgency.

They melded together as one.

CHAPTER TWENTY-NINE

Arising late, and delaying further to extend their thanks and gratitude to the townspeople, a weary group left Paddy the following day to return to the mine.

Adam drove the wagon, with Eve and Simone on the seat beside him. Sam rode on a horse alongside the wagon. Conversation was minimal. All were too sleepy to share whatever was on any of their minds. Finally, after about an hour, Simone spoke up. "Bailey certainly missed some delicious food."

"Serves him right," Eve grumbled. Bailey's attitude was a sensitive issue to her. She felt that his ideas about marriage were responsible for Sam and herself being born bastards.

She straightened up and began rubbing her back to ease the aching muscles. The move did not go unheeded by Adam. "Your back hurting again, honey?"

"I guess I'm out of the habit of sleeping in a bed. Either that, or it's this wagon." Adam and Simone exchanged a knowing smile. Eve's dislike for riding in the wagon was no secret to any of them.

Adam shifted the reins into one hand and hugged her to his side. "We'll be stopping in about an hour to rest the horse, and you can stretch your legs. Maybe that will help." She was grateful when he finally pulled the wagon into a shady copse.

Being out of the hot sun felt good to Eve. She sat down and leaned back against the trunk of a tree. Adam stretched out on the ground beside her, placing his hat over his face.

"How much longer will it take to get to the mine?" Eve inquired.

"A couple more hours," Sam said. He was lying with his head in Simone's lap. "With the late start we got, we'll be lucky to get there before nightfall."

Suddenly, without moving, Sam asked calmly, "Adam, do you have your rifle?"

Adam lifted his hat and raised his head. "It's in the wagon, why?"

"Don't look, but something just flushed some grouse in the trees to the right."

Slowly Adam sat up. "A grizzly?"

Sam shook his head. "I don't know." He sat upright and, at the sound of a pheasant calling to its mate, he looked at the trees to the left. The fowl took flight with a flutter of wings. "Not a grizzly. Whoever it is, they're on both sides of us." He began inching his hand toward the rifle on the ground beside him.

Eve and Simone sat stiffly with eyes alert. Adam rose to his feet and casually brushed himself off. He walked to the wagon and reached for his rifle. A shot rang out; a bullet whizzed past his head, slamming into the wagon.

With rifle in hand, Adam dove to the ground and rolled over to Eve. Several more shots kicked up the dust. Sam began firing to their right.

"Keep your head down," Adam shouted to Eve. He pumped several shots into the trees on the left.

The sound of the gun blasts spooked the two horses and they pulled to break free from restraint. Sam's horse succeeded and galloped down the road.

No bullets had yet found their mark. Either the attackers were poor marksmen or they couldn't get a good bead on any of the four without exposing their positions. The heavy barrage of firing ceased. The two couples moved together, seeking the protection of a huge boulder. The two men flanked Eve and Simone, who huddled together in the middle.

"How many you figure, Sam?" Adam asked.

"Six, maybe more." Sam checked the chambers of his pistols, then reloaded his rifle. "How many rounds you got left?"

"About twenty," Adam replied after a quick check.

The information was not good news to Sam. He frowned, deep in thought. "Damn! We'll have to make every shot count."

"Well, I'm a better shot with a rifle," Adam mumbled.

Sam shoved his rifle over to Adam. "Let's switch. I like a six-shooter."

In Eve's eyes the combination of Adam and Sam was an invincible force, and she had felt surprisingly secure until she heard the ammunition was low. That narrowed the odds considerably.

"Who could be shooting at us?" she asked.

Sam shrugged negligently. "Bandits, or maybe Cayuse? They've been on the warpath up north. Might even be Colomas."

"Colomas?" Adam remarked in surprise. "Sutter uses that tribe for labor at his mill. I thought they were peaceful."

Sam nodded. "They were, but the miners stopped that, killing them and raping their women."

A bullet ricocheted off the rock above their heads, halting further conversation.

"Looks like someone's got into position to do some damage," Adam warned. They remained crouched, hoping one of the unknown attackers got careless and would expose his position. Until then, Adam and Sam had no sure target.

At nightfall they were still pinned down, an occasional bullet striking near them.

"They'll rush us by dark," Sam cautioned. He

threw a concerned glance toward the two women, huddled together.

Sam slipped one of the guns back into the holster. "I've had enough of this." He handed the other pistols to Adam. "Keep these until I get back."

Simone felt a rising panic. "Sam—?"

"I've got an idea where those shots are coming from," he whispered, and slipped a knife out of his boot. "Keep your eyes open." He crawled away into the darkness.

The minutes seemed to pass like hours in Sam's absence. Seeing Simone's gaunt and pale face, Eve reflected that Sam lived daily with violence, moving from one crisis to another. Loving him could only led to heartache. She was anxious for her brother, but she knew that her feelings could not touch the apprehension Simone must be feeling at this moment. Eve reached over and squeezed Simone's hand. It was icy cold.

After what seemed an eternity, Sam appeared out of the shadows as silently as he had gone.

"Get ready. They're getting set to rush us."

Adam handed Sam the pistols. "Are they Indians?"

"No. My friend from the saloon yesterday. He brought the troops."

Eve was aghast. "You mean that bully from San Francisco? I thought he left."

Sam nodded. "He should have. He won't be going anywhere again."

As Simone gasped, Sam shifted his eyes to his

wife. He had avoided looking at Simone since his return.

"Are you hurt?" Simone asked with a ghost of a smile. The color had returned to her cheeks.

"No, mouse. Not even a scratch," he replied in a measured tone.

"They?" Simone asked.

Sam avoided her gaze and shrugged. "We've got two less to worry about." Simone closed her eyes in a gesture of despair.

All at once, the night was rent with the sound of gun shots and shouting as the Hounds charged from two sides. Bullets zinged around them and over their heads. The women crouched lower. Adam took down two of the attackers. Sam doubled the count. Then, as quickly as the assault began, it ended.

After about an hour without further attack, Adam turned to Sam. "Do you think they've pulled out?"

Sam nodded. "We'd have had more action by now. They must be shot up pretty bad. I'll check to be sure."

He was back within minutes. "They've cleared out."

That was all Eve wanted to hear. Shivering, she ran to the wagon, snatched the blankets out of the back, and tossed one to Simone. "Let's get out of here. I'm freezing."

"Perhaps we should stay here tonight," Adam said. There was a somber line to his jaw.

"Oh, no. I'm not sleeping in the woods surrounded by corpses," Eve announced emphatically with a toss of her dark head. "I don't want to even think about what's out there."

"This is a savage land," Simone said quietly. Taking Sam's hand, she continued, "I agree with you, *chérie*, I want to get away from this horrible place . . . before anything else happens." Each knew she had Sam's welfare in mind.

"Then let's get going. We've got a long ride in the dark." Adam lifted Eve into the bed of the wagon, then swung Simone up beside her. "You girls will have to ride in the back."

Adam waited for Sam to climb up on the seat beside him. There was no humor in his eyes as he commented, "I think we've rested the horse long enough."

Traveling through the mountains at night was an arduous task. The wagon bounced and rattled over rocks and ruts, jarring its occupants.

Sleep would not come, so Eve lay on her side with her hand tucked under her head watching Adam's grim profile in the moonlight. She knew she would be affected by the thoughts lying beneath his sullen frown.

They reached the mine in the middle of the night. Bailey had waited anxiously. "I had a good scare when Sam's horse wandered back to camp," he told them. "Didn't know what happened. I was going to start out at dawn to look for you."

"We'll talk about it in the morning," Adam offered. "Right now, we're all going to bed."

They left Bailey standing, scratching his head perplexed.

Eve awoke convinced that every bone in her body was bruised. She peered out of the tent and saw the others seated at the campfire. She dressed as fast as her aching bones would allow her.

"I'm glad to hear that, Sam," Adam was saying as she walked up behind him.

"Glad to hear what?" Eve asked, resting her hands on Adam's shoulders.

"Sam's thinking about hanging up his guns and taking up ranching. I offered him some land near the Oregon border that would be great for a horse ranch."

Simone held her breath expectantly awaiting Sam's answer. He shoved his hat to the back of his head. "Well, now that we've got this money, no sense in drifting around the country. We'll take a look at it. Wouldn't mind a small spread to run cattle and horses."

"If you like, it's yours," Adam declared.

Sam held up a hand. "If we like it, we'll *buy* it from you," Sam corrected.

Eve smiled at Simone. The woman looked as if her life had been given a reprieve. The thought of settling down and not having to encounter the challenges that put Sam's life on the line, was more than she ever hoped for.

Simone smiled joyously at Bailey, who was frying some salt pork. "You missed some delicious food, Bailey."

His blue eyes twinkled with pride. "Bet the cooking wasn't as good as yours. I'm going to miss it when I leave."

His answer took Eve by surprise. "Where are you going, Bailey?" Eve asked.

"It's getting about time to pack up old Socrates and move on. This mine's just about run out."

Adam knew what was coming. He had tried to spare Eve this moment. "What are talking about, Bailey? Aren't you coming back to Sacramento with us?"

"Heavens, no, girl. Never could stand city life. Heard tell there's been silver found in Nevada. I was thinking of trying my luck there."

Eve was unable to believe that her father was willing to leave so soon after they had found one another. She looked with constricted eyes to Sam, who had turned away, standing stiffly. Simone's eyes were filled with compassion as she watched Eve's torment unfolding. Adam slipped his hands on Eve's shoulders. "Come on back to the tent, honey."

Eve shrugged out of his grasp, her face stricken as she faced Bailey. "Aren't you even interested in seeing your grandchild?"

Bailey didn't raise his head from the task he was doing. "I'm sure I'll make it back again some day."

Eve was still unable to accept his decision as she struggled for an explanation. "What about your gold?"

"I thought I would take enough to give me a grubstake, and you can divide the rest between you," Bailey replied.

His eagerness to leave was incomprehensible

to Eve. She turned away, unable to contain her tears, and hurried back to the tent. Shortly, Adam joined her. He gathered the heartbroken woman into his arms.

Eve sobbed against his chest. "No one means anything to him. Not me, not Sam, not even the baby."

"I tried to spare you this, honey. I once tried to tell you that Bailey was the kind of man who chases dreams."

Her cheeks streaked with tears, Eve faced him with resentment. "Why, Adam? Why did you have to be right about this, too? Why couldn't I have a father who loved me?"

"You have a brother, honey. Isn't that enough? Sam and Simone will always be close." Adam started to lift her in his lap but Eve winced with pain. "What is it?" he asked distracted.

"I'm a little sore from last night."

Adam was not convinced. "Let me look at you." He lifted her gown and his face hardened. "My God, Eve, you're covered with bruises." His face settled grimly. "That settles it, we're going home tomorrow."

Eve stared at him, aghast. "What are you talking about? There's still a couple of weeks' mining to do."

"It'll be done without us," he asserted. "I'm sorry about Bailey, Eve, but right now, I have to consider your physical well-being. I've had enough of my wife—*my pregnant wife*—being terrorized by bandits in these mountains. Last night was the final straw. Like it or not, we're going home tomorrow. There's the baby to consider, and I've neglected my business responsibilities too long." He stormed out of the tent.

Eve knew it was useless to argue when Adam was in this kind of mood. Perhaps he was right.

The following morning, she tearfully said goodbye to Bailey. Sam and Simone decided to stay until he left and promised they would come to Sacramento later. As the wagon rolled away, Eve turned back on her seat for one final, lingering look. Bailey's white hair fluttered in the breeze as he took off his hat and waved farewell.

CHAPTER THIRTY

With few roads and trails to follow, progress in the wagon was slow. Adam did not want to put physical strain on Eve or the horse, so he was exceptionally cautious.

"I think I could walk faster and not feel worse for the wear," Eve lamented as they stopped that evening to make camp.

"Once we're out of these mountains, we'll move faster. I don't want you jarred around too much. How are you feeling?"

Eve stretched her aching muscles. "I feel fine, Adam. Just a little sore. Don't worry about me. I'm not a Dresden doll."

Adam grinned at her annoyance. "I know you're not, Eve, but I am not going to take any chances with you or the baby. How about a back rub? Maybe that will help."

Eve made them a bed with pine needles and blankets. When they bedded down for the night

Adam slipped his hands under her shirt and began to knead her aching muscles.

She closed her eyes with a sigh of contentment. There was nothing like the feel of Adam's hands. His long firm fingers could effortlessly arouse her body to a mindless, writhing ecstasy or, as now, move in soothing pressure to lull her to sleep.

Eve awoke sometime in the night curled up in Adam's arms. She savored the moment. How she loved him. No matter how much she tried, she could never remain angry with him. Loving or fighting, Adam was her life, and she would not leave him again.

Her hand slid down to curve around the rounded swell of her stomach. *I hope it's a boy*, she thought wistfully, gazing lovingly at the face beside her, so boyish itself in sleep. A smile curved softly on her face and she closed her eyes and returned to slumber.

The day dawned gray and overcast with low-hanging clouds pressing down, threatening to pour out a torrent. With a thick stick and the tarp, Adam erected a simple tent in the back of the wagon.

After eating a hasty breakfast, they got under way.

At midday, the rain began falling in a drenching downpour that turned the countryside into quagmire and slippery rock. Progress was reduced to a snail's pace. Adam insisted that Eve crawl into the back of the wagon under the tarp, but several times she had to climb down while he pried a wheel out of a rut.

Adam began to cross a rain-swollen stream when a rear wheel wedged between two rocks. He jumped down, waded to shore, and found a sturdy stick to use as a lever.

Several times, as he tried to release the wheel, Adam lost his footing in the flowing water. The horse pulled at the reins, but the wagon wouldn't budge.

"Eve, I have to lighten the load," he shouted in the force of the downpour. Just as he reached up to lift her, the wagon ripped away from the anchored wheel.

The wagon was caught in the swift current, and Adam dove and grasped the tailgate as the wagon careened into midstream. By the time he pulled himself onto the bed of the wagon, Eve had worked her way to the seat and tried to grab the loose rein that floated like a streamer in the water beside them.

"I can't reach it," she gasped breathlessly as Adam scrambled into the seat beside her.

"Sit down and hold on," he ordered brusquely.

Eve expected him to lean out to grab the reins, but instead he lowered himself into the water and, hand over hand, worked himself along the shaft.

Eve could only watch, helpless to be of any assistance to him. If he lost his hold, he could fall beneath the wagon and be struck in the head. But his grip held firm, and when he reached the end of the shaft, he swung a leg over the floundering horse.

His legs gripping the sides of the animal, Adam leaned over the horse's head to reach the reins. Once they were firmly in grasp, Adam turned the animal toward the shore. Finally the weary horse found footing and reached the opposite bank dragging the broken wagon behind it.

Exhausted, Adam slipped off the horse, his strength waned by the effort of fighting the current and maneuvering the horse. He lay on the ground with the rain belting his face.

Eve climbed down from her shaky perch and hurried to kneel at his side. Her hair hung to her shoulders in sodden hanks as she bent over him with an anxious frown. "Are you all right?"

Adam nodded and sat up. "Yep . . . soon as I catch my . . . breath. What about you?"

Relieved, Eve said through chattering teeth, "I'm fine . . . but I'm freezing."

Adam pulled her into his arms, holding her tightly against him. Then he lowered his head and kissed her. The kiss was a blending of relief, need, and love, as the two figures remained locked in one another's arms, oblivious to the rain that continued to pour upon them.

Although most of the wagon's contents were wet, Eve was too cold to be fussy. Shivering, she pulled off her clothing and wrapped herself in a damp blanket. She couldn't remember when she had been so cold and miserable.

It was over an hour before Adam found enough dry wood to get a fire started. Eve got a pot of coffee brewing as he went to find more wood. By the time he returned, she had hot beans and salt pork waiting for him.

That night they crawled wearily beneath the tarp and curled up in each other's arms.

Eve awoke to the boom of thunder and flashes of lightning piercing the distant sky. Sometime during the night the rain had stopped, but it was evident that the storm in the distance would soon be upon them.

She sat up and gingerly rubbed her aching lower back. Adam walked over and handed her a cup of coffee. "Good morning. As soon as you eat, we'd better get moving. I've packed as much as the horse can carry in the saddlebags."

Nodding, Eve pulled on her clothing. Most of it was still damp. "Are we going back to the mine?"

"Of course not. We'll both ride the gelding. He's strong enough to make it to Sonora."

Eve watched Adam fold up the blankets in the tarp as she chewed a hard biscuit and gulped down the remains of her coffee. When he finished, he tied the roll to the saddlebags.

Eve was irritated at Adam's insistence to press on. It was unreasonable. "Is there any reason we can't wait a day to rest and dry out?"

Exasperated, Adam looked at her and sighed. "We can't dry out here. Take a look at that sky. I'm hoping we make it to the cabin. So, please, let's not argue."

Having heard that determined tone often enough in the past, Eve knew further discussion was useless. But old habits die hard; challenging Adam's decisions was second nature to her. "I don't understand why we don't go back and wait for Sam and Simone to leave. What's another week or so?"

"Another week could bring a snowfall in these mountains. The baby could end up being born in Paddy, or worse, at the mine." He led out the saddled horse and mounted it.

"Well, what would be so bad about that?" she persisted.

Adam reached down, and Eve took his hand reluctantly. He pulled her up so that she sat sidesaddle in the circle of his arms. "Eve, running off into these mountains in your condition was a crazy damned thing to do. I've been more than patient about this."

"I wasn't sure I was pregnant when I left San Francisco," she snapped defensively with a sideward glance at him.

"Either way you had a responsibility to be certain." His rebuke triggered memories of the Adam past: smug, opinionated, and dictatorial.

"If I would have waited, Sam and Simone would have left without me." Suddenly her eyes widened in shock as she felt a stabbing pain in her lower back.

Unaware of her problem, Adam continued to state his opinion. "All you could think of was getting away from me, no matter what the consequences. Well, whether you like it or not,

Eve, my child is not going to be born in a mining camp."

Eve was seized by another pain. Worriedly her eyes swung to his face. "Adam, I think I'm in labor. But it's too soon. Much too soon."

At her frightened glance, he cursed softly. "Damn! I knew we should have gotten out of here sooner. Are you sure, Eve?"

"I'm not sure. I've never had a baby before. Maybe I'm wrong." In a few minutes the pain struck again, leaving no doubt in her mind. "I'm sure the baby's coming, Adam, but it's too soon."

The quarrel was forgotten. Adam's calm voice masked his anxiety. "Maybe you miscalculated when the baby was due. I've got to get you to Sonora. Don't worry, honey." He hugged her protectively and goaded the horse to a quicker gait.

Her pains continued throughout the morning. Adam stopped only long enough to rest the horse. By noon the rain began falling again. He stopped to cover her with his poncho.

The pains were not any closer together, but their intensity had increased. Eve cowered in his arms in severe pain, but she forced herself not to cry out.

Within the hour, the distant rumbling had moved overhead. Each jagged, silver bolt streaking the sky was followed by a thunderous crash echoing through the valley.

Seized with a severe pain, and trying to restrain a whimper, Eve stiffened in Adam's arms.

Her eyes opened in panic, glazed with pain. Adam could tell that her contractions were worse, and yet she wouldn't complain.

Still five miles to the cabin, and at least fifteen miles to Sonora, Adam wondered how much longer she could bear the pain. The town would have medical supplies and maybe a doctor or, at least, women who would know what to do. If Eve could hold out, it would be wiser to get her to town. He hugged her tighter, trying to shield her from the rain.

A bolt of lightning struck a nearby tree, splitting it in half. The tree flared into flames and the horse reared in terror with front legs pawing the air. Adam struggled to maintain his hold on Eve and bring the animal under control.

Fighting the rein, the horse stomped down, jolting Eve just as her body was seized with another contraction. Unable to withstand the pain, she screamed in agony. That settled his doubt; he turned the horse toward the cabin.

They reached it at dusk. To Adam's relief the cabin was empty. Nothing appeared changed since their earlier stay. The chopped wood was stacked neatly the way he had left it.

Eve was shivering uncontrollably when he laid her down on the bunk. He quickly built a fire, which soon took the chill and dampness out of the tiny room.

Eve's eyes were closed when Adam returned to her side. "Honey, I have to remove your wet clothing." She opened her eyes and nodded but lay listlessly, impervious to his actions as he removed the sodden garments. Adam covered her with a blanket, then rubbed her legs and feet to restore the circulation. "Sweetheart, I don't want you to worry about a thing," he said gently.

Eve smiled feebly. "I'm not worried, Adam. I know you would never let anything happen to me."

Eve closed her eyes again. Adam was uncertain whether or not she had dozed off. Her body was seized with another contraction and her eyes opened. She smiled at the sight of the concern on his face. "Have you ever delivered a baby before?"

Adam shook his head and grinned crookedly. "I've seen my share of colts born, though."

"My intuition tells me this is going to be a little filly."

He grasped her hand and squeezed it. "I hope so."

"Really? I thought all men wanted a son." Eve gasped from the pain of another seizure.

Adam reached out and gently stroked her cheek. "I want a little girl who looks just like her mother." He bent down and lightly brushed her lips with his own.

Eve's body arched convulsively and she bit down on her lip, drawing blood. "Don't try to hold back, honey. Cry, scream if you must," Adam pleaded. He brushed away some strands of hair clinging to her face.

"Make one of your miracles, Adam," she

411

teased through the pain gripping her. He could feel her hand tighten convulsively as she gasped for breath.

"Oh God, honey, I wish I could."

Eve's eyes closed again and she seemed to doze off. Adam went out in the downpour to unsaddle the horse and get the animal under the tarp.

Eve was awake when he returned. "I thought maybe you might have decided to leave. I haven't been very pleasant company."

Adam picked up her hand and brought it to his lips. "I think that's just wishful thinking on your part. You should know by now I'm never too far away."

The rain beat a steady staccato on the roof of the cabin. The measured cadence lulled Eve into whatever sleep she was able to steal until the intensity and rhythm of her contractions increased. Her labor continued throughout the night, and Adam never left her side.

By dawn her strength was exhausted. Adam had shifted to the foot of the bunk and was helping the delivery as much as he could.

"Adam, I can't bear it," she cried.

"The head's almost out. Just another push, honey."

Eve fainted from the effort of the final thrust. The baby slid out of the mother's womb; the hands of the father were there to receive it, dwarfing the tiny body in his cupped palms. Deftly, Adam cut and tied the cord that bound mother to child.

Adam picked up his daughter. The little form barely filled his hand. His finger smoothed the silky, black down that covered her head—a rich ebony, so like her mother's.

The infant's eyes were closed—never to open.

Tears trickled down Adam's cheeks as he picked up a perfectly formed hand. He pressed a kiss to each of the petite fingertips, which had long turned to blue. He laid her down and gently washed away the stains of mucus and blood. Then, tenderly, he shrouded the small lifeless form in a blanket.

When Adam returned to Eve, he laid his ear to her heart and found her breathing was shallow but steady. Turning his attention to her needs, he disposed of the afterbirth, and noticed that Eve's body felt excessively warm to his touch. Adam took two clean spare shirts from the saddlebags and ripped one into strips. He cleaned and padded Eve in one, then dressed her in the other.

Eve's usually luxuriant hair lay dankly on the pillow, seeming plastered to her head. Large purple circles had formed beneath her eyes against the ghostly pallor of her face.

That day, he left her bedside only long enough to bury their daughter. When he returned, Eve was tossing in a delirium. Adam agonized, listening to her cry out to her mother, to Simone, and to him. Sobbing his name in anger and in love, Eve thrashed in torment, reliving her suspicions, their quarrels, and also her need for him.

Through it all, Adam held her hand, and though she heard it not, he expressed his love and his grief.

Adam Rawlins could not witness the suffering of the woman he loved without taking on the burden of her pain.

He blamed himself.

He alone was responsible. His domination and deceit had driven her to the brink of desperation; a desperation that had driven her from the security of her home to the savagery of these mountains, a desperation that might destroy her, as their baby had been destroyed. He had brought Eve nothing but heartache and grief from the moment he entered her life. Entrusted with a precious gift, he had abused that trust.

Adam swore to himself that if Eve pulled through, he would steel himself to leave, and get out of her life. She would have the freedom she wanted and deserved.

Some day, if there was a forgiving God, maybe Eve could forgive him as well.

Adam rarely slept in the days that followed, dozing occasionally while he sat at Eve's bedside holding her hand. Lovingly he sponged her feverish body with cool water, changed her padding, and lifted her head to trickle water through her parched lips. He re-covered her every time she shoved the blanket aside.

On the third day, Eve opened her eyes and saw Adam sitting at the bedside, his head slumped on his chest. Her first sensation was an awareness that the pain was gone. She remembered the pain. Her eyes swept the cabin and her jumbled thoughts began to take shape. With the recollection came the reason for the pain. She raised up, her eyes searching for the small bundle. When she saw there was none, Eve fell back sobbing.

Adam awoke with a start to the sound of her weeping. He was overwhelmed with relief to discover she was awake, and he knew the reason for her tears. Shifting to the bunk, he gathered her into his arms. Her tears needed to be shed; they were a healthy sign. The misery had to be released.

Eve cried herself to sleep. But this time her sleep was not a delirium. Adam placed a hand on her forehead and was relieved to find her fever had broken.

For the first time in days, he was able to leave her without fear. He set a snare for a rabbit, then gathered up the soiled clothing and took it down to the river.

Laundering was unfamiliar to Adam Rawlins, but he relished the task because he was doing it for Eve. As he washed the clothes, he grinned when a thought crossed his mind. Maybe Eve would laugh if she could see her domineering husband doing charwoman's work, just to fill her need for fresh clothes. Then his face turned solemn as he thought of the future. From now on, Eve would no longer need him or his money —for anything. Once safely back in the city, he would honor his vow to himself.

He would leave her.

Then she could get on with her life in the manner *she* wanted.

Eve awoke to an empty cabin. She wanted Adam, she needed him. He would make everything right again; he always did. With a plaintive sigh she thrust aside the painful thought of her lost baby. They would have other children, and one day they would be a family. For now, she must not sink into gloom. She had been enough of a burden to Adam already.

She raised her arm and saw she was wearing Adam's shirt. Eve lifted the blanket. Gradually her face flushed red. In the deep self-effacement of an immature girl, she was mortified at what Adam had been forced to do while she lay unconscious.

Adam entered the cabin carrying a skinned rabbit, and he smiled at her. Only minutes earlier Eve had yearned for his presence. Now, she felt as awkward as if they were strangers. She turned away from him.

The move did not go unnoticed. Adam sobered, believing he understood her response. She simply couldn't bear to look at him; he was responsible for the loss of their child. In despair and silence he went to the fireplace and began to prepare a stew.

As the smell of the frying rabbit assailed her nostrils, Eve felt the bile rising in her throat. She covered her mouth and ran to the door. After retching several times, she realized Adam was there with an arm around her waist to support her.

Damn it! Hadn't he cleaned up enough of her gall? She took several deep breaths of fresh air. Her legs trembled from the exertion as she allowed him to lead her back to the bunk.

Adam hovered above her. "How are you feeling?"

"Fine. I'm fine," she snapped. "I just want to go back to sleep."

"Won't you try to eat something, Eve? You haven't eaten in four days."

"Perhaps later. Just a cup of tea for now." Adam brought her the tea and Eve began to slowly sip it.

In a short while, the hot brew had an energizing effect on her and she felt almost human again.

With the stimulation came a feeling of shame for the way she was treating Adam. Eve knew she was reacting out of embarrassment, but she couldn't help herself. As she lay unconscious, he had ministered to her body's most intimate needs. In her heart, a stigma was attached to her dependency and vulnerability.

Much harder to face was her guilt. Adam had shouldered the burden of the past days, all because of her stubbornness. How many times in the past months had he asked her to return to Sacramento? He had remained only for her sake.

Now he had withdrawn from her, and his silence was deafening. She concluded he wanted nothing more to do with her. Only his code of decency kept him here.

As she sipped her tea, she watched Adam's movements at the fireplace. He did everything effortlessly. Even though servants had waited upon him his whole life, he adapted to these primitive conditions easily and without annoyance.

Painfully aware of his reticence, she broke the silence. "Adam, I won't ask you to talk about it again, but please tell me about the baby."

Adam was bent over the kettle stirring the stew. His spine stiffened and he straightened up slowly. "It was a girl."

Eve's chin quivered, but she forced back her tears. "How long did she . . . did she—"

"She was stillborn. Never opened her eyes." He turned to face her, and she saw the glint of moisture in his eyes. "She had dark hair, just like yours."

"Or yours," Eve interjected with a trembling smile. "Was she . . . disfigured?"

"No, Eve. She was perfect. I think her little heart just wasn't strong enough." He paused, then continued with a measured tone. "I named her Mary MacGregor Rawlins." He stopped and swallowed the catch in his throat. "She's buried beneath the large oak near the river," he said softly.

Eve's heart swelled with gratitude at the name Adam had given their child. Her violet eyes shimmered against the pallor of her face. "Thank you, Adam." Her long lashes dipped to her cheeks as she choked back her feelings. Then she turned her head to the wall.

Eve fell in and out of sleep thoughout the day. Adam spent most of the daylight hours outside the cabin chopping wood, filling the water barrels, and doing whatever menial tasks he could find to keep busy.

He caught a fish, and that evening for supper Eve nibbled on the catch. The conversation remained stilted and guarded, she suffering guilt and shame, he consumed with remorse.

After they ate, Adam made himself a pallet by the fireplace and then came over to the bunk. "I'll change your padding for you before I bed down." He began to raise the blanket.

Eve snatched it out of his hand, her face distraught. "I'll do it myself, thank you."

Adam ignored her and reached again for the blanket. "You're still too weak, Eve."

"Oh, good heavens, Adam. Can't you let me have *some* dignity?" she uttered querulously.

Adam straightened up. "What has this got to do with dignity?" To Adam her question was senseless.

The tragic events of the past days had imposed a costly emotional toll on both of them. Tension, stretched to tautness since she regained consciousness, now snapped in stinging reproachfulness.

"You obviously wouldn't understand." Eve glared in resentment.

"I think I understand much better than you do, Eve," he said quietly. "It's not your dignity.

It's your vanity that's been hurt. You just see us as lovers, not husband and wife. Human beings with frailties would shatter the romantic illusion."

Fearing that he had touched on the truth, Eve watched painfully as Adam moved to the mantel and gazed into the fire. "I'm supposed to be the knight on a white horse, and you, the maiden fair. But a hero will not lie and a princess does not bleed. No deception of mine nor illness of yours dare enter the ivory tower."

He sat down, his shoulders slumped in defeat. "But hell, why am I criticizing you? I lived in a fairy tale too, Eve," he said sadly. "I thought you were ready to be a wife to me."

Adam removed his boots and lay back. The night wore on. They remained isolated from each other, both wearing the black mantle of sorrow.

CHAPTER THIRTY-ONE

The following morning, there was no conversation. They spoke in monosyllables, and only out of necessity. Each felt responsible for Mary MacGregor Rawlins' death, when in truth, Fate had deemed her dead. Each brooded on the future apart; Adam was resolute to give Eve her freedom, Eve was certain that Adam no longer loved her.

Soulmates bound by the sorrow of death, yet rent asunder by lovers' misunderstanding, they could not communicate.

To make the silence more bearable for her, Adam busied himself with outside chores. Eve moved around the cabin, gingerly at first, and then took the kettle from the fireplace. Warmed by the tea she made, she sat for a long time, entranced by the glow of the fire, and therein tried to fathom the embers of her life.

Finally she thought that being dressed in her own clothing might help her feel better. Resolutely she got up and slowly moved to the laundered pile, all neatly folded. She smiled, wondering if there was anything Adam couldn't do.

When noon came, Eve had prepared a simple meal. Looking out of the window, from afar she saw him sitting on a boulder with his back to the cabin. Apparently engrossed, his head was bent over a piece of wood lying across his knee.

"Adam," she called from the door. "Would you like something to eat?" He put the wood down, sheathed his knife, and walked to the cabin. When he entered, he sat down at the table absorbed in thought. He said nothing.

Finally she broke the silence as he took a second cup of coffee. She broached him tentatively. "Adam, I feel better, and Sonora is not so far from here. Could we please leave today?"

He was inwardly pleased that she felt well enough to dress, but thought it risky for her to travel so soon. Lowering the cup from his lips, he answered calmly, "No, not yet. Today you still need to rest." Seeing her downcast expression, he quietly added, "Tomorrow is soon enough." Her eyes looked up to meet his as he thoughtfully completed his remark. "Tomorrow, Eve . . . one more day is all you have to wait."

After a few seconds, he dropped his eyes and returned his attention to the cup. He rose from the table and started toward the door, then stopped to say, "I'm going to fish for a while."

Solemnly he fixed his eyes on her saddened face. "I'll be close enough to hear you call if you need me." He walked out the door, heading toward the stream.

Eve lay down on the cot and slept. The afternoon passed.

She woke to the sound of Adam scraping the catch on a tree stump close to the cabin. When he came in, she lay still and closed her eyes while he tended the fire and cooked the fish. She managed to eat some of the fish, but still few words were exchanged between them.

Later, Eve was stirred from her slumber by the familiar and reassuring sound of Adam's breathing as he slept. Carefully she got up and went over to him. Adam was stretched out on the pallet with his hands clasped behind his head, sound asleep. For a few moments, she gazed at him. Handsome and vital awake, he was as handsome in sleep, yet different. With his eyes closed, features relaxed, his countenance took on an ethereal quality. If only she could touch the strength of spirit in Adam's face, so much in evidence as he slept.

She turned away and tiptoed to the door. With a backward glance, she quietly left the cabin. Eve had to walk hesitantly down to the stream, halting a few times. As she paused the last time, she knew Adam was right . . . she did need one more day.

Reaching the bank, she had no trouble finding the stately oak. From afar, it stood above all others. Tears trickling her cheeks, she approached the tree. Seeing the fresh mound before it, she stopped, startled at what her eyes beheld. Firmly planted to mark the grave stood a roughhewn cross. Carved thereon, in neatly formed letters:

Mary MacGregor Rawlins.

Tears flowed freely now as she put her hand on the cross, and sinking to her knees, she sobbed, releasing the emotions that choked her heart—utter grief for the child and consummate love for the man.

An hour later, Adam found her crumpled next to the grave. Blessed sleep had relieved her torment.

As he carried the limp form back to the cabin, Adam knew they could not travel tomorrow. Eve would have to wait a few more days to leave this place of anguish.

Laying her gently on the cot, he reflected on the need she must have felt to visit the spot where their child was buried. Covering her, he made a decision. When he got back to Sacramento, Richard Graves could make the arrangements with the bank; the oak and surrounding acres of land would be hers, forever.

The following day, Adam was bathing in the river when the sound of approaching horses caused him to bolt from the water. Not wanting Eve to be isolated in the event of trouble, he grabbed his clothing and rifle and dashed to the cabin.

Eve let out a cry of alarm when Adam dashed

naked through the door. "Get my gun belt," he barked. "Someone's coming."

Frightened, with her harrowing escape from the bandits still vivid in her mind, she obeyed him immediately. Adam had his trousers on by the time the first rider came into view.

Standing at the window with his pistol aimed, he suddenly relaxed, and then grinned. Sam Montgomery rode up to the cabin, with Simone close behind.

Adam sighed in relief and released the bar on the door. He stepped outside to greet them in his bare feet.

At the sight of Adam, Sam climbed down from his horse. "I figured we'd find you here when there was no word of you in Sonora. We waited a day, then turned back and headed here."

Eve appeared at the cabin door, and, with a squeal of delight, Simone leaped off her horse. The two women hugged and kissed, then Eve burst into tears, and they disappeared into the cabin.

"Eve went into labor, so we were forced to stop." By Adam's tone, Sam knew the news was bad. "The baby didn't make it. She was stillborn."

"I'm sorry, Adam," Sam said succinctly.

"Eve had a rough time of it. She's still pretty distraught, and I realize now that I'm just an irritant to her. I've decided that when we get to Stockton, I'll leave her and go back to Sacramento alone."

Sam was silent for a long moment. Then he said, "I've heard tell that sometimes women go off the deep end for a while after having a dead baby. Maybe Eve is just having a bad time adjusting," he offered.

Adam smiled glumly. "Just having a hard time adjusting to *me*, Sam. The loss of the baby was the final straw. She'd be happier with me out of her life."

The subject was a closed one. The two men continued talking for a short time, discussing the mine.

When they entered the cabin, Simone put a finger to her mouth cautioning them to silence. Eve had just cried herself to sleep. Reaching for his boots and shirt, Adam went down to the river bank. Reflecting that the arrival of Sam and Simone would make the situation less awkward until Eve was able to travel, Adam sat down on the ground to pull on his boots. In a few minutes Simone joined him.

"I'm sorry about the baby, Adam."

He nodded in acknowledgment. "She would have been as beautiful as her mother."

"It wasn't an easy time for you, was it?" she said sensitively.

"It was a lot easier for me than for Eve. She had all the pain."

"I don't think so, Adam. I don't think Eve bore all the pain. You and Sam are so alike. Always trying to hide your scars behind indifference. You're a strong man, Adam Rawlins, and a very brave one."

Smiling briefly, Adam picked up her hand and brought it to his lips. "Don't offer me sympathy, Simone, or I'll fall apart in front of you." Sobering, he turned to her, his handsome face now etched with heartache. "I wanted that baby so badly."

"I'm sure you and Eve will have others," she offered consolingly.

Adam shook his head. "I doubt that very much."

"Oh, Sam told me that you're talking about leaving Eve, but I don't believe it." She put her hand on his knee. "I know how much you love each other."

"Sometimes love is not enough. Eve and I got started out wrong and, whatever happens, we seem to end back on uncommon ground."

"Please reconsider, Adam. Once Eve is healthy and her old self again, things will be different. I know she'll come back to you. True love really does find a way, Adam."

Adam's expression changed, as if he were in a far-off dream. "I can only pray so, Simone."

Two days later, they began their ride to Stockton. The long journey was quiet for all of them. When they finally arrived, Adam got Eve safely settled in a hotel room and took the room across the hall. He left for Sacramento at sunrise.

Waking to an empty room, Eve yearned for Adam. She wanted to see him, to touch him. Because his presence was always reassuring, his absence left her feeling completely desolate.

She realized with extraordinary force that Adam had become her reason for living. She saw that, whatever she did, it was to please or to spite him, but she could never be indifferent to him.

Last night she had wanted to admit this to him, but the trip had exhausted her. *Adam had been right about that, too,* she thought with a tender smile.

In the past few days she had plenty of time to think about his assessment of her fairy-tale world. Everything he said was true. As devastating as the loss of her baby was to her, his words, spoken after the tragedy, made her see herself in a true light for the first time. She had been no wife to Adam. She had never given their marriage a chance. Every time Adam had displeased her, she had condemned him and run from him.

Conversely, Adam had tolerated her shortcomings because he loved her. It was time she finally grew up. She was long overdue in accepting the responsibility to be worthy of his love.

Eve couldn't wait to tell him.

Quickly she got to her feet, then grasped the bedpost for support. The room was spinning around her. She took one step toward the door before blackness overcame her.

When Eve opened her eyes she found herself back in bed. Simone leaned over her with a worried frown. Eve thought she couldn't have fainted for more than a few minutes, because Sam was standing at the window with the sun streaming through at the same angle. "How do you feel, *chérie?*" Simone asked.

"I feel all right," Eve managed to respond feebly. "How long have I been unconscious?"

"Since yesterday morning."

"Yesterday!" Eve couldn't believe her words. Her memory held nothing beyond getting out of bed and the whirling room.

"Where's Adam? I want Adam." Eve closed her eyes and was asleep before Simone could reply.

Eve was in and out of sleep in the days that followed. When she regained consciousness, a lamp was lit on the stand next to her bed. Eve looked about groggily. The room appeared different to her.

"Adam," she called out. At once Simone appeared in the doorway from the connecting room. "Where am I?" Eve asked, confused.

"Don't be alarmed, *chérie*. We've moved you to a different room. Sam and I are here right next to you."

"Where's Adam?" Eve asked in panic.

Simone's smile was forced. "He's not here right now."

"I want Adam," Eve cried out.

"Hush, *chérie*. You have been very ill. Your fever has flared up again. The doctor has sedated you, and he said you must remain still."

"How long have I been like this?" Eve could feel herself being drawn back into the dark eddy.

"Almost two weeks."

"Two weeks?" Eve questioned, uncertain she had heard Simone correctly. Then nothing mattered. She had plunged back into the whirlpool.

It took another full week for Eve to recuperate. When Simone told her about Adam, Eve was devastated. If only she had told him her true feelings before he left, she was certain it would have made a difference.

It was six weeks before Eve was on her feet and healthy enough to leave. In an effort to remain anonymous, Sam had patiently borne the boredom of the town, passing up the saloons for the seclusion of their room. As a result, Simone suspected she was pregnant. Her joy was unbounded, except for her concern about Eve.

"Where will you go to have your baby?" Eve asked them when they told her the hopeful news.

"As far from the gold fields as possible. Sam wants to buy the spread up north that Adam told him about, and settle down to a life of peace and quiet."

"I'm really happy for both of you." Eve paused, thinking of the coming event. "Just think, I'm going to become an aunt."

"We want you to come with us," Simone interjected. "We were all raised without much family. We don't want our children to grow up without knowing their relatives."

Eve smiled at her thoughtfulness. "Your offer is very kind, but I can't see myself growing old on your ranch." Her face relaxed as she thought of an alternative. "Maybe I should consider opening a bakery again. After all, it was the one thing I did without any help from Adam."

Sam, who had remained quiet throughout the conversation, now cleared his throat. "Not really, Eve. It's time you learned the truth about that."

Eve turned to Simone, expecting to see some awareness on the face of her friend. Simone shrugged in innocence.

"Adam had been looking out for you from the beginning. Even the arrangement you made with Captain Grant for supplies for the bakery was his doing. Adam picked up the extra expense to make sure you got the supplies you wanted."

Both women's eyes were wide with astonishment. "I don't understand," Eve said perplexed. "How do you know all this?"

Sam knew he had backed himself into a corner. But it was time she knew the whole story. "Eve, it wasn't a coincidence that I was at the wharf the night you arrived in San Francisco. Adam had sent me a message by stage. I was hired by him to protect you."

"You mean all this time you have been working for Adam?"

"Up until the time we left San Francisco for Bailey's mine."

The two women looked at each other in disbelief. Eve turned away. The truth was overwhelming. There was much to sort out in her mind. "But how did he know I was going to San

Francisco?" She guessed the answer to the question as soon as she asked it.

But Simone answered for her. "Of course, Captain Grant."

Sam nodded. "The *Senator* is owned by Adam."

Simone responded with a nervous laugh. "And I thought Captain Grant's intentions were dishonorable. He was just obeying orders." Sam nodded.

And Adam had talked about her fairy tales?

All their hard work and the long hours they had worked through the night at the bakery! She hadn't had the independence and success she had supposed. Adam had assured her success by paying her way, just as he bought everything and everyone.

She turned back to Sam, tears misting her eyes. "I guess I never proved a thing by running away from him. He guided my life the same way he did when I was under his roof."

"You proved you had courage and the spunk to try the bakery, Eve. You gals would have found a way, with or without Adam's help."

"But as usual, Adam was afraid to let me make decisions for myself. He simply didn't trust my judgment, and protected me as one would a child."

"As his ward you *were* a child. Then, after Paris, he saw the woman the child had become. So he protected his interests, as you might say." Sam smiled at his allusion to Adam the businessman. "He kept right on doing it, protecting his filly, giving her just so much rope so she would not get into trouble outside the corral," Sam drawled with a wry smile, hoping Eve would accept Adam's overprotectiveness.

Eve digested his thought and returned the smile. Sam continued to fill in the picture. "So then, when you bolted, naturally he followed, crawling around these Sierras, dodging bullets, and digging for gold. Anything you wanted. Not surprising . . . for a man in love."

Eve looked at him squarely. For a few seconds their eyes met in understanding, and Sam concluded his thought. "A man in love will do anything in his power to keep his woman from danger."

My knight on a white horse, Eve thought. She dropped her eyes, feeling remorse for not having seen the obvious truth long before now.

But she still needed the answer to one more, very puzzling, question. "Sam, why didn't Adam tell me about you and Bailey being my kin?"

"I figure he had his reasons. Springing *that* nest of rattlesnakes must have been hard to do. You saw for yourself how Bailey is. And with my reputation, well, he probably thought he was doing you a favor. Anyway, when the time came for the truth, he told us, didn't he?" The question was answered; she knew Sam was right.

Deep in thought, she walked to the window, staring out to the horizon as Sam's words collected in her mind.

She *had* been spunky enough to leave Adam, and now she was financially independent of him. So, in truth, she had accomplished what she set out to do.

Adam *had* chased after her, taking all the risk and danger on himself. Yes, he must have loved her to do all that. As for Adam keeping her kinship to Bailey and Sam secret, well, he had been trying to protect her feelings as well.

What a child she had been. She had not understood Adam at all.

Now she was caught in a trap of her own making. Financially independent though she may be, she would never be emotionally independent of Adam. She loved him too much, and knew in her heart that life would be unbearable without him. Her reasons for constantly vexing him and then leaving him bore as much weight as a feather in the wind.

Unaware of her shifting thoughts, Sam interrupted her rueful concentration. "Eve, I suppose Adam could have played his cards different," he said gently. "A man in love does a lot of damn fool things he's sorry for later. He may have his ante in the pot, but he's not always playing with a full deck." He smiled crookedly at Simone, embarrassed by having said as much as he had.

Simone sensed the misgivings of her quiet man, knowing that Sam Montgomery did not meddle in the lives of others. She returned his smile to offer him the encouragement he needed. In a role alien to him, Sam awkwardly reached for his sister's hand. Eve looked up to find him studying her intently.

"It was never my way to poke my nose into other people's lives. I just did the job I was hired to do and moved on. But since you two women came into my life, it seems I've been doing an awful lot of interfering in other people's business." His dark eyes filled with a steely glint. "You're my kin, Eve, and I don't want to see you hurt. Now, if you don't love Adam Rawlins, I'll see to it he never bothers you again. Is that the way you want it?"

Eve closed her eyes, unable to bear his intense gaze. Of course it wasn't the way she wanted it. She wanted Adam. She wanted his arms around her, his lips on hers. There was no denying this. No deceiving herself. She loved him. Everything they had suffered and struggled through together in the past months had proven how much. In those perilous and often tragic hours, she had grasped the fulfillment of everything she had ever wanted or dreamed about. She would not let her pride allow happiness to slip through her fingers now.

But had her immaturity finally consumed his patience, and destroyed his love? Would he be able to forgive her mistakes and understand that it had been necessary to prove her independence to *herself*, as much as to him?

Eve opened her eyes to discover that Sam and Simone appeared to be waiting for her answer with baited breath. Despite the seriousness of the moment, she couldn't help but smile at their grim expressions. *Good heavens, did either of them actually believe she wanted Adam out of her life forever!*

"Sam, I know you disapprove of the way I've been treating Adam. I know I foolishly doubted his motives, accused him, and ran away from him. It's all difficult for you to understand, because you and Simone have no doubts about each other. The two of you liked each other first, and before you knew it, you fell in love. Your love is beautiful and will last forever.

"Adam and I were just the opposite. We began with accusations and suspicions. We actually fell in love without even liking each other. He thought I was self-centered and childish; I thought he was manipulative and despotic. It's taken me this long to recognize Adam for the man that he really is—a selfless, generous, caring person. You said it all yourself. I only hope it's not too late to convince him that I've finally grown up."

Her smile widened to the width of her face. "So, whatever gave you the idea that I want Adam out of my life? My goodness, you two, of all people, should know I could not live without him."

Sam threw his hands up in the air in total bafflement. "Women!"

Eve winked at Simone and watched her slide a hand into Sam's. He grasped it tightly, all the tension easing from his body, before he pulled her into his arms. "A man's a fool for messing with the female mind."

"As soon as I can muster up enough courage, I intend to go to him. Adam Rawlins did a lot of manipulating to get me. Well, he's got me now, whether he's changed his mind or not," she announced saucily.

The closer they got to Sacramento, the less confidence Eve felt. What if she couldn't convince Adam that she had finally grown up, and he threw her out of the house?

When they arrived in Sacramento, Eve wanted to dress, and checked into the hotel with Sam and Simone. She took special pains with her appearance to prepare for her visit. She selected a violet organdy gown that hugged her tiny waist and flared over her slim hips. She brushed her hair vigorously. When they were alone Adam always loved to see her hair flowing loose to her shoulders.

Simone sat on the bed smiling, watching the changing expressions on Eve's face as she twisted around several times in front of the mirror, studying her figure. "Do you think I've got my former shape back, Simone?" Eve asked, frowning worriedly. "I know it's vanity, but I have to look my very best today."

"I think Adam will be so glad to see you, he won't even notice how you look," Simone chided lightly.

"I sure could use that black satin gown I wore in San Francisco. Adam was crazy about it." Eve slumped down desolately on the edge of the bed. "I'm afraid I'm going to need every weapon I can get."

Simone smiled in understanding. She knew Eve too well not to sense the doubts that were plaguing her. She reached out and placed a hand on Eve's arm. "Would you like us to come with you, *chérie*?" she asked gently.

Eve smiled gratefully. There was comfort in knowing that Sam and Simone would always be there when she needed them. But not this time. "No, Simone. This is something I have to do for myself. Nobody can help me."

An hour later, as the carriage stopped at the entrance of the tall white house, those words echoed through her mind. Eve stepped out and dismissed the driver. For several moments she remained quietly staring at the scene before her. It felt good to be home again.

Home. Why hadn't she realized sooner that this indeed, was her home? Why had she fought it for so long, closing her eyes and heart to Adam's love? But the foremost question plaguing her thoughts was: *Was it too late?*

Eve took a deep breath and approached the door. It opened before she could reach it. James greeted her with a welcoming smile of pleasure.

"Miss Evelyn . . . I mean, Madame Rawlins. How good to see you again."

Eve returned his smile. "It's good to see you, James. Is Adam here?"

His smile creased into an austere frown. "The

master's in his study, madam. I'll announce you," he said, assisting her with her cloak.

"That won't be necessary, James. I'll announce myself. Oh, and, James, that will be all for tonight," she added with her former spunkiness, which brought a relieved smile to his face.

"Very well, madam." He extinguished the lamp.

Eve's heartbeat quickened as she crossed the foyer in the darkness. She paused outside the closed door and waited until the sound of James' retreating footsteps no longer echoed through the hall.

The door that had always seemed so foreboding in the past now still stood as a barrier between her and her happiness. Her thumping heart threatened to bludgeon her chest as she turned the handle.

The room was empty. Eve whirled in a momentary flight of panic. A crack of light glimmered from beneath the door of the drawing room in the darkened foyer. It drew her like a moth.

Adam sat slumped in a chair. A half-filled glass of brandy dangled from a hand slung negligently over the side. Her heart leaped to her throat as she stared longingly at the beloved figure. He was in his shirt sleeves; his cravat and vest had been carelessly tossed aside. The shirt was wrinkled, and his dark hair was rumpled and hanging over his forehead.

Several days' growth of beard darkened his

jaw. He looked incredibly masculine, yet forlorn and vulnerable—the man-boy she had glimpsed on rare occasions in the past. Eve was torn between wanting to comfort him or rushing across the floor and flinging herself into his arms to make love to him.

He was staring desolately at the portrait of his grandfather. Eve almost lost her nerve at the sight of the deep scowl on his face until he began to speak aloud.

"Well, Grandfather, I made it through another day without her, but it's getting harder. How did you ever do it?"

Absorbed in his own thoughts, Adam was unaware that Eve had entered the room. He was wallowing in self-reproach. He wasn't the man his grandfather had been. He could never be that man. If Eve loved him, she would have come back weeks ago. She was lost to him forever; her love had been destroyed by his lies and deceit.

Eve tiptoed across the room and sat down on the floor at Adam's feet. She looked up at the painting. "You do resemble him in many ways."

Her voice startled Adam out of his dolor. He sat up. The words must merely have come from his imagination.

"You both have a tendency to be tenacious." He was speechless with astonishment. She had to turn away to conceal the smile tugging at the corners of her mouth.

Adam steeled himself at the sight of her, not daring to read too much hope into what her presence might mean. He found enough of a voice to offer a reedy reply. "I never thought of Grandfather as tenacious." The high, piping pitch sounded as ridiculous to his own ears as it did to hers. He cleared his throat and concluded the thought. "He was purposeful in directing his energies."

"Obsessive," she corrected. "You're just like him."

Adam had regained enough of his composure to begin weighing the true significance of her presence. Eve turned to him, and for the length of several heartbeats, they stared at one another with the unspoken message that their hearts longed to declare.

They had reached this point so often together, and then, for whatever reasons, had always allowed it to escape from their grasps. "And I don't know if I can change, Eve," he said with regret.

Eve's eyes pleaded for understanding. "Censure me. Dominate me. Manipulate me." Her voice became a throaty plea, "But don't ever give up on me, Adam." Eve picked up his hand and pressed it to her cheek. "Because I love you so much."

A smile crept into his eyes, breaking the solemn line of his face. He dropped his glass as he reached for her, lifting her onto his lap.

His kiss was filled with urgency and desperation. Eve flung her arms around his neck and molded herself to him, offering her mouth to his as she accepted the kiss with the same driving urgency as his. Only now, she no longer harbored doubts. She knew they would be together forever.

Adam buried his face in her hair, breathing in the sweet essence of her, whispering her name over and over, still unable to believe she had, at last, really come to him. He rained quick, fervent kisses on her face and eyes, amidst husky declarations of his love.

Tears of joy welled her eyes as breathlessness forced the lovers apart. Adam cupped her cheek in his hand and gazed down at her, cosseting her in the warmth of the love that glowed from his eyes.

"Oh, Lord, I love you, Eve, and I've done everything wrong. Will you ever be able to forgive me for all the heartache I've caused you?"

She placed a finger over his lips to stem the flow of his words. "No apologies. We have both made mistakes, my love. I've been foolish and immature. It's time we put the past all behind us. The only thing that matters now is the future."

Tears shimmered in her violet eyes as she smiled up at him. "And, Adam, the future does belong to us."

Sighing contentedly, she lay her head against his chest and gazed up at the portrait of David Rawlins. Thank God, Adam had inherited the old man's steadfast determination to win the woman he loved. And thank God, she was Adam's woman, because her own stupidity would have driven away a lesser man long ago.

"I'm glad you're like him, my love. I wish I could have known him."

"I'm not really like him at all. I wouldn't have been able to bear waiting ten years for the woman I love. Look at me, I'm a total wreck after only a month."

"No, you're like him, Adam. You have all the strengths of that grand old man. And I know he looked as great on his white horse as you do on yours."

"White horse? Honey, you know Equus is bla . . ." Adam halted at the sight of the playful smile on her face. He chuckled and placed a light kiss on the tip of her nose. "You're an incorrigible vixen."

Eve's brow curved provocatively. "Do you really mind if on special occasions I still make you my knight in shiny armor?"

He grimaced in pretense. "I'll try to live up to the demands of the role."

Adam hugged her tighter and looked up with a secretive grin at the face in the portrait. "Ah, sweetheart . . . there is one thing I haven't told you about my grandfather."

Eve raised her head inquisitively. "I do lack his patience," he said. Eve waited with increasing curiosity for Adam to continue.

Adam rose to his feet, carrying her in his arms. She buried her hands in his hair, her fingertips tingling as the thickness curled around them.

"Patience?" she questioned, nuzzling her lips against his neck.

He stopped at the base of the stairway to smile down at her, the deep sapphire of his eyes brimming with love and laughter.

"You see, Grandfather was already fifty-one years old when his only heir was born."

Eve frowned adorably, weighing the remark. She began to giggle when she grasped his train of thought. "You're not suggesting that Grandfather might not have been the man of action you led me to believe, are you?"

"I certainly am."

Her wide mouth curved into a mischievous smile. "Perhaps a little *too* patient?"

"Much too patient." The gleam in his eyes telegraphed his intent, and she blushed, burying her now flaming face against his chest.

Adam threw back his head with a roar of laughter, mounting the stairs two at a time with Eve in his arms.